Tomorrow's Dead

*And Other Stories of
Crime and Suspense*

Praise for David Dean

"David Dean is incontestably one of the best of Ellery Queen's Mystery Magazine's regular contributors over the past several decades. Although not exclusively a short-story writer (he's produced three novels!), he began his career as a writer, in 1990, with a short story, and he's had more than sixty stories published since then, the majority of them, including his fiction debut, in EQMM. He's a master at creating unease and suspense out of the small, ordinary incidents of daily life, and he's adept at bringing characters to life through his appreciation of the big consequences seemingly minor frailties often have. What I find most compelling about this writer is the depth he brings to his stories. Like all of David Dean's work, the stories you'll find in this book are thought-provoking as well as entertaining."

—**Janet Hutchings**
Editor-in-Chief, Ellery Queen's Mystery Magazine

"Like the great miniaturist painters, David Dean is a master at creating world-class art on the smallest of canvases. Dean's medium is the short crime-fiction story, and he is without a doubt one of the contemporary masters of his craft. A two-time winner of the Ellery Queen's Mystery Magazine Reader Award, his years as a police officer in Avalon (NJ) bring an unrivaled realism to his work. But his range goes far beyond stories of law enforcement, as you'll see from the twelve tales collected in this volume. If you're already a fan of short crime fiction, you need this book. And if you aren't yet a fan, Tomorrow's Dead is bound to convert you!"

—**Josh Pachter**
Award-winning author and translator of crime fiction

Tomorrow's Dead

And Other Stories of Crime and Suspense

David Dean

Genius
Book Publishing

Milwaukee, Wisconsin USA

Published By:
Genius Book Publishing
PO Box 250380
Milwaukee, Wisconsin 53225 USA
GeniusBookPublishing.com

ISBN: 978-1-947521-93-3

220727 Digest LH

Contents

Introduction

In 1990 my first story was published by *Ellery Queen Mystery Magazine*. In fact, all of the stories contained in this volume, but one, originally appeared there. This was also the first story that I'd ever written to completion and it was a police procedural.

My writing debut was done in strict adherence to the time-honored adage, "Write what you know" and at that time I was a police officer. Many of my stories in the following years would continue in this vein, just as I continued in my law enforcement career. In time, I would branch out from the procedural into other sub-genres of crime fiction. Many of these efforts will appear in collections that follow this one. The subject of this initial volume is police work and the people who do it.

Tomorrow's Dead contains twelve tales of law enforcement personnel, the last of these lending its title to the whole. The cast of characters run the gamut of patrol officer to chief, dispatcher to detective, prosecutor's investigator to cybercrimes officer; there's even a priest who, though obviously not a police officer, plays a role as friend and advisor to one. Both he, and Julian Hall—the officer he befriends—appear together in this volume and two of the other collections that follow. I've tried to lend authenticity to my characters, so all are flawed, some fatally so. Some redeemable, others not. All, I hope, are quintessentially human.

The stories are not presented in chronological order and beneath the title will appear the year of publication. As these stories are procedural in nature, the editor thought it might be helpful to the reader. Why? Because police work—like most other professions—has changed rapidly due to both technological and societal influences. In the stories I wrote earlier, for instance, the use of DNA evidence (I can only speak to New Jersey) was restricted to homicide cases, and juries were allowed to assign it whatever weight they might agree upon. Just a few years later, the use of DNA evidence became as unassailable as fingerprints, and utilized in everything from burglaries to aggravated assaults.

I've been retired from law enforcement for a decade now and stopped writing procedurals a few years ago. It became obvious to me that my institutional knowledge was rapidly becoming that of an historian rather than authority. What hasn't changed, however, is the human being that is the police officer, and the unique profession that person practices. There is no other like it. This is what *Tomorrow's Dead* is about. Truth lies at the heart of good police work, and good story-telling should always be entertaining. I hope you find both requirements satisfied within the covers of this book.

My heartfelt thanks and gratitude go out to Leya and Steven Booth of Genius Books for their incredible contribution to this, and the collections that will follow. Their tireless efforts and faith in my work were invaluable in the creation of *Tomorrow's Dead*. I would also like to thank Janet Hutchings, the editor of Ellery Queen Mystery Magazine, and Josh Pachter, the editor of *Only the Good Die Young*, for having originally published these stories. Lastly, I wish to express my gratitude to my daughter, Bridgid Dean, whose keen eye and candid observations have kept me on target for so many years.

David Dean
2022

Copy Cat
(1999)

The chief sat at his cluttered desk and studied the photographs. His secretary had gone home to prepare supper for her family hours before and left him alone in his darkening office. His wife had not called. Most likely, she would not be there when, or if, he finally did arrive home. Quite possibly, she would be seeing the realtor who was handling the sale of their house. It was much too large for them now that the children were gone.

His senior investigator had, in a touchingly offhand manner, offered to look into the matter of the realtor, but the chief quietly declined his offer without ever acknowledging its implications. He had no wish to dissuade his wife from her affair, and even less to see his old friend's career destroyed by accusations of strong-arming his wife's latest lover. He was too tired to waste what little energy he mustered each day in fighting unwinnable battles, and a certain private peace lay in this acceptance. It was his wife who was in turmoil and paid the greatest price for her sexual wanderings, and it was for her, not himself, that he felt pity.

At five foot, nine inches tall, two hundred and forty pounds, with a gimpy leg (due to the only shooting the town had experienced in the last twelve years) and an unreliable heart, he could no longer satisfy the passions of the woman who had made the nights of his youth incandescent. With the leaving of their children, those passions had grown inexplicably white-hot, and she had passed from his life like a comet in a winter sky. In the end, he knew, age would quench and destroy her. Meanwhile, the kids refused to visit, and people talked.

Opening a drawer in his desk, he withdrew a pack of cigarettes and an ashtray he kept hidden there, and lit up, inhaling deeply. A breeze wafted in from an open window and ruffled the photos that lay before him. He adjusted his glasses and spread them out. Their color and clarity were impeccable, the subject matter appalling: The horror of the victim forever captured for posterity.

The tramp, as the chief had come to call the white male, had never been identified, despite every effort. He had carried no papers or licenses that would aid in identification, and his body had gone undiscovered far too long for fingerprints or facial photographs to be of any assistance. No one in town had gone missing and he matched no missing-person reports, or rather, his almost generic corpse matched too many to be of any assistance. In the end, he had just become "the tramp."

The location of his body had added weight to this conclusion, being discovered partially concealed by debris in a wooded area at the edge of town, near the park and its small zoo, and not far from some switching tracks known to be frequented by freight-hopping winos. In the county's small law enforcement circle, it was generally agreed that the tramp had been the victim of a fellow hobo, now long departed; killed over a bottle of cheap wine or for a pocketful of change. The townspeople seem to agree. After the initial alarm had worn off, and it had been determined that the victim was not one of them, the local population had lost interest with surprising alacrity.

But they had not been there and seen the body, thought the chief. The pitiable and desolate end to a fellow man who, presumably, came from the loins of woman, as they all had. For some reason, the townspeople's lack of caring fueled the chief's own sense of personal responsibility for this nameless man, and he found himself overly occupied with a case that he could have safely shelved.

Had he been less preoccupied, he might have noticed that the mayor and council found his concern morbid and distasteful, an opinion shared by most of their constituency. His recent absences from council meetings and his increasingly disheveled appearance had been duly noted, while their probable cause had been debated in public places and private homes. There were two camps of thought: The public-at-large attributed it to his obsession with the unsolved murder; those closer to him laid the blame on his wife's blatant infidelities.

Unaware of this, he studied the pictures on his desk, occasionally referring to his copy of the medical examiner's autopsy report. Even with the use of a magnifying glass, no revelation leapt out at him. Not even a small, but overlooked, clue to give him fresh hope. Both body and scene remained well documented, yet unyielding and mute.

The wound favored by the M.E. for the cause of death was evident as a gaping tear in the blackened parchment of the skin tissues at the throat. Within, the upper vertebrae were twice deeply scored, evidence of the force of the slashing. The neck was broken as well, whether by violence or the result of scavenging animals could not be determined.

The rest of the body evoked similar equivocation. That the breast cage had been rent open and the abdomen eviscerated were apparent. Whether it was the work of the assailant, or a host of carrion feeders, remained an open question. The M.E. refused to commit on a corpse, "at least six weeks old," that had been dry-baked in a compost of forest litter by an unusually hot September sun and worried by animals.

The chief yawned and stubbed out his cigarette. Pushing himself to his feet and scooping the grisly photos back into their folder, he thought for a moment of his bed. He dropped the folder back into a drawer and closed it, anxious his secretary not discover the disturbing pictures, then limped over to his worn leather couch, a relic of a long-forgotten predecessor.

Kicking off his shoes, he lay down, pulling up the old army blanket he kept hidden under the couch and tucking it around him. Reasonably comfortable, he reached up and turned off the overheads. There, in the swimming darkness, he wondered if his wife would return home that night and regret the empty bed. He wished that he didn't care, but he did—terribly. And with the bleak honesty that besets weary men, he knew that a large portion of his obsession with the death of the tramp was simply a device to avoid the more immediate concerns of the living. After a short while, he fell asleep.

ɔ

The runner stood at his sink drinking from a glass of filtered water. The predawn world outside his window remained dark and hidden. This did not bother him, as his mood was one of ebullience and well-being. He was twenty-seven and in his prime: tall, lithe, and finely muscled. His thoughts strayed for a moment to the night before and a smile spread across his face. The memory of his sexual escapades with a woman twenty years his senior gave him an added sense of power; her lewd appreciation of his toned, handsome body and, later, her grateful cries of ecstasy aroused him even in the cool, damp of the morning. The knowledge that she was the wife of another man, and the chief of police at that, gave the liaison an added edge, a certain illicit and dangerous flavor. She was a lovely, voluptuous woman for her age, he had to admit—if a bit worn at the edges.

Setting the glass in the sink, he bent at the waist, touching his toes. After a few moments, he sat on a rug on the polished wooden floor and began a series of stretches and warmups. He was anxious to be out, but his regimen dictated he be properly prepared for his run to prevent injury. He was well rested despite the evening's exertions, having bid a reluctant goodnight to his pliable real-estate client by ten-thirty. By eleven o'clock, he had showered, brushed his teeth, and was asleep. He controlled his schedule very carefully.

Stepping out onto his deck, he took several gulps of air, slowly exhaling each.

When the sun, a red ellipse on the horizon, began to break through the patchy morning fog, he came down onto his back lawn and began to jog across the wet grass to the tracks that ran behind his house, swinging a five-pound running weight in each hand.

He had used the presence of the railroad as a bargaining chip to bring down the price of the house when he had been negotiating for it. In reality, he knew that the freight trains were an infrequent event, and that he was such a sound sleeper even their occasional passing would have no effect on him. In fact, he had desired the house partially for its proximity to the tracks. The well-worn path that ran along the side of the rails had long been one of his favorites, carrying him through miles of solitude and forest, to arrive at a smoothly asphalted bike path that bisected the tracks as it entered the county park. Once there, he would make a right and jog through the lovely, deserted, early-morning grounds, past the rather forlorn zoo, to arrive at the town's main street. From there, it was another right and home for the single cup of caffeinated coffee he allowed himself each day.

Gaining the tracks, he turned north and began his jog in earnest. It was darker than he had expected; the overhanging trees and abundant undergrowth effectively shading the path and giving it a tunnel-like effect. In spite of the warmth of the season, the days were growing shorter, with the sun rising later and later each morning. Today, its appearance seemed tardy, and he looked at his illuminated watch to ensure that he had not mistaken the time. He had not, and the knowledge gave him a certain sense of foreboding, as if the night were attempting to prolong its stay.

He increased his stride in an attempt to outrun this feeling and after a few moments, as his heart began to pump the oxygen-enriched blood through his system, he began to feel better. His eyes, too, began to adjust to the dimness, and the soft, gray, cottony shapes that loomed to each side began to take on definition.

To his left, the low hummock of the tracks could be seen, with its twin rails stretching into the distance like a great fallen ladder. On his right, the dripping shrubs and weedy, second-growth trees separated into distinct forms and less mysterious shapes. Even a subdued color began to bleed into his surroundings, like a chameleon gaining a green leaf. Then, like an announcement, sunlight began to pour over the tops of the trees to his right, striking the far wall of his man-made valley and throwing it into sharp relief. With the sun near to escaping the horizon, his heart felt lighter.

He felt the pounding of that organ with a great sense of pride, knowing the promise of strength and speed it hammered out, and began to pump his arms more vigorously, the weights like gloves on his hands. By his calculations, the entrance to the park lay three minutes' distance, and he lifted his face to the sky as if to hasten the sun's warming ascent.

Ahead, something low to the ground streaked silently towards him. Like him, it ran in the deep shadows of the path, apparently oblivious to his presence. He slowed to a stop, breath catching in his throat, looking for a way to avoid it.

The fox, orange-red in the early autumn light, saw him at the last minute and braked itself some twenty yards away, nearly sitting on its haunches with the effort. For a moment they stared at one another: the fox, its long, red tongue lolling across its black lips, panting; the man, panting as well, steam rising from his overheated body in the still-cool morning air.

Before the runner could react, the fox fled like a flame into the undergrowth, turning not so much as a stone with its silent departure. The runner was left in sole possession of the track. He stared down its length and saw nothing.

After a few moments, he began to jog again, slowly regaining his former pace, but his recent, and brief, peace of mind had fled with the fox.

As he traveled north, he saw the last tendrils of fog rising into the air above the trees like thin, ghostly streamers heralding the promise of another hot day. He also saw the killer of the tramp.

Had he not kept glancing into the brush with the nagging fear that the fox, grown bold with rabies, would come dashing out to bite his bare legs, he might never have seen. But now it was too late… as if not making eye contact could change the outcome.

His heart fluttered and lurched in an alarming manner, making him gasp aloud in a high, girlish voice. His knees buckled and he stumbled with the surge of adrenalin furnished by this certain knowledge, despite his brain screaming that he should run as never before. In the midst of all this, his thoughts shot upward like a covey of startled quail, flying in a dozen different directions, re-forming in revelation, then scattering again at the terror revealed.

It was like him to have been unconcerned that his favorite jogging path took him daily past the murder scene. He could truly say that it had never given him more than a moment's pause. It had been an isolated event amongst persons that these things happen to, and his strength, status, and confidence precluded any other conclusion. What little thought he had given it were evidenced in the five-pound weights that doubled as deterrents to violence, and that he now threw to the ground in a mindless flight from an undiscriminating death.

❧

The killer, unlike the runner, loved the brief time betwixt night and day—that quiet teetering of the balance from darkness to light, when the world is given over to the fortunate prey and the predator slips unobserved to its lair. But, being a predator, the killer understood too that as the sun drove back the darkness, it deepened the shadows and lulled the unsuspecting with its false promise of peace. The dawn presented a last, and best, opportunity.

He had watched the runner for some minutes as he approached, panting and wary, yet determined on his course. A course that would take him within feet of the killer. The killer had heard the steady crunching of the gravel beneath the runner's feet for some time before he hastened to his vantage point beside the trail, disturbing some small animal as he did so. There, he lay on his belly… waiting. Then the steps ceased.

He was tempted to stick his head out and look but resisted. Like all hunters, he understood patience as the thin wall that separated those that would die from those that would kill. He lay there in the wet grass, enjoying the anticipation, the… *almost* uncertainty.

The footsteps resumed and gained in speed. A few moments later, the runner came into his view, his head swiveling from side to side, disturbed and wary. He willed himself to remain still. He could see that his victim was large and healthy. This was unlike the last and gave him pause. That one had been easy. Even after years of confinement it had been an effortless kill, and the memory of it thrilled him and filled his mouth with the taste of iron. All those years, unable to do what he wanted… needed most!

Then the runner was next to him; a body's length away. At the last possible moment before his passing, the runner turned and saw. His eyes met the killer's, and all was understood between them: the role that each must play.

The killer broke from his cover in that same instant and began his silent pursuit of the stumbling, sobbing runner. In a moment, he was upon him, slashing him to the bone with his first, joyful blow. The slanting rays of the new sun crept over them as the killer celebrated the dawn in a welter of blood, punctuated by the occasional grunt of satisfaction. The victim, like the rest of nature, had grown quiet and still.

With the same caution he had exercised with his previous victim, the killer dragged the corpse to a spot deep in the woods, carefully covering it with the litter and debris of the forest floor. Satisfied with his work, he turned and hurried east towards the park. He knew, from years of watching, that soon the park attendants would be arriving, and he could not risk their observing him. He would not risk his greatest secret. Not after waiting so very long to enjoy it.

As the first service trucks approached the garage area, the killer watched from a perch in a large tree that overlooked his compound. Calling greetings to one another, the men hurried into a Quonset hut for their morning coffee. The great cat hesitated a moment longer, gathering strength in its haunches, then sprang from the branch, clearing the fence and inner moat, and landing lightly within.

When the first zoo attendant made his rounds, he found the old Bengal in its favorite spot beneath the ancient oak tree, carefully preening itself, for all the world, like a big house cat. The tree bore deep scores in its venerable trunk, testifying to years of service as a scratching post to the mangy old tiger that had dwelt beneath its ever-spreading branches. As he turned away, satisfied that his charge was well and secure for another day, he briefly wondered if it weren't high time for the grounds division to give the old tree a serious pruning. Its great branches shaded nearly the entire enclosure, narrowing the big cat's choices for sunning himself to fewer and fewer spots with each passing year. Making a mental note of this, the aging keeper continued on his rounds.

The tiger followed the old man with his round yellow eyes until he vanished from sight, then resumed his careful grooming, removing the last of his victim's blood from his fur with a broad, raspy tongue, pink as a flower.

എ

That morning the chief arose stiff and cranky from a fitful night's sleep on the lumpy couch, unaware that eventually another body would be discovered and that when it was, he would become the prime—and in the public's mind the only—suspect of the copy-cat murder of his wife's latest lover.

Road Hazards
(2005)

Rueben had lived in the same house for twelve years and held the same job for two more. He considered himself a steady man and a good neighbor, or at least an undemanding one. So how, he asked himself on his drive home, had he ever offended anyone? In what way? Why did he now have to dread returning to his own neighborhood each night after work? When had the comfortable routine of his solitary existence become so threatened?

These were not new questions that Reuben grappled with but a mantra of dissatisfaction, unease, and frustration that was recited nightly on his long way home from the police department. He already knew the answers to the why and when of his questions; the agony lay in the "What to do?"

He was a good, even exceptional, dispatcher—an important, if unglamorous, profession; the first voice that the frightened, desperate, and irate heard when they dialed for help. When he'd had a few too many at the annual Christmas party, he was often heard to remark that without him (meaning all dispatchers presumably) help would never arrive. There were few desperate situations that his disembodied voice had not been a party to, and yet, unlike the officers that he sent to the scene, he had never experienced the actual blood, vomit, and tears of unruly life, and in truth, was glad.

Rueben contemplated the idea (for at least the hundredth time) of asking one of these officers to pay his neighbor a visit and, as always, dismissed the thought. The officers would see it for what it really was: a strong-arm demonstration, shady and gangster-like, and would refuse. Worse, they would view him with contempt for not being man enough to do his own dirty work. Rueben squirmed at the thought as a sudden gust of wind shoved his car toward the center line.

An oncoming pair of headlights appeared from around a curve and began to flash high beams in an angry warning. Rueben twisted the wheel to the right, startled from his reverie by an accompanying blast from the other driver's horn as the car flew by. Gravel played a metallic tattoo on the undercarriage of Rueben's ancient Ford as it rode onto the shoulder at too high a speed. "Sonofabitch," he muttered, twisting the wheel yet again and resuming the roadway. "Concentrate… concentrate."

The nightscape seemed to reflect his turmoil—wherever his headlights fell, movement and shadow grappled and receded. A small white branch shot out of the darkness and skittered across his windshield like a ghost crab. Rueben slowed the car.

Somewhere far ahead, just beyond the reaches of a lone street lamp, there was movement. At least, Ruben thought he saw movement, though he could see nothing now. Yet, there was something that had drawn his attention. Even now, like a ripple in a pond or a disturbance of the mist, there was the suggestion of something. Rueben strained his eyes in the gloom. Yes, there it was again, on his side of the street! Linear and purposeful… nothing out of nature certainly and moving right towards him. Rueben felt a drop of perspiration form beneath his heavy, long-out-of-fashion moustache. "What on earth," he breathed. Car and phantom closed on one another.

A figure began to form at the murky outer fringes of his headlamps: tall and wobbly, a shifting dark kaleidoscope of flapping wings, limbs, and even tentacles, rushing headlong towards the car.

Then it arrived full-blown into the glare of the headlights, the face a rigid, unshaven mask of discomfort; eyes squinted almost shut behind skewed taped glasses that returned the car lamps' brilliance in miniature. The tattered old army overcoat that the man wore waved and flapped about him as he pumped along on the spindly, rusty bike, and his filthy scarf and hair whipped this way and that in the wild wind. He glared at Rueben through the windshield, though it was impossible he could see in. Rueben feared that he might intentionally collide with the car; he followed the white shoulder line so closely. He rode as if to challenge the oncoming driver.

"You idiot!" Rueben screamed as he swerved to the left at the last moment and the apparition was swallowed up by the night. "You idiot," he repeated more softly, chancing a backwards glance and half expecting to see the hated cyclist following. He wiped each palm on his trouser legs as more beads of sweat popped out on his upper lip (the real reason he had never shaved the unfashionable face hair).

"*Him…* " Rueben fumed, "… was there no getting away from that demented lowlife? How had he ended up with such a neighbor? And to pop up just when he was thinking about him. What were the odds—out here, in the middle of the night?"

"It hadn't always been so bad," he recalled, picking up speed again. "No, it wasn't that bad before Curt died. Uncomfortable, yes. But now…"

If Rueben had been less distracted by his train of thought, he might have been forewarned by the events of his drive: the wind, the branch, the other car; even his hated neighbor—bounding in front of his car the first deer vanished into the darkness of the other side of the road before his brain could signal his foot to brake. The fawn that followed was not so fortunate.

In the split second that it took for Rueben to react, he saw a flash of tan and white, as the smaller animal attempted to make the same crossing as its mother. The sickening thud that followed was simultaneous with the scream of his tires attempting to grip the asphalt. The deerling was flung back in the direction from which it had sprung.

Managing to stop the car on the shoulder of the road some fifty yards away, Rueben clambered out into a haze of burnt, stinking rubber that hung in the air like a fog. It was as if the hideous impact had silenced the very wind, and the night world now watched with held breath. By the light of his remaining headlamp, Rueben examined the damage as best he could. Besides the lamp, he could see that the grill was smashed, and with a frisson of horror, that several tufts of fur were caught in it, but as no fluid appeared to be seeping from the car and the engine was apparently unaffected, he had only the tire to be concerned about. A long streak of blood led him to the wheel well. Cautiously, so as not to smear himself, he felt about until he was satisfied that the tire was not damaged nor impeded by the crumpled quarter panel. Rueben stood and carefully inspected his palms but saw only road dirt.

Stumbling along the roadside in the direction from which he had come, Rueben scanned this way and that for the injured animal, as small stones skittered from beneath his shoes. He prayed that it was not still alive and suffering, as he had no idea what to do in such a case and doubted that he had the nerve to put it out of its misery if he did.

No nerve was required, however. Rueben found the small, broken body at the wood line, and even by the phosphorescent moonlight, it was obviously dead. Staring down at it from the edge of the lonely road, he was struck with the enormity and finality of death, as evidenced by this tiny, frail, yet once vibrant creature. It already had the deflated look of the absence of life, and even the large, bright eye that he had glimpsed the second before collision was filmed and sticky-looking.

"You were goin' too fast."

Uttering a cry, Rueben took several steps backwards, almost losing his balance.

"*Way* too fast." The phlegm-choked voice challenged again from the darkness.

Rueben's dilated pupils were now able to make out the dim figure that stood like a statue in the greater darkness of a nearby oak. He could just discern the bicycle that the figure leaned on. With a fresh outbreak of sweat on his upper lip and a sick feeling in his stomach, Rueben acknowledged what he already knew—that his hated neighbor was now a witness to his crime against nature.

"I… I didn't see it until… well, it was too late," Rueben stammered as the figure detached itself from the moon shadow and approached, still wheeling the bicycle. "He just sprang out from the woods." Rueben hated the wheedling, defensive sound of his voice. Why did this man always elicit this kind of reaction from him? Of course, the fact that he was evidently some kind of demented night crawler might explain some of it, he thought, but what was he doing out at this time of night? It was after one in the morning.

"Her," the neighbor corrected, bending low over the carcass. "It's a female."

With a shock of revulsion, Rueben saw that he had lifted the poor creature's tail to expose the hindquarters for his benefit.

"Yes, I see…" Rueben acknowledged.

Still squatting, he turned his face up to Rueben and smiled. This time it was the wan light of the moon that pooled in the grimy lenses of his skewed glasses, hiding the bloodshot piggish eyes that Rueben remembered so well. The same light delineated his face like a stark black and white portrait: each detail stood forth from the composite whole as unattractive in its own right, independent of the unpleasant picture they all conspired to create. The crown of his lumpy skull was nearly exposed, with only a few lank wisps trailing down to join the true hairline that began just above his large hairy ears. Allowed to grow to shoulder-length, the hair was so filthy that it looked like that of a drowned man: wet and twisted into greasy ropes by the currents. Dirty-looking stubble covered the drawn, lower face. In the thousands of days that Rueben had watched his neighbor lounge about his property his appearance never changed: the facial stubble; the lank, wispy moustache that draped the thin upper lip, the glasses sporting some amateurish repair. He was like some prehistoric insect trapped in amber, Rueben thought—hideous and unchanging.

The face continued to grin up at Rueben as if awaiting an answer that would surely be wrong. Rueben stared back, unable to shift his gaze or just walk away; aware for the first time just how much the man frightened him and how that fear resembled hatred.

"That might'a been me," the neighbor observed, standing. "Dead, like that." He nudged the carcass with the toe of his engineer boot to emphasize his point. "Almost was me."

"You were on the wrong side of the street," Rueben squeaked, outraged and made nervous by the insinuation.

"I've been runned over before," he went on, pointing to the left side of his face and turning his small, round head to best advantage in the moonlight.

Rueben was horrified to see a whorl of scar tissue at the man's left temple that appeared to extend into the eye socket. Face on, with the glasses, it was almost hidden, but from the angle he presented, it appeared as if a spike had been driven into his head and wrested out many years before. He could barely contain his disgust.

"My God," Rueben whispered, "How did that…"

"Speeder… like you," The neighbor offered, his tiny teeth an uneven row of mottled corn kernels. "Left me for dead." As an afterthought, he added. "But I wasn't."

For the first time Rueben felt a spark of compassion for the man.

"Danny," Rueben tried the name like a foreign word; he hadn't used it since Curtis, Danny's poor, broken father, had died. "When did this happen… your accident, I mean?" He gestured at the scar.

Danny seemed startled at the use of his name. "Right about when you moved into the neighborhood." He stared into Rueben's eyes and smiled.

Now it was Rueben's turn to be startled. "You're not insinuating that I… you're not serious!"

Danny stopped smiling. "Might'a been you…. It almost was tonight."

"I was nowhere close to hitting you," Rueben protested, the sweat breaking out on his forehead now. "You were on the wrong side of the street! Besides, what are you doing out here at this time of night, anyway? And with no lights or reflectors?"

"Gimme ten dollars," Danny countered, taking a step closer.

"What?"

"Ten," Rueben repeated. "The Bealwood closes in half an hour."

The Bealwood was a local watering hole; not the kind of place Rueben patronized. "You want beer money?" Rueben gasped, taking a step back.

"Ten," Danny repeated and shot out a grimy, black-nailed hand. "Then we'll just keep this to ourselves."

"Keep what?" Rueben protested even as he pulled out his wallet and extracted a five with shaking hands. He was disgusted and ashamed of his easy capitulation, but the nearness of this man, the smashed animal at his feet, and the eerie solitude of their situation all conspired to deprive him of what little courage he possessed.

Danny snatched the five from his grip. "I said ten."

Humiliated, Rueben dug out several more bills to find another five, only to have Danny snatch the remainder from his grasp and crush them into a ball without even bothering to count. Smiling now, he slapped Rueben on the shoulder and asked, "Wanna come get a drink?"

Shaking his head, Rueben looked at his feet to hide the tears that welled up in his eyes.

"Aw'right, then," Danny acquiesced. "But I aw'ways shut the place down." Climbing onto his shaky bicycle, he grunted and puffed until he vanished into the darkness.

"I could have him arrested," Rueben told himself as he stared after his antagonist, knowing that he would never do it. The additional humiliation of explaining to officers, people who he saw on a daily basis, how he was robbed without a blow or a weapon was too much. He could easily imagine the sly, exchanged glances and barely concealed smirks. No, he would tell no one. It would be unbearable.

Danny had been in his late teens when Rueben had bought the house next door, and even then, Rueben had sensed all was not well with his neighbors. Curtis and Dot were quiet, friendly folk who had made a point of welcoming Rueben to the neighborhood with an iced cinnamon cake baked by Dot herself. They had arrived at his door without their son, and never once mentioned him throughout their brief, chatty visit. Rueben might never have known he existed if not for his sullen, beer-drinking presence camped out for hours at a time in their backyard, ensconced in a lawn chair and glaring at Rueben whenever he ventured into his own. Apparently, he did not attend school, as Rueben (who had always worked the four-to-twelve shift) found to his dismay when he wished to enjoy his own yard.

It was unsettling to be the subject of such intense and, seemingly, malevolent scrutiny, but Rueben kept his peace, not wishing to upset Curtis or Dot, who obviously bore a heavy, and what must have been disappointing, burden in their son. Rueben's attempts to break the ice with a friendly wave were met with a toad-like stare, the occasional curt nod, and more than once, the "finger." If things had continued in this manner, then Rueben might not have found himself standing on a lonely roadside twelve years later with a dead deer, an empty wallet, and worse still, a gut-sick fear that was rapidly evolving into murderous hatred.

It was typical, if destructive, boyish pranks at first: a full garbage can left at the curb for pick up, turned upside down, the lid vanished; impossible to right without emptying the entire stinking contents into the street. A jack-o-lantern smashed against the siding of the house, orange gore dripping and a stain that took great effort to wash away. A paper bag set aflame on his front step that Reuben found, after stomping it out, to be full of excrement (he never cared to discover whether it was of animal or human origin). In every case, he could count on looking up and finding Danny watching, a cigarette dangling from his lips.

Events grew more alarming, and not just for Rueben. It seemed no one was exempt, even if Rueben was especially singled out. One neighbor got a brick through the windshield of his brand-new automobile left parked on the street. Another awoke to find his newly-filled pool fouled in a manner reminiscent of Rueben's porch incident. There were accusations and recriminations, and even Rueben joined in after he awoke to find his front door spray-painted with the word "FAG" in bright yellow. It took several coats of enamel paint to conceal the epithet and Rueben noticed that several men in the neighborhood were cool to him afterwards.

Rueben was shocked at the appearance of Curtis and Dot when they warily answered his rings on this occasion. He had not seen them but at a distance for several years, so cool had relations become in the neighborhood as a result of their son's depredations. He found them shrunken and timid: hollowed out with shame and something else... fear, Rueben thought. They looked ancient. He hadn't the heart to do anything other than ask them to keep an eye on Danny and beat a hasty, embarrassed retreat.

Danny was sitting on the front steps when Rueben came out and gave him a terse nod. After he hurried past, a cigarette butt arced past his head like a tiny comet. He spun about to find Danny staring off into the middle distance, making perfect smoke rings.

Rueben's cat did not return home the following day. A week later he found the old tom curled up on the patio with his head tucked neatly beneath his tail—frozen solid and slowly defrosting in the blazing summer sun. In the adjacent yard, Danny leaned from his rickety lawn chair and retrieved a cold beer from the refrigerator plugged into an outside outlet that he kept for his convenience, and with slow exaggeration, rolled the sweating can across his sloping brow. Rueben fled into the house, tears of shame and rage choking him in a slow, steady grip.

As Danny could and did roam at all hours (he never held a job, to Rueben's knowledge) and could, therefore, strike at will and without witnesses, the neighborhood simply hunkered down and tried not to gain his attention. Any complaint to the police resulted in inquiries at Danny's door, which had the unfortunate result of identifying the complainant. Retribution was sure to follow.

Curtis and Dot suffered the silent scorn and universal condemnation of the community. Though their abhorred son had long ago reached adulthood, it was they that were anointed the status of "non-persons": they were invited nowhere, spoken to only from necessity, and soundly, firmly, and most pointedly ignored. The kindly, middle-aged couple shrank from public scrutiny over time and was seen less and less often. Even as their closest neighbor, Rueben only caught glimpses of them as they ran the most necessary errands. *After all, the beast must be fed,* Rueben thought on more than one sighting. Yet, he could see the toll taken on them. They looked ill, and frailer than their years should have made them. Dot died the tenth year of Rueben's residency of ovarian cancer, and Curtis followed a scant two years after from a heart attack.

Both funerals were surprisingly well attended, though Rueben suspected baser motives at work than the simple act of mourning might portray. He suspected because he recognized the cowardice at work in himself. But if the crowd expected a softening from the son in the face of their apparent grief, they were to be disappointed. Each time, Danny simply sat at the foot of the coffin like a drugged though still dangerous guard dog, staring out over the uncomfortable gatherings as if he were in an empty room.

The neighborhood was also to be disappointed in yet another way. With Curtis's death, hope raised its head and happy speculation circulated from house to house. The watch for the "For Sale" sign to appear was a happy and expectant one. It was not to be, however, for the truth eventually supplanted the rumors, and Danny was found to be the sole possessor of a mortgage-free home. If this was not disappointing enough, and infuriating for all those who would work thirty years to attain the same status, it also became known that he was the recipient of some mysterious source of income: not much, but enough to meet his basic needs. The neighborhood fell back in dismay and awaited the next blow.

That blow had yet to fall, and this was almost worse than the campaign of depredations. Rueben and the rest of the neighbors existed in a state of tension, an unbearable condition of expectation and dread; like beaten dogs they seemed to scurry, not walk, always looking back to see who, or what, approached.

Danny's lassitude only made matters worse. His lizard-like posture on his front porch was ascribed as planning, his forays on his bike were interpreted as reconnaissance, and when lights were seen in the windows of his house in the small hours, it was understood to bode ill for someone.

All of these thoughts raced through Rueben's head as he stood at the edge of the road, the wind beginning to rise once more as evidenced in a murmuring of dried leaves.

"Enough," he hissed. "I don't deserve this! Who the hell does he think he is?" Rueben kicked the small, broken body that lay at his feet, and stepped back immediately with a stifled cry of horror and disgust at what he'd done. From across the street came an answering report of a snapped branch or twig, and Rueben spun about, expecting to find Danny returned—but saw only darkness. Hurrying to his car, he drove away with only the one lamp to light his progress.

એસ

Rueben waited until the following morning to request an officer for an accident report. He reasoned that he would need it for insurance purposes, but as no one had been injured and it had not involved another vehicle, it could wait until after a night's rest. The officer, an affable fellow named Blaise, arrived at ten to find Rueben hollow-eyed and nervous after a fitful sleep, standing next to his car in the driveway.

"Mornin', Rube," Blaise huffed as he bent to examine the damage.

Rueben gritted his teeth in annoyance. Though the nickname was almost universally employed by the officers of the department, it seemed to hold a particularly demeaning ring this morning.

"Good morning, *Blaise*," Rueben returned stiffly.

Blaise glanced up, "Somebody cranky this mornin', Rube?"

Rueben tried a strained smile. "Yeah," he agreed. "I'm a little cranky… I hit a deer last night—a baby deer."

"What were you doin'? Drivin' drunk?"

"No… of course not! I just got off from work! You know that! I was just…"

"Whoa." The officer held his hands up from his still-kneeling position. "Take 'er easy, Rube! I was just kiddin'. Maybe we *should* go out and knock back a few—sounds like you need it," he chuckled.

Rueben put his hands to his head and massaged his temples. He *did* feel like he had a hangover. "Sorry… sorry." He sighed. "It was all just a little upsetting." Rueben glanced at the house next door, and for the briefest of moments considered telling the officer everything that had happened.

Blaise stood up, dusting his knees. "Well, the important thing is that you're okay, and the car ain't that bad, really. In any case, I'll have the report ready by tomorrow and you can pick it up at work. Where'd you say you left the deer? I'll notify animal control to pick it up."

"What..." Rueben mumbled, his thoughts jumbled, as if he were trying very hard to remember something, "... oh, yes, the deer."

Ⴊ

After the officer left, Rueben placed a call to his insurance company and then to a garage on their approved list. He got the head mechanic after a half-dozen rings.

"Yeah, sure, bring it in today. Things are kinda slow 'round here. We should be able to get to it over the next few days."

Rueben couldn't believe his good timing. He had off the next two nights and wouldn't even have to make arrangements for a ride to work. "That's great..." he began, then trailed off. For the second time that morning he felt his thoughts intruded upon, as if something were moving beneath his consciousness, trying to rise from the gray depths into the light. Clearing his throat, he asked, "How about Friday? Could I bring it in then?" That would give him two nights.

"Sure," the mechanic replied in a puzzled tone. "But we might be busy by then; could take longer."

"Well, that'll be fine," Rueben assured him. "Friday, then," Rueben said, and hung up the phone.

What had lain hidden now burst forth: bits and pieces of the previous night scrambled this way and that, glowing with import. Rueben stood stock still and forced himself to examine each telling moment—Danny's half-hearted accusation, his inadvertent (or was it?) revelation that he always closed the Bealwood Tavern, and of course, the fawn. Was that just bad luck... or Providence? He could see it all now as clearly as if it were already done.

⚮

As Danny staggered from the bar, Rueben smoothly accelerated from the dim parking lot across the street and glanced at his watch. It read two a.m. "Right on time Danny, just like you promised," he whispered.

Though he couldn't know exactly what route Danny might take home, Rueben was certain of one thing: The stretch of county blacktop that they had met on the previous night was unavoidable. It was the only link to their subdivision.

Rueben calculated that he had at least fifteen minutes before the drunken Danny could possibly arrive into what he now thought of as the "kill zone."

His plan was simple—drive up and down the road until Danny was spotted, then, if the coast was clear, run him down. The only real challenge, as Rueben saw it, was that the impact must occur where the car had suffered damage the night before. Not that hard, really, and Rueben felt equal to the challenge.

Since Danny insisted on being a traffic hazard and using the wrong side of the road, it would be a simple matter of swerving to the right at the last possible moment, at a high rate of speed of course, and then just continuing on. If Danny happened to survive such a head-on impact, the headlamps would prevent him from identifying the vehicle. Even one headlamp, so long as it was set on high-beam, would blind him. In any event, Rueben did not expect him to survive.

The wait was not long. In less than fifteen minutes he spotted the wobbling bicycle approaching. Even in the gray, hazy light provided by the occasional street lamp, Rueben's flapping, fluttering, scarecrow-like silhouette was unmistakable. Far from the terror it had inspired the previous night, this time Danny's presence was welcomed—Rueben felt elated; not a trace of nerves. In fact, as he began to accelerate, climbing steadily beyond the fifty-mile-per-hour limit, the sense of inevitability, and yes, invulnerability, that he had first felt grow warm during his conversation with the mechanic now positively blazed. He hit the high beams.

If there was such a thing as a God-anointed mission, then this surely was it. Rueben chuckled. Hadn't the hated, Caliban-like Danny suggested it himself ,even an appointed time and place? Danny knew what he truly deserved, and like the animal he was, he should be put down. Was he any better than that poor little deer, beautiful and unoffending, whose only instincts had been to stay with its mother? The speedometer had passed the sixty-mile-per-hour mark and was still climbing.

Smiling, Rueben now leveled the car at sixty-five, not wishing to risk loss of control. Danny could be seen clearly, one arm raised against the intensity of the light bearing down on him. Easing the speeding vehicle to the right, Rueben placed the passenger side wheels onto the shoulder. Ever defiant, Danny remained close to the shoulder line, waving the oncoming car away with imperious slaps at the air, infuriating Rueben.

The car struck bike and rider with a metallic clack, Rueben shouting at the same moment, "Yes!... Yes, you bastard!" The rest followed so rapidly and silently that he was unsure as to what had happened. He sensed, rather than saw, something large and dark sail past the passenger side of his car at incredible speed and vanish into the darkness.

That was it... all of it.

With only slight difficulty, largely because he was breathing so hard, he regained his lane and began slowing. Not a single

other car was in sight. He reached an intersection a mile down
the road and executed a careful U-turn. Within moments he was
passing what he was sure was the very spot.

There was nothing. The undergrowth by the side of the road
had swallowed everything—man and bike. With a smile and the
satisfying sense of a job well done, Rueben headed for home.

ॐ

Since he had accomplished what he set out to do on the first
night, Rueben now had the second to get through before he took
the car to the body shop. After inspecting it in the security of his
garage, he was pleased, though not surprised (he had somehow
known it would be like this) to find almost no additional damage
to his old Ford. The lamp housing was twisted even more to the
outside of the car, but not alarmingly so; he doubted whether
Blaise would note the difference even after having previously
inspected it.

There was one unsettling moment though, when he discovered
a tuft of what was obviously human hair caught between that
same housing and the front quarter-panel. With meticulous care
and a gagging disgust, Rueben extracted it with tweezers and
disposed of it down the toilet, scrubbing his hands afterward.

There was surprisingly little blood. Besides the smear that
had been left by the fawn, only wine-colored droplets were
spread across the passenger side of the car. Warm water, soap,
and a brush made short work of both.

Now, as night was upon him once more, Rueben found
himself at the Bealwood Bar and Grill enjoying a cold beer. He
felt flamboyant, though of course no one there could possibly
know that he had slain one of their steady, and he was sure,
unwelcome customers. The day's paper had made no mention

of a hit and run. Still, it felt deliciously dangerous, and Rueben thought he had never tasted such wonderful beer in his life. He was a little disappointed though, that not one person in the bar remarked on Danny's absence.

After several more beers than was his usual, Rueben set out for home, retracing his victim's ride of the night before. Humming with the radio, he turned left onto the county road and began to accelerate.

Pulsing red lights reflected off the trees as he rounded the curve, and for one gut-wrenching moment, Rueben considered braking and turning the car around. The chase car parked in the greater shadows to his right convinced him of the folly of that. Swallowing the beery, acidic gorge that rose burning into his throat, he slowed for the roadblock that the police had engineered.

Two patrol cars facing opposite directions sat in the center of the road, the overheads rotating in a riot of red light. Beyond, a second chase car also crouched in the darkness, awaiting anyone from the opposite direction who might wish to avoid the police. Rueben came to a stop behind one other car and watched as an officer (he couldn't tell who due to the glare) seemed to chat amiably with the driver. Rueben used the few moments of respite to collect himself.

No one saw anything, he reassured himself. They must have found the body sometime this afternoon or evening and conducted the autopsy. That's why they're here now. They know the approximate time he died, and this is just the routine roadblock to interview everyone who normally passes at this time. They don't *know* anything; otherwise they wouldn't be bothering with this.

The officer waved the other car on and Rueben eased forward. Damn! He didn't recognize this kid! He must be a rookie. For Christ's sake! Of all the times to draw the wild card! He could see the kid's brow puckering up as he played his flashlight over the damage to Rueben's car. He shot his hand up, as if to say far enough, and began walking the length of the passenger side, his head at a tilt.

A sudden wave of hilarity came over Rueben and he could barely contain it. "Look kid. Look all you want," he whispered.

Having worked his way around the car, the young officer arrived at the driver's window. "Good evening, sir," he greeted Rueben. "May I ask what happened with your car?"

Rueben didn't like the rookie's no-nonsense attitude and wasn't used to not being recognized by the officers—it unsettled him, made him feel like just another civilian—and his mood quickly evaporated. He tried to smile but felt his cheek muscles twitching and let it drop.

"A deer," he replied. "I hit a baby deer."

"A deer…?" The young officer looked dubious, and his eyes drifted to the damaged headlamp.

"Yeah… a deer," Rueben repeated, beginning to enjoy the game; that overwhelming feeling of euphoria returning unbidden. "You know… Bambi." The smile arose naturally now, and he could feel laughter bubbling dangerously close to the surface. He could see the kid didn't like it but was powerless to stop it.

"And when did this happen, sir?"

"Night before last," Rueben replied, the smile threatening to split his face. "There's a report. Blaise took it… Officer Lamanna, that is," Rueben added.

The rookie seemed challenged by this and took a step back. "Wait here, sir," he directed, and marched off toward the other patrol car. Rueben placed a hand over his mouth to suppress the giggles.

Presently, he made out the rookie in the company of an older, larger officer, stumping back. He couldn't believe his luck (then again, yes he could). It was Blaise! Rueben was so pleased with the turn of events that he shouted out a greeting and slapped the veteran officer on the shoulder as he leaned down to Rueben's window.

"Rueben, what the hell are you doin' out? I'd a' thought you'd learned your lesson the other night," he joked. Then he took a sudden step back and began to fan the air in front of his face. "Whoa… so you did take my advice, huh?"

Rueben grinned stupidly at Blaise. "I'm on my way home," he offered.

The older officer leaned in and grinned back at him. "Listen, you're damn lucky I'm here—I switched shifts with Billy MacDougal as a favor; otherwise, this young lion," he tossed his head back at the now sullen, younger officer, "would be locking your ass up for DWI… pronto."

"I appreciate it, Blaise, I really do," Rueben gushed.

Lowering his voice to a stage whisper, Blaise hooked his thumb over his shoulder, saying, "Thought he caught a *killer* when you pulled up with all that damage."

In the nick of time, Rueben remembered that nothing had been in the news. "What's this all about?" he asked with a sweep of his hand indicating the roadblock.

"Hit and run, ol' son, hit and run… some son of a bitch run down a bicyclist and left him for the flies. Hell of a thing… hell of a thing." He paused, then added, "In fact, you ought'a know 'im—he was a neighbor of yours, if I'm not mistaken."

Rueben's mouth became cottony and dry. "You're kidding… who?"

"A scruffy looking character name York… Danny York. Know 'im?"

"Yeah, of course I do. That's a shame." Rueben did his best to sound sincere.

"Yeah… well, since I'm here, let me do a walk around to satisfy the rookie," Blaise announced and began to walk in front of the car playing his flashlight along its surface.

Rueben almost protested but stopped short. He felt the eyes of the rookie watching his face. It didn't matter, he reassured himself, it didn't matter.

Blaise sauntered along, reaching the far side of the car and beginning to work his way to the rear. He stopped almost opposite Rueben and appeared to be studying something. Rueben felt his breathing get shallow and rapid. What was he looking at? What could he possibly have missed?

Blaise tapped on the passenger window, indicating that Rueben should roll it down. Leaning over, Rueben noticed that his hand was shaking as he worked the crank. He prayed Blaise couldn't see it.

"What happened to your mirror here?" The officer tapped the outside rear-view, making it spin uselessly on its axis. "I don't remember this, Rueben."

Rueben shrugged, unable to speak for a moment; he had no idea what his expression must be. "It was there, Blaise," he lied. "The day you came over, it was that way." For the life of him, he couldn't think how he could have missed it. Danny's bike, or body, must have struck it and broke the retaining screws, and yet, it somehow remained in place. Hell, rust must have held it together for a little longer! For all he knew, it came dislodged when he ran over a pebble a quarter-mile back.

Blaise glanced past Rueben to the young officer waiting and whispered, "Hell, you think I just missed it?" He paused again, his seamed face a mask of concentration. "Wouldn't surprise me," he exhaled, at last. "I'm not a young buck, like that one." He nodded at the rookie. "Well, straight home, Rueben, I mean it, okay?"

"Okay, Blaise," he answered in a small, contrite voice, though he wanted to shout to the skies.

With a quick glance of contempt at the younger officer, Rueben put his car in gear. "Seatbelt," the rookie snapped and pointed at his chest. Rueben ignored him and drove away.

As soon as he was out of sight of the roadblock he pressed the accelerator to the floor and began to howl and bang the roof with his fist. "I knew it," he shouted over the cool wind whistling through the open window. "I knew it! There is a God…. There is justice! The meek shall inherit the… sonofabitch!"

The deer seemed to be waiting, standing in his lane as he rounded the curve, gazing calmly at the oncoming vehicle.

Everything slowed down inside Rueben's head. He watched as his hands seized the wheel and wrenched it hard to the right. It was instinct, but such a mistake in this case, he thought with remarkable calm. Oddly, he recalled the snapping of a branch in the darkness the night he had run down the fawn—the feeling of yet another witness watching from the darkness.

His foot had barely touched the brake when he rammed the elm. Worse, his old car had no airbags, and he had neglected to fasten his seatbelt as the young officer had directed.

Even as Rueben completed his high-speed exit through the windshield, the deer bounded into the wood line, vanishing without a sound.

Trial by Fire

(1995) Nominated for Shamus Award

The tavern was nearly empty, and I had just slammed my tumbler on the bar and was about to call for another when they walked in. The sight of them choked off my words. It was just past three in the afternoon and I was keeping my usual appointment with Jack, Jim, Hiram, and the rest of the gang. I had a pact with myself that I'd never start drinking until the rest of the working world did, even though I was no longer part of that scene, being prematurely retired. It helps to have some sort of structure to your life.

I recognized the other patrons as regulars, like myself. Of course, in a dive like this everyone's a regular. You wouldn't just walk into this place off the street, you'd just keep walking. They count on people like me and they don't run tabs. That's why the couple snatched my attention away from that all-important follow-up shot. They weren't regulars here or anywhere else for long, I'd bet.

The man led the way, with the woman enough paces behind him to cover his back. I tend to notice little things like that, being an ex-cop. Usually, when a man and woman enter any establishment, they either walk side by side or the lady remains within touching distance of her escort. These two entered the joint like they were about to take it down. He walked hard and fast, making straight for the office in the rear, his trench coat swinging with his forceful gait, and sparing nary a glance for the losers at the bar. She, on the other hand, scanned the entire crew, almost walking backwards at one point, so as to include the door they had come in. A large woven bag was clutched to her ample bosom and seemed to contain something heavy that she was keeping close to hand.

Tall and powerfully built, the man had an acne-scarred face partially concealed by a short, dark, curly beard that matched his hair. Throwing open the door to the office with his left hand while keeping the other concealed in his coat pocket, he stormed in as if late for an important meeting. The woman reached the doorway and stopped, swinging slowly around, the bag at the ready. My palms had gone wet and I had a death grip on the tumbler. Locking eyes across the expanse of the horseshoe-shaped bar, I think we both stopped breathing.

She had the face of a fortyish hard drinker: pouchy and swollen, looking as if it were molded out of putty and about the same color. The eyes, peering out from the swollen lids, reminded me of green cat's-eye marbles, and showed about as much compassion. The mouth was wide and froglike. These attractive features were framed in bottle-blonde, shoulder-length hair that had once been styled so artfully that she hadn't seen fit to touch it since. The eyes flickered like a snake's tongue and her hog nostrils distended. The right hand slipped into the bag. I began to reach around to the small of my back, feeling for the off-duty piece that I no longer carried.

Stepping between us, his broad body blocking my view, Murray, the barkeep, shoved a shot glass brimming with amber liquid in my direction. "Here's your second," he said. "You look like you could use it." With that, he scooped up some of my cash from the bar and sauntered over to the register. She was gone. The doorway was empty and dark.

I'd caught myself unawares in the mirror and it was a sobering sight. My image in the murky, fly-blown mirror behind the stacks of bottles looked like a resurrected floater with its shock-white face and drowned-looking hair and clothes. I wasn't used to allowing anything to intrude on my carefully guarded reality these days and the last thing I expected was to start thinking like a cop again. Using both hands so as not to spill any, I lifted the tumbler from the bar and lowered my face to it. Years of waking with the shakes had perfected my technique.

*

I awoke the next morning with the usual cottonmouth and a vice grip loosely fitted to my skull. No headache, just the hovering threat of one. I've found that if I'm careful and make no sudden movements or bend over, I can escape undue punishment. It's a matter of practice. One false move, however, and the vise tightens accordingly. I only had to get to three o'clock, I thought, and it was already eleven. Piece of cake.

These days I don't usually arise till elevenish. The shorter the day, the better. If I do wake up early, it's because of my vivid, color-filled dreams and the pounding of my heart against my rib cage. Not a good way to start the day. What's worse is that I can never get back to sleep. That makes for a long day… which is a bad day. Today was starting off well.

I'd just settled down to a nice big breakfast of scrambled eggs, fried onions, Italian sausage, and A.1., when I remembered my couple from the bar. They never did come out again and I was there till last call. Actually, after a few more shots, I forgot about them. They must have had business with the owner, who's a fat Lithuanian with bad breath and an associate of mine from the old days. I'd like to say friend, but that would be stretching it. I probably bring back too many memories he'd rather forget. Nonetheless, he seems to have a kindly tolerance for me and that's good enough to keep me going back there. I can't afford to be choosy these days.

It was funny that after all these years I should pick up on those two as bad guys. It wasn't as if I didn't see crime and scumbags by the tubful in this neighborhood, but since I'd turn in my badge, I hadn't once felt the need to do something about it. If I wasn't needed, so be it. John Q. was on his own. Even so, there was something about those two. I'd ask ol' nasty-breath about them tonight when I reported to the bar for roll call.

❧

I didn't get to ask any questions of the Lithuanian that night and he wouldn't be answering any in the future. The bar was closed… permanently. When I strolled up it was just a smoking ruin wrapped with a bright yellow ribbon that stated, "Crime Scene—Keep Out." I wouldn't even have recognized the place but for the bodega and check-cashing shops on either side.

It was from Luis, who ran the bodega, that I got the lowdown. He said the place had gone up sometime shortly after closing and the Lithuanian with it. The building had been so fully engulfed by the time the fire department arrived that it was all they could do to keep it from spreading to adjacent buildings, and for this, Luis was eternally grateful. He had chased his family from their walk-up above the store into the street where they had watched the whole show. Arson investigators had arrived as the last of the flames were doused. I had already kind of figured on arson due to the crime-scene tape. I hadn't been a cop for nothing, I guess. The rest of it took me by surprise.

Just about the time Luis was given permission to return to his apartment, a body bag was brought out and deposited in the medical examiner's van. One of the uniforms on the scene, a local boy, told Luis that they believed the charred carcass to be the owner of the bar.

It hit me then. The couple from last night. The long stare from the woman. She had recognized me. After thirteen years, I don't know how. I don't even recognize myself half the time. I'm twenty pounds heavier and a lot more grey and grizzled than the last time we saw each other. Of course, if I had been in her shoes, I would remember too. I was surprised she didn't kill me on the spot. She was sure as hell mulling it over.

Kathleen Vichter... dope-pusher, hold-up artist and, the piece de resistance, torture-murderess. Quite a resume for someone sent up for life at twenty-seven. She hadn't been so chunky then, or blonde. Otherwise, she was still the essential Kathleen, brutal-looking and ugly. I should have made her right off and if I hadn't been for years of pickling my brains, I would have. A little late for Jogaila, though. That was the Lithuanian's name.

The man with Vichter was called Gunnar Bergstrom. I kid you not. He was the only Swedish thug I ever arrested. Actually, he was second or third generation and didn't look like the stereotypical Scandinavian, being dark and curly-haired. The beard was a new addition, as well as fifteen extra pounds of what looked like solid muscle. State prisons tend to have pretty good gyms and the prisoners have a lot of time to use them. The complexion wasn't cream-fed either, as I mentioned earlier. His face was so acne-scarred that it looked like someone had set it on

fire and put it out with an ice pick. His disposition gave weight
to that theory. So did his M.O.

He was the one I should have thought of first, because arson
was his calling card. Someone must have convinced him early
in his career that fire destroys all evidence, because after his
first stint in prison, at eighteen, he helped to justify half the fire
department's manpower increases. Every crime scene, including
a number of murder sites, was left smoldering rubble. Sherman
would have loved him.

I guess the worst was when he set fire to an ex-partner of his
over a business dispute. He had, with Kathleen's able assistance,
bound the hapless bastard with copper wire, squirted lighter
fluid all over him, and lit him up. Where he wasn't scorched, he
was cut to the bone by his efforts to escape the wire and flames.
The pathetic part was that he lived for several days afterwards…
begging to die. Actually, with no lips and blackened, cracked
teeth, I couldn't make out what he said, but I'd bet it was
something along those lines.

The dynamic duo had met up some two months before
Gunnar dissolved his partnership and it was love at first sight. I
don't know how they met, but they were never far apart from that
time on. Their violence seemed to escalate from that point also. I
guess they brought out the potential in each other, as happens in
any good relationship.

What got them sent up wasn't murder of the partner, though.
We knew they did it, but we couldn't prove it. It just got us
looking extra hard at their activities. What got them put away is
why I know they were the ones at the bar last night. It had to do
with the Lithuanian. More to the point, his son.

Jogaila used to be the owner of a liquor store in this same
neighborhood. Needless to say, it did a profitable business in this
part of town, especially in pints and halfs. I ought to know, I was

one of his most frequent customers. This was toward the end of my illustrious career with the police department.

Jogaila's mistake was that he let his first American-born son run the shop more and more frequently as he spent time with his fellow immigrants at the Lithuanian-American Social Club. The Soviet Union was still going strong in those days and I think they spent a lot of energy trying to figure out ways to get relatives over to the States.

The son, Johnny Joggs, as he was known in the neighborhood, was as American as you could get. He couldn't have cared less about what was happening in Lithuania, Russia, or the next street over. He was twenty-one, healthy, good-looking, smart, and had plans. He saw Pop's business as only the first step in a city-wide chain of Jogaila and Son stores. They were making money hand over fist here and he didn't see any reason to stop at that. Like a lot of kids, he had big plans. Those plans, however, did not include making payoffs to local thugs for the privilege of running his own store. Unbeknownst to Pop, he stopped making the payments and hid the money in a lockbox in his room. The elder Jogaila had instructed his son in the making of payoffs as a natural course of business in the U.S. of A. Coming from the old country, he was only too happy to be allowed to make bucks on his own, and if that meant a small tax to the local warlord, he was glad to pay it. Well, maybe glad was too strong a word, and the tax was a little stiff, but when in Rome, etc.... In any case, the kid didn't buy it. He began to put aside a nest egg for future endeavors. Only for him, there would be no future.

Gunnar and Kathleen let him slide through about three payments. That's how they were making ends meet in those days, strong-arming for the big boys. They had made such a fearsome reputation for themselves with their Bonnie and Clyde act that the Mafia put them on retainer for collections and enforcement.

Kind of like letting Dobermans patrol a meat locker, in my opinion.

Anyone who knew anything about them paid up when they made their rounds. In fact, they probably threw in a few extra bucks for putting them to the trouble. Everybody but Johnny Joggs. Why he should try such a foolish thing, I can't figure. He grew up around there and knew the score as well as anybody. Like I said, he was a smart kid, except about this one thing.

Why the Bobbsey Twins let him go for three payments, I don't know either—though shortly before they waxed him, he came home one night with both eyes closed and missing two front teeth. He had also been thoroughly doused with the only good Scotch they carried. That should have told him something. His statement to the cops was that he had been robbed by person or persons unknown. His assailants had not taken a thing from the till. That should have told him something, too.

They could easily have drawn the balance of what he owed, plus some, from the register and been on their merry way. Johnny misunderstood them. They really didn't care if he paid or not. In fact, they probably hoped he wouldn't. That's why they left the money alone. They were leaving it to him to make things right or give them the opportunity to do what they really liked to do. They got paid either way and fixing him would just be a bonus. Johnny must've thought his resistance actually put them off. Only a very young stud could think like that.

They didn't let the fourth time pass. When I got there he was a smoldering black mummy. The store itself had suffered minimal damage due to the sprinkler system, but it was too little, too late for Johnny Joggs. The elder Jogaila was being restrained outside the store by two poor uniformed saps and calling out to the heavens in his native tongue, but that didn't stop him from breaking free and taking a roundhouse swing at me. I ducked it easily and the uniforms drove him to the sidewalk. "You," he gasped in his heavy accent. "You do nothing to protect us! My boy! Give me back my boy!" Then he began to howl like a beaten dog as the tears streamed down his sooty face. It was hard not to feel sorry for him. He had played the game according to the rules but had failed to see to it that his son did likewise. Now he needed someone to blame. Cops always make easy targets.

When I stepped through the doorway, the stench was enough to gag a jackal. I popped open the nearest bottle to hand and poured some peppermint schnapps into my handkerchief and slapped it across my mouth and nose. The boy was worse than I expected. He was charred over seventy percent of his body and still smoking. What was left of his clothes was melted into his skin. The body itself was curled into the fetal position so common to burn deaths. The M.E.'s report stated later that he'd had both arms and legs broken prior to being set ablaze. All he could have done was scream, until the oxygen was sucked out of his lungs.

I knew right then that this was Gunnar and Kathleen's handiwork and that I was going to get them. No matter what, I was going to get them. Nobody deserved this. No matter how they played the game or bent the rules. Nobody should have to die like that. Nobody.

It only took me four weeks to nail them. It's funny how simple things can be once you make up your mind. I convinced Jogaila to take his name down from the door and go out of business. When it reopened a week later, yours truly was behind the counter.

It didn't take long. On their first visit, they explained the rules of the game and extracted fifty from the cash register as a sign of my good faith. They assured me that they would be back the following week. On their way out the door they helped themselves to a fifth of cheap vodka. Kathleen glanced back over her shoulder, smiled, and said, "Asshole." Gunnar stopped and turned to face me, waiting to see if I was stupid enough to respond in kind to his beloved. My palms were sweating, and I could feel the blood draining from my face. I managed a sickly, simpering smile and nodded my head up and down like a puppet. They both laughed and walked out into the night.

Yeah, I was scared. Knowing what I knew about those two, I was plenty scared. But I was also mad. Madder than I had ever been. I had seen their work several times and now I had met them up close. Now I knew what it felt like to be toyed with by them. To be a victim. What scared me most though was a line of thought that had been going through my head during our little encounter.

I was thinking how easy it would be to kill the bastards. All I had to do was to let them get in the door for their next collection and cut 'em down like dogs. My report would read that they had attempted a strong-arm robbery and deadly force was required to protect my life. End of problem. But that wasn't me, not then. I believed in the system. Most of all, I wanted to kick over their rock and scoop them up, slimy and squirming for all the world to see, and deliver them to justice.

My partner walked in as I was mulling this over and informed me that the wire was good and he had been able to hear and, more importantly, record everything that had been said. He'd even managed to get a few good shots with the telephoto of them rummaging through the cash drawer. We were well on our way to a conviction.

The plan was to make the first couple of payments, then start stalling. I wanted to get their spiel on tape of what they would do if I stiffed them and their bosses. What I got was even better.

It was their fourth visit. They were both standing on the other side of the counter listening to me blubber about how bad business was, with Gunnar all stone-faced and crazy-eyed and Kathleen looking like she knew a good joke and was just busting to tell it. Then Gunnar made his big mistake.

He reached inside his fake snakeskin jacket and yanked something out and slammed it down on the counter. At the same time, Kathleen grabbed a good handful of my hair and pulled my face down to within inches of the object. She chuckled. She had a hoarse, boozy chortle that sounded like a guy in drag. I didn't resist. I knew that Gunnar was just hoping I'd take a swing at his little sweet'ums. Not a chance. I was too busy sweating and not breathing to do anything that constructive. I was also trying to figure out why I was looking at his wallet. Though I had to admit, it was a lot nicer than mine, being genuine hand-tooled leather.

With a flick of his wrist he snapped it open, and then I understood. It wasn't a wallet at all. It was his very own pocket-size photo album, and in pride of place was Johnny Joggs, almost as I had last seen him. The same scorched, ruined face with its lipless mouth stretching open in a scream that would never stop. The only difference was that he was still burning.

From somewhere far away I heard Kathleen's voice saying, "I took that, ya know, and it wasn't easy. Came out pretty good. I didn't even need a flash!" And they started to laugh. That was the joke she'd been dying to tell. I stopped thinking then.

With my left fist I straight-armed Gunnar in the solar plexus with everything I had. At the same moment, I clamped Kathleen's hand to my head with my right so that she couldn't step away. I heard Gunnar grunting and wheezing from someplace far off as I snatched her hand away from my head, bringing a clutch of hair with it and pulling her off balance towards me. As she slammed into the edge of the counter, I let go with my right, drew back, and hit her with everything I had. Her head snapped back, and her body began to follow her abrupt change of direction. She quick-stepped in reverse, colliding with a rack of whiskey bottles, and went down in a cascade of amber liquid and shards of glass.

Gunnar's grunting had gotten louder, and he was beginning to snort in rage as he pushed up from the floor. I didn't waste a moment. Seizing the truncheon I kept under the counter, I vaulted over and struck him an overhand blow to his left shoulder, just where the muscle rises to meet the neck. I saw his left leg go wobbly. Then, without hurrying, I did the same to his right shoulder. Now the right side of his body went numb too, and he fell face forward. I stepped out of the way and let him fall… hard. His head bounced once and he was still. I straddled him like the Colossus of Rhodes and raised the club high over my head with both hands. I wanted to get this just right and then I'd see to the woman. I never heard my back-up crashing through the door and shouting my name. It took three of them to get the club out of my hands. Kathleen and Gunnar left on separate stretchers.

I didn't see them again for nearly three months and then it was only for their sentencing. The D.A. had wimped out, as usual, and let their attorney go for a plea bargain. They would plead guilty to the murder of Johnny Joggs and *accept*—I especially like that—accept a life sentence, in exchange for the other charges being dropped. As the D.A. explained to me, the other charges were lesser ones, little things like extortion, arson, robbery, jaywalking, etc.… This would save the state the expense of a lengthy trial and the Jogailas the anguish. They never would have gotten the death sentence in any case. Not these days, not with this governor.

I didn't like it. We had a damn good case and I'm not so sure a jury would have been so lenient. But it was a done deal before I was even told about it. The last I saw of my lovebirds, they were being hustled out separate doors and bundled off to his and hers prisons upstate.

Now I was sitting in Captain Walter Dravidian's office, hat in hand, shaved, wearing my only suit, and sober. Though I admit to one little eye-opener in the a.m., just to steady me after my shocks of recent days.

I figured if anyone could, or would, give me an update on how my two lovebirds flew their respective coops, Walt would. We go back a few years and Walt had never turned his back on me. Even when I decided I hated everybody in the department and "retired," Walt would give me a call now and then just to see if I was still alive. We started out together in the academy and drew the same assignments a number of times over the years. He was the best cop I knew, besides myself, and went on to bigger and better things in his career. I went on to make Detective Sergeant and an early "service-related" medical retirement. Even that, I owed to Walt. If he hadn't pulled a few strings with his fellow brass, I'd have been out on my ass, no pension, no benies. Drunks with guns didn't meet the department's new and improved image of the eighties. Good old Walt... nobody knew me like he did.

"So, you had yourself a little eye-opener before droppin' in, did ya?"

Like I said. Better than anyone.

"So what's so important that it actually brings you to stand next to a razor and attempt to look like a citizen again? Not that you succeeded, by the way. You look like someone I'd warn my grandkids about."

Did I also say that old Walt has a droll sense of humor and can be an unlikeable son of a bitch? He'd never forgiven me for falling into the bottle. He'd once remarked that he'd always be my friend, but that didn't mean he had to like me.

I cleared my throat and began, "Well, since we've decided to dispense with the pleasantries..." I gave him one of my hurt looks. "I need a little information of the official type, and since you're the only one in the department that still talks to me, or remembers me, for that matter, I thought I'd drop by."

Walt didn't answer, he just let it hang there, eyes closed and arms crossed. I noticed that his desktop was as barren as ever. I used to wonder how he did that. Mine had always been awash in paper. I decided on a different tack.

"Of course, if you're too busy, I understand. I can see that you've got a lot of pressing business… coffee to be brewed, donuts to be ordered—and that's no easy task these days with all the new varieties they've come out with—a secretary to chase around, et cetera…. Is that why you keep your desktop cleared? I've always wondered."

One baleful eye had opened and was regarding me with some distaste.

"If this involves money passing from my hands to yours, forget it. I don't bankroll alcoholics."

I felt my face getting hot. I didn't like that word.

"No, it's not that," I choked out. "A phone call. An official phone call to the upstate wardens. I want to know the status of Gunnar Bergstrom and Kathleen Vichter."

Now both eyes were open.

"Their status is that they're both in the slammer for life. You know that. We put them there."

If I didn't mention it before, Walt was my partner on the liquor store setup. Remember? The one who took pictures and stayed clean. Dapper Walt.

"I saw them the other night. At Jogaila's place. You know, the dive that got torched?" I could see that I had his interest now.

"You saw them?" he asked.

"At Jogaila's place," I repeated. "Think the department might be interested? You've got motive. Old Jogaila helped set them up. You've got means, that goes without saying with their track record. And you've got opportunity. I can place them at the scene."

Walt took a long pause before answering. "Were you drinking?"

I felt my face getting hot again. "What do you think, Walt? It was a freakin' bar." I could see where this was going, fast. "I'd had my first of the day, for chrissake! One!"

Walt was sitting upright now and carefully ignoring the fleck of spittle that had landed on his pressed pinstripe. Picking up the phone, he spoke quietly to his invisible secretary. After a few instructions, he hung up. We sat there looking at each other. To break the tension, I helped myself to a mug of his gourmet coffee since he wasn't going to offer any. I felt like a steel rod had replaced my vertebrae. My hands were shaking as I stirred in my third sugar. The phone rang and I spilled some of my coffee onto his cream-colored carpet.

I came and stood over his desk while he had another of his infuriating whispered conversations. "Yes…. Yes…. I see." Long pause. "Yes. Thank you." He gently replaced the receiver.

I stood over him waiting. He continued looking at the phone. I was getting damn sick of his long pauses.

"Where are they?" I asked at last.

He looked up as if he had just noticed me standing there.

"They're in prison. Just where we left them," he replied. "No parole, no special privileges. Life."

My legs were shaking, and I had to set the mug down on his immaculate desk even though I knew it would leave a ring.

"You didn't even speak to them. How can you be sure?" I could hear how lame I sounded.

"That wasn't necessary. My secretary spoke to the wardens of both prisons. I don't think they would lie about it… do you?"

I didn't care for the tone of that question. It sounded like a reality check.

"Walt, I saw them. They've changed, sure. Who wouldn't after thirteen years? It was them, Walt! I'd bet my life on it!" I was backing towards the door. The office felt close, stifling.

Walt was standing now. I'd about forgotten he could do that. Through the roaring in my ears, I could just make out fragments of what he was saying. Words like treatment, help, drinking problem. He looked pale and stricken, human at last. My friend was calling my name as I slammed the door to his office and fled the building.

⁓

If there's anything worse than a useless drunk, it's a drunk who thinks he's useful. My ears burn when I think of myself in Walt's office. I know what I must have looked like. A burned-out, used-up alcoholic—there, I've said it—ex-cop attempting to worm his way back into the fold with tales of bad guys from his heyday. Unverifiable, unsupported tales. Hallucinations. It must have been pretty sickening for Walt. "Think the department would be interested?" It made me want to vomit.

What was even worse was that now I wasn't sure. About anything. If that wasn't Vichter and Bergstrom I'd seen in Jogaila's, then I was further gone than I ever realized. I was lost… seeing ghosts. You'd think that if God was merciful, I'd have been visited by shades of lovers past. Like that full-breasted Italian beauty that used to make such a fuss about me so many years ago. Instead, I got the couple most likely to burn in hell. Actually, the couple most likely to burn… period! Har, har, I kill myself! What a sense of humor! And humor is important to the drinking man. Without it you might go insane.

I decided to raise a toast to myself and my ghosts and let the devil take the hindmost. When you're surrounded by friends like Jim and Hiram you've no need to fear phantoms. Even they cannot follow you into oblivion. With my friends' able assistance I'd become a ghost myself and wander these vaguely familiar streets. Maybe I'd bump into someone who remembered me, and I'd haunt them instead!

∾

On the third day, I rose again. I had no idea where I'd been or who I'd been with. I was reasonably certain that I'd been rolled, as my ribs were sore as hell and my cash gone—even the reserve I kept in my left shoe. The shoe was gone too.

I woke up in a doorway that smelled of urine, covered with newspapers. The sun was still below the horizon. In the grey, murky light of a tenement dawn, I lay among the trash and wondered if I was human anymore. I couldn't even picture my own face.

A sooty breeze fluttered the papers that covered me and I rolled over to my stomach and forced myself up onto all fours. Even that effort had drops of sour sweat trickling down my face and armpits. It seemed important to get on my hind legs if I was ever going to resume human form again.

After dry-heaving a few times from the exertion, I managed to pull myself up using the security bars that covered the door. I stood there, holding on and praying that I wouldn't faint from the throbbing inside my skull. After a few moments, it subsided enough for me to take stock of my surroundings. I recognized the street. It would appear that I had missed finding my own doorway by only three blocks.

I tossed my remaining shoe into the gutter. What good would it do me now? In my tattered stockinged feet I trudged towards sanctuary like a pilgrim in Palestine.

Eventually, I arrived within sight of my building, my feet cut and bleeding. I guessed it was a Sunday morning as the streets were still deserted when I approached my address and leaned against a friendly wall to catch my breath. It was then that I smelled it. Burning death. It was coming from the doorway of my building.

Sweat started pouring from my body and my legs got so wobbly I started to slide down the wall. I think I might have whimpered a little. I didn't want to look into that doorway. I didn't want to see. But I was also terrified that nothing would be there and I really was losing my mind. I had to find out.

I peeked around the doorframe into the shadowy interior. The sweetish smell of burnt flesh was overpowering. Its source lay just inside the cramped foyer on the cracked, dirty tiles: a curled, blackened fetus of a man, shrunken by the flames that had consumed all recognizable humanity. A bottle of Mad Dog lay just beyond his reach. A bum in a doorway, just like I had been. Only he picked the wrong doorway. I felt myself weeping.

The tiles of the floor and walls were scorched, as was the interior metal door. The fire must have been intense but brief and exhausted itself quickly with nothing else to feed on. My fellow tenants had been lucky. They probably never heard a thing. This poor bastard never knew what hit him. By the time the flames roused him from his stupor, he wouldn't have had enough oxygen to scream. The pity is that he was just a substitute.

I stepped over him and pushed open the inner door. I could see the pry marks near the latch, just where I expected them. There was nothing to fear now, Kathleen and Gunnar had gone. They'd just left me their calling card in the foyer.

My room on the third floor had also been jimmied. They hadn't really bothered anything, just taken a quick look around to make sure I wasn't there and left. There was the faint smell of an accelerant in the air. They had come prepared, of course. Finding the wino in the foyer on their way out must have been irresistible. They would fight back. First Jogaila, then me. Simple. Revenge.

I threw my shaving kit, some clean clothes, my checkbook, credit cards, and a few other odds and ends into a flight bag and split for the YMCA to get cleaned up. I left my friends Jim and Hiram behind. I wasn't going back.

☙

I laid low for a few days, drying out and thinking about what I knew. Which wasn't much. First, Gunnar Bergstrom and Kathleen Vichter. I knew with absolute certainty that I'd seen them, booze or no booze. And for now, it was no booze. Second, the time of the first murder—the wee hours of a Saturday morning. I had spotted them coming into the bar on a Friday afternoon. After normal work hours. The murder of the wino had been accomplished in the small hours of a Sunday morning. Both killings had been on a weekend, a week apart. Third, they were after me. Not really a lot to go on, so I theorized.

My theory was this: They were coming here from somewhere else. Too many people remembered them around this town, on both sides of the law. None of them had much reason to be friendly. The mob wasn't too happy with them for pleading to the Johnny Joggs murder and causing the uproar that ensued about cleaning up the city. A lot of wise guys had had to go underground, and a lot of business was lost as a result. I'd heard that the feds were having a field day right around the time I left the force.

So now I was testing my theory by sitting on the rooftop of a factory building that was across the street and two doors down from my old address. It was closed on the weekends and they had no security. I just wheezed my way up the rear fire escape and set up camp with an old lawn chair and a thermos of coffee. Occasionally, I scanned the street with a set of binoculars that I never turned back in to the department.

I figured they'd come at night. Even the gruesome twosome had to exercise some discretion. So I was just waiting and watching. Since I'd quit drinking—this was my seventh day—I didn't sleep anyway. Maybe two, three hours a night.

I'd done something with my appearance too, though not what you might think. I'd grown myself a pretty full beard. It was a little on the grizzled side, but not bad. Along with the horn-rimmed reading glasses I'd picked up at the pharmacy and a decent-looking suit, I came off as almost professional. I'd even sprung for a nice leather attaché case to complete the picture. A professor of criminology, specializing in arson murders.

☙

The sound of a car's idling engine gradually worked its way down into my consciousness and a tiny alarm went off. I woke with a snort and leaned cautiously forward over the parapet of the rooftop. I didn't know how long I had been dozing. My watch showed four a.m., Monday. The street was completely deserted. The only sound came from a late-model Chevy four-door that stood idling with its lights off near the corner. It almost looked like an unmarked, but there were no telltale antennas.

I fumbled the binocs up to my eyes and adjusted them. I couldn't see anything inside the darkened automobile. Suddenly, there was silence as they killed the engine. Still nothing happened. Even from where I was I could hear the clicking of the cooling engine.

Both doors flew open and they stepped out. The interior light never came on. They had unscrewed the bulb. Very professional. They eased the doors shut and began to walk away from the car. A man and a woman. I had to wait for them to reach a light before I could get a good look. I was wrong. It wasn't a man and a woman. It was Gunnar and Kathleen.

I waited until they entered my building. Kathleen's throaty, clotted cackle wafted up to me as they crossed the charred foyer. Past pleasures remembered, I guess. When I heard the soft pop of the new lock being forced, I dashed for the fire escape.

My breath was coming in gasps by the time I reached their car. Gulping air, I gave it the once-over. Clean, impersonal. The glove box yielded a registration and a rental agreement. The registration showed that the car belonged to one of the rental agencies at the airport. The lease papers identified a Mr. and Mrs. Charles Schlosser of Cleveland as the lessees. Right. I came up for air and glanced at the window of my apartment. The lights came on.

It wouldn't take a moment for them to determine I wasn't home. With my palms sweating so that I could hardly hold the pen, I scribbled down the information, including the make and model of the car and its plate numbers. I looked up again. I could see their shadows on the ceiling crisscrossing one another. One detached itself and reached out towards the window. It quickly foreshortened as its owner approached. Suddenly, Kathleen was there looking out into the night. With one move, I swung my legs into the car and pulled the door closed. Lying across the front seat, I could still see her through the windshield. She pressed her face to the glass, cupping her hands around her eyes, and looked directly at the car. I prayed I wasn't visible by the streetlight. After a long moment, she stepped away. The shadow dance resumed on the ceiling.

They would be on their way out any second. I sprang from the car, eased the door shut, and melted into the darkness of the storefronts. If they couldn't hear my heart pounding up on the third floor, they were deaf. I hurried around the corner to find a usable payphone. My theory having been proved, I now had to put a plan into action. Phase one was to dial 911, like any concerned citizen. Then a dash for the airport.

After giving the dispatcher a story about arsonists at my old address, I made sure he had a good description of Gunnar and Kathleen, as well as their car. At the very least, after the murder of the wino, I knew a patrol unit would respond. If Kathleen and Gunnar had any alternate plans, like last time, I hoped the appearance of the cops would discourage them. At best, they'd be caught with their pants down and arrested for conspiracy to commit arson, and fingerprint comparisons after booking would hopefully do the rest. The mystery of how they waltzed out of prison every weekend would get solved when their actual identities became evident. To hedge my bets, I beat feet to the airport after waking a startled cabbie.

There was no traffic on the road yet and we made it in twenty minutes. I had the cabbie drop me off at the agency that had rented the Chevy to the Schlossers. After waking another denizen of the night, a bloodless-looking clerk with a Heavy Metal hairdo, I got directions to the turn-in lot. At this rate I'd have half the town up before dawn.

I'd just gotten settled in a dark little niche when I heard tires squealing up the ramp to the lot. The big Chevy careened onto the platform and slammed into the nearest slot, clipping the car parked next to it. The doors flew open and the "Schlossers" spewed forth. Obviously, whatever had happened as a result of my 911 call had shaken Gunnar and Kathleen.

Gunnar opened the trunk and retrieved an overnight bag. Kathleen took a moment to pat her helmet of hair back into some semblance of shape. The heavy-looking knit bag she'd seemed so fond of before was missing. She must have ditched it back in the city in preparation for the metal detectors and X-ray machines of the airport. They walked rapidly away without a backward glance. After a few moments, I followed them into the terminal.

At this hour the airport was only sparsely populated. Most of the airline counters were closed and deserted. The only activity seemed to be at the international gates and in the commuter-flight waiting areas, where clusters of people sat or reclined in various attitudes of exhaustion. It was easy to keep sight of my quarry, but a challenge not to be obvious about it. Especially with the ever-vigilant Kathleen. My only comfort was that I could be reasonably sure they were unarmed. I was less confident of my new look.

They showed their tickets to security and passed through the detector without a pause. I watched them stride down the corridor and turn into a waiting area marked B-2. I stepped back and looked at the bank of monitors in the main concourse. After scanning for a few moments, I found it. Gate B-2 for Cleveland, boarding in thirty minutes. I'll be damned, I thought… Cleveland.

I ran to the ticketing counter.… This time, I didn't have to wake anyone, only get their attention. With the clock ticking down the minutes until flight time, the clerk seemed reluctant to break off her phone conversation, which appeared to be with a man and had become very friendly and animated. Five a.m. I couldn't imagine. She put him on hold and came to my aid, though she was careful not to rush. Haste makes waste. Yes, she reassured me, there were several more seats available. There were almost always some empties on these red-eye commuter flights, she explained. All of this in the most languid manner, even as the flight she was booking for me was making its first boarding announcement. Naturally, my credit card needed scanning as well and that took several more minutes. She liked my beard. I thought of the poor bastard on the other end of the phone. I hope he wasn't in a hurry… for anything.

I fled down the corridor and almost made it through security. The buzzer went off and they had to look at my binoculars and camera. The waiting area was empty. I walked on board, trying to look preoccupied with my pass and keeping my face down. The flight attendant ushered me into an aisle seat near the front of the plane. We were already starting to back away from the terminal by the time I got my seatbelt fastened.

The three rows in front of me revealed no familiar heads. That was good. With any luck, they would never have to pass me while in flight and I would beat them off the plane upon landing. It was killing me not to look back and see where they were, even though my neck was so rigid with tension that I doubt I would've been able to accomplish it.

With great reluctance and regret, I passed up a Bloody Mary and stuck to coffee. The perfect drink for the overwrought. The rest of the flight passed without incident and we landed right on time an hour and a half after takeoff.

I was the first off the plane and sprinted up the incline to the concourse. As soon as I hit a crowd, I stopped and turned around. Here they came. Gunnar, head and shoulders above the rest of the passengers, and Kathleen, pallid and angry-looking, with a face that would've given a pit bull second thoughts. They didn't seem to be watchful now, and they were in a lot less of a hurry, though they were still moving with a purpose. I fell in behind them.

We entered the long-term parking lot along with hundreds of others as the working world kicked off another week. The Ohio sky was slate grey in keeping with the complexions of most of my fellow travelers. Lurch and Morticia made for a sporty-looking Beamer, fire-engine red... of course. As Gunnar unlocked the doors, Kathleen swung around suddenly and looked hard in my direction. If she was going to recognize me, now was the time. I didn't break stride. With nary a glance at them, I walked over to a Lincoln parked opposite their row and slammed my attaché case onto the roof. She was still watching. I patted myself down for keys. Still watching. Grunting with irritation, I dug through my pockets. Still on me. With my hand shaking so much I knew she had to notice, I began to try and fit my apartment key into the car lock. A drop of sweat ran into my eye. A car engine roared to life and two doors slammed. I turned in time to make out the license plate as the BMW roared out of the lot.

This time I had to remember it, as I couldn't force my hands to work the pen and pad.

☙

Inside the car rental agency, I tried the phone book for Charles Schlosser. Nothing. I gave Information a call and got the same. Unlisted. Meaning, I presumed, that somewhere out there in metropolitan Cleveland, a Mr. and Mrs. Charles Schlosser did exist. Without a subpoena, the operator would not part with an address or telephone number.

I sat in the nondescript Olds that I had rented and pondered my options. If I called Walt and asked him to run the BMW's plate through DMV, he would want to know what I was doing. Since I really wasn't sure myself, I would be hard-pressed to answer that. Any answer I did give him I knew he would find far from reassuring. Besides, the plate could very well be under yet another alias, getting me no farther down the road.

I pulled out the crumpled piece of paper on which I'd jotted their rental information. The address stared back. *22 E. Rosemont*

Ave. Could they be so cocky as to have used their actual address? Hell, yes! For two felons who were supposed to be locked up in another state, they seemed to have the world by the ass. What I couldn't get over was that no one seemed to be missing them. Why wasn't the countryside being scoured for these scumbags? Being of an inquiring mind, I consulted my complimentary city map, put the car into drive, and embarked for the pleasant-sounding Rosemont Ave.

cs

The neighborhood was one of those older, middle-class sections that had largely escaped urban blight. Most were attractive, well-built homes from the fifties and holding up well, though they exhibited some signs of neglect. I surmised that this was due to the fact that most housed their original owners, who were not as spry as they had once been. Occasionally, an old pensioner would sally forth to do battle with weeds and other gardening chores.

A number of homes appeared to have fallen to the younger generation as evidenced by new paint jobs, additions, and children's toys in the yards. All in all, a very comfortable, neat community. With one glaring exception: 22 E. Rosemont.

The lawn was knee-high with overgrown grass and weeds, and broken lawn furniture was scattered across it as if to impede the unwary. Dusty-looking curtains covered every window and the white stucco of the walls was sooty and streaked with dirt in places. It had the look of a house where the former owners would likely be found buried in the crawl space.

The attached one-car garage was closed when I arrived and hadn't opened since, so I had no idea whether the red Beamer was there or not. No one had come or gone, and I'd seen no signs of life. School had let out about an hour ago and the neighborhood kids were beginning to notice me. If their parents had done their job, one of them would report home with their "suspicious man" story soon and Mom would probably call the local station for a patrol car. I figured I had thirty more minutes, at most.

A knot of kids were using the Schlossers' driveway as a skateboard ramp. Occasionally, there was a surreptitious hand-off of a well-worn pack of cigarettes and one of their number would drift off behind some shrubs. Lazy tendrils of smoke rose into the late-afternoon air to reveal the secret smoker's position. I felt myself starting to doze. I couldn't remember the last time I'd really slept.

The garage door began to rise; there was the whine of an automatic opener. I shook myself, trying to wake up. The kids pantomimed hasty goodbyes. Behind me, at the corner, I heard the screech of tires. My rearview mirror showed a red car making a hard left onto the street. I glanced back at the garage, which was now fully open, and saw that it was empty. The kids scattered, keeping to the sidewalk. They not only knew the Schlosser's routine, but with the unerring intuition of the very young, had guessed something about their personalities. They surrendered the street as the car hurtled past and made another hard left into the drive. I just had time to catch a glimpse of the occupants and the license plate before it vanished into the garage. The door was closing before they'd even gotten halfway under it. I half-expected the Beamer to continue on through the back wall of the house as the heavy wooden door slid to a stop. From deep within, I heard the sound of two doors being slammed. The Schlossers were home.

The local stop-and-rob provided me with enough nutritious rations to see me through the night, and I returned a little after dark. I parked a few doors down and pondered my options. Going in and arresting them was out of the question. First of all, they would kill me, and I didn't want that. Second, I wasn't a cop anymore and even if I had been, I was way out of my jurisdiction. Third, I didn't have anything but circumstantial evidence that they had committed the murders back home, and as far as their being fugitives, I seemed to be the only one who thought so. It all boiled down to proving that the Schlossers were, in fact, Gunnar Bergstrom and Kathleen Vichter. If I had that, Walt would have to act. At the very least, official inquiries would be started. I had faith that the rest would come out in the wash.

With that in mind, I carefully cleaned the telephoto lens of my thirty-five millimeter and waited. Sooner or later, I'd get a shot of then. More than that, I intended to break into their cozy residence and help myself to a few well-handled objects. Fingerprints don't lie.

The twin beams of the headlamps caught me before I had a chance to slump down in my seat. I sat very still as the car swung to the curb in front of Schlossers' and stopped. I was praying for invisibility as a trim man in a business suit hopped out and waded through the yard to the Schlossers' front door. It occurred to me that he knew his way through the jungle pretty well. He only knocked once before the door was opened and the darkened porch flooded with light. I could hear Gunnar's greeting float across the street to where I sat. Gunnar was smiling as he clapped him on the back and ushered him in. Business Suit was smiling also. Just before the door closed I heard Kathleen chirp, "Get you anything to drink, Bill?" What the hell? I expected the Beav to come pedaling up any moment.

Easing the car door closed, I trotted over to Business Suit's car. Chevy Caprice four-door. Late model. Two antennas mounted on the rear. One was for a car phone. Pretty typical these days. The other was for a two-way radio. I risked a look at the interior with my pocket flash. Sure enough, a police band radio was mounted under the dash. I wobbled back to my car and sat.

Business Suit came out after about an hour and drove away. I gave it a couple of beats and followed. It wasn't hard. He was used to doing the tailing, not the other way around, and never looked back. When he turned into the garage for employees in the federal building, I kept going. I knew all I needed to know. Business Suit was a federal agent. Gunnar and Kathleen were in the Witness Protection Program.

On the flight home I tried to think things through, but all I could think about were the cocktails being served to my fellow travelers. It seemed like everybody in the plane was knocking them back. I think they were even serving the kids. I could almost hear the tinkle of glasses raised in toasts behind the closed cockpit door. I closed my eyes and squeezed the armrests.

Now it all made sense. The feds must have picked them up even before they got to trial. That explained the easy plea bargain and why the prison bureau carried them on their rolls. They never spent a day inside. They were too valuable, too busy being pumped for information on the workings of the mob to risk in prison.

It also explained why the feds were so successful with mob enforcement after Gunnar and Kathleen got "sent up." All us local yokels thought it was just a crackdown as a result of the hue and cry over Johnny Joggs's burning. It was, of course, but it was a crackdown with inside information. The feds had made a bargain with the devil, devils actually, and the end justified the means.

Now, over a decade later, the leash on Bergstrom and Vichter had grown long and frayed. Nobody was paying them much attention anymore. They did what they promised to do and kept their noses clean in the meantime. Occasionally, once a week or so, an agent dropped by to see how they were making out. Only on workdays, of course. Why spoil their weekend? No guns or drugs in the house… have a nice day. See you next week. So they burned and tortured a few people to death. Basically they were good kids.

Who could I turn to? I felt certain Walt didn't know anything about the arrangement and even if I convinced him, what could he do? Go to the feds? They would send him packing posthaste. None of your business, it's a federal matter.

If I went to the feds myself, they would want proof, not allegations. After all, they had a lot on the line here. This could be a major embarrassment. It would be easy to discredit a broken-down old ex-cop with a drinking problem.

I fell asleep and dreamt of the old days. Old friends and old enemies, cops and robbers, good guys and bad. Some dead and a few still living. The bump of the tires on the tarmac woke me just as a tumbler of amber liquid reached my lips.

ဢ

The public library has become one of my favorite spots on earth. I love the quiet, restful murmur of the place. It's very much like a church that way. I discovered it shortly after my return from Cleveland when I came in looking for out-of-town newspapers. I spend most afternoons here now and the employees are kind enough to wake me only when I snore.

Today I had to go to the desk to ask for change for the copy machine. The librarian actually smiled at me when she handed me back my quarters. And these are public employees! She pointed out the location of the copier and asked if she could help. Even though I wasn't too familiar with their particular model, I decided to go it alone. I wasn't really too keen on her seeing the article I wanted copied. She might have thought I was a little strange.

The article concerned a couple by the name of Schlosser in a suburb of Cleveland. It seems they were burned to death in their own home sometime during the night. The fire department was able to salvage most of the house and the police were labeling the fire as arson and the deaths suspicious. Interestingly, the FBI was also investigating, though agents there would make no comment to the press on their interest in what would normally be a local case. The article quoted a neighbor as saying that the Schlossers kept pretty much to themselves.

Now I can't tell Walt about what I found out and how I was right about Gunnar and Kathleen. In fact, I haven't told anybody except one person. A nobody, really. Just an old snitch who used to bring me the odd tidbit of information back when I was on the streets. Of course, I can't vouch for who he might have told. You know how snitches are. When they've got information that's worth something, they usually find the persons it's worth something to.

Somewhere back in Cleveland there's an agent in trouble. Business Suit is probably racking his brains trying to figure out how the mob found the lovely Schlossers and torched them. I chuckle thinking about the whole situation, and the librarian gives me a curious look. I smile back at her and she blushes. You've got to admit, the boys who did that job had a sense of irony.

I hang the newspaper back on its rack and make for the door. I tip my hat to the librarian on the way out. Walt and I have an appointment this afternoon. He's agreed to drive me over to my first AA meeting and hold my hand.

A Matter of Trust
(2021)

"Take a look at this," the lieutenant said, tossing a screenshot of a webpage onto Sergeant Russell Turner's desk.

Picking it up, Russell studied the printout. It read:

SPOUSE REMOVAL SERVICES
When legal recourse no longer makes sense or provides proper satisfaction.

Beneath these words were two photos. The one on the left showed a young man, smiling and carefree, striding through a crowded bar as slender women eyed him hungrily over the shoulders of their escorts. The second photo featured a good-looking woman driving a convertible, also sporting a smile, her blonde hair flowing behind her, a young male model at her side, gazing at her profile in rapt adoration, the road ahead undulating toward a beautiful sunset above a dramatic coastline.

Along the bottom of the page was printed an email address.

Russell had little doubt that both photos had been "shopped" from glossy ads that had nothing to do with *spouseremovalservices.com*.

"Is this serious?" he asked, offering the printout back to the lieutenant, who stood over him, muscular forearms exposed by his rolled-up sleeves, handsome face composed as always. "It's a joke, right?"

But it did not appear as if Lieutenant Steven Wallace agreed, his easy smile vanishing like something best forgotten. "That's for you to determine, Russ—your *job*, last time I looked."

Doesn't even bother to call me sergeant, Russell thought. *He knows an inferior when he sees one.*

He tried again, slapping the paper with three pudgy fingers. "It's got to be a joke, LT. Nobody in their right mind would advertise something like this." A lock of his dark hair slipped down his forehead. In brushing it away, he managed to knock his glasses askew.

The lieutenant looked on as if witnessing something sad. "You too busy, Russ?"

This was a trick question: Russell's boss knew exactly how little he was working on at the moment.

"How did you come across this, anyway?" he asked, trying to salvage a little dignity.

Lowering his lean rump onto the edge of Russell's desk, the younger man explained, "A patrolman was given it yesterday at a coffee shop, owner says he found it tacked to a corkboard. Didn't know who put it there and hadn't given anyone permission to do so. He didn't like the looks of it, so we—no, *you've* got it. Check it out and get back to me if it's anything."

The lieutenant strode out of the detective bureau's cybercrime unit, which consisted solely of Sergeant Russell Turner, without another word.

Taking a deep breath, Russell gazed 'round the small institutional-green office he occupied in the basement of Wessex Township's police department. Besides his cluttered desk and computer, there was little to see. The only window was at ground level and covered with heavy wire mesh. His view of the outside world was of his fellow officers' shoes and boots passing on their way to their more robust tasks of patrolling the streets, making arrests, effecting rescues.

The only decoration in the room was a photo of him and Claire on their honeymoon eight years before—she honey-haired and clad in a white two-piece bathing suit, smiling indolently at the camera; he, a much trimmer version of his present self, also in a bathing suit, tanned and confident.

He had been a patrol officer then and up for promotion. The world had been spread out before him, and he had been happy and in love. Claire had been—and still was—everything that mattered most in his world.

Then it had all gone wrong. A routine stop on a car drifting in and out of its lane, a kid so nervous his hands were trembling when he passed Russell a driver's license not two days old. Taking pity on him, Russell had issued a mild warning and welcomed the lad to the driving world. Returning to his patrol car, he couldn't hear the boy's vehicle over the roar of passing traffic.

The teenager—still shaken by the encounter—inadvertently placed his car in reverse and gunned the accelerator to merge. Russell was struck down, his left leg run over. He remembered nothing more until he came to in the ER, too groggy from painkillers to appreciate how bad the damage was. In the end, he kept the leg, but would never be able to walk without difficulty. His days of active police work were over.

Thanks to his stellar record and a benign police chief, he was retrained for the newly instituted cybercrime position—and, three years later, there he remained, softening into a man he barely recognized… a man who devoted hours to the contemplation of the deaths of his wife and her new, unknown lover. Given those unspoken thoughts, this flyer for "Spouse Removal Services" seemed to him a cruel cosmic joke.

His suspicions had begun at the Christmas party Claire's boss threw each year. He drank too much, and they'd had a tiff over it. At some point, he lost track of her.

Later, making his way through the crowded banquet hall rented for the occasion, he caught a glimpse of Claire standing near the coat racks, almost hidden by the winter garments clustered against the wall. Leaning back against someone's fur coat, she was sheathed in a sleeveless red dress that ended mid-thigh, her white teeth bared in a glistening smile.

Concealed within the deeper shadows of the alcove was another figure, a tall male in a dark suit. Russell couldn't see his face, but he appeared to be stroking Claire's hip.

He hurried toward them, his hobble aggravated by the exertion, and arrived flushed and sweating to find Claire alone.

"Who was that?" he demanded, his slur pronounced even to his own ears. "He had his hands on you!"

Out of the corner of his eye, he saw the exit door closing.

"I have no idea, Russ, somebody's husband or boyfriend, I guess. He was as drunk as you are and stopped to wish me a Merry Christmas on his way home."

She handed him his coat, snagging the car keys from the side pocket. "I'll drive," she announced.

After that evening, Claire's job—which had seldom before required her to travel or work weekends—suddenly began demanding both on a regular basis.

He knew she must be having an affair.

The grief of loss and betrayal weighed on Russell's heart like a stone, but he was so fearful of what might happen if he confronted her that he didn't push the matter further. He couldn't decide which was worse, facing a moment of truth that, once revealed, could never be forgotten, or trudging along in willful half-ignorance, the poisonous seed of jealousy growing within him like a cancer.

He shook off these unhappy thoughts and typed the URL from the bottom of the flyer into his browser.

"I'll be damned," he murmured as the page loaded.

On the screen appeared a velvety royal-blue background with ornate lettering reminiscent of a Victorian funeral announcement.

Russell selected the "About Us" tab and clicked on it. On the same background as the home page, a block of text appeared:

> *It is a sad statement of our times that divorce has become commonplace. Yet as necessary as the ending of a marriage may be under some circumstances, the usual handling of such a wrenching decision is unsatisfactory to many people. If you are reading this page, you may be—and probably are—one of those people. For you, the matter is anything but a routine legal action to be undertaken by unfeeling lawyers. Instead, it is something far more significant. The issue is not just freedom from an unhappy marriage, but freedom from a person who has caused you great sorrow. In some cases—yours, perhaps—divorce will not provide proper satisfaction and meaningful resolution. Something more is called for, and that something is what we at Spouse Removal Services provide: the ultimate state of control, marriage dissolution, relationship erasure, true and complete closure.*

In addition to the emotional rewards provided by such a service, there are other benefits to being divested completely of an unhealthy relationship. Consider, for example, the long-term financial stability achieved when all costs associated with the end of a damaging entanglement can be eliminated after only two payments.

If what has been described here sounds as if it might be of interest, please contact us at...

"This is a joke," Russell said aloud to the empty room. "It has to be a joke. You'd have to be crazy..."

The sentence trailed off.

On the screen, his cursor winked on the email link.

He thought of Claire in the arms of another man.

A car horn and the slamming of doors jarred him from his trance. Muffled voices and the scuffle of footsteps passed his basement window, reminding him that it was four o'clock and shift change. Shutting down his computer, he rose, slipped on his coat, and limped out, locking the office door behind him.

☙

Two hours later, Russell received a text from Claire: "Jill got engaged last night! Impromptu office party for her after work. Okay?"

Putting his beer down, Russell pecked a question onto the tiny screen: "Where? Maybe I'll join you."

After a long wait, his phone dinged with a reply: "Not decided yet but it's all girls. Sorry!"

"Have fun," he answered.

She had made the mistake several weeks before of giving him the name of a restaurant where she and "the girls" were supposedly celebrating another impromptu occasion. He'd stopped in unannounced, but neither she nor her fellow workers were there. When he'd questioned her later that night, she'd looked him in the eye and said, "It was too crowded, so we went somewhere else."

When did she become so cold? Russell asked himself. She had always been such a happy, passionate girl. Now, he hardly knew her.

Rising, he hobbled into the kitchen and poured himself a generous shot of bourbon. Bringing the tumbler to his lips, he saw that the amber liquid was trembling and set it back down, spilling some onto his hand.

"Goddamnit, Claire," he whispered, a tear running down his cheek, "I don't deserve this."

✧

Russell entered his office the next morning with the dull throb of a hangover pulsing in his skull. His wavy hair was tousled, his eyes bloodshot. Flopping down at his desk, he flicked on the computer, removed the lid from the cup of coffee he had bought on the way in, and took a sip.

Claire had come home after midnight. Taking a furtive shower in the guest bathroom, she had slipped beneath the sheets of their bed with the hiss of flesh against fabric. Moments later, she was breathing deeply.

Despite everything, he felt a deep longing for her. It had been three months since they had last made love, and he missed her touch even more than the sex itself.

He slept fitfully, woke long before Claire, rose, dressed, and left the house. He was thirty minutes early for work.

With dull resolve, he surfed to *spouseremovalservices.com*, clicked the email link, and typed, "Interested in your service. What next?"

He understood that he was taking a great risk in using a police computer but reasoned that it could also provide the perfect alibi. After all, hadn't Lieutenant Wallace assigned him the task of investigating the site? *If* anything came of it, and *if* things went awry, he could fashion an explanation: a sting gone terribly wrong.

He stared at the screen for several minutes, waiting, then closed the browser. Rising, he limped to the men's room, feeling as if a void had opened within him. As if in sympathy, his stomach clenched like a fist around a bird. The men's room was empty. He staggered to the nearest stall and vomited.

℃℈

When Russell returned to his office, he found a response to his email: a telephone number and the words "3 PM." Nothing more.

He stared at the message. *It's not too late to back away*, he told himself.

He opened a case file—an unsolved series of threats and cyber-stalking—and studied it, but his thoughts kept returning to Spouse Removal. Though common sense and long experience told him the "service" was most likely a hoax or scam, he couldn't deny that he was curious.

With a *frisson* of terror, it occurred to him that the site could have been designed by the Feds, a way of trolling the net for would-be murderers. Perspiration broke out on his skin at the thought.

Still, he had been assigned to look into the site, and he was committing no crime by doing so. Not yet.

He forced himself to concentrate on the stalking case, and the hours shambled on toward three.

ભ

His call was answered by an automated message that advised him to leave a number and promised he would be contacted as soon as possible.

Russell paused, the moment made anticlimactic by the mundanity of the robotic voice, and then he gave his personal cell number and disconnected, his palms sweating.

He had crossed a line—an invisible line the nuns had warned him about, the line his instructors at the police academy had assured him a cop treads close to every day but should never, *ever* cross.

His cell phone rang. The words "Caller Unknown" appeared on the screen. His heart pounding, Russell answered.

"Yes?"

There was a crackling noise, like signal interference. "You called us," an electronically modulated voice replied.

Russell couldn't tell if it was a man or a woman on the line. "Yes, I did," he replied.

"And you are?"

"Steve," he lied, giving his boss's name, "Steven Wallace."

"That's not the name registered to the phone you're using," the tinny voice informed him. "You are Russell Turner. Is that correct?"

"Yes," Russell admitted, feeling foolish and a little frightened. His phone's settings should have prevented his name from coming up for an unknown caller. "Who are you?"

"I am with Spouse Removal Services. That's all you need to know, Russell. It's better for both of us this way." The words warped and woofed, the speaker didn't even sound human. "What is it you want from us?"

"You know what I want," Russell answered, piqued by the question and the casual use of his name.

"Say it aloud."

He felt his annoyance grow far out of proportion to the situation.

"What do you think I want? What does anybody want when they call you?"

"Say it."

"Spouse removal, goddamnit! Are you happy?"

"Thank you."

"You're recording this, aren't you?" Russell challenged. He did the same thing in his own investigations.

"She's hurt you, hasn't she? I can hear it. Do I presume too much when I say *she*?"

Russell felt himself sag. "No. Her name is… Claire."

There was no going back now.

"Can I safely assume she's taken a lover—broken her marriage vows? Would that be correct?"

"What difference does it make?" Russell answered, his earlier anger giving way to sadness and shame.

"We promise *complete* resolution, Russell. In cases like yours, where our client is so obviously suffering—as opposed to those cases driven only by cold financial concerns—we would be happy to include the other party for half our usual charge."

"He might be married," Russell heard himself saying, "might have children. I couldn't live with that."

"Do *you*?"

"Have children? No… no, we don't."

"That makes things easier, doesn't it?"

Russell thought the voice was clearer now, less modulated, almost human.

"How much?" he asked, his own voice drained of emotion.

"Fifty thousand dollars—twenty-five up front, the rest once the dissolution has been completed. Is that acceptable?"

"It's a lot of money—I don't think I could come up with that kind of cash and Claire not find out about it."

"You shouldn't worry about that, Russell. Once the down payment is received, things will move rather quickly. You'll see."

"Will she be hurt?"

"Do you care?"

"Yes."

"Then no, I can promise you that she won't be hurt."

Russell wondered about the use of "I" language. "Do you work alone?" he asked.

"No questions of that nature, please. Since you are a police officer, the less you know the better."

"How—?" Russell began, then caught himself.

"I've run quite a thorough background check on you, Russell," the voice explained.

"Then how do I know this isn't a trap?"

"I *understand* you, Russell—your life, your love, your hurt— and I believe I can trust you. When all's been said and done, it boils down to a matter of trust, doesn't it? You know that better than I—having suffered the loss of it. It may comfort you to know that you're not the first law-enforcement officer I've assisted. Now, as to the money, it's to be transferred electronically to the following account—are you prepared to write it down?"

Russell scribbled the information onto a pad.

"If questioned, you can say you're investing in Timmons and Westlake Financial Ventures. Payment within forty-eight hours, please. You'll be—"

"Forty-eight hours!" Russell erupted. "I can't—"

Spouse Removal Services disconnected, and Russell sat there with his silent cell phone in his hand.

"Any progress on that spouse-removal thing?"

He spun around to find Lieutenant Wallace leaning into his office from the corridor.

"No," he stammered, wondering how long the man had been standing there. "Not yet. I sent them an email and got a number to call, but no one picked up." He forced his pulse to slow. "I think some kid put it up as a hoax."

"How about the website itself? Anything there—graphic photos, threats?"

"Nothing explicit. It's all pretty vague, actually."

"All right, then. Keep me posted if anything develops."

"Of course," Russell answered to an empty doorway. The lieutenant had already gone off to attend to other, more important matters.

ɛ⁄ɔ

At lunchtime, he drove to Claire's office. He wasn't sure why, but he suddenly had the urge to see her. In spite of what he had just done—perhaps *because* of it—he was overcome with a sudden tenderness for the woman he had fallen in love with and married.

He was greeted by one of her co-workers, a young woman with a dark complexion and long shining hair. He thought she was called Rita.

"Hi, Russ," she waved. "You just missed Claire."

"Did I? I didn't think she'd take off for lunch *this* early. I was going to surprise her."

"That's sweet, but she had a doctor's appointment and said she wouldn't be back. Did you forget?"

Russell felt his face coloring, but not for the reason Rita might think—he wasn't embarrassed at forgetting something he'd never been told.

"Oh, right." He managed a smile. "She mentioned it at breakfast—I *did* forget."

"My husband would've, too," she assured him.

Nodding, Russell turned for the exit. He wondered if Rita knew what Claire was up to. Maybe the entire office did. Since he'd been at the Christmas party, her mystery man was almost certainly one of her co-workers—or one of their husbands.

He drove straight to his bank and transferred the money to the numbered account.

ఌ

When Claire arrived home, Russell was on his third drink. "Went ahead and ate," he announced, a little too loudly.

"Am I that late?" she murmured. "I should've called."

"I'm used to it," he replied, studying her distracted expression. She sat on the sofa, almost within touching distance.

"Did you get something to eat?" she asked.

"I just *said* I did," Russell snapped. "You should've had your *doctor* test your hearing."

Claire's head snapped up. "I felt like I was coming down with something—she said I'm run down and should get more iron."

"That's a lie, Claire, and you know it."

His phone rang. The screen read: "Caller Unknown."

"It's work," he said, and headed for the bedroom.

"When did you start using your own phone for work?" Claire demanded as he shut the door behind him.

"We have the money," the mechanized voice crackled in his ear. "Thank you. That was prompt."

"What now?"

"Does your wife leave for work before or after you do?"

"After. I leave around seven-thirty, but she doesn't have to be in until nine."

"You're scheduled to work tomorrow?"

"Yes."

"Then go to work at your normal time."

Despite his hurt and anger, Russell felt a moment of doubt. This was going to happen.

"Tomorrow? That seems so—"

"It's like ripping off a Band-Aid, Russell. Best to do it quickly."

"Do I—?"

"Just come home after your shift as usual."

"Yeah, but what'll—"

The caller was gone.

When Russell returned to the living room, he found it empty. He could hear the shower running in the master bath. For one crazy moment, he thought of joining his wife there, surprising her, as he had done in the earliest days of their marriage, when such things had been spontaneous and joyful.

Then, recalling where she'd been and what he'd set in motion, he stalked into the kitchen and downed another shot of bourbon.

৩

The following day was an agony of waiting in his cell of an office. Unable to concentrate on any one thing, Russell was only vaguely aware of the comings and goings of his fellow officers. Overly warm one moment, he grew suddenly cold and clammy the next. The only thing he could think of was what was going to happen—might in fact already have happened—to Claire. The hands on the wall clock appeared to have stopped altogether, then jumped forward whenever he managed to distract himself for what seemed only moments.

It was almost lunchtime when the lieutenant threw open his door and leaned in. "Anything on that... what was it called again?"

"Spouse Removal Services," Russell managed to answer over the blood pumping like thunder through his ears.

"Yeah, that. Nothing?"

"Nothing," Russell echoed.

"Gonna write that up, Russ? Give me something to close out?"

"Yeah, sure, I was just getting started."

Crossing his arms, Wallace leaned against the doorframe and asked, "What's wrong with you?"

"What do you mean?"

"You don't look well. You're kinda pale. You sick?"

"I'm fine. Some indigestion, maybe."

The lieutenant appeared unconvinced. "Go home if you're sick, Russell," he said without the slightest note of sympathy in his voice.

Home, Russell thought.

&

When he pulled into the driveway, he found Claire's car in the garage. She almost never got back from work before six. It was now half past four.

Russell climbed out of his car on wobbly legs, the damaged one feeling as if it might give way altogether. The door connecting the garage to the mudroom was locked.

He fumbled his key into the slot and opened the door. Stepping inside, he stopped and listened. All he could hear was the soft rush of heated air through the floor vents.

It occurred to him that Spouse Removal Services might still be inside the house. That he—or she, or they—might be waiting for him, either to demand the second payment or, just as likely, to kill him, too… or *instead*. Perhaps they'd allowed Claire to pay them to switch their attention from her to him.

He drew his gun and eased his way down the hall.

His pistol held out before him, he stepped around the dividing wall and into the living room.

Claire sat silently on the sofa, her eyes widening at the sight of him, then filling with hate.

Something cold and metallic touched the skin where his neck met the back of his skull, and a familiar voice said, "Lay the gun on the carpet, Russ, and don't make any sudden moves, okay?"

Russell did as he was bid.

Claire stormed across the room and slapped him hard across the face. "You sick bastard!" she hissed. "Steve told me everything!"

His face stinging, Russell thought, *Steve…*

"Sit down, honey," Steven Wallace told Claire. She did so, and the lieutenant took a step back, his own gun aimed at Russell's heart.

"*You're* Spouse Removal Services?" Russell asked.

"Hardly," Steve replied. "Spouse Removal Services is a pimply twenty-six-year-old kid, who is crying his little eyes out as we speak. He's apparently pulled this scam off several times already. Never actually killed anyone, of course—that would've required him to leave his parents' cozy basement. None of his 'clients' ever complained—but how could they, after commissioning him to commit a murder?"

"But—"

"I heard enough of your side of the conversation yesterday to realize you were up to no good. When I confirmed that you were using your private phone to communicate with the target of an investigation, I called in a little outside help from the State. It was easy from there."

"You and Claire…?"

"Since Christmas."

Russ remembered the silhouette of a tall man stroking his wife's hip. "So now what? I go to prison?"

"That's the way I see it."

"You've got it all figured out."

"You handed it to us, Russ."

"There's just one thing," Russell said, feeling a resolve he had not felt for a very long time.

"Oh?"

"I'm gonna go for my gun… and if you don't kill me first, I'm gonna kill you." Glancing at Claire, whose expression had gone from fury to fear, he added, "Her, too."

"Don't be an idiot, Russ! You'll be dead before you can get to it—and it'll be a justified shooting, you know that."

"Will it? The DA's office will have to investigate, and *everything* will come out. Once they know about you and Claire, I wonder how the Grand Jury will rule. Any guesses, *Steve?*"

The uncertainty on his wife's and her lover's faces were all he could have hoped for.

Russell Turner took a slow breath. "The kid at Spouse Removal Services was wrong," he said. "It *never* was a matter of trust."

And with those words he reached for his gun.

Lady Anne's Friend
(1995)

The kitchen of their little ranch house was darkening as Julian settled himself at the counter to watch Anne making dinner. From the back of the house he could hear the voices of Ina and Conner raised in debate on some, no doubt, compelling issue. He gave it two minutes before intervention became necessary. Two more minutes in which to watch Lady Anne.

Ever frugal, Anne switched on only the light over the stove, throwing a soft golden glow over her features. Julian was content to remain at his post in semi-darkness. She glanced over at him and favored him with a quick smile mingled with a perplexed look. Julian knew that she was wondering at his silence. With the normally quiet-natured Anne he did most of the talking. Only now he could not trust himself to speak. He wanted only to savor his secret until the right moment. He smiled back and she returned her attention to the task at hand. The children's argument grew louder in the background.

He loved these moments before dinner when he could immerse himself in the warmth of his family. They only came around for one week a month. On the four to twelve shift, he was at home when Anne was at work and the kids at school. When they returned for the day he had already left for duty. On the midnight shift, like the living dead, he rose in darkness and moved about the house like a phantom, wraithlike and insubstantial, feeling out of synch with the human race. Only on day shift could he play the part of a normal father and husband and pretend that being a cop was a job like any other. In fact, today it was a job better than any other. He choked back the stupid grin he felt spreading across his face and returned to Anne.

"Anne." He spoke hoarsely, waiting for her full attention. She was engrossed in the poppings and cracklings of some stir-fried dish, her slender neck bent over the task. Her delicate head turned towards him, the green eyes distracted. The children's dispute was erupting into civil war. He plowed on.

"Something happened at work today." Her eyes came into focus as the lips settled into a grim line. Something happening was usually not good.

"It seems the chief screwed up and promoted me."

Anne stood there, uncomprehending. The kids burst forth from their room, each vying to be first to present their case against the other.

"Honey, I'm a sergeant now," he clarified.

It was then that he saw the tears standing in her eyes and he came around the counter and held her. The children arrived just in time to be silenced by the spectacle of their mother crying. Julian smiled at them over her shoulder. The Lady Anne was happy.

It took over a year for them to sell their old home, find a new and larger one, finance it, and move in. Julian swore that he would never be involved in another move and, in fact, would be buried in the backyard of Anne's dream house. She happily agreed to this, with the proviso that she would be able to extend her flower garden over the spot and that there would be no gloomy headstone.

It was during this time that Julian noticed the car. He had just gotten home from a midnight shift and was about to pull the curtains of his bedroom, when he saw it. A large, grey car parked at the end of his street, the driver a motionless shadow behind the wheel. The man appeared to be watching Julian's house.

Julian continued closing the curtains, being careful to leave a small opening between them. He walked downstairs to retrieve his binoculars. When he returned to the window, the car and driver were gone.

As he undressed for bed, it occurred to him that he had seen the car before... somewhere. He lay in the silent house—Anne and the children were at their respective schools—and tried to remember, but only succeeded in falling into an uneasy sleep. In his dreams, the faceless man came to the door and tried to hand him a painted stick with feathers tied to one end. Julian woke up gasping and shouting, his cries echoing through the empty, day-lit house.

It was weeks later, during day shift, that Julian was summoned to the chief's office. These summonses were as rare as the chief himself, who managed to enter and exit the police building each day without encountering the men he commanded. Considering that there was but a single entrance for police personnel, this was quite a feat of timing.

Julian checked himself over at the bottom of the stairs to ensure there were no obvious omissions in his uniform, then began his ascent. He had to assume that since the chief had bypassed the captain in his request for him, this was not a disciplinary matter.

He gained the landing and strode past the chief's secretary, who nodded him through. Julian didn't read anything into this, as she always behaved nervously around the uniformed officers and, like her boss, seemed to avoid them whenever possible.

The chief sat behind his massive desk, awash in paperwork, and waved him in. "Come in, come in!"

He smiled at Julian from across the wasteland of his desk, a place referred to as the "black hole" by the officers of the department, indicating its uncanny ability to draw onto its surface requests, requisitions, and suggestions, and never yield them up again.

"Well... well, well, well. How's Julian? Just about through with your probation, aren't you? How have things been going? No problems?"

He paused while Julian pondered which of these questions he was expected to answer.

"Actually, Chief, I finished probation a month ago. "

"Ah... yes," was the chief's mock-thoughtful reply. He tended to be clownish when he was nervous and now he put a finger on his pursed lips. "When *did* we promote you, anyway? Has it been that long? Damn, time has a way of slippin' by doesn't it?"

Not in some situations, Julian thought. "Yes sir, it does. You wanted to see me about something?"

The chief glanced at Julian. "It's nothing to worry about. There's just this letter."

"Letter?" Julian repeated.

"I had it looked into and it's completely unsubstantiated. I knew it was bullshit," he finished with a self-satisfied grin.

"A letter?" Julian repeated, feeling stupid and alarmed.

The chief began to paw through the mounds of paper on his desk. "I guess you want to read it, huh? Well, if I can find it, you can!" He laughed aloud at this.

When the chief came up waving it in the air, Julian almost snatched it from his hand. Then, composing himself, he began to examine the envelope, working from the outside in, forcing himself to slow down and be methodical. The chief, not smiling now, watched.

It was an ordinary, white envelope, the paper worn and soiled by much handling. The stamp was recent and common. The postmark, barely legible, was two months old and indicated that it had been mailed from a town in New York state. Julian did not recognize the name of the village, but the name of the sender, Sean Molly, rushed at him, grabbing him by the throat and choking off his air. Blood began to pound and roar in his ears. He knew, or more correctly, knew of, Sean Molly.

The familiar writing on the outside was large and shaky, done in block letters. Julian carefully withdrew the single ragged sheet of lined writing paper from the envelope and unfolded it. There was no heading or date. It was brief and to the point. Julian's hands were shaking by the time he finished.

It was a plea to save Anne from her husband, Julian Hall. Julian was vilified as a drug-dealer, wife abuser, and… worse. The writer also alleged that Julian allowed others of his kind to abuse Anne; in fact, encouraged it. It made him sick to have Anne mentioned in such a context. Did the writer actually believe this trash? He sounded so sincere, even desperate for Anne's well-being.

Then, in the final paragraph, the writer's apparent concern veered into what was clearly fantasy, even to the unschooled eye. He accused Julian of storing large amounts of plutonium in their home. Julian felt the room growing darker around him. He's mad, he thought.

The writer had learned of Anne's predicament through a phone call, he claimed. A call Anne had made out of desperation and in secrecy, fearing for her life. He lent credence to his allegations by stating that he and Anne had attended the same high school together and grown up in the same town in north Jersey. He closed by giving the Halls' address and pleading for immediate action.

Julian looked up at the chief, who looked very uncomfortable. He had read it too.

"Why wait two months, Chief?"

"Two months?... Oh! You mean since we got the letter. We didn't see the point of upsetting you if it was all unfounded. The detectives had to make a few calls to get to the bottom of it. Seems this fellow is some nut living in a religious community in upstate New York. We spoke with the local constable and he says this Molly character showed up about six months ago and is a real loony! This particular area has a number of communes of one kind or another and he's got more nutcases wandering around than Carter's got pills!" He guffawed.

"So, I'm cleared then?" Julian asked in a quiet voice.

"You were never under suspicion! We have to check out any and all allegations against our officers. It's for your own good. We wouldn't want any half-baked rumors floatin' around."

Julian took a deep breath and replied in a calm and offhand manner. "You're right, Chief. I understand. I take it we haven't heard anything further from Mr. Molly since his letter?"

The chief smiled, relief showing on his face. "Not a thing. I doubt we'll hear from him again. It was a fluke. He picked your name out of the phone book or something. He's probably forgotten all about you by now. Like you said, it's been two months."

"Yeah, probably. You mind if I keep this letter and have a copy of the detectives' report? Just in case he starts up again."

The chief looked uncomfortable for a moment. "Well, I guess that would be okay. Get copies from my secretary on your way out."

Julian took his cue and rose on unsteady legs. He managed a smile at the chief and walked to the door clutching the envelope.

"By the way," he said when he reached the door, "since this is a closed case and there's no harm in knowing, have you had a car watching my place?" Julian felt as if he were standing on the edge of a precipice waiting for the answer.

Indignant, the chief fired a reply at him. "Hell no! If I had really thought there was anything to these charges you would have been offered a polygraph by now!"

"Thanks, Chief."

"And get that plutonium out of your house!" the chief called out as Julian stepped into the hall.

の

Julian ignored the speed limit on the way home, something he was usually very conscientious about, especially in uniform. Today he didn't care. He just wanted to see Anne and the children, to be where he could watch over them. He knew two things that the chief did not, and they filled him with a sense of helpless anguish and fury. If the department had not been having him watched, then presumably, the man in the car had been Sean Molly. A Sean Molly who had not found their address in the phone book, as the chief assumed, their number having been unlisted since their move to the new house, but through someone they both knew. Maybe one of Anne's unwitting high-school classmates. The chief had assumed also that Anne had no knowledge of any Sean Molly. In fact, they had indeed gone to school together. He had been class president. It wasn't the first time they had heard from Sean. For reasons he didn't fully understand, Julian had chosen not to enlighten his chief.

As he drove, Julian debated with himself the wisdom of revealing any of this to Anne. He knew that after her initial panic subsided there would come the dawning realization that Julian could not stand guard indefinitely. In a week, he would return to the midnight shift. After that would come the swing shift when he wouldn't return until after midnight. Only one week a month would he be home after dark.

As he turned onto their street, dusk was already settling over the houses, draining the color from the landscape and leaving an orange hue in the western sky. Late November leaves, russet and desiccated, scuttled across the asphalt like scorpions, lodging themselves against the tires of parked cars or becoming trapped in pools of water left by the last rain.

Julian slowed his car and studied each of the automobiles at the curb. He looked closely for signs of condensation on the interior of the windshield or driver's side window. Nothing. No food wrappers or other accumulated trash on the dashboards. No telltale piles of clothing in the backseats.

He turned into his drive and stopped the car. Getting out, he quietly closed the door, wanting just a few more moments to study the neighborhood and compose himself before going in. Across the street the well-lit and cheerful homes of his neighbors glowed warmly as a soft misting of rain blew gently from the south. Julian noted how easily the interior of the homes could be viewed from the darkening street, the people inside going about their tasks oblivious of his watching. It seemed every yard was crowded with shrubs and trees that grew ominous as the light bled away.

As he entered the house, both kids looked up and said, "Hi, Dad!" in unison. Julian could hear Anne rattling around in the kitchen. The house felt warm and welcoming. He hung his coat up in the foyer and walked over to the children, kissing each on the top of the head. They remained intent on their game. He didn't mind. In fact, it felt good to know that they were so sure of him that they could take him for granted. He turned toward the kitchen.

Anne was just retrieving a loaf of bread from the oven as he entered. Soda bread, by the smell of it, Julian thought. His mouth watered and he was instantly ravenous… and not just for food. He pulled Anne to him and kissed her, wanting to envelope and protect her. Her body, at first tense with surprise, gradually relaxed and conformed to his. When their lips finally parted, she gazed at him with a touch of mischief in her green eyes.

"My goodness, Sergeant, I may have to file a complaint about your behavior."

"Yes ma'am," he replied , "If you'd like to step up to my office, I'm sure I've got the paperwork you'll need. Naturally, I'd like an opportunity to respond to any… complaints you may have. Perhaps we can work things out between us."

Anne looked tempted.

"Guess what?" a voice behind them asked.

Julian looked over Anne's shoulder as she extricated herself, and felt a sense of déjà vu, remembering a similar scene—was it a year ago?—in their old home. Conner waited for the proper response.

Julian smiled at Anne, who was now busy at the counter, her back to them. "What?" he asked in return.

"Mr. Olivera says that somebody's been campin' out in his shed."

Julian's momentary sense of well-being drained away. He knelt down to speak to Conner.

"When did he tell you this, son?"

"Couple'a days ago. I forgot. He wants you to come see."

"All right. I'll stop over after dinner."

Conner wasn't finished. "He said it was weird. He thinks it's a crazy person."

Julian felt rivulets of ice begin to course through his body. "Why did he say that, Conner?"

"'Cause of the stick men. The crazy man made little stick men out of twigs and stuff and

stuck them all over the shed."

❧

Dinner was a subdued affair, with Julian's edgy replies to any attempt at conversation causing a fog of uneasiness to settle over the table. More than once, he caught Anne watching him. As soon as the meal was finished, he excused himself to make the promised visit to Mr. Olivera's.

Olivera lived two doors down on the largest lot in the neighborhood. He was an elderly man whose wife had died several years before. He now devoted all his energies to his home and property, setting the standard for the neighborhood. He was proud of this and seldom hesitated in giving advice to his more slatternly neighbors—this being the prerogative of the standard-bearer.

Julian rang the doorbell and had only to wait a moment before the door was flung open by the energetic Olivera and he was greeted by his critical visage.

"By God, it's about time the police took an interest! Lucky for me this wasn't an emergency!"

Julian had the feeling that Olivera had been standing behind the door counting the minutes since he first dispatched the ten-year-old Conner two days before.

"Sorry, Mr. Olivera. Conner just remembered to tell me about your shed a little while ago. You know how boys are."

Olivera was not interested in excuses, however, and was already leading Julian through the house and out the back door to the shed.

"Could've been murdered in my sleep," he murmured, throwing an accusing glance over his shoulder at Julian.

"Worse could happen," Julian mumbled in reply.

"What's that?" Olivera spun around, coming to a stop in front of the outbuilding and eyeing Julian with suspicion.

"I said, what exactly happened?"

"See for yourself. I left everything as I found it, even though anybody could see that it's been broken into."

Even the cops? Julian wondered.

Olivera removed the padlock and flung open the double doors revealing the interior. At first glance, Julian did not, in fact, notice anything unusual. It was as much as he would expect of Olivera, crowded with tools and lawn equipment, yet a place for everything and everything in its place. It was only at the back of the large, roomlike shed that he noticed another's influence.

Underneath a swing-out window was the intruder's "nest." It consisted of several lawn chair cushions laid end to end on a bed of pine needles to form a divan. Julian guessed the needles were for insulation against the cold that would seep in through the concrete floor and into the plastic-covered cushions. Several pictures were pinned to the wall over the bed, and Julian stepped closer to look.

As he leaned over the lair, his nostrils were assailed by the animalistic odor of old sweat and unwashed clothes. He drew back and noted old man Olivera nodding in satisfaction. Obviously, he too had encountered the same stench when he discovered the mess.

Julian blew out through his nose and leaned forward again, crouching down as he did so. The pictures, garishly brilliant reproductions torn from the pages of a book, laughed back at him. Each page depicted the beautifully developed body of a man or woman surmounted by the head of an elephant or monkey and cavorting in gleeful abandon. Some wielded swords and others musical instruments. One serene beauty had retained the head of a woman and was captured mid-step in the dance, her blue, voluptuous body frozen with a shapely leg raised and cocked to one side, each of her eight arms clutching a curved and gleaming sword as she advanced on the viewer. The full lips of her sensual face curved upwards in a lazy, beatific smile of pleasurable anticipation of the destruction she promised.

Julian squatted on his haunches, staring, his breath becoming shallow, and remembered back to a time, years ago, when he had stared at the same pictures. It was about six months after their marriage that a package had come in the mail for Anne. He had stood by while she opened it like a schoolgirl at Christmas. She had assumed it was a late wedding gift.

The plain, brown paper wrapping was torn off to reveal a thick, hardbound book. When she opened it, a note fluttered to the floor. Julian retrieved it while Anne flipped curiously through the pages. She halted at the illustrations, a funny, fearful look coming over her face.

Julian, meanwhile, was trying to decipher the meaning of the shaky, block writing as its author rambled incoherently about her soul and his desire to see her attain a higher plane through Krishna. A wrinkled photo of a smiling Indian guru was pasted to the note.

What... what does this mean? Julian? She pushed the book away, unable to tear her eyes away from the depiction of Kali advancing. The same picture that Julian was staring at now in his neighbor's shed. " Who sent this?" she asked. Julian could hear the fear creeping into her voice. "I never ordered anything like this!"

He handed her the note. "Somebody named Sean Molly."

Her face looked more bewildered than ever. "Sean Molly," she repeated. "Sean Molly... I don't know a Sean. Oh my God! Sean Molly! He was our class president in high school! He must be playing a joke! Read the note! It's probably some sort of five-year reunion gag."

Julian passed it over to her, saying, "I did read it, honey, and I don't think it's a joke."

He watched as she read it in silence.

"Julian, I don't like this. It seems so strange that he should send this to me. I hardly knew him. What does it mean? What does he want?" She never looked up but continued to stare at her clenched fists.

There was no threat, veiled or otherwise, that Julian could decipher, yet he had been made uneasy by it too. Moreover, his sense of protectiveness was aroused.

Later that night, they had quarreled, Julian accusing Anne of hiding some prior relationship with Sean Molly. Anne denied it, insisting that she had known him only in passing and had never so much as dated him. In the end, he had believed her, feeling ashamed of his own insecurities and mortified at his evident self-centeredness.

The following morning, exhausted from sleeplessness, he had risen early, repackaged the book, and mailed it back to its origin. Anne and he had agreed not to speak of it again and to return any other communications from the unbalanced Molly.

Five years later, they received another package from the now forgotten Molly. This one had contained a crude wooden rattle, daubed with various colors of oil paint. There was no explanation in the accompanying note, only the even more incoherent ramblings of a fanatic. Anne was admonished to chant her mantra and "get right." The tone was stern and fatherly.

This time, Anne was crying after she read the letter and Julian smashed the crude instrument before mailing it back. When he returned from the post office, he held Anne in his arms for a long time without speaking. After all, what could he say? Once again, there was no threat; in fact, Sean Molly's concern for her welfare was obvious, if outlandish. In time, they forgot again.

Until now. The illustrations in the shed left no doubt in Julian's mind that Molly had been there. Years after his last contact with them, Sean Molly had resurfaced… and this time in the flesh. Or almost.

Behind Julian the cranky voice of his neighbor was saying something about the window and pry marks. It was then that Julian saw the stick figures perched up on the sill, tiny warriors about four inches high. He picked one up. The stick comprising the body had been carefully chosen. It was forked for half its length and these branches provided its legs. The arms were simulated by the attachment of a single crosspiece held in place by a rubber band. The head was depicted by the simple expedient of painting the tip of the body red. Julian took it that the figures were intended to be male, for their creator had removed the bark everywhere but the fork. On this remained a scaly pair of black trousers.

The figures were unmistakably martial. The left arm of the one Julian held clasped a shiny, serrated holly leaf as a shield, while its right brandished a sewing needle for a lance, its point mere inches from Julian's face.

Julian looked out across the lawns, through the trees and intervening shrubbery, to a home. A home with a well-lit family room that was easily visible. Inside, a woman and her two children moved about within the glowing warmth, gesturing and interacting in a pantomime of family life. Just an ordinary family waiting for the father to return. Oblivious to being watched from the wet darkness and dreamed about in the rank foulness of this nest—Julian's family. He looked at them as Molly must have done for many nights and as his tiny surrogate was doing even now.

Julian cupped the manikin in his hand like an ember left behind by Molly's smoldering madness. He looked again at his wife and children and decided to track down and kill Sean Molly.

⋘⋙

That night, after the children were asleep, he brought Anne into the living room. He couldn't bear the idea of them sitting exposed in the family room at the back of the house. Its open-air quality now seemed a foolish mistake, a bold challenge to the darkness and what lay concealed within it.

He could see that he had made Anne apprehensive by his unusual actions and dreaded even more the revelations that he knew he had to make. In spite of his desire to protect her from all knowledge of Molly's new and unprecedented actions, his policeman's experience told him that only through awareness of the threat could she take the precautions necessary to protect herself and the children.

They sat in the semidarkness of their new house and Julian, smiling with embarrassment, handed her the letter. He had hidden the detective's report in his desk. He couldn't bring himself to reveal to her that he had actually been the subject of an internal investigation, however bogus the allegations. His ears burned with shame just thinking about it, and he had a brief vision of pounding Molly into something unrecognizable.

Anne took the proffered letter with a shaking hand, looking hard into his eyes as she did so. Her pursed lips and wary eyes told him that she was expecting bad news.

She sat there without reading it and asked, with a tremor in her voice, "Is this about another woman?"

Julian stared back, uncomprehending for a moment, her response was so unexpected.

"It's from Molly," he answered.

"Who's she?" Anne whispered.

He took her hand. "Sean Molly… your old class president. It's from him."

Hours later, in the breathing darkness of their sleeping home, he eased out of bed and made his way downstairs. With the expertise of one who has worked half his life in darkness, he removed Anne's high school annual from the bookshelf and took it into the kitchen. Using only the light over the stove, he opened it to the M's and scanned for Molly. His finger came to rest on the clear and hopeful face of a boy about to begin his journey into manhood. Smooth and unlined, it gave no hint of the madness that must have been brewing even then beneath the innocuous surface. Julian noted that he proudly sported a full set of sideburns and had the longish hair that had been all the rage then.

Memorizing each bland feature, Julian tried to age it—an exercise in mental Identi-Kit. But every time he managed to conjure a face, it would drift away, insubstantial as smoke. Now and again, he would glance at the windows, wondering if Molly would be there, drawn to the unusual light like a moth, his face pressed against the screen.

There was only darkness.

Julian brooded and pondered the web he and his family had been drawn into, and that he himself had begun to weave. He had lied to Anne—lies of omission. He had not told her of his discovery in Olivera's shed, nor of the contents of the detective's report. Specifically, the interview with the New York constable. This he had kept to himself, nursing its hideous implications. Unfolding the report now, he smoothed it onto the tabletop. Smarting with fatigue, his eyes sought and held one paragraph in particular:

What really got my attention about this fella was a phone call from the local hardware store. 'Course, I'd noticed him before, he's kinda hard to miss, what with the topknot and face paint and stinky clothes, but this was about a check. Seems he'd bought himself a hatchet and wrote in the memo blank, For Weapon. There's no law against that, but naturally, I filed it away for future reference and have tried to keep my eye on him. That was a few months ago and I haven't seen much of him since. According to some of the locals, he's part Hare Krishna and part Mansonite… thinks blacks are going to rise up and kill all white people. And just for variety, he's convinced Hitler's still alive, just layin' low.

"Hitler," Julian said aloud, the name hanging in the air like poison gas. He got up and retrieved a locked box he kept hidden in the house and placed it on the table. He opened it with a tiny key and gazed at the contents. Musty papers and letters, a few curling black-and-white photographs. In one of them, his father, younger than Julian was now, smiled back at the camera, bedecked in his WWII uniform, a Europe in rubble in the background. Julian carefully lifted the picture, drawing scant comfort from the confident young soldier, and withdrew a 7.65mm Mauser semi-automatic pistol. War booty taken from a slain Nazi officer in 1944, now a family heirloom. Unregistered and untraceable.

Julian knew that it was still operable, as he had test fired it on the police range a few times. It wasn't very powerful, being designed primarily as a last resort weapon. Julian knew it would do the job at close range. The irony of its origin and its intended victim was not lost on him, but gave him no joy, the black weight of the gun as heavy on his heart as it was in his hand.

⁁⁃

The trip to the village, nestled in mountains overlooking the Hudson River, took five hours of nonstop driving. Julian made a point of checking into an overpriced motel on the highway, where he could count on a steady flow of travelers to blend in with. The village itself was another half mile down the road. The room was reasonably clean, but had a damp, unwholesome feel to it.

He noticed ancient stains in various places on the worn carpet. It was easy to imagine that in such a place, so devoid of character and promising such anonymity, a man could lose himself. Anything could happen.

He threw open the curtains and saw his nondescript rental car. His own was garaged at Newark Airport—an added precaution. Sitting in a mushy armchair he stared out, dully aware of the intermittent traffic beyond. On the horizon, tendrils of mist rushed headlong over the mountaintops.

It had not been hard to get here. Julian had accumulated a lot of vacation time over the past year, and in his newly promoted zeal, had not used a day. That, and the understandable stress that Sean Molly's allegations must have caused him and his family, ensured the captain's signature on his leave request.

Anne had been fearful when he told her of his plans, but he had assured her in his most logical and policeman-like way that it was necessary. By going to New York, he would be able to assess the threat more realistically and make it clear to the constable that he was very concerned about the safety of his family. Something a phone conversation could not convey. Besides, it wouldn't hurt to get a good look at Molly, in case, someday, he needed to identify him for charges. It all made good sense... and it was all a lie.

On his way out the door, after holding each of his children for a long moment, he had remarked to Lady Anne that his service weapon was locked up in the bedroom, though it was unlikely she would have any need of it, as the constable in New York had assured him by telephone the day before that Molly had resurfaced there, more disheveled and psychotic than ever. He could see Anne's relief. The mistrust and lurking fear in her eye had vanished. He knew she would never remember the Mauser.

⁊

It was just after dusk when he found the address in the police report situated at the end of a cul-de-sac. The steeply descending street was potholed and erupted, looking as if it might slide down the mountainside. The lone two-story house gave the appearance of struggling to free itself from the clinging vegetation it was immersed in. All the paint had peeled off achieving a uniform weathered grayness that produced the effect of it gradually diminishing in the growing twilight. As he watched, it vanished, like a witch's house.

Raising his binoculars, Julian trained them on the space that the house had occupied and waited. The outline of the house returned first, then details began to reappear. At the edge of his vision, something toppled from the overflowing garbage can in the front yard and quickly scurried into the overturned and crushed one next to it. The can rocked slightly on its warped sides. Still no light appeared behind the uncurtained windows.

Moments later, a small flame leapt into life, spluttered, then died, briefly illuminating a figure through the smeared glass of a second-floor window. A faint and flickering glow followed, gradually resolving itself into a small tongue of fire that began to travel like a will-o'-the-wisp from room to room, its bearer invisible in the greater darkness. Mesmerized, Julian followed its progress as it appeared and disappeared from each window, first on the second floor, then on the first. Once done, the inspection was repeated, as Molly returned to the second floor and then again to the first. Ceaselessly walking his rounds, searching for, or guarding against, something only he could know or perceive, haunting his own house. Sometime after midnight, with the eerie pantomime still in progress, Julian fell asleep.

☙

The cold awakened him, shivering and stiff, with the sun's oblique rays piercing his bloodshot eyes. A blanket he had brought along lay on the seat next to him, forgotten. His neck felt like it was in a vise and he had no idea of the time. He glanced at his watch. It read eight-ten. The day had cleared, the sky scrubbed blue and huge, but the temperature had dropped. He considered starting the car to run the heater, but decided against it, knowing it would create plumes of exhaust in the frigid air. Instead, reaching for his thermos, he hoped that the coffee within was at least tepid.

It was then that he saw Molly striding down the center of the short street toward him. It was too late to duck down. Cursing his carelessness, he thrust the thermos away and rested his hand on the gun tucked into his waistband. Sitting up, he unlatched the door in case he needed to open it quickly. Then, for the first time, he studied Molly in the flesh.

Like an apparition, Molly kept coming, his saffron robe billowing from his tall, lank body like a ship in full sail. His narrow, shaven skull, capped by a strip of hair that ran down the back of his head, moved neither left nor right, his protuberant, hot-looking eyes focused on the horizon beyond. The wide straight mouth appeared to be working, the strained tendons in his scrawny neck rising and falling in tortured unison. Julian felt the hairs on the backs of his hands rising.

As Molly reached the front of the car, he could see the starved-looking face more clearly. A swastika was crudely tattooed in black on his left cheek and his forehead was daubed with yellow, a drop of it having run between his eyes and onto the bridge of his straight nose. In his left hand he was carrying something wrapped in brown paper.

Julian swung open the door to block Molly's passage. Unfazed, Molly simply gave it a wide

berth, his eyes never once straying from their distant hold, and strode on, mumbling audibly now. Julian caught a glimpse of familiar writing on the package.

"Molly!" he shouted at Sean's retreating back, rage rising like vomit in his throat, hot and sickening. "You know who I am, you Hare Krishna Nazi bastard! You've watched me and my family enough! Now it's my turn! How's it feel? Do ya like it?" He wanted to choke the life out of this useless, frightening creature. "Stop, goddamn you!"

Molly halted and turned a little, his face contorting like rats under a blanket. Raising his right hand in the air, palm open, level with his head, he screamed in a high, girlish voice, "I could just slap you silly!" and stomped the ground with his booted foot. With that, he resumed his headlong march without a backward glance, his incongruous army boots slapping the broken asphalt. Never once had he looked at Julian.

☙

Julian was waiting for him when he entered the post office, pretending to fill out a change of address card. Molly's *outré* costume and pulsating madness filled the tiny customer-service area as soon as he entered. Two elderly women, who had previously been engaged in a fascinating discussion of current weather conditions, decided that it wasn't that cold out after all, and fled the building. An old man gaped, transfixed, mouth loose and watery eyes blinking rapidly behind his thick, smeared lenses.

Molly's aggressive demeanor altered abruptly as he approached the counter. His head drooped to his chest and his stride became a shuffle. Humbly, he slid the package forward like a slow student with a late report. The lone postal worker continued to sort through the morning's take at a worktable in the rear, oblivious to the offering.

Julian's hand shot out and grabbed the parcel, spinning it around so that he could read the address. Molly gasped and began to mutter, never lifting his eyes to the interloper.

"I can save you the postage, Sean, and deliver this personally, since it's my house you're sending it to " Julian said quietly, his eyes never leaving Molly's face. Molly began to wring his hands in anxiety. "In fact, why don't we open it now? The suspense is killing me." With that, he shook the box. Inside, something slid from end to end with a dry rattle.

Molly sprang to life with a small cry, snatching the box from Julian's grasp and rushing toward the exit. Over his shoulder, he cried out, "Devil! Devil bastard!" Then he began running, crying loudly, "Help! Help! Help!"

Julian sprang after him into the street. "You crazy son of a bitch! Leave my family alone! Do you understand me? Leave my family alone or I'll kill you!" he screamed at Molly's fleeing figure. The impotent rage and fear of the past week exploded from him, leaving him drained and almost tearful on the streets of a town where no one knew him. All around people had stopped to stare. Not at the robed lunatic he had chased out of the post office, but at him—a violent, threatening stranger. He had never felt so cast adrift, so separated from humanity. Avoiding meeting anyone's eyes, Julian began the long walk back to his car, consciously squaring his shoulders and pretending that he was not ashamed.

☙

It was long after dark when he checked out of the motel. He had spent the day sleeping and had packed immediately upon waking. There was no point in staying on. He had failed in his self-appointed mission. Molly was still alive... still a threat, an uncontrollable force that might remain static or suddenly blow into a storm with unpredictable results Yet, Julian knew that he could not strike him down, provoked or not, and was disgusted that he had sunk so low as to have attempted to bate a madman.

Praying for some insight, he pulled away from the motel, pondering the hodgepodge of beliefs and rituals that gave form to Sean Molly's persona. Shortly afterwards, he found himself parked with his lights out in the now familiar street facing Molly's shack.

For a long while, he watched as Sean went through his ritual of lighting candles and marching from room to room, and he thought of the walls that madness erects, brick by brick. He thought too, long and lovingly, of the Lady Anne and his misguided knight-errant quest to protect her. Of how easy it was to love her vulnerability and how even someone as lost as Molly might remember her and cherish that memory of unrequited, simple boyhood love and want to protect her, just as Julian had been doing. It was only when he heard the high-pitched squealing that he realized that the house was on fire.

Julian sat dumbstruck for a moment, unable to move. The flames were leaping from room to room, eagerly consuming the dry-rotted walls, as the figure of Molly rushed to and from, upstairs and down, without once making for the door. For just a moment, Julian wondered if this was not God's answer to his prayers. Then, he began a mad sprint for the house, carrying the wool blanket he had kept in the front seat for his surveillance.

Kicking open the front door, he was greeted with a great rush of scorching air and fell back. Taking a deep breath, he crouched and waded in under the smoke that was beginning to flow through the newly created exit, holding the blanket over his head. In the hallway, he shouted Molly's name and got a mouthful of choking smoke for his trouble. Above his own coughing, he heard Molly's beseeching squeals and saw a figure wearing robes of flames streak across the hallway from one room to the next. Julian rushed after him, only to be bowled over as Molly ran back out again like a comet. Blindly, Julian reached out and snagged an ankle. With a crash that shook the floorboards, Molly slammed into the floor, his squeals now hellish screams of pain. Using the blanket, Julian climbed on top of him, smothering the flames as he went.

Flipping the unconscious form over on top of the smoldering blanket, Julian now began to crawl backwards, pulling Molly, sled-like, towards the door. The heat and smoke had become so intense that he felt as if he would combust spontaneously any moment, and it was only by sheer will power that he didn't abandon Molly and run screaming for air. Somewhere, far-off it seemed, there was the sound of sirens, and he struggled toward the sound, hoping that it was leading him in the right direction.

Suddenly he was surrounded by glass-faced figures that seized him roughly and rushed him into the blessed night air. Through his squinting, reddened eyes, he saw Molly being placed on a stretcher and medics bending over him. The house was an inferno, the frame shimmering like a ghost within the flames and groaning like the damned in hell. The firefighter was saying something and slapping Julian on the back.

"You saved his life, bud! Hell of a job! He a friend of yours?"

Julian managed a smile and lied, "No, I was just passing by."

ᔌ

Before he checked out of the hospital the next morning, Julian stopped in to see Molly. He had been lucky. His burns, though painful, had not been severe. His arms and back had suffered the most and he was heavily sedated for the pain. For the first time, he focused on Julian, his eyes rolling and sliding with the effort.

Julian leaned down and whispered, "Sean, do you know who I am?"

Molly nodded a little.

"Do you remember what happened?"

Again, a nod.

"Do you understand what it means?"

Molly only stared, a puzzled look in his eyes.

"It's karma, old friend. You know what that means, I know. You believe in karma, don't you?"

A look of comprehension dawned quickly, then a nod.

"It means all this had to happen for me to be in the right place, at the right time, to save your life. Now it's done and we can stop. We've completed the circle and you can leave me and mine in peace. You've been released. This is what it means."

Julian saw tears forming in Molly's eyes and knew he had understood. His protectorship was finally at an end. "Thank you," he croaked.

Julian stood and patted his hand. As he was going out the door, he turned. "It was meant to be," he said softly and, walking away, thought of his return to the Lady Anne, his sword unbloodied but the grail firmly in hand.

A Prayer Answered

(2010)

Father Gregory parked the old, black Buick a half block from his destination, running it up onto the curb in the darkness. Driving was still a new experience for the priest. In his native India his diocese had been far too poor to afford such luxuries as automobiles and, he thought with a sigh, he had been much thinner in those days as a result. With a grunt, he slid out of the tilted vehicle onto the street. In one hand, he clutched the valise that contained the Sacraments, while the other struggled to keep the white stole 'round his neck from being blown off in the rising wind.

A policeman approached him from a cluster of emergency vehicles pulsing with red and white strobe lights that made him appear to shift from side to side like an apparition. With what seemed impossible speed for a walking man he loomed ever darker and larger. Father Gregory smoothed his black shirt over his plump belly and smiled. "Hello," he called out. "I am sent for by Chief J, I believe... yes, um... yes, I think so."

The officer was suddenly in front of the priest, as tall and broad as a tree that had miraculously sprouted forth from the asphalt. *How do Americans grow so large*, Father Gregory wondered as he awaited whatever the policeman might choose to do.

"Father Gregory?" he asked, then, not waiting for an answer, added, "Follow me, sir, the Chief is inside." Turning on his heel, he indicated the house surrounded by the police cars and set off once more. Nearby an ambulance sat idling, its occupants slumped in their seats, bored-looking and unconcerned in the flickering red wash of lights. Next to them, a white panel van sat empty on the lawn, its rear doors thrown wide, revealing nothing but a greater darkness within. On its side were printed the words, "Medical Examiner."

Hurrying to keep up with the striding officer, Father Gregory managed to ask, "Is there more than one person hurt?"

The policeman glanced back over his shoulder, "Nope... just one."

"Then why..." The priest struggled with both his English and his shortness of breath. "Then why is the ambulance still here, may I ask? Surely the injured should have been taken to hospital by now?"

The officer slowed and turned, and Father Gregory thought he could discern an expression of concern on the young man's face. "We had an 'injured' when we got here," he said, "but she's beyond all that now." He nodded towards the panel van, his face hard and set once more. "The meat wagon is for her; the ambulance is waiting for the 'go-ahead' on her husband... he's paralyzed, you know... fell down a flight of stairs while giving his wife a drunken beating years ago. The Chief is holding on to him until we remove the body... there's no way he wouldn't see her otherwise, so we're leaving him in his bedroom until you… do whatever it is you do." Then he added, "I'm not a Catholic, Father, and I don't really understand why you're needed here in the first place, but I'll let the Chief give you the rundown, he's the one that said you should be called."

The "Chief" had been amongst the first of Father Gregory's new parishioners to welcome him to Camelot Beach and invite him into his home. This had gone a long way to breaking the ice with the rest of the islanders. Though the venerable Monsignor Cahill was still the head pastor, his slow, painful demise by cancer was steadily robbing him of his vitality, and his availability had been curtailed as a result. Many had found the dark, little man with the almost incomprehensible accent a jarring change from the dour, old Irish prelate. But with time, an improving grasp of the language, and a sincere devotion that needed no translation, Father Gregory had gradually come to be embraced by the community at large. He had heard it remarked of late that his homilies were nearly always understood. By his own calculations, the congregation laughed at his jokes at least half of the time, and this delighted him, as he felt strongly that he was an inspired humorist.

The house he had been called to was a throwback to the seventies and one of the last of its kind on the island. Most of the older homes and cottages had long ago been devoured by the jaws of the wrecking machines and replaced by four-, five-, and six-bedroom vacation homes that were only used in the summer months and on various holidays. Instead, this squatted amongst its silent, dark neighbors like a cringing, old dog awaiting a kick or a curse. Even the color, to Father Gregory's eyes, participated in the allusion, being the mangy yellow of an unwelcome cur.

The priest had not been told who occupied this home, and he could not remember ever having visited it before, but he assumed the victim within was one of St. Brendan's parishioners. Certainly the man standing in the doorway was. Chief Julian Hall was engrossed in a murmured conversation with a thin young policeman who stood beneath the clouded porch lamp. He held in his hands a notebook, and Father Gregory heard his nervous laughter float out from beneath the bug-filled globe above his head. Patting him on the shoulder, Chief Hall turned to go back inside, then spotted the little priest.

Stepping around the rookie officer, he hurried down the few steps. "Father, I'm so sorry to drag you out this late." The two men shook hands as the freshening wind off the ocean several blocks away swirled 'round them.

"No, please, it is my duty to come to those in need. However," Father Gregory paused to arrange his words, "this man tells me that I have come too late. I sincerely hope not, Chief J."

The police chief paused. "Well, yes and no, Father. When I had you called, Mrs. Fischer was still alive, if just barely…" now it was his turn to choose his words with care, "I could tell from her wounds that she didn't have much time left so I had you contacted to respond here instead of waiting to get her into the hospital… it turns out I underestimated the damage… she died before we could even get her on a stretcher."

Father Gregory still grasped the Chief's hand and now patted it gently, as if Chief J were one of the bereaved. He knew Mrs. Fischer, of course, "Kitty," as she was known to everyone— though why she should be equated to a young cat the priest was at a loss to understand. He blamed his imperfect comprehension of the language and promised himself that before he returned to Goa, he would master the intimacies of American speech. "I see," he murmured. "I quite understand, dear man." He patted the Chief's hand once more before releasing it. Behind him he heard a snort. Unperturbed, he demanded, "Take me to her, Chief J."

Julian responded with, "Prepare yourself, Father," then nodded at the officer with the notepad who stood aside to let the two men pass. As they did so, Julian said to him, "Father Gregory Savartha…" then added for the benefit of the puzzled rookie whose pen remained aloft, "common spelling on Savartha." He led on with only the ghost of a smile.

The sixty-five-year-old woman lay on the grimy linoleum of her kitchen floor within full view upon entering the house. Father Gregory found that he was not prepared, saying only, "Oh… oh, dear lady."

In spite of all the medical packaging that lay strewn about her, clearly none of their contents had been useful—she was quite shockingly dead. The blood that had leaked from the numerous gashes in her skull had congealed into a black pool and she lay with the back of her head resting in it, her features grey and slack, the whites of her eyes gone the color of dirty sheets flecked with red. Even to his untrained eye, the priest could see that she had originally been face-down in the mess and had been turned over by the officers and rescue personnel attempting to save her life. As a result, one half of her face was war-painted a sticky scarlet—a final indignity for a woman he knew as a quiet and devout member of his flock.

"She was always kneeling and praying," he murmured. "I believe she must have lit a thousand votive candles in the brief time I have been here—such a shame."

"I don't need to tell you not to touch anything, I'm sure," Julian nonetheless reminded the priest, "though the scene's been pretty thoroughly photographed and processed up to this point. In fact, I think the investigators from the Prosecutor's Office have already cleared." He glanced over at the Viking-like patrol sergeant who filled the doorway behind him, completely obscuring the young rookie on sentry duty. The sergeant nodded once but made no move to enter the room. "These folks," and here the Chief indicated two figures suited up in what appeared to be paper pants, shirts, and caps, and wearing surgical masks and gloves, "are our M.E.'s best." The two sexless, faceless figures appeared to glare at the senior policeman over their masks. "They're a little annoyed with me," he continued in a mock confidentiality meant for the entire room to hear, "they're anxious to package up Mrs. Fischer, the cadaver that is, and be off—it appears we are holding them up with our superstitious ways."

"I see," Father Gregory replied. "Well, this shan't take but a moment, I am thinking, as the time for the Viaticum has unfortunately passed. Some patience is in order, however, for a simple prayer." He set his valise on the floor, no longer requiring its contents, and knelt next to his unfortunate parishioner, though being careful to stay well out of the blood. As he drew closer an odor began to reach him, cloying and carnal, that would shortly become rank. How distressingly mortal the poor body is, he thought, even as he grimaced at the smell of new, and violent, death.

Sketching a cross in the air above the corpse, he intoned, "In the Name of the Father, the Son, and the Holy Spirit," and began to pray for the soul of one Katherine Denise Fischer. Julian automatically followed suit and crossed himself, but refrained from kneeling due to some unarticulated concern over his professional reputation. Nonetheless, he bowed his head for the prayer. Out of the corner of his eye, he saw that Sergeant Dunbar and the Medical Examiner's investigators were all but tapping their feet.

In what seemed an almost inappropriately brief time, the priest completed his prayer with an Amen, and rose once more. With a sigh, Father Gregory removed the stole from his shoulders and returned it reverently to his valise. "Such a shame," he repeated while studying the sad remains. Suddenly the little priest appeared to remember something and said, "I was too late to administer to her, of course, but perhaps she had last words that I should be informed of. Is this possible?" he asked the Chief.

Julian looked inquiringly around the room, meeting the blank, hostile glare of the M.E.'s people and coming to settle on the sergeant. "Anything?" he asked out of politeness.

Sergeant Dunbar backed out of the doorway while seizing the rookie and thrusting him bodily in through the same. "He was first on scene," he spoke from the porch. "Says she made some kind of statement—read it," he demanded of the thin, young officer who had suddenly become the center of attention.

With the slightest tremor in both his voice and hands, the officer flipped back through several pages of the notebook he held and appeared to find the passage in question. Taking a moment to clear his throat and draw himself up to his full and uncommanding height, he read aloud, "My prayers have been answered… thanks be to God." He slowly closed his book and looked up to gauge the effect of his reading upon his audience. Everyone stared back at him.

"That's all she said?" Chief Hall asked.

"Yessir," the rookie confirmed. "That's it."

Julian grunted in dissatisfaction. "I guess it's too much to expect that she should name her killer."

Father Gregory stared up at him in seeming astonishment. "Chief J," he asked, "may we confer in private?"

Julian gave the nod to the Medical Examiner's investigators, even as he took his parish priest by the arm and led him into the living room. The last thing he saw in the kitchen was the hasty unfurling of the body bag.

Once in the musty, over-furnished front room, he turned back to Father Gregory. The little man squinted in the dim, dusty light that filtered in through the kitchen. "Is it possible for me to be included in the details of the case?" the priest inquired.

Julian studied Father Gregory's round face with its large, dark eyes and white shock of wispy hair. At last, he spoke, "If... and this is very important, Father... *if* I can rely on your discretion. You do understand that we have a murder here?"

"Indeed, Chief J, I do. As to discretion," the cleric paused with just the slightest of smiles, "you can't be serious, my friend... I am a priest."

From the kitchen came the clack and clatter of the gurney as it received its sad burden. "What we have is an apparently motiveless murder, as Mrs. Fischer was neither robbed nor raped. There was no forced entry—like many folks in town here, they never locked their doors—the locals consider it a point of honor." The chief paused to roll his eyes, then continued, "As she lived alone with her husband and they kept largely to themselves; the 'charming' Mister Fischer being paralyzed from the waist down, it is hard to imagine how they might have any enemies." The chief paused to arrange his thoughts, then resumed, "As to evidence, the only obvious thing we have is the murder weapon—a ball bat."

Father Gregory repeated this last in puzzlement, "Ball bat, Chief J?"

"Yeah, a baseball bat we found in the yard..." It occurred to him that the Indian curate was unfamiliar with the instrument. "Like a..." he struggled for the appropriate analogy, "... like in cricket?" He raised his eyebrows hopefully, but in vain, then continued, "you know, a bat... a club... a shillelagh," he laughed.

"A cudgel!" Father Gregory cried, catching on. "Oh yes, I do understand! From whence did it come?"

The chief stopped smiling, "We don't know yet. It could have come from here... nearly every house in America has at least one in the closet. The victim's husband," Julian winced at his own attempt to distance himself from his newly murdered neighbor, "is too 'distraught' to be of much help right now." He threw a glance down the hall to a closed door.

Father Gregory picked up on the policeman's emphasis and asked, "You do not think much of this bereaved man?"

"I knew Charlie back in the days before he was a… *victim*, Father." Julian hooked a thumb over his shoulder at the bedroom. "If all this had happened twenty years ago when he was still walking around, he would have been my prime suspect.

"In fact, if it had been left up to him, Kitty would have been dead long ago, and it wasn't for the lack of trying on his part. My God, the beatings he gave her…. That's why he's in there now. He dragged her to the top of the stairs one night by a belt he had looped around her neck, and though Kitty denied it, I think he was going to try and hang her somehow. In any case, fate intervened, and he lost his balance and fell down that same flight, breaking his ugly neck on the way down and landing him on his back permanently. In all my years of policing, I've never seen a more hateful, jealous man, nor with less reason to be so. Kitty was a saint."

Father Gregory remained silent, studying the outraged young officer that had suddenly appeared in place of the steady, middle-aged man that governed Camelot's Police Department. It faded once more into obscurity even as he watched, leaving the drawn and creased face with pale, washed-out blue eyes with which he was familiar.

"So certainly there is your motive," Father Gregory pointed out. "Vengeance is a strong motive… it often crops up in the scriptures… Old Testament mostly."

"Vengeance," Julian repeated. "Wouldn't that require that the suspect be able to stand on his own two legs, Father? She was struck repeatedly on the top of the head; I seriously doubt she knelt down for Charlie to have a go at cracking her skull."

"Fingerprints?" Father Gregory queried.

"Yes," Julian answered with a shake of his grey head, "plenty of those. But it will be some time before we can determine whose are whose… chances are they all belong to Kitty and Charlie… possibly the killer. Though if we don't develop any suspects, or his prints aren't on file, they won't do us much good."

"What if they are on the bludgeon?" Father Gregory persisted.

"Same," Julian answered.

"What if you find only Mister Fischer's fingerprints on the weapon?"

Julian thought longingly for a moment of the days when he smoked cigarettes. "Father let's not play cat and mouse. We played this game once before and you know I find it irritating." He was referring to a case a few months before, when the Indian priest had uncovered a murderess within the pages of a discarded journal. "Spill it."

Father Gregory appeared to think the proposition over carefully before answering. "I believe Mrs. Fischer… Kitty," he tried on the nickname for size and found it uncomfortable, "has named her killer for us."

"And when did she do this?" Julian asked.

Father Gregory smiled at this seeming encouragement. "In her dying, and recorded, declaration."

"I don't recall that being in her statement," the chief declared.

"No, no, perhaps not," the priest began. "But she did say," he cocked his round head like a bird with the effort of memory, "My prayers have been answered… thanks be to God!" He brought his hands together in an attitude of prayer and shook them at the policeman. "A miracle," he whispered, "a miracle!"

"Father, are you telling me that Kitty prayed that Charlie would walk again… and that he has?"

"Yes, yes, this was her most fervent prayer! She has told me many times! The prayers of a pious and devout woman carry great weight! I knew that you, if anyone, would understand this."

Julian stared back in amazement, unable to speak for several moments. "No," he said at last. "No, I don't. You don't honestly believe that her prayers were answered with murder!"

The joy fled from Father Gregory's face at the policeman's logic and he appeared to consider his previous declarations, then answered, "You are only half right, Chief J—the good woman's prayers *were* answered; her own words testify to it. As to the husband, I believe this odious man has squandered God's precious grace in that most pernicious act—revenge. For him, I reserve my greatest pity."

"Pity," the policeman repeated while studying the closed door of the bedroom and thinking that Kitty had been found as if fleeing from someone coming from that direction—she had been running to the kitchen door, not from it. "Revenge for what?" he muttered.

Father Gregory cleared his throat and appeared embarrassed at the question. "Well, as to that it… it is awkward, dear man. You see, it was told to me in confession… but as she is now no longer among us, I can say at least this—on the night of his terrible 'accident,' he had, or *believed* that he had, discovered the proof he had been unable to beat from her on previous occasions."

"Good God," Julian breathed. "Please don't tell me she shoved him down those stairs."

Father Gregory stared back at him. "He did try to harm her," he added at last.

"Father," Julian began after a pause. "You do understand what you're saying here? If what you believe is true, it means that Charlie Fischer had to keep this a secret once he discovered feeling had returned to his legs. That he had to exercise himself for weeks, or months, without Kitty knowing, and prolonged and denied himself the pleasure of walking out in the fresh air—all these things, just so that when he was strong enough, he could both surprise and kill her. Do you understand what all that would mean—the hatred, the… the evilness?"

Both men remained silent for several moments, then the chief spoke once more. "What do you expect me to do with this?"

"You cannot arrest this man?" Father Gregory asked in obvious disappointment.

"Based on what?" the chief fired back. "I don't intend to haul him before an ecclesiastical court, Father. I need proof, or at least a good circumstantial case."

The cleric was not to be deterred. "Is Mister Fischer not a good suspect? And one that sits like a spider in this web of suspicious circumstances? If he could walk, would you not be interrogating him at this moment?"

"*If* he could walk, Father…"

Someone cleared their throat and the two turned to find the ambulance driver standing in the doorway to the kitchen. "The M.E.'s people have taken Mrs. Fischer," he said. "Should I get Mister Fischer loaded up now?"

It had been Chief Hall's intention to have the victim's husband evaluated by the emergency room physician for stress and shock, as he had been a witness, at least an audible witness, to the horror of his wife's murder. He stared back at the plump, unshaven young man awaiting his answer, even as he felt the eyes of Father Gregory upon him.

"No," he murmured, "not just yet, Justin. Give me a few minutes with the poor man."

Unconcerned, Justin nodded and began to back out of the room.

"Oh, and Justin," Julian halted the young man, "you've got an EMT riding with you… right?"

Justin nodded. "Yeah, Chief, we've always got one on board… you know that." Then another thought occurred to him. "Is someone else hurt, Chief? We thought there was just the one victim."

"No," Julian reassured him, "the only victim was Mrs. Fischer… just checking, that's all."

As the young man completed his exit, Julian extracted a long needle from a pile of sewing that lay in a basket next to the couch and held it up to the light. "I have been assured that he has no feeling from the waist down," he said out of the corner of his mouth.

Father Gregory stared at the needle gleaming like truth in the dim obscurity of the room. "You are indeed a man of faith, Chief J," he said with admiration.

"Probably an unemployed one as of tomorrow," Julian replied as the policeman and the priest approached the closed door at the end of the hallway.

လ

The arraignment of Charles Fischer for the murder of his wife created a small sensation as the facts of the matter became public. Chief Hall, for his part, received a letter of censure from the county prosecutor for his rather extraordinary actions in exposing the killer. Surprisingly though, the accused chose not to challenge the probable cause that led to his arrest but, instead, accepted a plea bargain that guaranteed him twenty-five years in prison—a certain death sentence at his age. This was a decision he declined to discuss with the press, except to say that he was, indeed, guilty of the crime of which he stood accused and was deeply sorry.

Charles Fischer's thoughts and feelings, beyond those few words, remained private to all but his confessor, Father Gregory

Savartha, who was most pleased to have been able to grant absolution to the wretched man, knowing that he was truly contrite, and now restored to full humanity.

Night Class
(2017)

Rachel Lally had her back to the screen door as they approached, but could hear their muffled voices, their shuffling footsteps coming up the drive. Chopping carrots and potatoes occupied most of her attention, so she didn't bother turning 'round to greet her son and his friends returning from their night class. She was pressed for time preparing a late supper before starting the graveyard shift at County Convalescent.

Blowing a lock of unruly hair out of her left eye, she winced as the door slammed behind her. From the living room a distant voice chirped merrily that thunderstorms were in the local forecast.

As if in confirmation, the billowing curtains above the sink suddenly reversed with a soft snap against the screen; the rising wind through the leaves beyond mimicking the sound of rushing water.

Rachel glanced out to see a tall bank of boiling clouds revealed in a silent flare of light over the hidden sea. Nearby, a car burned rubber in its haste to be elsewhere.

"It's a good thing you guys got in before…" Rachel began, then stopped, confused. Instead of the usual banter and wisecracks, she heard a gargling noise behind her, almost like someone using mouthwash. In the same moment she also registered that there was only the scrape of a single pair of shoes. Turning now, chopping knife still in hand, she saw her eighteen-year-old son.

He leaned against the wooden kitchen table where they shared most of their meals. Propping himself upright with both arms, his mouth was open, the awful sound issuing from his throat, his face white with panic.

Eyes wide, and straining, he pushed off suddenly from the table and staggered toward her. She heard the knife she had been holding clatter onto the kitchen floor.

"Stephen," she managed, "what is it?"

His hands had now risen to his throat as if he were choking or trying to strangle himself. Launching himself forward, he shunted his much smaller mother aside, knocking her to the floor as he stumbled to the sink.

Looking up at her only son, she began to scream as he convulsively emptied his life's blood into the basin. "Stephen," she cried, trying to regain her feet, terror making her limbs weak and rubbery. "Stephen!"

But before she could raise herself, he collapsed as well, arms and legs pumping and drumming. Crawling to him, she took him into her arms, trying to hold on to him, to still him.

An arm shot out, striking her hard in the face, knocking her nearly senseless.

Then he went still… completely, utterly still.

In the sudden, profound silence, she could hear the first heavy drops of rain begin to tap on the dusty windowsills, the ticking of the cat clock on the wall, her own labored breathing.

Stephen remained mute and cool as clay.

With tiny, furtive concussions, the rain drops grew rapidly in both number and intensity, soon becoming the muted roar of a deluge. As the spring monsoon swept over the small house, Rachel's wails were muffled and contained, the streets and sidewalks cleansed of anyone who might hear her cries.

℀

"We ain't got a lot to go on here, Boss," Detective Sergeant Gavin Wolfe informed the chief of the Camelot Beach P.D. "There's a few possibilities—a half-filled container of radiator fluid in the garage, an open bottle of clog-buster in the bathroom with a little missing. But the M.E.'s investigators say neither's likely."

"Why's that?" Julian Hall asked, glancing through the screen door at the brilliantly lit activity within the house. The two men were standing in the darkened side yard of the property. Nearby, trying to catch a glimpse as well, perhaps gather a tidbit of gossip, a small clump of curious neighbors shuffled restlessly on the sidewalk. The tourist season was still a month away, and Julian was glad they didn't yet have to manage the army of drunken revelers that would bring to the Jersey Shore. The policemen conversed in low voices.

"The blood trail actually starts outside on the porch." Gavin nodded at the small concrete landing protected by a roof. Yellow tape fluttered in the breeze that remained after the storm; a young uniformed officer stood sentry in the shadows. "Most of it got washed away by that squall, but it continues right on into the kitchen where things got worse… a lot worse. It just don't appear he had time to ingest anything inside the house."

Julian looked beyond the large, heavy man that was his senior investigator to the small kitchen that appeared to be the set for a horror film, gouts of blood gone dark as port decorating the floor, the sink, the adjacent cabinets. His thoughts raced, recreating what the mother had witnessed but could not explain.

He remembered the unhappy looking young detective that he had last seen escorting the victim to the morgue.

"How's your protégé making out, Gavin?"

Shrugging, the older detective ran a hand over the reddish buzz-cut hair that covered his small, round head. "About as well as you might expect, Chief. He wasn't all that thrilled with morgue duty, I can tell ya." Chuckling, he added, "Maybe he'll quit now—go back to patrol."

After a moment's silence, he cut his eyes to Julian's profile, then away again. "He may not be cut out for this line of work, Chief… he's a little… *different*," he added.

"Aren't we all?" Julian replied. "He just needs a good teacher."

"You're the boss," Gavin rumbled. "You know best."

"He wasn't cutting it in patrol, Gavin. Just wasn't meshing. But I think he's got the makings of a good investigator. Give him some time."

"But no special treatment, Chief… I gotta draw the line at that."

"God forbid."

"Good," the big man exhaled, "cause I'm treating him like everybody else."

"Then I already feel sorry for him," Julian replied. "By the way, what's the rush on the autopsy? The medical examiner usually waits till regular office hours."

"The manner of death, Chief—he's concerned whatever Stephen ingested is still at work, so he wants to get in there before there's any more damage to *his* crime scene."

"Jesus Christ," Julian muttered. After a few moments of silence, he asked, "Do we know yet *how* he got home? Did he drive himself, or was he dropped off?"

"His mom seemed to think that someone might have been with Stephen but walked away before she saw him… or them." Gavin nodded his bristly head at a car in the driveway, "She says that's their only car and it's been here all evening, that he was picked up by friends—she didn't see who. Someone dropped him off; then got the hell out of Dodge."

"Any idea of who that was?"

"Maybe." Julian could see Gavin's gap-toothed grin in the yellow cast-off light from the porch. "Our boy had friends in low places, Boss. You know he was part of the crew we've been looking at for that rash of winter burglaries, right? Bit of a hanger-on, he was, but it wouldn't have been his first time at the rodeo. Remember?"

Julian did remember—Stephen had been an active juvenile, dabbling in petty thefts and shoplifting. Drugs had come into it, as well, which had been no surprise considering his long-absent father's track record. But after a period of mandatory counseling the boy had fallen from their radar.

"So you know some names, Gavin?"

"I know all the players, Chief, all the players…" he tapped his temple with a beefy finger. "… Traci Mendel, Blaise Aubrey, and maybe even McAfee the Magnificent. It's a tight-knit little group of local turds. Fancy themselves some kind of 'posse' these days.

"Stephen was supposed to be at Wessex Community College tonight. I'm gonna check that out tomorrow. If he was playing hooky, he had to be someplace… with someone. These things, and more, shall be revealed to the enterprising detective and his Boy Wonder."

"Keep me informed, will you? I want to know what you know as soon as you know it." Julian turned for his car.

"Like we was twins, Chief..." Gavin called to his boss and friend of many years. "... *Telepathic* twins."

When he heard Julian laugh, the big man smiled.

ↄ

"God, I'm so exhausted," Detective Tyler Errickson moaned from his seat, his pale, slightly crooked face wedged between his fists, his back hunched over in his loose, ill-fitting suit.

Framing him between size eleven shoes that rested atop his cluttered desk, his boss regarded the slender young officer.

"Tired, are ya?" he asked with feeling.

"I've only had a few hours' sleep," Tyler responded, shaking his dark, close-cropped head. "I just couldn't get that autopsy out of my mind... and that smell! My God, I showered twice, but that smell kept waking me up."

"Aw geez, that's a shame. What was I thinking sending you there all alone?" Gavin asked the office at large.

"That was not right of me," he answered himself.

Tyler glanced up, pushing his dark-framed glasses onto the bridge of his narrow nose.

"Maybe we need to get you started on some vitamins to build you up a little," Gavin offered with concern. "Or some testosterone... you may have *Low-T*! I've seen that on a commercial. They're making great strides, you know."

"That ain't right," Tyler protested.

"No...?" his boss inquired with puckered lips. "Well then, how 'bout you dry your little eyes and give me the run-down from the M.E.—what killed our boy, Stephen? Think you can manage that much?"

Detective Errickson appeared close to rebellion, but murmured instead, "The doc says that he died from massive hemorrhaging, but he won't know the exact cause until the contents of Stephen's stomach have been analyzed. He thinks the caustic material was an alkali; that's his best guess for now."

Gavin's fleshy face screwed up in concentration, "What's an alkali when it's at home?"

"It's a base... not an acid..." The young detective shrugged. "That's what he said."

"Uh huh," Gavin grunted, squinting hard at his subordinate. "Well, that clears things up considerable."

"I'm not a doctor," Tyler muttered.

"Among many things you're not," his boss replied.

Slamming his big feet onto the floor, Gavin rose from behind his desk, seizing Tyler's elbow. "This is the first day of the rest of your career..." he crowed, leading the younger man through the door and into the corridor, then added, "So what d'ya say we go roust some innocent citizens and see if they know any more than we do—which shouldn't be hard, since we don't know squat!"

Two patrol officers coming out of the breakroom nudged each other. Grinning at their former colleague, one of them opened his mouth to comment. But, as the big man turned his baleful gaze upon them, all thoughts of levity fled the scene.

∾

Tyler had to trot to catch up to his boss as they approached Traci Mendel's bungalow, a leftover from the seventies that had the battered, surly look of a survivor. Inherited from her parents who had died in a car crash two years before, it was shaded by its much larger and newer neighbors, hunkered down in perpetual damp and gloom.

"Good cop… bad cop," Gavin instructed over his shoulder.

"Which one am I?" Tyler managed as his sergeant gave the faded door a few good whacks.

With an appreciative glance over his big shoulder, Gavin said, "You're a great kidder, ain't 'cha? Haw!"

The door opened on a chain, and a pale, too-thin, young woman peered out at them, her dark frizzy hair forming a nimbus round her sallow face. Upon seeing the sergeant a trembling hand rose to her throat as if she feared throttling.

Gavin held his badge and ID card at eye level. "Traci Mendel," he stated, rather than asked. Before she could answer, he continued, "We need to ask a few questions about your friend, Stephen Lally. May we come in?"

"Um… I don't know… I've got some things…"

"… to do?" Wolfe completed her sentence. "Well, your friend, Stephen, doesn't, Ms. Mendel. Not anymore."

Even within the shadowy doorway, they could see her go a shade whiter. The trembling hand crept toward her mouth. "What do you mean…?"

"Open the door and we'll discuss it," Gavin insisted.

The chain fell away and the big man pushed in, followed by his protégé. Traci was already walking away from them down the dim hallway. Leading them into the living room, she plopped herself into a faded yellow chair, the arms pockmarked with cigarette burns. She waved vaguely at the remaining furniture. Drawing her feet up she pulled a dingy sweatshirt over her bony knees.

"Is he… alright?" she whispered.

"What do you think?" Gavin asked back. He remained standing while Tyler took a seat on a couch that wobbled beneath his slight weight.

"I don't know what you're getting at," she replied. "What's this all about? Am I under suspicion for something?"

"Ms. Mendel," Tyler interjected, his large eyes pools of compassion behind his thick lenses, "we're under the impression that Stephen may have carpooled with you to school last evening. So you may have been one of the last people to see him alive. Naturally, we'll be questioning all his friends."

Gavin favored him with a scowl.

"What do you mean… the last to…" she began; then Tyler's words sank in. "… Oh my God… Stephen!" The remainder of the blood in her face drained away.

"Was Stephen sick when you brought him home?" Tyler continued.

She hesitated before answering, then replied, "Who said that he was with me?"

"Wasn't he?" Tyler persisted. "Didn't you and Stephen have some night classes scheduled yesterday—his mom seemed to think so."

"I… I was sick yesterday," Traci sputtered. "I've got hepatitis C. Sometimes I have to stay home and rest."

"Dirty needles, was it?" The sergeant inquired cheerfully, then asked, "Did you and Stephen do any drugs last night, Traci?"

"How dare you," she hissed, rising several inches in her chair, giving the appearance of levitation.

"Sweetheart," he replied, "I've popped you for dope before, so let's not put on airs, shall we?"

"I think you two should get out of my house right now!"

Tyler rose to comply, while his boss remained standing, feet firmly planted apart. He appeared to study the young woman. "It won't be hard to find out if you're telling the truth, Traci, but if we find that you're lying, or keeping something back about your friend's death, you'll be charged with obstructing an investigation… at the very least. Think it over." He turned and strode for the door, Tyler on his heels.

"You can't threaten me!" she screamed, leaping from her chair.

Opening the door, Gavin ushered his detective through and turned, announcing, "And *you* can't withhold information about a homicide investigation… unless, of course, you need to take the fifth to protect yourself."

"Homicide…?" Traci repeated, anger draining from her voice and posture.

"Yeah," Gavin confirmed, "as in manslaughter… possibly murder. Who knows?—deep waters for poor swimmers, little girl. I'll be visiting the rest of your entourage, and only one lucky person will be granted a deal." He grinned. "Which one will it be?"

Closing the door slowly, he added, "I bet you're already trying to figure that out, ain't 'cha? First come, first served! Have a nice day."

As the detectives walked to the unmarked, Gavin asked, "You notice that flat screen down the hallway?"

Tyler shook his head.

"Jesus," the big man exhaled. "It was the size of some cars these days." He gave Tyler a disapproving glance. "It was also unmounted and didn't have any packing material around it. It's what we detectives like to call, 'suspicious.'"

"She never asked what happened to Stephen—how he died," Tyler countered.

Raising an eyebrow, his boss said, "Well don't start bawlin' about it."

❧

"This kid, Blaise, I don't get—what he's doing with Lally and his roving band of losers," Gavin remarked, heaving his great bulk nearly sideways within the tight confines of the Chevy's passenger seat, "Star athlete at Wessex High, got some scholarship nibbles from Rutgers, Towson, a few others. If he plays his cards right there'll be some four-year school that'll snatch him out of county college before his freshman year is over."

"Some people are just loyal, Boss," Tyler responded. "It's not like these island kids have a lot of choices in friends to begin with, and they tend to stick together. Blaise and Stephen were best of friends from what I've heard."

"Oh, thanks for that pungent observation," his superior huffed. "I can see that you've got a lot to teach me about human nature."

"*Poignant...*" Tyler corrected him; concentrating on his driving, "... I think you meant poignant, Sarge."

"I meant *pungent*, Nancy Drew... as in 'stinks.'"

Tyler remained silent during the rest of the short drive.

"She'll have called ahead," Gavin warned his partner as they strode up to Blaise's address. A ripple ran through a curtain on the second floor.

Mrs. Aubrey opened the door before they could knock. She looked as if she had been crying. "I just can't believe it," she greeted their badges, "little Stephen Lally dead! I can't tell you how many times we've had him over for dinner when his parents were going through their bad times. He was like Blaise's brother—they were that close! I think he spent as many nights here as he did in his own bed."

"How is your son dealing with it, Mrs. Aubrey?" Tyler inquired.

"He... we... just got the news! He's devastated, as you can imagine."

"Yes, ma'am, I would think so, especially after he had just dropped Stephen off from school last night."

"Yes," she replied. "My God, you just never know, do you?"

Gavin broke in, "We need to speak with him, ma'am, if you could just show us the way."

"Oh no," Mrs. Aubrey cried, "Blaise is far too upset to be disturbed right now."

"I see," the detective sergeant replied. "Well, ma'am, Stephen's far too *dead* to help us, and the delightful Ms. Mendel was less than forthcoming, shall we say, so we'll have to insist on a moment or two with your son, if you don't mind."

"Oh," she managed, "oh… well, I…"

"Let 'em up, Ma," a voice spoke hoarsely from the top of the stairs behind her.

Mrs. Aubrey stepped aside, saying, "Well… if you're sure you're up for it, honey."

The two policemen mounted the stairs, then followed the tall, broad-shouldered Blaise as he led them into his cluttered room. He wore his wavy blond hair long and was attempting to grow a goatee.

Sweeping a football off one chair and a stack of Sports Illustrated from another, he offered the two investigators seats, while plopping himself on the edge of his rumpled bed. At a glance they could see that he had been crying; his eyes still puffy and red.

Tyler jumped in first, "Blaise," he asked, "was Stephen sick yesterday when you were together?"

"I didn't see him yesterday," Blaise answered after a long beat.

Tyler was shocked at the obvious lie, "But your mom just confirmed that you dropped him off at his house yesterday evening!"

There was a sudden buzzing noise in the room, and Blaise glanced at his cell phone on the nightstand but refrained from answering it.

"Naw… umm… Ma was mixed up. She just thought that. I didn't go to classes yesterday after all."

Tyler noted a light sheen of perspiration on Blaise's forehead.

His boss rose with a grunt, taking a few steps to look down at the unanswered phone. "Wanna get that?" he asked with a pale smile, shoving it toward Blaise with his fingertips.

"It's okay… it can wait," Blaise sputtered.

"Oh, look who it is…" the older detective cried, "… Traci… *again*… she must have forgot to tell you something important… go ahead and take it." He nudged the phone closer yet. "We can wait."

"That's okay," Blaise whispered in a husky voice.

"So what did you do instead?" Tyler asked him.

"Well…" His broad face screwed up in concentration, "… I went for a run."

"Where?"

"The county park in Wessex Township… you know, near the zoo."

The buzzing stopped at last.

"In the dark…?" the Detective Sergeant took over with a smile; still hovering over the phone.

"Yeah… there are some street lamps."

"*Are* there… really?"

Glancing up, Blaise answered in a faint voice, "Yeah… a few. I know the way, anyhow."

"In the rain you run…?" Gavin persisted.

"I don't mind it."

"… anybody with you?"

Blaise shook his head after a moment, "No… nobody… I was alone."

"Alone…" Gavin repeated, his big, rubbery face mournful, "… that's sad; makes me a little weepy to hear it."

Blaise cut his bloodshot eyes to the senior officer then quickly away again. "I just felt like being alone," he said. "There's no law against it."

"Hey, what are the scouts telling ya?" the big man asked out of the blue. "Hear you've got a few nibbles on the line, might mean big things ahead!"

"Yeah," Blaise agreed, relieved at the change of subjects, "there's been a few talked to me. They want me to get my GPA up at Wessex Community. So far, so good with that—I'm hoping to hear something by summer."

"They're talking full scholarships, are they?"

"Yeah," Blaise confirmed. "That'd be great, too; money's a little tight around here since Dad's real estate company went bust and he took off."

"Detective Errickson," Gavin barked at his subordinate, startling both young men. "Stop mooning there and let's go— places to see, Blaise, people to do!"

"Sarge…" Tyler began.

"We need to run by the school, Junior, and find out who the hell *did* attend night classes yesterday." He swiveled his great bulk gracefully back to Blaise, seizing his hand in his big paw, pumping it, "It was a real pleasure, Blaise. I look forward to watching a few of your games on TV this fall! I was a big fan of yours when you played at Wessex High."

He leaned in confidentially, then stage-whispered, "You might want to call the lovely Traci back, my young friend, and let her know that you kept your end up, she'll be worried. And while you're chatting, ask about that offer I made her—first come, first served, good through Friday only at a participating P.D. near you." He released his hand and Blaise fell back from the ogre-like policeman. "I bet she didn't mention it when she called to prep you on our visit, did she?" He waggled his spiky, red brows.

"Offer…?" Blaise repeated, "… for what?"

"Oh, now that's a matter between old friends, I think. Come, Boy Wonder," Gavin cried, stalking out of the room.

Tyler locked eyes with the college athlete for a moment before following.

დ

"He was genuinely upset, Boss, I think if we'd kept at him a little longer he'd of…"

"Coughed up the whole ball of fur…?" Gavin finished for his younger counterpart as they climbed into the car. "Not likely, Junior. He needs orders from on high."

"You mean Traci?"

"Maybe…" Gavin agreed. Then, as if coughing up his own fur ball, proceeded to make throaty sounds until he could launch the wet results out the driver's window.

"Jesus, that's disgusting!" Tyler complained.

"… But maybe not," his mentor continued, gunning the car into the street. "Remember these birds came under our scrutiny for those unsolved burglaries, right?"

Tyler nodded.

"Well let's not forget Chris McAfee—local tough guy and proud graduate of Southern State Correctional. If these kids are involved with those break-ins, then C-Mac's fencing the goods if not running the show." Gavin reached across the seat and punched Tyler in the bicep. "You're the one that posted the intel report on seeing his car parked next to Traci's house this winter. Maybe that's who's muzzling the crew here—maybe *he* put the kibosh on our victim."

Tyler knew of McAfee, or C-Mac, as he was commonly referred to, but he had never had any direct dealings with him. Somewhat legendary on Camelot Beach Island as a brawler and all-around thug, he stood only five foot, six inches tall, most of it muscle. As if in compensation for his premature balding, he wore his dark, curly hair long at the neck, as well as a full, and unkempt, beard. More than once, Tyler had seen him stop on the street and stare challengingly at his patrol car as it swept by, giving him the one-fingered salute. With his dark, sunburnt complexion, and taste for gaudy necklaces worn with open-necked shirts, he looked more like a beached pirate than a modern criminal.

After a quick stop at Wessex Community College, they eased up to the curb a house down from McAfee's current address.

Gavin turned in his seat, "Not a one of 'em went to class like they was supposed to—and them paying for the privilege!" he observed, shaking his cannonball head in wonderment.

"Well, Sarge," Tyler shrugged, "what's that leave us, besides the fact that they were all up to no good *somewhere*, doing *something*, which we kinda knew to begin with?"

Gavin's face went slack, "You know what you are, Junior? You're a pessimist; a little Debbie Downer—always mopin' around. That's why you never get invited anywhere—have you ever thought about that?" He wagged a finger in admonishment, "You got a reputation, old son." Throwing open the car door, he climbed out.

"I *do* get invited places," Tyler snapped back, knowing it was a lie, but stung. He was well aware that he wasn't popular in the department, had never quite fit in and was regarded as prematurely stodgy and overly cautious. Exiting the vehicle in a fluster, he shouted in defiance of all this, "I get invited *lots* of places, but how the hell would you know, since they aren't the kind of dives you pass out in!" He felt something rising up within him. "You may be my boss, but that doesn't give you the right to judge me, or make comments about my private life, or to call me *Nancy friggin' Drew!*" He just managed to refrain from stomping his foot on the sidewalk.

An approaching couple decided to cross the street before the intersection.

Gavin hitched up his sagging trousers to tower over his trainee. "Goodness, little man, I struck a sore spot, didn't I?" He stuck his big mug close to Tyler's lean, flushed face, adding, "Okay, here's what we do—I'm gonna hang back on McAfee and let you do the talking. He and I have a little history that doesn't bear repeating, so I'm letting you take the lead on this one. Ready?" Without waiting for an answer, he turned and began striding down the walk to the next house.

"What...?" Tyler said to the space his boss formerly occupied.

As he caught up to him, Gavin hooked a thumb at a wooden garage nestled at the end of a weedy drive. "He lives up there," he said, indicating an apartment with peeling white paint perched atop the slightly leaning structure. "Go ahead."

Looking back at his boss with suspicion, Tyler proceeded to approach the residence. A voice behind him, said, "Don't be afraid now... I'll be right behind you."

Tyler felt his face flush with anger again, but before he could think of anything to say he was at the rickety stairs that led up to the door. Throwing a poisonous glance back at his boss, he climbed up and gave the door a couple raps. When there was no answer, he drew back and pounded it a few times.

"What...!" A shirtless Chris McAfee shouted in his face, having suddenly thrown the door wide.

Tyler reared back, managing to flip open his badge and ID carrier. C-Mac glanced at it with contempt for a moment before returning his bleary gaze to Tyler's face. "So...?" he asked.

Until this moment, Tyler had thought McAfee to be in his thirties, but close-up he realized he was off by a number of years—and they had been hard years. "We need to talk to you, Mr. McAfee. May we come in?"

"Who's *we*, Junior G-Man? You got a mouse in your pocket, or somethin'?"

Tyler suddenly realized that Gavin had not followed him up; was nowhere to be seen. C-Mac began to close the door. "Get a warrant if you wanna spend time with me, sweetheart," he advised.

Jamming his shoe between the door and the frame, Tyler was suddenly very, *very*, pissed, "Don't close that door on me, you low-life scumbag! You're on parole, and I'm a police officer… *sweetheart!*" And with that, he gave the door a good, hard shove, dislodging the surprised thug and throwing the door wide again.

C-Mac stumbled back over a low, flimsy coffee table loaded with empty beer bottles, sending several of them spinning and clattering to the floor.

Tyler stalked in, his anger only growing, "And another thing, you mini-golf pirate-lookin' SOB, when a marked unit cruises past, you show some goddamn respect from now on. The next time you give a patrol car the finger, you better start running…"

"You can't roust me," C-Mac shouted back, struggling to regain his feet, balling his fists. "I'll kick your ass you mother…"

"Detective…!" A large shadow fell across them both and a familiar voice demanded in unfamiliar outrage, "What's going on here?"

Tyler froze in the act of advancing upon his suspect. He saw C-Mac's narrow eyes widen at the sight, and size, of the newcomer filling the doorway.

"No, you don't," Gavin warned Tyler as he lumbered into the small room, "Not again you don't! Stand down, detective!" Tyler felt the greasy-looking floorboards bow beneath their new burden.

Suddenly his boss was there helping C-Mac to his feet, murmuring apologies for his trainee's *enthusiasm*. "He's only been with the bureau a few weeks, Mr. McAfee; he's just trying to make an impression. He's young, you know." He grinned over C-Mac's head at Tyler with his big teeth.

"Rookie's gonna get his ass kicked, he tries that stuff with me!" C-Mac promised, while allowing himself to be seated on a nubby, brown sofa littered with popcorn.

"Mind if I sit down?" Gavin asked with real concern, still resting a big, protective paw on C-Mac's bare shoulder. Tyler felt as if he had entered another dimension.

C-Mac nodded, still glaring at the young officer, "Let's get this over with," he agreed. "But I don't talk to him!" He stabbed a thick, heavily ringed finger in Tyler's direction.

"No... of course not," Gavin promised, squeezing his wide buttocks into the confines of a chair that matched the couch, popcorn and all. "Detective Errickson," he addressed his subordinate, "maybe it would be better if you wait by the door until you cool down."

Tyler stalked to the open door and leaned against the frame, watching the two of them from the corner of his hot eyes. In spite of knowing that he had been played, he was helpless to stop acting his role. Realizing that his lower lip was jutting out, he stood up straight and willed his face to relax.

"It's been a while, Chris... mind if I call you Chris?" he heard his boss asking C-Mac.

"No, man, it's cool... we've got some history, you and me, so it's cool. I respect *you*."

"Thanks, Chris... and please call me Gavin. I think enough water's passed under the bridge that we can offer each other that much, huh?"

C-Mac lit a bent cigarette from a crumpled package of Marlboro menthols, coughed once, and then laughed, "That was quite a dust-up we had back in the day, bro!"

Tyler heard his boss chuckle in agreement, "Yeah, I got thirty days suspension for that arrest."

"And I got six months in county," the smaller man responded. "That was a good fight, though."

"Chris," Gavin went suddenly serious, "I need your help here. You've heard about young Stephen Lally's death, yeah?"

C-Mac nodded just a little.

"And you know some friends of his, right?"

This time he shook his head and shrugged, "Umm... I don't think so. That's a young crowd, man."

"So you *do* know 'em..." the detective sergeant grinned "... Traci Mendel... Blaise Aubrey?"

"I mean I've seen 'em around, of course..."

Tyler saw the dark, troll-like, little man straighten up from his slouch. "Hell, Camelot Beach ain't that big a place, man—everybody knows everybody."

"Exactly," Gavin agreed, "and you've been seen with them, Chris. You're banging the girl, right?"

"Wait a minute..." he protested, raising his broad, grimy hands.

"Are they boosting for you, Chris? Or are they just bringing the swag here for you to move? Trust me on this, my friend, the important thing is that we find out what happened to that boy—he had a very ugly death. I'm just including you in on my one-time offer for old time's sake. The expiration date is ticking down—both the girl and the jock are already thinking it over.

"What d'ya say, Chris... C-Mac... my man? You've got the most to lose—wanna grab that ring before it's too late? You've got to know that you make the best suspect—you're an ex-con, after all. Maybe you didn't mean for him to get hurt. But if that's the case, you'd better start explaining now before someone else beats you to it."

Even from across the room, Tyler could see the stress lines etching themselves into the already seamed face, Chris's dark eyes sliding left to right, right to left. Then, suddenly... he smiled. "Oh goddamn..." he waggled a finger at Gavin, blowing out a deep breath in relief, "… oh, goddamn… you had me goin' there for a tick, Boss. Listen," he spread his arms, "you wanna search this place, be my guest; I've got nothing illegal on the premises— no swag—no drugs." He glanced over at Tyler standing by the door. "Have your little Rottweiler do the honors. I know he'd just love to rip this place apart."

Leaning forward, his smile gone sharkish, he spoke directly to Gavin, "If you really had anything, I'd already be in cuffs, fat boy. But you're just fishing here, aren't you? And those kids haven't said anything, because there's nothin' to say. I'm not goin' back inside, Five-O; I'm gettin' way too old for that shit—nobody's tellin' *you* jack!"

Tyler watched his boss extricate himself from the chair, some popcorn adhering to the seat of his shiny trousers. Leaning over, he smiled down at the seated con, "You'd best hope so, shorty. But think it over quickly; it's only good until I hear from *one* of you." He took a breath, the smile vanishing, "But I've got to be honest, Chris… I sure hope it *ain't* you that squeals, 'cause I'm gonna love seeing you back at Southern State; especially when those corrections officers start telling your fellow yardbirds how you killed that kid because he was *cheating* on you. You're gonna be very popular in the shower room, Chrissie… *very* popular, Dawg!"

Laughing, Gavin turned his back on C-Mac's glare, and stomped away.

Following his boss down the shaky stairs, Tyler hissed, "You set me up in there!"

Tossing him the car keys, Gavin replied, "Felt good, didn't it… getting those juices flowing? Besides, I was tired of playing the bad cop."

Climbing into the unmarked, Tyler went on, "I could file a grievance, you know! This is not right—supervisors cannot treat their officers like this!" He sped off from the curb.

"Oh, I'd hate to see that," the big man remarked, "a promising, young career like yours...."

"What the hell does that mean?" Tyler asked, suspicious and uneasy again.

"Well," Gavin explained, "there'd have to be a hearing, you know, all the circumstances illuminated—that temper of yours, and you knocking down a suspect, and I don't even like to think what you were about to do when I caught up to ya. That scared me a little."

Tyler's mouth opened... closed... then opened again. Before he could frame a suitable response, his boss went on, "I screwed up in there. I shouldn't have made McAfee the offer. He's been around the block too many times and figured my hand right off. I should've just mentioned the kids and left the rest to his imagination."

Tyler's mouth remained open—Detective Sergeant Gavin Wolfe had just admitted a mistake. "Yeah," he agreed, after a long beat. "Now what?"

"It's Good Friday, stud. Let's call it a day, go home, and get some shuteye. We'll figure it out tomorrow."

❧

"God... I'm so exhausted," Tyler moaned, unconsciously mimicking his performance of the day before. "I'd just gotten to sleep when dispatch called." His third cup of coffee, half drunk, was cooling at his elbow as his head rested on folded arms atop his desk.

"You gonna finish this?" Gavin asked while helping himself to Tyler's coffee with a loud slurp.

Glancing up, Tyler started to protest, then sighed. "Knock yourself out."

His boss proceeded to doctor the beverage with several packets of sugar from his pencil drawer. "Needs sweetening," he murmured, then, "It's *them* again, you know," referring to the latest burglaries discovered the previous evening. Beyond the shuttered blinds the brilliant light of morning warmed the returning spring visitors, the sidewalks busy and humming for Easter weekend.

The younger detective raised his head. "Yep," he agreed, "it's them—same M.O., same neighborhood. They like that area 'cause of the older homes—a lot of them still don't have security systems even after that last wave of burglaries. A couple of the places had even been hit before, and *man*, were those homeowners pissed. They blame us, of course, not the burglars… or themselves."

"So that places this latest rash between St. Paddy's weekend and now," Gavin rumbled. "And considering what's happened with our suspects, I'm thinking it was before Stephen Lally's untimely demise. What say you, Boy Wonder?"

Tyler nodded, coming alive a little at actually being asked his opinion. "Yeah," he agreed. "That's how I read it. Though it's possible some of these were committed even earlier, only the owners just hadn't been down to find them."

"I bet our little crew was scheduled for night classes when these were done," Gavin mused. "Burglary 101, no doubt."

"No doubt," Tyler repeated, "but even if we found security video at the college showing them leaving during classes, we still don't have definite dates on the break-ins to tie them to—they only hit unoccupied summer homes."

The big man belched. "That pork roll I had for breakfast might'a been off," he warned with a pained expression, then went on, "True enough, Junior. On a positive note, I bagged a cigarette butt from the deck of one place where the owner says nobody in the family smokes."

"Marlboro menthol…?"

Gavin's eyebrows went up, "And here I thought you was pouting the whole time at C-Mac's. No such luck, amigo—it was non-menthol. You find anything?"

"Patrol found a couch pillow the burglars had taken from one house to muffle the window they broke to get into another. I let a Sheriff's K-9 take a sniff and he followed it right to where they had entered. Then, I had them take the dog around the perimeter and he seemed to pick up the scent again and followed it to a house across the street.

"Only the owner there said he hadn't been broken into. I remembered him from the last batch; he had been furious then, a real dick! But he was nice enough this time, a little smug maybe—said he had gotten hooked up to a security system."

"I'm happy for him," Gavin remarked. "So what happened?"

Tyler shrugged, "Nothing really, Boss. The hound picked up the scent again on the sidewalk, followed it a half block, and stopped."

"They got into a car."

"That's what the K-9 officer thought too."

"Send both our items to the state lab and let's see what happens."

The phone rang and Tyler picked it up.

After a few moments of silence, he placed a hand over the mouthpiece and said, "Dispatch just got a call from Traci Mendel's aunt—her car's at home, the house is unlocked, and her cell phone's still there. There appears to have been a struggle."

His boss's reply was succinct and obscene.

☙

"I've been calling since yesterday evening…" the aunt wailed, as Tyler's boss loomed over her, "… house phone, cell phone—but nothin'!" The aunt was five-two and weighed in at two hundred pounds. Her bleached hair was cut short and spiky, with a tattoo of what appeared to be a lantern fish festooning a flabby bicep. She was sweating bullets as she stood in the middle of the wrecked room. "We always get together for breakfast on Saturdays! I got worried and come over to find this!"

"You didn't touch anything, right?" Gavin rumbled.

She glared up at him, "Of course not… I know a crime scene when I see one."

Sergeant Wolfe patted her doughy shoulder with a big paw. "I bet you do," he murmured. "Detective Errickson, take your thumb out and canvass the place for anything that might be useful, and check her cell for recent callers—be careful of prints."

"We've got to get a warrant for the phone, sarge," Tyler warned. "There's that ruling, remember?"

Ushering the aunt out the door, Gavin responded over his shoulder, "Screw that ruling, and the horse it rode in on! This is an emergency situation, Junior, and I'm declaring martial law." Shutting the door behind the aunt, the big man spun and crossed the room to meet Tyler. "Get some DNA samples, too, while you're at it—just in case. Check her hairbrush, coffee cups, dirty panties… you know the drill."

Tyler hurried down the hall toward the bedroom.

"And get the serial number off that flat screen in there and check it against any that have been reported stolen! And get the lead out, will ya!"

Tyler heard the front door slam, shaking the house, then realized he was alone. A moment later he heard a car roar into life and go screeching down the street.

℣

Patrol already had C-Mac in custody by the time Gavin pulled into the station. From his appearance, the detective sergeant could see that he had offered some resistance and was looking the worse for it. The two young patrolmen guarding him appeared unruffled and very satisfied.

"Out," Gavin commanded, squeezing himself into the tight confines of the interview room.

As the two officers slid past, one, sensing his dangerous mood, whispered, "Don't forget the camera, Sarge."

Gavin glanced up at the unblinking lens poised in an upper corner of the room. "Shut the door," he instructed the officer.

McAfee was still shirtless, and sporting some fresh, sore-looking abrasions on his elbows and right cheek. Gavin smiled in satisfaction at the tiny bits of gravel and dirt ground into them, while Chris studied the linoleum, one wrist shackled to a bar set in the wall.

"Let's cut to the chase," Gavin growled. "I want the girl... now. What have you done with her?"

Shaking his shaggy, balding head, C-Mac murmured, "I don't have her, man. I've got nothin' to do with that... I swear it."

"You've got everything to do with it, Dawg! I've got your DNA at one of the burglary scenes; the girl's, too," Gavin lied with gusto. "She was gonna come talk to me and you found out and did something about it. Remember what you said to me, C-Mac, '*I'm not going back inside.*'"

"No, man, that can't be right..." McAfee protested, "... you *can't* have my DNA—I was never *at* those burglaries! You're making that up!"

Leaning in, so that his big, ugly face was within spitting distance, Gavin whispered, "After I snagged a couple of butts from your place, I took care of that, you nasty, little runt." He stood back up with a smile. "How *long* you're going back in for is the only option you have left... *if...* is no longer on your wishlist, sport."

Gavin's prisoner considered his situation for several long moments, then sagged in his chair and said, "I just picked the places and set up the sales with some dudes I know in Philly. Those kids did the jobs. I didn't *want* anything to happen to *anybody!* But when that Stephen kid croaked, Blaise went nuts, dude. They was like brothers and he was really tore up... couldn't understand what had happened. None of us could. Then you guys came snoopin' around with your 'one-time offer' and he got scared... real paranoid, man. He told me he had too much to lose with the scholarships and all, and he was worried about Traci, said she was thinkin' one of us had poisoned Stephen to get his cut—thought she might be next—crazy talk. *He* took her; I had nothin' to do with it!"

"You had everything to do with it, scumbag," Gavin replied as he dialed the phone, paused, then asked, "Mrs. Aubrey is your son at home?" After listening for a few moments, he said, "We'll start looking for him right away, ma'am, don't you worry about that."

Placing the receiver back in the cradle, he turned to McAfee, "Where are they, Chris?"

Pointing at the plastic container the arresting officers had placed his belongings in, C-Mac replied, "A trailer on the mainland, I think. Number twenty-seven. The key's in there; it's tagged Blue Creek Campground. It's where I store the swag until I can move it. They don't open until Memorial Day weekend, so it's nice and quiet."

"You better hope it's not *too* quiet, loser," Gavin growled, dumping the contents of the container onto the countertop and snatching up the key. Before McAfee could respond, the big man was out the door.

☙

"Patrol's running the samples over to the lab right now," Tyler informed his boss as the low, heavy car careened along the blacktop. He checked his seatbelt as they swept the shoulder of the road. Diving out of their way, a bicyclist repairing a flat threw his helmet after them.

"As for the flat screen," Tyler went on, glancing back at the irate cyclist, "it's not in our property inventories and hasn't been reported stolen. Even so, I sent a request to the manufacturer asking them to trace the lot number. Once we know what retailer it was shipped to, and where, we can ask for a record of who purchased it. Maybe they don't know it's been stolen yet." He waited for his boss to be impressed.

Still looking in the rearview mirror, Gavin snorted, "Spandex! Haw! Can you picture me in something like that?"

Tyler winced at the unbidden image.

"On the left," Gavin pointed out as they sped beneath the canopy of overhanging branches. Spraying gravel as he turned into the drive, he pulled to a sudden halt at the gate. "Open," he commanded, tossing Tyler the key.

Moments later they were hurtling through a scattered array of campers and trailers nestled beneath oak, sassafras, and sweet gum trees. Here and there, delicate pink blossoms floated on the graceful fronds of mimosas.

"Shouldn't we sneak up, Sarge? I mean…"

"Sneak up…?" the big man asked incredulously. "Do I look like I can sneak up?" The car accelerated.

"Does that say twenty-seven?" Gavin aimed the car at the worn numbers next to the door of a camper-trailer streaked green with mold and resting on cinder blocks.

"Yeah," Tyler confirmed, feeling his mouth go dry. "… shouldn't we be…?"

"When I knock, you run in the door and effect an arrest," Gavin directed.

"What…?" was all Tyler could think to respond.

Slamming on the brakes at the last minute, the big man slid the car into the trailer at a sedate ten miles per hour. The entire box-like structure tilted, defied gravity for a long moment, and then miraculously fell back onto its supports, askew but upright.

"I knocked!" Gavin shouted at Tyler.

Leaping from the car, Tyler raced up the displaced steps to the now off-set door. Behind him, Gavin heaved himself free of the automobile. "Go, for Christ's sake!" he yelled at his subordinate.

Throwing the door wide, Tyler rushed in with his gun leveled. He had no idea what to expect.

The interior was a shambles—televisions lay toppled onto sound equipment, power tools amidst luxury kitchen conveniences. There was even a rack of expensive shoes now strewn over the limited floor space. In the midst of this, Blaise Aubrey was desperately trying to gain his feet.

"Police… don't move!" Tyler heard himself shouting. "You're under arrest!"

As if coming up from deep water, Blaise stared at him in amazement, then asked, "Was it an earthquake?"

From the welter of stolen property on the floor behind him, something tightly wrapped and taped into a blanket began to squirm and moan.

The trailer shifted once more as Gavin stepped in.

"She's alive, boss," Tyler announced with relief, nodding at the bound girl.

Looking around the chaos with ill-disguised pleasure, Gavin replied with a smile, "Bingo!"

℅

Watching the ambulance lumber down the rutted drive to the gate of the campground, Gavin remarked, "Not a bad day's work, Junior—you have covered yourself with glory—under the guidance of my steady hand, of course."

Still shook up after ramming a free-standing structure containing human occupants, Tyler threw his boss a murderous look. "You could'a got me killed," he complained. "Damnit, Sarge, you could've killed everybody!"

Shaking his bristly head, Gavin sighed, "Always the buzz-kill ain't 'cha?"

A patrol car rolled through the dust plume left by the ambulance, Blaise Aubrey in the backseat. The big policeman pointed and asked, "You believe him about some poisoned booze at one of the break-ins?"

Shrugging, Tyler answered, "It would've helped if he could've remembered which place it was exactly. I don't recall any Scotch bottles being seized as evidence at any of the scenes."

Slapping the younger man hard enough on the shoulder to stagger him, Gavin said, "Me neither. Now let's go drop a murder charge on Mighty Mite to round out our lovely day!"

He had taken three steps before he realized his junior partner had not moved.

"Oh hell," Gavin moaned at Tyler's long face. "What now, *Nan...*" he caught himself. "Damnit... what's the problem?"

"We don't know McAfee killed Stephen. I don't think he did," Tyler declared. He took off his glasses and fiddled with them nervously. "There's no evidence. We can't prove it."

The big man reared back as if encountering a foul odor. "Prove it?" he echoed. "It's simple, ain't it? He's what passes for the mastermind of the outfit, right?"

Tyler nodded just a little.

"Well, he got greedy and wanted to keep Stephen's share, or got wind that the Lally kid was gonna rat them out—hey, maybe the kid was even trying to blackmail him! C-Mac's got a temper on him, if you haven't noticed."

"So he got him to drink some kind of highly caustic fluid, then relied on Blaise to provide a cover story for the murder of his best friend—*really*?" Tyler returned his glasses to his long nose.

"I can't make sense of everything that happens in the world—that's God's problem."

The chief pulled up and rolled to a stop next to them. "Nice work, you two," he remarked.

"Thanks, Chief," they both mumbled.

His eyes came to rest on the off-kilter trailer and the police unit with the smashed grill. "Problem with the brakes?" he asked.

"It's a wonder we're still alive."

"It's a wonder anyone's alive," Chief Hall murmured, then asked, "Any news for Stephen's mom?"

The big man's eyes cut to his junior partner for a moment, then away again. After a pause, he replied, "Nope... not yet, Chief."

Julian nodded his greying head, then put the car into drive. As he pulled away, he asked, "Will that heap get you back?"

"It's all cosmetic," Gavin assured him.

"Happy...?" The sergeant growled at Tyler, as the chief drove away.

Tyler's phone rang. "Detective Errickson," he answered. After a brief conversation, he disconnected and said, "That flat screen was traced to a Lawrence Fortescue."

"Do we know him?"

"Yep," Tyler answered, an odd look on his face. "He's the homeowner that gave us such a ration about his house being hit over the winter, then said he got hooked up to a service and the burglars gave him a pass this time around, even though the K-9 tracked to his house."

Gavin perked up a little, "Well, he'll be happy to get his TV back."

Tyler shook his head, "He didn't report this TV being stolen, boss—it's a completely different model than the one he said was taken—I remember 'cause he was such a dick about it."

"Then how did this set...?" They looked at one another.

"Sonofabitch..." Tyler breathed. "Boss, you don't think...?"

Gavin was already lumbering toward the car as Tyler hurried to catch up.

∽

By the time the detectives were able to obtain a search warrant, the sun was disappearing into the sea. Now, as dusk stole over the island, Julian Hall stood in the darkening yard of Fortescue's vacation home. Within the brilliantly lit residence, figures in paper suits shuffled about their business, reminding him of a similar evening just two days before. Nearby, but hidden, a whippoorwill cried out from time to time.

Suddenly the front door was thrown open, and Detective Sergeant Wolfe and his protégé strode out, marching a handcuffed Lawrence Fortescue toward a marked unit.

Seeing Julian, the sergeant sang out, "Got 'im, Chief!" He pointed at the gaunt, older man. "Don't look like much, does he?" he asked, hustling the suspect over for Julian's inspection. "He's a chemical engineer in Delaware, it turns out. Lied to us about not being burglarized a second time, the little scamp," he gave the arrested man a shake, "and never really got a security system—just a sign he stuck in the yard after he saw his little trap had worked."

"I'm being humiliated by this buffoon," Fortescue hissed at Julian even as he gave Gavin a poisonous glance with muddy, blood-flecked eyes. "I won't be treated like a common criminal! I'll be suing your entire goddamn department," he promised.

"Shut up," Gavin instructed him while grabbing his underling by the shoulder with his free hand and shoving him toward his boss. "The kid put it all together, Chief! He's finally starting to show some promise! Tell 'em, Junior," Gavin demanded, while dragging his elderly prisoner away.

Smiling at the attention, Tyler hooked a thumb at the departing suspect, "He set them up, Chief—Stephen, Traci, and Blaise. After the first break-in he bought the most expensive flat screen on the market, put it where it could easily be seen from the street, then set up a bar full of something he concocted for the job and left the house unlocked. We found the ingredients inside. He didn't care if he killed them all—he's a sick puppy. As it turned out, only Stephen stopped long enough to take a slug of what he thought was Scotch. We found bloodstains hidden beneath a brand new carpet inside. I'm pretty sure it's gonna match Stephen's DNA."

Taking a breath, he concluded, "Traci and Blaise didn't understand what was happening, and panicked. They drove Stephen home and dumped him out. After that, it was every man for himself."

"Thanks, Tyler," Julian said. "You've done good work here today."

Smiling even wider now, Tyler answered, "I'm learning from a pro, Chief."

After the detectives had departed with their prisoner, the evening quiet returned, only the whippoorwill's plaintive cry piercing the distant thunder of the sea. In the cool dusk of late spring, as his town prepared itself for the bright festivities of summer, Julian pondered the dark lessons of Stephen's final night class, then turned toward his car and the task of informing Rachel Lally of the arrest of her son's murderer, knowing full well it would bring her no comfort.

Falling Boy
(1995)

The small, single-engine Cessna thrummed and shuddered as it coursed its way through the autumn night, buffeted occasionally by unseen turbulence. The tired young man in the cockpit was concentrating on the instrument panel, glancing up and out the windscreen only when the monotony became too great and he needed to rest his eyes and ease the tension in his back. He would only allow this for a few moments, aware of the disorientation that would quickly seize any pilot flying in these conditions of poor visibility. With the earth invisible below and no horizon in the distance, spatial delusions, like harpies, hovered at the edge of consciousness. With no earth below and no sky above, were you right-side up, or upside down?

Snatches of grey cloud raced by the windows as if torn from the greater whole and flung away. The young man, staring straight ahead now, felt as if he had entered a tunnel, the stratus clouds fleeing the vortex that he was hurtling into.

Little by little, it occurred to him that the wraith-like moisture was not escaping past him in a horizontal plane, he was heading up into it. Naturally, he began to adjust, bringing the nose of his aircraft down. Yet nothing seemed to change, the cloud cover continued to stream downward past him, therefore he must still be ascending!

Beads of sweat formed on his upper lip. It seemed impossible to stop his climb, so he pressed harder against the wheel. Outside, a whining sound began to reach his ears. A small voice said, "Look down. Look down... now!"

With an effort so great that he felt his neck muscles creak with strain, he forced himself away from the mesmerizing windscreen and checked his instruments. Airspeed... gaining. Horizon indicator... horizon indicator! He was nosing over into a dive! Vertical speed was increasing!

With forced control, he eased the wheel back, correcting the plane's attitude, and inadvertently raising his head as he did so. The whining sound had vanished. The night world still rushed past his cockpit. *I was never climbing to begin with*, he thought with a chill.

Down, boy! he commanded himself. Scan the instruments, damn you. There's nothing out there to see, anyway.

But there was.

Something had flashed, small and white, out to his left, at almost the same altitude. Oh, my God, he pleaded, don't let it be another aircraft. I've got enough on my plate now without playing Dodgem. He would call the nearest airfield and ask if they had it on their radar. He had the right of way here.

It was too late. Out of the corner of his eye, he saw it coming. At right angles to his aircraft, it rushed for him as if in joyous greeting, resolving itself into something coherent. Instinctively, he began to descend, desperate to avoid collision. The instrument panel completely forgotten now, he gaped in horror, white-faced through the tiny window.

Tumbling and falling through the night, it came on. He could see it clearly now, little arms and legs thrashing, a plump body spinning. Sometimes the face would flash into view, the eyes seeking him, only to spin away once more. His amazement was so great that he only dimly registered the phenomenon of an object falling sideways and not down.

With a soft thud, the boy struck the cockpit and stayed, his face pressed against the glass, his sleepy almond-shaped eyes roaming the interior—"Jesus Christ!" the young pilot screamed. He was incapable of any further action or thought.

Meanwhile the boy continued his perusal, seemingly oblivious to his plight. His pudgy, short-fingered hands grabbed at the window as his thick lips curved in a lazy smile, smearing the glass. He appeared fascinated with the instrument panel, gleeful. The pilot couldn't see how he was holding on. He was just there!

At that moment, the boy looked into the pilot's eyes as he cowered in the dark of the cabin, and the boy's heavy, moon-shaped face lit up. Pounding on the cabin door with obvious excitement, he pointed at the young man, his small mouth working in silence. The pilot saw the door handle begin to turn and lunged for it, feeling the calm, heated air of the cabin already rushing out into the turbulent atmosphere. With a gasp, he seized the door and forced it shut again, shouting and cursing now. When he looked up again the boy was gone.

"Help me! Help me!" he cried aloud as his plane continued its erratic and spiraling descent through the clouds, seeking the earth on its own.

☙

Sitting in the grey cubicle that was his office, the psychologist awaited his next patient. The day's paper, its headlines screaming of fresh horrors, lay folded next to his chair. Murders, rapes, and kidnappings heralded each day in a fresh parade. *How many of the perpetrators of these atrocities*, he wondered, *had sat across from him in his tiny office over the years?*

Were they insane at the time of the act, or did they understand the difference between right and wrong? That's all the court wished to know. It had been his distressing experience that the majority had been perfectly lucid when they killed or tortured.

He sighed aloud at the memory of fifteen-year-old murderers, parents who had smothered their infants, and old women who poisoned their decrepit lodgers for their Social Security checks. He no longer found humor in *Arsenic and Old Lace*.

Attempting to clean his thick glasses with an old and not-so-clean handkerchief, he admitted to himself some interest in this new referral nonetheless. Here was something different and unbloodied. Possibly a true psychological puzzle.

He had been requested by a local FAA official to do a workup on the young man waiting in his reception area, with the understanding that the patient would pick up the expenses. The FAA was simply affording the young man the opportunity to clear himself and regain his aviation license, which had been suspended pending investigation.

Brushing some dandruff from his shoulder, the psychologist flipped through the reports that had been made available to him. The papers gave the young pilot's name as Ernest Thorvald, white male, twenty-four years of age, a college graduate, and a pilot for six years. Urinalysis and blood samples taken within hours of his "incident" had shown no traces of narcotics or alcohol use. A full and lengthy physical conducted over several days had showed him to be free of any disease or organic problems that might affect his judgment or performance. That left only the mind, that shrouded and shifting landscape that resisted microscopes and X-rays, yet affected its host far more profoundly than any physical stimuli.

Leaning forward, the psychologist spoke into his desk intercom and then stubbed out his cigarette, fanning the smoke with his small hands as he did so. As a final concession to the patient's comfort, he tilted his overflowing ashtray into the wastebasket next to his desk, spilling several butts onto the floor for his efforts. He looked up to see the young man standing in his doorway.

Thorvald was tall and slender and stood with an athlete's easy grace, in spite of his fidgeting. The little man behind the desk could clearly see that he was troubled. His plain, youthful face was pale, the cheeks hollowed. The eyes were red-rimmed and puffy, a painful suffering evident in their nervous travels. A poster boy for college recruitment in his better days, the psychologist thought with subjective envy. He himself had graduated college at seventeen and been derided for his small stature, dark-complexion, and love of opera. A nerd. Yet now he must help someone who years ago, had they been contemporaries, would probably have made him the butt of cruel dormitory humor.

Pushing his plump body away from his cluttered desk, he stood to his full five-foot, five-inch height and, indicating the chair opposite, said, "My name is Anthony Valerian, Mr. Thorvald, please have a seat."

Thorvald folded himself into the proffered chair and nodded. Valerian said nothing for a few moments, watching the workings of Thorvald's face. "So, Mr. Thorvald, you've had a problem recently," he began without preamble. He often found going straight at a problem the best method, eschewing smarmy platitudes and reassurances. Most patients were too intelligent or neurotic to be lulled by them in any case. He also knew, from long experience, that there was no immediate need for them to like the man who was probing into their thoughts and feelings. Trust and confidence were things that he would have to earn along the way.

Thorvald pulled himself upright in his chair and clasped his hands tightly together. "Yes, I guess so… a problem."

Valerian said nothing. The silence went on into the uncomfortable zone.

"An unauthorized landing," Thorvald resumed. "On a closed airfield," he clarified with just a touch of indignation creeping in. The silence returned.

"Is that bad?" Valerian asked.

Thorvald looked directly at him now.

"Yes, it's bad. I'm looking at permanent revocation of my aviator's license. I think that's pretty damn bad," he finished on a rising note.

"Why is it bad?" Valerian persisted.

"What?" exploded out of Thorvald. "It's my living. I need that license in order to fly airplanes, which happens to be how I make my living!"

"No, no, Mr. Thorvald. You misunderstand me. Why is an unauthorized landing on an abandoned airfield a bad thing? What's the harm?"

"It's dangerous. Not only to the pilot and his crew and passengers—though I was flying alone at the time—but also to other aircraft in the area. You see, you're supposed to stick with a flight plan and observe certain air traffic control rules along the way."

Valerian could see that he was warming to his subject and nodded to encourage him to go on.

"When you enter an air traffic control zone, they give you altitude and air-speed instructions in order to lessen the chance of midair collisions. They watch the big picture on radar and know better than you could what's out there.

"So, when you suddenly go sliding off-screen, with no explanation, they've got to scramble. They've got to get any other aircraft out of the area, because they don't know what you're doing or where you're going.

"As far as landing at a closed airfield, well, anything or anyone could've been on that strip, I could've plowed into an old fuel truck or a carload of kids sittin' out there drinkin' beer. As it turned out, I got lucky. It's an airfield that hasn't been closed long and was in pretty good shape. What's even luckier is that I'd flown that field before, a number of times actually, and remembered the layout. Which was good, because it was darker than hell out there."

"Um, yes, I see. I guess you were lucky, then." Valerian replied. "But what made it necessary to change your flight plan, Mr. Thorvald?"

Thorvald was looking away now, the classic body language of the liar. After a moment, he turned and faced Valerian, looking him in the eyes for the first time.

"I just blacked out, I guess." Thorvald's gaze slid away to his left.

"Have you ever experienced such a thing before?" The psychologist already knew that he hadn't, having read his medical history.

"No, not that I remember."

"Never in school? Or when you were a child?" Valerian continued.

"No, never."

"Perhaps your parents might remember. Your mother. Would you mind if I called her?" It could be very risky bringing up a patient's parents. However, Thorvald was not here for long-term therapy, only an evaluation, and Valerian didn't have much time for niceties.

"No! I mean, yes! I would mind. I'm telling you I've never had a blackout!"

Valerian guessed that he had told his mother the truth. They often did. "Exactly, Mr. Thorvald. You have never experienced blackouts. Blackouts, if they are not organic in nature, and your medical records show no sign of this, are usually brought about as a result of great stress. Now, given that you are an experienced flyer and were piloting an aircraft that, according to your instructor's evaluations, you were comfortable with, and the weather conditions, though challenging, were not overly demanding of someone of your experience, *where* was the stress? The *episode?*—was it prior to the flight or during?"

"Episode?" Thorvald spluttered, leaning forward, then back, then forward again. "I'm not sure what you mean."

"Event, Mr. Thorvald. The event that brought about your blackout." The pilot glanced up. "As you have pointed out, you have no history of blackouts and for the moment that rules out a long-standing psychosis, which leaves us with the present, or at least the very recent past.

"Understand that the details of our conversation will remain confidential. The only issue that the FAA board is concerned with is your fitness to fly again. Something you wish for as well, I think. Naturally, you must be forthcoming, or my report will simply read, 'No conclusions possible.' Whenever you are ready, Mr. Thorvald."

With a deep, slow exhalation, Thorvald began.

◊

When he had finished, dry-mouthed and exhausted, Valerian said nothing for some time.

Outside, in the hallway, two people walked by the closed door of the office in subdued conversation. One of them laughed at some shared joke. Valerian looked up at last and asked,

"Did anything strike you as unusual about the boy?"

Thorvald stared at him for a moment, as if trying to grasp his meaning. "You mean besides the fact that he was clinging to the outside of my plane as I was racing home in a storm?" He laughed. "I thought that was unusual enough, at the time!" His laughter continued and grew in volume.

"What I mean," Valerian went on, "is that you actually gave a very good description of the boy. Forget for a moment the circumstances. What impression did he make on you?"

Thorvald's laughter began to subside little by little as he focused on the memory of the face pressed against the rain-drenched windscreen, the drooling smile, the thick-lidded, oddly shaped eyes.

"I think," he began, "I think he may have been *disabled*...is that the right word?"

"Yes," Valerian murmured." Mr. Thorvald, do you know this boy?

"Know him? How could I know him? He's not real! Even I know that! And if you don't, chief, maybe you and I should switch seats."

Valerian leaned sideways and reached for something on the floor, grunting with the effort. When he came up, he had a wad of newspapers clutched in his hand and began to smooth them out on his desk. Spinning one of the newspapers around, he pushed it in front of Thorvald. His finger rested on a grainy photo of a boy about ten years of age. "Do you recognize this child?" Valerian asked.

In answer; Thorvald slumped forward in his seat, unconscious.

෴

Valerian spoke quietly into the pay phone in the diner, not wishing to be overheard. "I believe that I have a young man who may be of some help in the Edison kidnapping." He waited for a reply from Captain Masterson of the prosecutor's office before continuing. Masterson and he had been thrown together a number of times over the years and had achieved something of a relationship. He knew what Masterson would ask next.

"Anthony, is this young man a patient of yours?"

Valerian understood the implications of the question and had anticipated Masterson's concern. If a trial resulted from information obtained through therapy, the defense would seize on the ethical violation of patient confidentiality and the whole case would be torpedoed. But there was a young boy missing. A boy with a serious handicap. How long would his captors tolerate the demands this put on them? Or had they planned to tolerate them at all? The clock was ticking.

"Yes," he answered. "He is a patient, a referral for evaluation, actually, but he has expressed a willingness to meet with you. Naturally, I do not intend to reveal what was said in our session. I'm not sure it would be of help, in any case."

There was a significant pause. "Then what can he do for us?"

"I'm not sure."

"Anthony." Masterson's impatience was beginning to show. "Is he a suspect?"

"Again, I'm not sure." Valerian answered.

෴

Masterson had agreed to the meeting nonetheless, acknowledging that they had precious little to go on in this case and hadn't the luxury to be choosy. A difficult, sometimes capricious, mentally challenged boy had been kidnapped from a prominent, local couple. The heir apparent to an aviation empire started by his father, dead now for several years.

His mother, a society girl from old and dwindling money, had married new money in the person of Franklin Edison, thirty years her senior. Brilliant, but grasping, bullying, and crude, he had amassed a considerable fortune in his time, saving marriage for his old age. He had sired but one offspring, hopefully christened "Thomas" after the great inventor.

Now, Thomas was gone. Taken, without apparent force from his own bedroom. That in itself was puzzling. Tommy was known to be a handful when angered or frightened. It was hard to picture him going quietly. Of course, they, whoever they were, could have been prepared. Ether, gags, and even suffocation could not be ruled out. Even so, it was hard to accept. The bed was hardly mussed. It was as if he had simply risen in the night and floated out his open window. No telltale ladder had been left behind in this kidnapping. His mother claimed the window had been closed when she had last looked in on him.

Had it not been for the computer-generated note left on the bed, there would have been doubts about an abduction at all. The note itself was useless. It might as well have been beamed down from Mars. It was virtually impossible to narrow down its source to any computer or printer without suspects, and naturally there were no fingerprints.

The note had simply read, "We have taken the boy. You will hear from us." No demands, rules, or threats. Just a conspicuous "us." Masterson wondered about that. Intended to mislead or an inadvertent slip?

That was three days ago and there had been no follow-up as of yet. There had been dozens of letters from various psychos and psychics, all claiming revealed knowledge or involvement, and even a bogus ransom note demanding a cool million in cash. All had been easily run down, including the high school gang that had demanded the money. None had furthered the investigation one iota.

Not that there weren't suspects. Masterson had two. The mother, Catherine, and her second husband, Roger Scrope. Obvious, really, but not a shred of evidence to connect them with the crime. They had opportunity, means, and motive. A powerful motive, in Masterson's experience. Gain.

Only Tommy stood between them and Edison's aviation empire. In a move typical of the irascible Edison, he had left his son his entire estate. His pining young wife became de facto regent for the young heir but stood to gain nothing directly so long as he lived. Masterson had learned through the rumor mill that this was done due to various indiscretions committed by his youthful bride. Especially with his senior executive, Roger Scrope.

Tellingly, the widow was married to the ambitious Scrope just a year later. There was something medieval about the whole arrangement, and now the heir apparent had vanished like Richard the Third's princely nephews, leaving the kingdom up for grabs. Masterson had no doubts that once Tommy was found dead, or was legally declared so, the courts would settle the fortune on the mother and, indirectly, her sinister husband.

Masterson had met and interviewed both of the Scropes and each had provided the other with an alibi. They were asleep in the same bed the night of the abduction. They had heard nothing and seen nothing and slept through the night undisturbed.

More than that, Masterson doubted that Catherine could have participated in such a scheme. In spite of her reserved, brittle manner, it was obvious that she was racked with grief and terror for her son. It had not escaped Masterson that during Tommy's young life, she had never attempted to hide him in spite of the embarrassment his condition must have created among her society friends. She had often been seen in his company at air shows and local events.

There was one troubling point in her vouchsafing of Scrope, however. She admitted that since her remarriage she slept very soundly and often relied on her husband to wake her when Tommy called for her.

Even so, it was difficult to believe that Scrope could lure the volatile Tommy away in the dead of night. It was well attested that Tommy had little liking of his stepfather, often having tantrums and other less pleasant episodes when forced to be in his company. In fact, when the family had to travel, mother and son traveled separately from the husband in order to avoid these displays.

Masterson's next step would be to place the couple on the polygraph, but she dreaded to do so. In the public's eye it would cast them as prime suspects and the press would make the most of it. The result would be a political firestorm that the prosecutor's office was ill-equipped to weather, especially if they came off clean. They were, after all, powerful citizens and there was no evidence that they were anything but grieving victims.

The office phone rang. It was the receptionist announcing that Captain Masterson's appointments were waiting in the interview room. Masterson hung up, straightened her pantyhose, and walked dispiritedly down the corridor to meet them.

ᴄ⁄ᴐ

Thorvald sat up quickly from his slouch when Masterson introduced herself. It had never occurred to him that "Captain" Masterson would be a female. Especially an attractive, if older one. She must be in her late thirties, he figured, judging by the worry lines around her eyes. Her legs, however, were those of a schoolgirl, long and shapely. She must take pride in them, he thought, as the skirt of her rather severe business suit was just a tad shorter than it needed to be.

Valerian had simply nodded in greeting and returned to studying the top of the table at which they were all seated.

"Well, Mr. Thorvald," Masterson opened. "I understand that you have some information about the Edison kidnapping that might be of use to us. Is that so?"

Thorvald looked up at her cool, appraising eyes and began to flush.

"Well, um, you see, I had this… " He glanced at Valerian, who was now engrossed in studying his shoes. "I was flying back from Memphis when… oh hell! I don't know! I saw something. I really don't know what you two expect from me! I was tired. It was raining.

"You tell me!" He pointed at Valerian. "You're the head doctor!"

Masterson's gaze shifted to Valerian. "Anthony? Care to enlighten me a little?"

Valerian roused himself and turned in his chair like a schoolboy facing his teacher. His small hands were clasped together on the tabletop. "It seems Mr. Thorvald had a hallucination that featured the missing boy. What struck me as potentially important about it was that during the experience, and for several days after, he did not recognize the boy as someone he knew. Someone he had been in contact with on many occasions. Memorable occasions, I would think. In fact, a very memorable boy.

"It came out during our session that Mr. Thorvald was employed by the boy's family as a pilot and often flew the mother and child on their trips and escorted them about once they arrived. He is one of the few adult males that the boy appeared to take a genuine liking to. His being a pilot no doubt helped in this, the boy being enamored of planes and flying in general."

Valerian paused, letting the facts sink in. "The night Mr. Thorvald was flying and experienced this 'episode' was the same night the Edison boy was abducted."

Masterson blinked. "Yes, I see... I think. You're insinuating that Mr. Thorvald had some inside knowledge of the abduction plans?"

"Wait a minute! I don't know—" Thorvald started, the color draining from his face.

"No," Valerian interrupted. "I don't mean that, exactly. I believe that Mr. Thorvald, subconsciously, perhaps, may possess some insight into the situation that could be useful to your inquiries."

Masterson stared at him for a while as silence settled on the room. She was unsure of the little

man's reasoning, yet based on their past associations, wanted to trust him. To what end, she didn't know. If Valerian thought Thorvald was involved, then he was treading thin ice professionally, but she could have that checked out easily enough. Thorvald was in the air the night it happened and would be remembered by airport personnel. His unauthorized landing had made a minor stir, which only served to clinch his alibi.

But what about the "hallucination"? Was Valerian hinting at a guilty conscience? She could have her office confirm Thorvald's movements, but what was she to do with him in the meantime? Being an investigator, she hated vagueness.

"Anthony, I'm at a loss here. What exactly is it that you want me to do?"

"I'd like to suggest that we visit Mr. and Mrs. Scrope at their home." He paused a beat. "All of us."

Masterson glanced over to Thorvald, who looked like he wished he was anywhere but there. "Would that be agreeable to you, Mr. Thorvald?" she asked.

"Yeah, I guess," he answered. "Though I still don't see what you people want from me."

"No," she concurred. "I'm not too sure myself." She glanced at Valerian. "However, I don't see what harm could come of a little visit."

She rose from her chair. "Shall we?"

∞

The Edison estate was a rambling, mock-medieval affair built of grey stone and occupying sprawling, well-tended grounds. Though charming at a distance, at close quarters it presented a rather somber façade, inadvertently achieving an effect shared with its genuine counterparts in Europe. The steep, slated roof gave it a brooding, secretive countenance that Masterson felt matched its new occupant, the usurper Scrope, very well. As she brought the car to a crunching halt in the smoothly raked drive, she thought, at least this will be interesting.

They were greeted at the door by Yolanda, a pretty German au pair whom Masterson had previously met. Too pretty, Masterson thought. Either Catherine is very confident or Scrope is used to getting his way. As a woman, she didn't like the looks of it.

"Gut afternoon, Captain." Yolanda smiled through her thick accent. "Haben ze an appointment?"

"Nein, fräulein," Masterson replied. She knew the girl could speak English perfectly when she wanted to. "Haben ze badge. Now run and fetch your master and mistress. It's a little cool to be kept waiting on the stoop."

Yolanda hesitated, annoyance beginning to cloud her smooth face, then thought better of it and ushered them in. Without another word, or taking their coats, she turned on her heel and walked briskly down the hallway, her tight skirt clearly delineating the movements beneath. Masterson turned to the two men with her and noted, with some annoyance, that both had come to attention in the presence of the lovely Yolanda and were entranced by her sinuous exit.

"Anthony," she snapped. "You might want to take a handkerchief to that drool on your chin."

He had actually begun to dig in his rear pocket before he caught himself.

"Men are so easy," she murmured.

Scrope startled them all, striding into the foyer and hailing Masterson. "Bridgid!" he called out. He had made a point of finding out her first name shortly after their initial meeting. "Come in, come in." Waving them into his office/study, he breathed good whiskey on her as he forced her to squeeze past him in the doorway. He stepped aside for the men.

"Ernest," he greeted the young man. "What brings you here? She hasn't got you under arrest, has she?" Masterson thought he sounded almost hopeful.

"No sir," he began. "They seem to think—"

Masterson cut him off. "We think, since Mr. Thorvald knew, um, knows Tommy so well and spent so much time with him, that maybe he can help us. Point out something we might have missed."

"And who's this?" Scrope asked, nodding at Valerian.

"This is Mr. Anthony Valerian, a professional colleague of mine. I asked him to assist me."

As they took seats in the overstuffed armchairs of the study, Masterson asked after Mrs. Scrope. Roger was still eyeing the other two men.

"Eh? Mrs.... Catherine? Much as you'd think. She's taking it damn hard. Lying down now, I expect. The doctor's got her on some pretty strong sedatives. Her only child, you know," he added by way of explanation to the men present. As if it would be any different if she had a dozen, thought Masterson. This reptile doesn't have an ounce of feeling for the missing boy or his suffering mother. She also noted that he had yet to ask of the progress of the investigation. Most victims didn't let you get through the doorway before they asked.

Scope returned his attention to her. "You don't need to question her anymore, do you?"

"I would like to talk to her, yes."

"Listen, Bridgid, we've done all we can to cooperate, now what I'd like to see—"

He didn't get to finish as his wife stumbled into the room. "Any news, Ms. Masterson? Have you found him?"

Masterson was shocked. Just three days before Mrs. Scope had still worn the facade of class and wealth. Not so now. The deterioration was marked. Her hair was askew, and her face, naked of makeup, was ashen and dry. Her eyes were sunken and dark, whites showing all round. She leaned against an end table for support, wobbling, as she clutched a damp handkerchief to her bosom.

Seeming to comprehend the effect she had created, she made a visible effort to compose herself. Masterson caught Scope looking at his wife with obvious distaste. The woman's eyes sought Masterson's and held. "My baby?" she pleaded.

Masterson was on her feet and guiding the wretched woman to a chair. "No news yet, Mrs. Scope. We've just stopped by to follow up on a few things. I know it's a bad time, but really, time is our enemy in situations like these. You understand, don't you?"

"Yes," she whispered, her voice hoarse and faint. "I do."

"Mrs. Scrope, you remember Ernest Thorvald of course." Masterson nodded in the direction of the uneasy young pilot.

The other woman turned in his direction, puzzlement, then delight rippling across her features. "Ernest!" she cried. "I'm so glad you've come! Tommy was always so glad to see you! It's so thoughtful of you to come by."

Thorvald was squirming in his seat with discomfort, his sense of participating in a subterfuge causing a blush to climb his cheeks. He managed to stammer, "The captain, that is Ms. Masterson, thought I should... well, since I know Tommy, that maybe I could help... or something."

Tommy's mother took no notice of Thorvald's discomfort. "Yes! Yes, of course! That's very clever of the captain. You know Tommy as well as anyone. He admired you so much!" Rising from her chair, her eyes bright with excitement, she went on, " You talked about boy things with him, didn't you? When I was dozing on our trips? I'm sure I heard you, though I tried not to eavesdrop."

Everyone present was frozen with embarrassment, knowing that such a conversation with Tommy was unlikely.

"Catherine, you'd best go lie down," Scrope barked. "I'll send Yolanda 'round."

She plowed on. "Tommy would confide in you, wouldn't he? About boy things. About hiding places and such?" Tears of hope had begun to slide down her drawn cheeks. She turned toward the doorway, as if to begin the search that moment, her movements now charged with energy. Yolanda had appeared, blocking her path, looking composed and capable, her former perkiness gone as if it had never existed.

Leaping up, Scrope shouted, "That's enough!" He spun on Masterson. "You happy now? You people clear out of here! Thorvald, you come see me first thing in the morning at the office."

"Roger, no!" Catherine wailed. "They've come to help, don't you see? They've brought Ernest along! He'll know where Tommy's hiding! He'll find him."

"Like hell he will," Scrope growled. "He can't find the goddamn airport for Christ's sake!"

Thorvald sprang to his feet, fists clenched. "You son of a bitch."

Stepping between them, Masterson placed one hand on Thorvald's chest.

"Take it easy. That's enough now," she murmured, looking into Thorvald's eyes. It took a moment for the pressure against her palm to relax. "Come on, maybe we'd better get out of here."

"Perhaps first, we could take a look at his bedroom?" It was Valerian, who had remained silent throughout, and was even now seated, hands folded in his lap, looking small and myopic. He had directed his question to Mrs. Scrope.

"Oh yes!" she breathed. "Please, let's look!"

Scrope fixed his gaze on Valerian for the first time, his face reflecting his contempt. "And who the hell are you?"

"Mr. Scrope," Masterson interceded, "maybe it wouldn't hurt for us to have another look in the boy's room. After all, Thorvald just might notice something we've missed. He did spend quite a bit of time with the boy.

"And I think it would calm your wife to see us making some kind of effort, don't you think?" she added with her back to the woman.

He looked as if he thought nothing of the kind, and was about to say so, but his wife had seized Valerian by the hand and was escorting him toward the hall. The unhappy Thorvald trailed behind like a forgotten chaperone.

"Well I'll be damned," he muttered. "It seems it doesn't matter what I think. You run along with your little friends now,

Bridgid, and have your look. But I just hope it's been worth it to you 'cause I am going to have your job over this. You've gotten nowhere with this investigation and now you're grasping at straws."

"I don't think you'd want it," she replied. "The job. You have to deal with too many people like yourself. It can be very unpleasant and not a little depressing." With that she smiled, turned on her heel, and went to join the others, wondering how she was going to explain her actions to the prosecutor. She prayed Valerian knew what he was doing.

She found the room much as she remembered it, large and oblong, with leaded pane windows overlooking an ill-kempt garden. Only now the bed was made and the windows closed. She noted a trace of fingerprint powder on the sill and thought how difficult the damn stuff was to get rid of.

Every conceivable surface was cluttered with the objects of Tommy's great, if limited, passion—airplanes. Toy planes clustered on every shelf and nightstand. Paintings and photographs lined the walls. Picture books of aircraft spilled from his bookshelves and desk. Even his quilt was stitched with them and the curtains framing his windows were an airplane print. Finally, in a crowning achievement, dozens of scale models dangled by invisible wires, festooning the very air in Tommy's room.

Tommy had made no distinction between the civil and the military but suspended them all in the crowded skies above his bed. Everything from the Wright Brothers' first effort to the space shuttle was represented. To complete the effect, the ceiling was painted a sky blue and laced with puffy white clouds.

At the far end of the room, Catherine Scrope was chatting to Valerian, her plumpish and distracted escort, pointing out each model as evidence of Tommy's incipient, if undiscovered, intelligence. Masterson smiled as Valerian nodded. Catherine could not have been more delighted at his responses. For the moment, she was happy again, playing hostess to this odd assortment of visitors, Tommy's room a source of joy and pride, the terrors of its vacancy held at bay.

Thorvald had been forgotten and was left standing over the missing boy's bed. Upon seeing Masterson, he glanced in the direction of Mrs. Scrope and her owlish partner and then hissed under his breath, "Great goin', Captain. Just great! Now I'm not only suspended, I'm unemployed as well.

"I want out of this! There's nothing we can do to help this poor woman. In fact, we've probably done more harm than good by coming here. She thinks Tommy and I shared some kind of secrets! I could hardly understand him when he talked, which wasn't very damn much. Mostly he just showed me his newest models when I'd come around to pick him and his mom up. Sometimes he'd even punch me when she wasn't looking."

Masterson couldn't hide her smile. Thorvald sounded just like an aggrieved older brother complaining of a rough-neck younger sibling. She wondered if he knew that combative behavior was sometimes an expression of love. At least, when she thought about her own boys, she certainly hoped so. It wasn't hard to see why Tommy might have loved this young man. Especially, when you consider Scrope as the alternative.

Out of the corner of her eye she saw Valerian waving them over.

"Mr. Thorvald," Valerian began. "Perhaps, you could tell us which of these aircraft,"—he waved at the ceiling—"would have been Tommy's favorite?"

Catherine Scrope smiled confidently at the young man. Thorvald hardly missed a beat.

"The B-17. Definitely. He was always wanting me to unhook it from the ceiling so he could show it to me. He had it hanging right over his bed." He pointed at the ceiling where a filament with nothing on the end twisted slowly in the air currents of the room. Thorvald's gaze darted from plane to plane, always coming back to the empty line. "I'm sure it was here, He especially liked that one because his dad, Mr. Edison, had one in mothballs stored out at the old…" Thorvald's face went slack for a moment and he seemed to lose his train of thought. "… the old airfield. The one I landed at that night."

"I see," Valerian replied, as if nothing out of the ordinary had been said. "Maybe we should take a ride out there?"

☙

It took several minutes for Masterson to realize she was looking at a crime scene. Once she had placed it together in her mind, replayed it for discrepancies and continuity, she believed she knew what had happened here.

Standing next to her in the dimly lit interior of the old bomber's fuselage, she and Thorvald stared down into the plastic bowl that projected from the plane's underside—the belly gunner's turret.

In Thorvald's hand he held the severed end of a length of hose that snaked its way into the turret and ended in an ancient, high altitude, oxygen mask, its deflated, insectile face staring back at them. Next to it lay the crushed remains of a plastic miniature of the aircraft they stood in.

Looking to Thorvald, Masterson saw that he had paled at finding these traces of the missing boy's passage. He was swaying and she thought he might faint.

Reaching over she removed the tubing from his grasp and said, "Let's step out of here now. Try not to touch anything else on your way out."

He obeyed and led the way to the ladder.

ᘓ

It had taken less than twenty minutes to drive to the airfield from the Scrope home. The lock on the double-gated, chain-link fence had yielded easily to the key supplied by Scrope himself. Masterson was sure that he had been on the verge of demanding she produce a search warrant when some warning device went off in his head, reminding him that victims, innocent victims, do not obstruct the police in a search for their children. Even step-children.

On their way out the door, almost as in afterthought, she had asked Scrope who else might have keys to the airfield. "The caretaker," he had spat. "Among others. How the hell should I know?"

Catherine had corrected him. "Oh no, Roger," she chirped, her mood buoyed with hope. "You dismissed him several weeks ago, don't you remember? And then changed the locks in case he tried to come back and damage anything. There's no one on the grounds anymore. You're the only one with any keys, dear."

Scrope's face was ashen as Masterson had eased the door closed.

On the drive over, she had made several calls from her car phone as she let Thorvald drive the route he knew so well. The first whispered, cryptic conversation was with her sergeant, whom she had given the task of verifying Thorvald's alibi prior to leaving the office.

It was much as she had thought. Assisting officers of the Nashville P.D. had confirmed his filing of a flight plan during the time in question and several of the airport's employees remembered his face from the grainy, black and white photo published in the local paper—an embarrassing commemoration of his inexplicable change in landing sites.

The second call had been to the detective she had assigned to keep the Scrope home under surveillance. "If he leaves the house, follow him—discretely. Don't put a stop on him unless I say so. Anything unusual, call me. Anything."

She hung up and glanced back uneasily at Valerian and Catherine Scrope in the rear seat. She needn't have worried about being overheard. Catherine was chatting with the taciturn Valerian like a schoolgirl on her first double-date, undeterred by her escort's lack of social skills. Masterson couldn't help but smile at the unlikely pairing.

☙

The corrugated metal doors of the antiquated aircraft hangar had presented more of a problem than the gates. The lock had yielded easily enough, but it had taken Thorvald several moments to get the heavy doors to separate and roll open on their rusty, dented tracks.

The cavernous interior was gloomy and echoed with their steps on the cracked concrete flooring. Above, a weak, greenish daylight filtered in through tinted fiberglass, giving everything a murky, underwater look.

The great warbird bristled with armament—a mechanical revenant of an era of heroes and just causes. Twin guns thrust from turrets located at its belly, top, and tail. An additional two were mounted at the front in stationary positions. Masterson glanced at Thorvald.

"All the firing pins and bolts have been removed," he explained.

Behind them Catherine Scrope called out, "Tommy?" She took a few halting steps toward the ancient World War II bomber, but Masterson, suddenly afraid of what she might find inside, forestalled her.

She took Catherine by the elbow. "Why don't you wait with Mr. Valerian while I take a look around? All right? It won't take but a moment."

"The gunner's turrets were Tommy's favorite," Thorvald said when Valerian had taken Catherine's hand and led her out into the sun. "He liked them so much that his dad, Mr. Edison, had their motors hooked up to the power in the hangar."

Masterson gave no sign of having heard him. Her face was pressed to the gunner's port beneath the plane.

"So now you can operate them," Thorvald went on. "That was Tommy's favorite thing. He would sit inside for hours with an old oxygen mask on and spin the turret around. All you've got to do is press on the foot pedals."

Masterson turned her face toward him, a smudge of dust on her cheek. "There's something in there. Can we get inside?"

It was the debris, obscure and dimly seen through the scratched and starred plastic of the belly-gunner's turret, that drew them into the fuselage. Inside, threading their way through a hanging garden of wires and cracked tubing, they were greeted by the smell of old leather and moldering canvas.

Peering into the belly turret with the aid of her penlight, Masterson could now make out clearly what she had noticed from outside. Evidence that Tommy had been there. Over her shoulder, she heard Thorvald murmur, "That's Tommy's model."

But it was the high-altitude mask that had her attention. One of the straps that secured

it to the wearer's face was broken, recently if she was any judge. The rubber tubing that led from the mouthpiece snaked its way up and out of the turret. She followed its course with the light, turning to her left. It ended, severed, within a few feet of a fire extinguisher mounted to the inner wall of the aircraft. The remaining half dangled from the ceiling.

On hands and knees, she crept to the extinguisher, playing the light across its metal surface. "CO2," she whispered. She noted the splayed end of the oxygen tube and compared it to the slightly flared nozzle of the extinguisher. A hot anger began to flush her cheeks. She knew what had been done here.

She walked back to the turret and stared down, an ugly picture forming in her mind. She saw a young boy, seated and strapped into the gunner's harness, high-altitude mask in place for added realism, grasping the handles of the neutered .50 cals., ready for action. She saw him pressing on the control pedals, spinning first this way, then that, to counter the enemy threat, blasting away at a sky swarming with enemy fighters. Oblivious to any distractions but the mission at hand. A happy and excited boy.

A boy awakened in the middle of the night and promised an unexpected treat. An adventure. A trip to the old airfield and its wonderful bomber! She saw the bargain of his cooperation and silence sealed with the treasured model that spun lazily over his bed. Always just beyond his reach.

She also saw a man. A man smiling down at the tiny warrior happily ensconced in the gunner's turret beneath him. She saw him unstrap a fire extinguisher from the wall of the aircraft and carry it closer to the edge of the turret, being careful, so as not to tug on the boy's mask and gain his attention. She saw the man sever the tubing and fit it over the nozzle of the extinguisher.

Still smiling the man leans over the rim of the turret and looks down at the boy. The boy, beginning to notice the lack of air, looks back at him, eyes widening in panic. His small hands begin to pluck frantically at the carefully tightened straps. But the man is quicker. He pulls the safety pin on the extinguisher and squeezes the release handle. A rush of freezing gas pushes its way through the tube and into the boy's straining lungs. His struggles are fierce, but brief.

She sees the man disengage the tube and return the extinguisher, pin intact, to its wall mount, then detach the tubing and remove the boy's mask. Straining, because of the acute angle, he lifts the boy's inert body out and carries it away to dispose of it. He fails to remember the scale model of the B-17 crushed beneath Tommy in his final struggles.

Turning to leave, Masterson sees Thorvald, puzzled and shaken, studying the cut tubing. She takes it from him and says something. She isn't sure what.

෴

Leaving Thorvald to guard the hangar, Masterson made a series of calls from her car phone. The first was to the assistant prosecutor assigned to the case. She wanted an immediate search warrant for the Edison estate and all vehicles garaged there. If Tommy's body had been transported from the airfield, it was probably in the trunk of a car. Fibers from his clothing would likely be found there.

She wanted included in the warrant all clothing worn by Roger Scrope. If and when they found Tommy, fibers adhering to his body could place Scrope at the scene. Lastly, she wanted a thorough search conducted for any sedatives, prescription or otherwise, that might be concealed in the house. Catherine's statement that since her marriage to Scope she slept soundly had taken on an ominous meaning.

Oh yes, she almost forgot. Fingerprints. She wanted both Scrope and the German woman printed for comparison to any latents they might find in the aircraft. He might be able to explain most of them away as part of his proprietorship, she thought, but the fire extinguisher and the model aircraft would be tough. Still, it was all circumstantial, and she knew it. She didn't have a body or the slightest clue where to look for it.

Her second call was to her sergeant. She needed him to get the evidence van and its crew mobilized and on its way ASAP and to make arrangements with the sheriff's office for a body dog. If Tommy had been buried nearby, and in a shallow grave, then the dog had a reasonable chance of finding him. To shore up their chances, she also asked that they coordinate with the state police for a chopper and an infrared scope. The heat generated by decomposition often produced red spots or "readings" against a cooler landscape. It could, at least, produce targets for the dog to check out.

Masterson sat back in her seat and surveyed the scene. Thorvald still stood at the hangar door, shifting from one foot to the other. Valerian and Catherine Scrope had found a seat on a grassy knoll nearby and seemed to be enjoying the sun. Sometimes, Valerian would glance in Masterson's direction with a quizzical expression. Perceptive, as always, he knew something was up.

In a short while, she thought, this tranquil scene would erupt with activity. Vehicles, searchers, dogs, evidence men, and helicopters would descend on them like an invading army. She decided to send the others back in her car. Once Catherine realized that it was a body that was being looked for, she would be inconsolable. Masterson knew that she would not have time to deal with that.

While she still had a few minutes and the privacy of the car, she mulled over the situation. Without a body and autopsy results her case was circumstantial at best. She felt her confidence and energy draining away but then an idea, small at first, but insistent and pugnacious, began to force its way into her consciousness. Climbing its way up from some darker part of her, it seized her imagination and demanded action. It challenged her to set aside such things as physical evidence and logic and come to grips with the enemy. If you have no strengths, it whispered, then probe for your opponent's weaknesses. She reached for the phone and dialed Scrope's number.

Yolanda answered on the second ring, "Scrope residence." Her voice was low and husky, with only the trace of an accent.

"Ah, Yolanda," Masterson purred. "This is Captain Masterson. I'm calling from the airfield. Is your boss available?"

There was a pause. Masterson pictured Scrope shaking his head.

"No, *Miss* Masterson, I'm afraid he's engaged with business at the moment."

Bridgid didn't miss the catty dig. "Well, look over your shoulder and tell him that it's very important. Then hand him the phone."

There was a hiss of breath. Masterson heard the receiver clatter onto a hard surface. A few moments later it was snatched up by Scrope.

"Yes?" he almost shouted.

Nerves, she thought. "Roger," she began, letting the use of his first name sink in. "I've some important news for you."

"By God, I should hope so, after all the upset you've caused around here. Where's my wife?"

Somewhere along the line, she heard the faint click of an extension being lifted.

"Yolanda? Is that you? Good. Stay on the line. This affects you, too."

Scrope burst in. "There's no one else on the line! What are you getting at?"

Masterson continued without answering his concerns. "We've come across several items of evidence in the hangar containing the old B-17. With some physical evidence to work with now, we'd like to begin eliminating suspects as well as family and household members."

"What…" Scrope sounded as if he was choking. "What kind of evidence have you found?" His tone was very reasonable now. A concerned stepfather.

Masterson ignored him. "Yolanda, is your hair naturally blonde, or does it come from a bottle?"

The question was so unexpected she forgot herself. "What? I am natural. What do you mean?"

Gotcha! Masterson crowed to herself.

"Yes, of course you are. It's just that we'll have to have some hair samples from you to compare to some we found at the airfield. Not to worry, the ones we have look bleached… I think. Besides, you've never had reason to go out there with Tommy, have you? At least, I don't remember your mentioning it in your statements."

This time there was no answer, just a long pause followed by the quiet click of a receiver being replaced.

Scrope stepped into the silence. "Where's this leading, Captain?" He had restored her rank. "I can vouch for Yolanda."

"Even at the time of night Tommy was taken from his bed? I don't think so, Roger. You were asleep then, remember? In any case, I'm not singling her out. I'll have to have prints from you both, as well as fiber samples from your clothes. It shouldn't take long. We can do it all right in your home."

"You suspect me, don't you?" Scrope hissed into the phone, fear and stress burning off his thin veneer of control. "You suspect I had something to do with Tommy's death—"

"Death? I thought we were investigating a kidnapping."

She heard a chair scrape across hardwood flooring.

"Just relax, Roger. My team will take about thirty minutes getting there."

She disconnected and immediately dialed another number. The investigator surveilling the Scrope home answered. "Yeah, boss."

"Stan, in about ten minutes, I think you'll see both Scrope and Yolanda leave the house in a hurry. Don't let 'em. Detain them both and separate them. I think she'll want to help us out with this thing. I've got a search warrant and team headed your way. Call me as soon as anything breaks and remember, keep them apart!"

"Right-o, boss. I'm on it."

ભ

The call came just as the evidence van was pulling up to the hangar. "Masterson, here."

"Well, boss, you were wrong. They came out in five, not ten minutes. I thought the house was on fire!"

"Anything, Stan?" Her temples were beginning to throb.

"Other than her spillin' her guts and claiming Scrope coerced her into the scheme? Nah, nothing much."

"Stan, you son of a... "

"Oh, yeah, there was something else. She says she's willing to cooperate and testify against Scrope, if we'll offer her a deal. She's pretty smart, huh? How long she been in this country?"

Masterson felt a sense of euphoria coming over her. "Give the big man a call and see what he's willing to go for. Remind him she's a foreigner. He'll have some calls to make."

The sight of Catherine Scrope reminded her of reality. "Stan, can she lead us to the body?"

There was a heavy sigh on the other end. "Yeah, that too. She says they planted him out by the runway."

Masterson's euphoria vanished.

❧

It was after midnight and the medical examiner's van had borne its small cargo into the darkness before Masterson had a chance to speak with Valerian. She had sent Thorvald and Catherine Scrope away after the arrival of the evidence team with no explanation of her planned activities. Now it would be her sad duty to meet with the wretched woman and break the news of her son's death and her husband's involvement. Her comrades' congratulations only served to make her feel jaded and cynical.

She turned and looked for a moment at Valerian, who stood silent and staring at the invisible horizon, floodlights from the adjacent excavations making his glasses opaque, his mood unreadable.

"Anthony," she began, "there's something that doesn't quite add up in all this."

He did not turn and face her or give any indication that he had heard.

"It's about Thorvald," she resumed. "When you first brought him to me, I thought you were taking a big chance. I figured you suspected that he had some involvement or inside knowledge of what had happened to Tommy and that that knowledge, that guilt, was what had caused the episode. I thought you were playing it close to the wire professionally by bringing a patient that you knew wanted to talk. But it didn't turn out that way. He really knew nothing."

A moisture-laden breeze drifted across them, causing them to draw closer together in the shadows of the arc lights. At the edge of the field, the same wind moved sighing through the pines and disappeared.

"So why, Anthony?" She was straining to see his face in the darkness. "Why did Thorvald land at this field? What did he see up there? If it was guilt, I could understand it. Anthony?"

When he began to speak, it was so softly that she had to bend her head down to hear him, though each word was distinct, as if he had thought on his reply for a long time. "Bridgid, when I brought Thorvald to your office, it wasn't because I believed he had guilty knowledge. Quite the contrary. If I had suspected that, ethically, I would have been prohibited from doing so.

"No, I knew he was telling the truth during our session. I've been in this business for twenty-five years. If anything, he was more bewildered than I was. I brought him to you because he seemed to have some connection to the case. I couldn't understand what myself. Yet I couldn't discount the coincidence of his episode with the disappearance of that poor boy. I had no idea if he had anything of value to offer you. As it was, he led us to this airfield. He had some connection to the boy. Or, more likely, the boy to him."

"Anthony, how…"

"I've no idea how." Removing his glasses, he began to absently polish them with his tie. "I've spent most of my life studying the mind and its workings, yet, I confess I know nothing about the movements of the soul."

They both turned, each with their separate thoughts, and stared down at the small emptied grave.

Don't Fear the Reaper
(1994)

Julian sat slumped in thought in the passenger seat of the patrol car, looking south down Island Drive. His partner, a summer officer, sat ramrod straight behind the wheel of the idling cruiser, his hands clenched in a death grip on the steering wheel.

Every summer, the Camelot Beach Police Department augmented its small force with a dozen or so Class II officers drawn from criminal justice programs at various colleges. All the communities on the Jersey shore followed this pattern during the tourist season, when the populations of the islands would explode with do-or-die fun-seekers. These hordes would occupy their newly acquired kingdoms from Memorial Day until Labor Day, when the call of unseen forces would compel them to fold their tents and move on, leaving behind their stunned, but richer, subjects.

Julian's musings came to a halt as the event they had been waiting for began. He sat up a little straighter in order to witness the nightly ritual of bar closing, and glanced over at his partner, who remained on alert, reminding him of a retriever waiting for a signal from his master. His gelled flattop almost quivered in anticipation.

"Think there'll be a fight?" he asked with a little more enthusiasm than Julian liked to hear.

"Um… could be. Possibly," Julian responded.

This was why they, and several other cars, were there. To forestall, as much as possible, the usual fights, vandalism, and the like, that tended to occur when several thousand drunk youths gathered together in one place. That place happened to be the Camelot Bar and Grill. A mammoth, rambling old hotel that occupied a city block, it boasted three separate bars, a liquor store, and pool tables. The actual hotel, which had rooms on the two upper stories, had been closed for many years now.

As they watched, the crowd began to pour out of the building, rushing through the now-open double doors that dotted the side of the structure, spilling onto the sidewalk and overflowing into the street. Many of them were drenched in sweat, their shirts plastered to their bones. Some seemed to be gasping for air, lifting their arms to the skies, as if thankful for deliverance from the crush inside. Julian felt a drop of perspiration slowly working its way down his chest and tugged his protective vest away from his body to let some of the heat escape. It was quite warm for two in the morning.

He pointed out one young woman to his partner. She was on her hands and knees at the curb, puking up her paycheck. "Well, at least someone had a good time," Julian remarked.

The mob spread out to block half the traffic circle in front of the Camelot. One of the other patrol units began to ease its way into the milling crowd, slowly cutting a swath through them, forcing them to cross the street or to get back up on the sidewalk.

Julian remained in place, ready as backup. He scanned the crowd for signs of trouble, alert for the arcing beer bottle that could turn this exodus into a melee.

"Where are they, do ya think?" he asked his younger partner.

"Who's that?" Franklin replied, a puzzled look on his seamless face.

"The piggyback couple." There was a pause while the young officer mulled this tidbit over.

Julian was amused to see a furrow of concentration form a cease on his shiny young forehead.

"Franklin, I'm shocked at you. You're not aware of the piggyback couple?" Franklin looked worried now, knowing he was being set up. "Soon they will come out of that bar, as they come out of that bar every night. As they come out of every bar in this town every night. Nay, as they come out of every bar in every town in this state every night, sooner or later. And yet you, a police officer, if only a Class II, know nothing of them. I'm disappointed in you, Franklin."

Franklin responded, "Oh yeah, right."

"Ah, here they are."

As if on cue, the piggy-back couple came jogging out into the night. A very drunk young man carrying an equally drunk young woman, squealing with delight, on his back. Julian chuckled. It never failed, no matter the bar. It was a phenomenon, peculiar to the summer perhaps, that cops witnessed with unfailing regularity. The couple made it to the corner before falling victim to gravity and the effects of alcohol. Teetering with ever-increasing speed, they disappeared, flailing, into some shrubbery.

"How'd you know that?" Franklin asked over an incoming call from dispatch.

Julian didn't answer him, but spoke into the microphone of the car radio, "Eleven-oh-seven will take that call. We're eight blocks south of it." He turned to Franklin saying, "Turn us around and take us to Thirteenth. A caller heard screams in the vicinity."

Franklin executed a hard U-turn, cutting off an oncoming car and slamming Julian against the door.

"Jesus, Frank, take it easy. I'd like to get there alive."

"I didn't hear that call," Franklin said, almost under his breath.

Julian could hear the self-recrimination in his tone and offered some consolation. "Yeah, I know. You were too busy worrying about the piggyback couple. It'll all be in my report."

Franklin floored the gas pedal and they careened northward.

As they approached the area of Thirteenth Street, Julian had his young partner slow the squad car down to a crawl and kill the headlamps. "Keep your eyes open for anybody wandering around down here," he instructed. "And roll down your window and listen." He reached over and switched off the FM radio and at the same time informed dispatch that they were in the area and that nothing was showing. He heard Eleven-hundred tell dispatch that they were in the area also, cruising south on Island Drive. Julian could just make out their darkened car, creeping ghostlike along the curb several blocks away.

Julian looked around, noting the desolation of the neighborhood after the press of the bar crowd a mere quarter-mile away. No one seemed to be out, and there were few houses showing lights at this hour. They were crawling past the public works yard, with its chain-link fence running the length of the block, when Julian switched on the alley light, throwing the various trucks, tractors, earthmovers, and surf rakes into sudden relief. There was no movement. No quarry was flushed from hiding. He switched off the light and told his partner to stop the car. They came to a halt at the foot of the water tower.

"I'm gonna take a walk around. You go ahead but stay close. If you stop anybody, call Eleven-hundred for backup. They'll be able to get to you quicker than I will on foot." Julian eased himself from the car. Leaning back in the window, he added, "Don't forget about me, okay?" then walked into the shadows.

As he waited for the patrol car to leave the area, he listened. Still nothing. Just an increase in traffic due to the bar break. Checking to make sure his portable was on low, he began to walk along the perimeter while keeping to the shadows, following the fence to where the water tower stood. There he stopped. A ragged piece of black fabric fluttered from the strands of barbed wire that topped the fence and he could just make out some lettering on it. It appeared to be "ALLICA." He noted that the strands were pressed down onto the chain-link, and that that section of the fence leaned out over the sidewalk as if crushed down by a great weight.

Looking up, Julian was struck square in the forehead by a drop of liquid. With a gasp he stepped back, his hand going to the spot. It came away glistening with water. The water tower was sweating in the warm night air. Peering up two hundred feet to where the vast squat tank rested on its enormous legs, he became aware now of an occasional plop of water on the nearby sidewalk. Risking a look with his flashlight, he saw nothing on the catwalk that girded the belly of the tower. His portable crackled into life, causing him to start.

"Eleven-oh-seven to Eleven-hundred, I'll be out with two subjects at Twelfth and First."

That was Franklin, and Julian began to walk quickly east on Thirteenth to back him up. As he reached the next corner, Julian heard Eleven-hundred sign out along with his Class II and slowed. He could see the little gathering just a block north of him now on First Avenue. Three officers and a young couple.

Julian approached from behind as the two Class II's let the full-timer, Shane McPherson, do the talking. Even though he was overweight and nobody's idea of a recruiting poster cop, Julian had great respect for him. What he lacked in appearance, he more than made up for in quickness of wit.

Sidling around to have a quiet look at the subjects, Julian thought they were not more than nineteen years old. The male's attention was focused on Shane's massive presence, a stupefied expression on his face. He was tall and thin, with a bad complexion and bangs that hung into his eyes that he kept nervously brushing away. Julian noted that his Blue Oyster Cult T-shirt was sticking to his starved-looking frame in several places. The girl seemed out of breath.

The girl noticed him right away and Julian thought he saw a moment's alarm flash across her white, fleshy face. It was gone in an instant, replaced by an angry determination that glinted in her small green eyes. She swung back to Shane and launched into a low, forceful monologue, forcing Shane to focus his attention on her. The boyfriend was shunted aside, literally taking a step back.

Julian drew closer to catch what she was saying and observed her right hand disappear beneath her great thatch of orangy-red hair and grip her neck, massage it, and drop again to her side. Standing with her short, plump body planted firmly in front of Shane, she explained, in exasperated terms, that, yes, she and her boyfriend had been in the neighborhood a few minutes ago taking a walk, as if that were a crime, and may have had a little difference of opinion on a few things. No big deal! The hand crept up to her neck again. It happened, or didn't the cops know that? Now, could they get on with their lives without any more police interference?

Shane looked amused. The boyfriend looked smug, staring in admiration at the girl. Then Shane took the lead back. "So, what are you sayin'? That you two had a fight and maybe you did a little screamin'? That's what the neighbors heard?"

Her voice dripping with contempt, she answered, "Yes, Officer, that's what I'm saying. Now, may we go?"

"So, why?"

"Why, what?"

"Why the screamin'? He hurt ya, or what?"

Glancing over at her boyfriend, a tight smile crept onto her face. "No, he didn't hurt me. No one hurts me. We're on a different plane than that."

"I kinda figured that," Shane replied without missing a beat. "So, you had a fight, you did some screamin', you didn't get hurt, and here we are."

She visibly relaxed, the hand went back to the neck. "Yes, exactly."

Julian stepped forward. "So, what's wrong with your neck?"

She swung to face him, the hand quickly retracted. Fury contorted her plain face into ugliness. "What?" she hissed.

Directing the beam of his flashlight onto her neck it revealed a livid red line beginning at her jugular and vanishing beneath her mass of hair. It looked like a rope burn, but much narrower, and recent. The throat area was unmarred.

"How'd that happen, miss?"

There was a pause as she mastered herself. Julian could almost hear her thinking. "In a volleyball game," she began, her voice low and her eyes focused on the ground. "We were having a volleyball game at the house, when someone's hand got caught in my necklace." Her eyes met his now. "It was an accident. Nothing to do with this. No concern of yours."

Julian looked over at Shane. They understood each other. There was nothing for them here. They had found their screamer and that would have to be that. If there had been violence between these two, there was nothing they could do with what they were getting. "You got some ID from them and a local address?" Julian asked as he began to walk to the patrol car.

"Yeah, just waitin' on dispatch to verify their DLs," Shane called to his retreating back.

As they drove away, Julian looked back at the newly-released couple. They were making their way down the sidewalk, their arms wrapped around each other as if for support. Their disparate gaits caused them to wobble as they walked, and they never looked back.

౪ఎ

It wasn't until after four a.m. that Julian remembered the patch of black cloth at the water tower. The Class II's had all been released at four and he was now teamed up with Shane. The sun was just starting to lighten the eastern sky with a rosy hue.

Pulling up to the base of the tower, he pointed it out to Shane. "This is what I thought was going on last night with the screamin'. I figured someone had tried to scale the fence to the tower and got cut." Julian opened the car door. "Let's take a look."

They ambled over to the damaged fencing and Shane pulled the fabric loose and studied it. "It's a torn shirt," he announced.

Julian peered through the linkage into the tall, yellow grass beneath the tower, spotting a brand-name sneaker lying on its side. Farther in, he could make out two large depressions in the grass, maybe some clothing.

"Yo, Jules, I think there's some blood on this shirt."

A slight morning breeze swayed the foliage surrounding the depressions and Julian felt sweat coating his palms. Turning to Shane, he said, "There're two bodies in there, and I think one of them belongs to the shirt."

ᕦᕤ

Within forty minutes of their summons, the scene was transformed from the breathless quiet of dawn to a place of controlled confusion and subdued chatter. Following procedure, Julian had had the dispatcher notify the detective on call, the chief, the prosecutor's office, and the M.E., and all had duly arrived in various stages of stupor. Even though the sun had risen well above the horizon, it was not yet five-thirty. The scene had been taped off and another patrol car had taken over shooing away the morbidly curious, though at this time of the morning they consisted only of the occasional jogger or elderly dog-walker. Even coffee had been sent for.

Various technicians, having completed the photography, now waited for the medical examiner to finish her preliminary examination before processing the scene. Julian stood over the body of a young white male as the M.E. crouched beside it, making some notes.

"So, you and Shane found the bodies?" she asked.

"Yeah," Julian replied. "There was a report of screams in the area around two a.m. We didn't find anything here, but I noticed the shirt and we came back for another look when it got light. We also found how they got in. The lock is missing off the maintenance gate. Accidental fall, do you think?"

She had started writing again. "Looks that way, or jumped, maybe. Do you know either of them?"

Julian gazed down at the broken body of the boy. He lay on his back, one leg almost completely folded under his body. The remaining flap of shirt showed the letters MET and a garish print of a guitar-playing skeleton. The chest, exposed where the T-shirt had been torn away, revealed numerous serrations made by the barbed wire and subsequent punctures from the top edge of the chain-link fence. He could see the purple-black line of lividity running lengthwise along the boy's back, where the blood had settled after his heart had stopped beating. It left the rest of him dead-white. The face appeared too large and asymmetrical as a result of the shattered skull shifting under its fleshy cover. Julian thought of the boy's parents and suddenly, yearningly, of his own children, safe at home, dreaming in their beds.

"Yeah, I know him. He lives, or did, a few blocks from here on First. He was seventeen. His name's Ryan Louper. The kids called him Loopy. I had him on a drug charge about two months ago and he'd agreed to supply me with some info on who's dealing LSD to the juvies around here. Acid has made a big comeback lately. I'd yet to hear from him."

The M.E. looked at Julian. "Think this has anything to do with that?"

"I thought you said they had fallen or jumped?"

After a short pause, she replied, "Yeah, I did." She turned and walked a straight and careful line to the next body. Julian followed, placing his footsteps in hers. When he reached the girl, he almost retreated a step. In spite of the fact that she had missed the fence and had less obvious damage, the result of the unbroken impact had been devastating. She looked as if a giant had stepped on her and carefully ground her into the earth. Her eyes were almost distended from their sockets.

Looking away, he said, dry-mouthed, "I don't know this one. I don't think I've ever seen her before."

The M.E. said nothing in reply and began jotting on her notepad once more.

"I don't think Ryan was the kind of kid that would kill himself. He knew the score. He knew that juvenile charges don't carry much weight. The worst he would have been facing was counseling or drug rehab. If he didn't want to snitch on the dealers, he would have just said so. It was no big deal. In fact, he hadn't snitched on anybody and probably wasn't going to. He was just stringing us along, more than likely." Julian stopped, realizing how defensive he sounded. And felt. He had been warned about using juvenile informers, how volatile they could be.

He looked up to the tower catwalk, then back to the sagging fencing that Ryan's body had struck. It wasn't far from the base of the tower, but would a simple slip and fall have taken him even that distance? And how did he explain the girl? How did she happen to fall also? Looking down at her shattered body a silly, adolescent notion came to him—maybe they had been holding hands at the moment of the fall… or jump. It was then that he noticed her clenched fist, two slender pieces of leather, or rawhide, dangling from it.

"Doc, what's she holding there?"

Turning her attention to the corpse's right hand, she pried it open. Lying there was a cheap-looking silver cross. Julian squatted down to get a better look. On closer inspection, he could see that the head of the cross ended in a loop. The leather thong was threaded through a small opening at the top of the loop and broken, ending in two pieces. It was obviously meant to be worn around the neck.

"I think that's called an ankh," the doctor murmured. "Egyptian, if I remember my history of religions class correctly. I believe it symbolizes eternal life." Neither chose to comment on the irony of this observation.

"Doc, do you think Ryan could have been wearing this?" Julian asked as he pictured the events in his imagination. "It would make sense that if she started to fall, she would reach out to grab something. Maybe she grabbed this necklace and pulled Ryan over with her."

The doctor looked thoughtful. "That's a pretty theory, but I saw no abrasions on the neck of the male during prelim. Still, an autopsy will tell us more. You can let the others know that I'm done here." She stood and stretched as Julian made his way to the cluster of officers.

As Shane pulled away from the curb, Julian looked back at the technicians fanning out beneath the tower, the bodies once again hidden from view. Even in the light of day, the water tower now looked evil to him, like a great, heathen idol, gloating over its sacrifices and its secrets. A shudder coursed through his tired body and a flash of memory surfaced like a striking fish—the memory of a girl on a darkened street rubbing the back of her neck and wincing in pain.

∽

The Loupers were home, as Julian feared they would be. He imagined they had had another sleepless night, thanks to Ryan.

He had not wanted to pull this duty, but since it was technically his investigation and there was the identity of the girl to clear up, it fell to him. He had Shane stop just around the corner from the Loupers' rented house. As they approached the home, they could see that the father's pickup was still in the drive, and the mother was visible at the kitchen table. She was still in her housecoat, staring out the window. Julian looked at Shane. They had already discussed what they would do.

As soon as they stepped into view, Mrs. Louper rose from her chair and took several steps toward the door. Her face was set and grey, vestiges of fear showing in her darkened eyes. As they climbed the steps, they heard her call out her husband's name. He appeared abruptly behind her as she threw open the door to their knock.

"Do you have him down at the station again?" she demanded.

Her husband's face was loose with exhaustion, frightened.

Julian began, "Could we come in for a moment?"

A spark of fear and suspicion animated the woman's face but was quickly subdued. Folding her arms across her chest she went on, "You've got him, don't you? Well, I hope you've put him in a cell this time! If he's going to keep fooling around with drugs that's what he deserves!"

Julian pictured Ryan's shattered body lying naked on a mortuary slab and wanted nothing more than to stop her from saying these things that she would have all her life to regret. Continuing up the steps, he forced the woman to step aside and entered the kitchen. "Ryan was with a young lady last night. Do you know who she was?"

The question threw them both off guard and he could see them relax a little. Problems with a girl, this was something normal. Something they could understand. Julian felt cruel, delaying the blow he knew he must deliver, but if he waited they might not be in any condition to identify the dead girl. After all, she too, probably had parents frantic with worry that she had not returned.

Mr. Louper spoke, "He went out with his girlfriend last night. She's from Bayshore Township." Bayshore was a down-at-the-heels town in the south of the county. Julian recalled that Ryan had run into some trouble down that way not too long ago. "He said they were going over to a friend's house to listen to some music. He promised me that it wasn't a party."

"Her name?" Julian asked.

"Becca… Rebecca Tournquist. Are they in some kind of trouble, Officer Hall?"

Julian ignored his question. "Could you describe her for me?"

Mrs. Louper answered, "She's seventeen, the same age as Ryan, has black, wavy hair just past her shoulders, and is kinda tiny… you know, petite. Is that what you needed to know?"

Julian faltered. That was the girl he had found. Now for the hard part. "Yes, Mrs. Louper, that's very helpful." He took a breath. "Now, I have some very hard news for you. Maybe we should sit?" No one moved. The Loupers, all color drained from their faces, remained immobile, waiting. "Ryan and Rebecca were killed last night in an accident." He stopped, he could feel his hands shaking. The woman began to sway, a low moan breaking from her ashen lips. Shane was quickly at her side, easing her into a chair. Suddenly Mr. Louper slammed his hand down on the tabletop, causing the dishes to jump and startling the officers.

"They didn't have a car, damn you!" he shouted. "It's still out front! They walked to where they were going! They couldn't have been in an accident!" he finished triumphantly, desperately.

"It was a fall, you see," Julian resumed. "They were on the water tower and fell." He refrained from mentioning any other possibility. "Mr. Louper, is there anyone you would like us to call? A priest or minister? If you like, we could get someone here to stay with you and your wife."

Mr. Louper, his hands still on the tabletop, supporting his full weight now, looked up. The hot tears were streaming from his eyes. "You're sure? You're sure it's Ryan?"

Julian nodded, and Mrs. Louper began to wail, a soft, keening sound. Her husband made no effort to go to her. Each was engulfed in their own grief and guilt. Julian heard someone clattering down the stairs from the second floor.

"Mom, Dad? What's wrong, what's happened?"

The little sister, Julian thought. I forgot about the little sister. Oh God.

೧

Several hours later, Shane and Julian were back at the station, drained and exhausted. They had summoned a doctor, who had medicated the survivors, leaving them zombielike in their quiet house. No TV, no radio. Just silence.

Before they left, Julian had secured permission from Mr. Louper to search Ryan's room. He had explained that it was normal procedure in a case such as this. Mr. Louper had simply nodded.

It was Shane who had discovered the sheets. There were three of them. Each had fifty hits of blotter acid on notebook-sized paper that was expertly perforated into fifty tabs for easy detachment. Each tab contained the LSD in the likeness of a dancing bear surrounded by roses. Childlike images. No suicide notes.

A quick field test confirmed their suspicions, and Julian packaged a sheet for examination by the prosecutor's lab for a definitive analysis. The other two he set aside for latent fingerprints. He was anxious to know who else had handled these sheets besides Ryan. Tomorrow, he intended to rattle some cages.

೧

Jacob Scotland was shooting hoops at the Rec Center when Julian found him the following evening—a small, thin boy of sixteen with a clear, milky complexion and a guileless, baby face. Julian noted that he held his own against the larger boys on the court. Since the age of fourteen, Jacob had successfully broken into a dozen or more homes, using a second-floor technique that required a good deal of dexterity and wiry strength. He had been caught twice already and showed little inclination to reform. In fact, his M.O. had recently resurfaced in a string of B&Es in the lagoons.

This was the person that Ryan and Becca told the Loupers they were going to visit on the night of their deaths. Julian waited for halftime and signaled Jacob over. He approached in his usual carefree manner, wiping himself down with a dirty-looking towel, as if being summoned by a cop during a basketball game was commonplace, His angelic face beamed.

"Officer Hall, how ya doin'?" he began.

Julian didn't smile back. He was in no mood for the usual adolescent banner.

"You know about Ryan and his girlfriend?"

Jacob's cherubic features clouded. "Yeah, it's all over town. Bummer, huh?" Then the smile broke through the clouds again.

Julian resisted the impulse to strangle this kid. "Yeah, Jacob, it's a bummer. I can see that you're real tore up about your buddy."

"Yo, man, Ry and Becca followed their own path. That's nothin' to do with me. They had free will."

Julian was caught off guard by Jacob's record jacket philosophy. "So, what are you saying? That they walked out of your place, climbed the tower, held hands, and jumped? Did you witness all of this, Jacob?"

Alarm rippled across the boy's face. "No, man! I wasn't there! They didn't even come to my house that night!"

Julian already knew that, having checked with Jacob's parents. He bluffed. "There's no law against suicide, Jacob, but there is one for assisting. If I find out you were there and did nothing, or helped them, by God, I'll have you tried as an adult."

The smile had completely vanished and looked like it might never return. That was what Julian wanted. "If they weren't with you before they went to the tower, who were they with? And this had better be the truth, Jacob, 'cause I'm gonna check."

Julian watched him weigh his options, and as usual he chose self-preservation.

"They were probably hangin' with some dudes over at Eleventh and Camelot. An old house on the corner. They went there sometimes when they told their folks they were at my house. Ry had been hangin' out there a lot since you guys busted him."

"Who are these people, Jacob? What's up with them?"

Jacob considered this for a moment. "It's a girl and a dude. They're a little older than us, eighteen or nineteen, but they're cool. A little different, maybe, but cool."

Julian felt his scalp tingle. "A red-haired girl and a tall, skinny guy?"

Jacob brightened a little. "Yeah, Gabriel and Morgan, you know 'em?"

There they were again. "Yeah, I've met them. Jacob, do a lot of people know about Ryan being busted?"

"It's been around town. You know Ry could never keep his mouth shut."

Julian digested the double meaning in Jacob's statement. If Ry had blabbed about his acid bust, had he also told everyone about how the cops wanted him to be an informant? The buzzer sounded for the game to resume.

"One last thing, Jacob. What makes you think they killed themselves? Why would they do that?"

Jacob had already started to walk away. He stopped in mid-stride, the towel slung over his shoulder. "You should talk to those dudes on Eleventh about that, man. All I know is that since Ry started hangin' there he's been different… or was different," he corrected himself. "They got a special way of lookin' at life over there. I'm not into it, but it's cool. Ry said they were teaching him not to be afraid."

"Afraid of what?" Julian asked.

"Anything, dude. Parents, cops, life, death, you know, everything."

"He said that? Even death?"

"That was the main thing he said they believed. If you didn't fear death, nothing could touch you. That there was freedom on the other side." Jacob walked away. Over his shoulder, the smile fully in place again, he called out, "Don't fear the reaper, man!"

Julian recognized the line from a popular rock song in which the singer urges his lover to commit suicide with him. "Bullshit," he muttered under his breath and walked away.

⋖⋗

Two days later, Julian received a copy of the medical examiner's findings. It contained no surprises. Both deaths were ruled accidental as a result of their plummet from the water tower. Suicide was not mentioned, both as a courtesy to the families and due to the absence of suicide notes or other corroborating evidence. The serology examination revealed traces of lysergic acid diethylamide, which was listed as a possible contributing factor in the deaths.

Julian pondered that for a moment. LSD kept popping up in this case. First, he nabbed Ryan with a sheet of acid several months ago. Second, Ryan agrees to put him on to the source of the local network. Third, Ryan, according to the possum-like Jacob, starts to hang out with the Eleventh Street couple. Fourth, Ryan and his girlfriend take a two-hundred-foot header off the local water tower and their autopsies reveal the presence of LSD in their bloodstreams. Finally, he and Shane find three sheets of blotter acid in Ryan's room.

A hundred and fifty hits was way too much for personal use. Had Ryan moved into dealing shortly before his death?

Had he cut into some other dealer's territory and suffered the consequences? It seemed unlikely. Money just wasn't a motive in street-level acid dealing. It was only three to five dollars a hit for God's sake! Acid dealers weren't like crack or heroin pushers. They weren't in it for the money. They tended to see themselves as purveyors of an alternate lifestyle. Modern-day shamans offering their followers a glimpse of paradise… or hell. It was a power trip, really, with the dealer as both holder of the key and the guide once you entered the gate. Among the very young, it could be a powerful, and dangerous, position.

Ryan just didn't fit the bill. He wouldn't have had the organizational skills for such a role. He was Loopy, remember? Essentially a good-time Charlie.

There was another possibility, however, Maybe Ryan had hidden those sheets as evidence, intending to turn them over to Julian. It would be just like Ryan to go half the distance and get distracted or change his mind. But had he shot his mouth off about that as well? Where money might not be a motive to an acid dealer, prison certainly could be.

Julian opened the bag containing Becca's clothing and belongings, which had been sent over with the M.E.'s report and withdrew the silver ankh with its broken leather thong. He had specifically requested a DNA test be run on any flesh found adhering to the leather at the point where it had been broken. The M.E.'s

office had been just as specific. In the absence of evidence of homicide and the lack of any suspects, no tests would be run. There was no way they could justify the expense and, besides, the use of DNA in forensic science simply had not yet reached a level where it was accepted as definitive by the judiciary system. At this point, the myth was a more powerful tool than the reality. There had been no mention in the report of whether the necklace had been identified by the girl's parents or not. He pulled the phone over to him and dialed their number.

Rebecca's mother did not recall ever having seen her daughter wear a necklace of that description, and it was unique enough that she would have remembered. Julian thought he knew its owner.

☙

The house wasn't hard to find, sitting exactly where Jacob had said it would be at the corner of Eleventh Street and Camelot Ave. It was a ramshackle Victorian monstrosity sprouting turrets and cupolas from unlikely places, a hangover from the days when the rich brought their servants with them to the shore. With three floors and an attic, there was plenty of room for everyone. Usually, the attic was where the servants ended up and were like rabbit warrens, cut up into a half-dozen rooms or so. They must have been insufferably hot in the summer, Julian thought.

As Julian approached, he noticed the paint had worn away in a number of places and that shingles were missing from both the roof and the siding. The broad, wooden steps leading to the wraparound veranda sagged under his weight and the wood looked spongy. The veranda itself sloped towards the heavy, ornate, front door, reminding him of a carnival funhouse where once you enter, you cannot go back. Julian glanced at the forbidding entrance, expecting to see a sign above the door that read, "Abandon Hope, All Ye Who Enter Here!"

He could see no one through the tall windows that fronted the house. The inside looked to have been better kept than the exterior, but still had a forlorn, shabby appearance, cluttered, dark, and dusty. Julian returned to the door and peered through the tulip-patterned etched glass framed in the woodwork. At the end of the dimly-lit hall he glimpsed a shawled figure gliding from one room to the next and felt the hairs rise on the back of his neck. He slammed the blackened brass door-knocker several times to dispel the goosebumps. Besides, this phantom had red hair.

After what seemed like a very long wait, Julian heard someone shuffling down the hallway towards the door. Gabriel's face appeared for a moment in the glass and vanished. Another pause ensued and Julian wondered if he was going to open the door or not. Just as he raised the knocker again, the door swung inward a few inches. Gabriel thrust his acne-scarred face out, his long, stringy forelocks covering one eye.

"Yeah?" he ventured.

"Is it Lurch's day off?" Julian asked.

Gabriel seemed to consider this. "Say what?" he finally responded.

"May I come in for a moment?"

Once again, the boy seemed befuddled, unsure. Julian could see a bead of sweat run down his long, dirty-looking neck as he turned to look back into the house. His face came around again. "Um, just a minute." With that he closed the door.

Was the girl standing behind him? Did he have to consult her before allowing the police in? He's either very stupid or very nervous, Julian thought.

After another long pause, the door opened again. This time it was Morgan. She was no longer wearing the shawl and her great thatch of orangy hair hung unbound to her waist, a mass of snarls and split ends that made her look like a flaming medusa. Her paper-white face looked serene and confident. She began to speak but had to stop to clear her throat. She tried again.

"How may I help you, officer?" she asked with just a trace of peevishness.

"I'd like to talk with you inside, if I may. With you both," he added.

She seemed to consider this. The door opened all the way and she said, "Come in, if that is what you choose." Gabriel was nowhere to be seen.

"Isn't that what Dracula said to Jonathan Harker?" Julian joked. Nonetheless, this house and these people gave him the creeps.

She turned back from the parlor entrance and eyed him without a trace of humor. "I don't know what you're talking about."

"You're right," said Julian. "I think it was 'Enter of your own free will.'"

Spots of color appeared on the girl's cheeks. Julian could see that she wasn't used to being toyed with. "You may come into this room," she said. "But no further. The rest of the house is off limits to you." Now it was Julian's turn to get steamed. Gabriel sat cross-legged on an antique sofa with the stuffing spilling out, watching this exchange. Julian walked on in, intentionally not replying, not acknowledging her implied control of him. Settling herself in an upholstered, wing-backed chair, Morgan regarded them both with an imperious expression.

Julian chose not to sit and leaned back against the mildewed wallpaper. "Gabriel," he asked, "when's the last time Ryan Louper and his girlfriend were in this house?" The boy's eyes looked fearful now.

The girl interrupted. "Officer, this is my house. I think I have a right to know why we are being questioned and what it's about."

"This is your house? When did you buy it?"

She was caught off guard at this. "Well, it's my grandfather's actually, but he's let me live here for as long as I choose." The spots of color returned.

That word again. "Choose." She seemed to avoid words like will and must. "I see. So it's not *your* house." He let that hit home and continued, "I'm investigating the deaths of Ryan Louper and Rebecca Tournquist, a young couple you're both familiar with, I've been told. You've read about it in the paper, I assume?"

"We don't read the papers," she responded. "They're full of lies, half-truths, and distortions. The real truth lies within."

Julian digested this for a moment. "Well, miss, the truth is that two friends of yours are dead. I found them myself. You can take it from me, they're as dead as you can get." Julian could hear Gabriel breathing through his mouth now, hoarse, ragged.

Morgan glanced in his direction. "What makes you think they were friends of ours? Who told you that? I'd like to know who that could be."

I just bet you would, thought Julian. "Miss, I'm just trying to determine their movements prior to the *accident*. It's pretty routine, actually. And seeing as how you two were in the vicinity of the water tower at the time of their fall, I thought you might have seen or heard something. In fact, I thought you all might have been together that evening." He finished up looking at Gabriel, who sounded as if he might have an asthma attack at any moment.

She was standing now, rigid. "We've already told you, Officer. We didn't know them, and they were never with us!" She wasn't going to give Gabriel a chance. She spoke for them both now. "We've told you all that we know which is nothing!"

"Actually," Julian cut her off, "Gabriel here hasn't told me anything. Have you, Gabe?" Julian reached down and patted Gabriel's knee. "Maybe we'll talk later." Gabriel looked ashen and terrified. Julian noted that it wasn't he Gabriel was looking at though, it was the girl. "Mind if I use the bathroom?" Julian asked, seemingly oblivious to the girl's blatant hostility and the tension-laden atmosphere. "Is it down the hall here?" He walked out of the room and turned left toward the back of the house.

The girl was instantly behind him. "I want you to leave now!" she hissed.

Julian kept walking and opened the door he had seen her come out of earlier. "This it?" he called over his shoulder.

The room he was looking into was radically different from the rest of the house. It was brilliant with a kaleidoscope of light supplied by a bank of large, stained-glass windows lining the rear wall. The furnishings consisted of mounds of cushions forming divans for reclining.

His attention, however, was captured by the inner wall, which was a pulsating mural of colors depicting a landscape of people meeting their deaths in a variety of graphic ways. Head-on collisions seemed to predominate. In each case, the person's soul was shown flying heavenwards, white-robed and rapturous, from the crushed or bleeding body. It was the end of the world and the beginning of the hereafter. Julian recognized it as a crude reproduction, with numerous liberties taken, of a frightening painting known as "The Rapture." It's like looking into her squirming little brain, Julian thought.

Morgan pushed by him and slammed the door shut in his face. "Get out!" she screamed.

"Oops, thought that might be the loo," Julian responded. He turned and started for the front door, leaving Morgan guarding her inner sanctum. Gabriel stood peering into the hallway from the parlor entrance. "I'm really sorry for all the upset, Gabriel. I was just hoping to clear up this accident business and I thought you guys might be able to help. Hey, cops are people, too. We all screw up."

Julian stopped abreast of the boy and leaned into him, removing something from his pocket and holding it in his closed fingers. "Listen, Gabe, I feel awful about upsetting your girlfriend. Maybe this will make her feel better. I found it right after we stopped you guys on First Avenue the other night." He opened his hand, revealing the ankh.

Almost smiling with relief, Gabriel reached out for it. "Morgan's ankh!" he breathed. "She was afraid she'd never get it back. It was so dark..." With a gasp, he stopped in mid-sentence and snatched his hand back like Julian was holding a scorpion. The realization of what he had just said was written all over his face. Over the boy's shoulder, Julian could see the girl, who had crept silently down the hall, witnessing their exchange. Her normally pasty face was even paler and the flesh hung loose with shock. Only the tiny, muddy, green eyes looked alive, glittering with malice.

Julian held the necklace up so that she could better see it. "Gotcha!" he said and went out the door.

Back in the car, he placed his head down on the steering wheel, trying to master his excitement and fury. On the one hand, he now knew with certainty that Morgan and Gabriel had been on that tower with Ryan and his girlfriend on the night of their deaths. The motive, now that he had caught a glimpse of Morgan's character, was just as clear. She had known, as Jacob and everyone else in their little circle had known, that Ryan was an informant for the police. That's why he had taken up with this odd couple in the last few months of his life. He was setting them up. But Morgan set him up first. There was no way that she could spend a day "inside." Not her. The queen of her domain, the mistress of her own fate. May not shall.

On the other hand, Julian knew that he didn't have a shred of usable evidence. In the absence of witnesses or a confession, they would continue as if they had never stood at the top of that bloated tower looking down at those shattered young bodies.

Julian thought of the mural and briefly pictured the souls of Ryan and Rebecca flying heavenwards, in terror, from the earth. He started the car and drove away.

Back at the station, a large, manila envelope was waiting for him. It was the report on the latents from the state police. Almost holding his breath, Julian tore it open and read the report.

೧

They hit the house at two in the morning with the search warrant. Julian was a great believer in visiting suspects in the wee hours, when they were at their physical and psychological low ebb. Defenses were down and truth tended to be less elusive.

The Automated Fingerprint Identification System, or AFIS, as it was more commonly called, had done the trick. Not only had it proven that the Acid Queen and her joker had handled the sheets of LSD that had been found in Ryan's room, thereby giving Julian a shot at a distribution charge, it also revealed that both had faced similar charges in the past. They could no longer deny that they had known the dead couple.

Morgan had been smart enough to destroy any sheets they had lying around the castle after Julian's visit, but she had underestimated the cops. Something Julian had counted on. The chemicals for making her brew were found in various locations throughout the house. In the servants' quarters, they found a paper perforator and a hand-operated silkscreen press. The stencil was a dancing bear.

Morgan had been carried out screaming that she was a chemistry major. Gabriel had remained silent. Julian saw to it that they were transported separately to the station and kept that way.

❧

Julian was sitting facing the door of the interview room when they brought Gabriel to him. He took a long moment to just look at the boy, who was shivering like someone with St. Vitus Dance. Looking down at the floor to avoid Julian's eyes, he wrapped his arms around himself. Julian, with careful enunciation, read him his Miranda warning, and Gabriel nodded his head to indicate that he understood his rights. He doesn't trust himself to speak, thought Julian.

"Gabriel," Julian began, "there's very little I need from you in reference to the drug charges you're facing here. I think the evidence will stand alone on that pretty well. Do you understand me?"

Gabriel's teeth began to chatter, making a slight clacking sound in the concrete room. He nodded again.

"There's another reason I have you in here. I think you know what that is, don't you?"

Gabriel looked up at Julian now. His eyes wet, beseeching. Julian couldn't tell if he wanted him to stop or go on and get it over with. His hope buoyed. If ever a suspect was on the verge of breaking, this was him…

"The water tower, Gabe, that's what we need to talk about." The young man began to rock back and forth, his eyes squeezed shut." I think you can tell me what happened up there that night, can't you? I know you were there, and I think you need to tell someone. If you help me with this, I'll go to bat for you with the prosecutor. I can't make any promises, but I'll try." The tempo of the rocking increased, and Julian saw that he was biting hard on his lower lip. Still nothing.

"It's the girl, Morgan, isn't it? Are you trying to protect her, Gabriel? Is that it?" Gabriel stood suddenly, still rocking like a crazy person. Julian stood, too.

"I know what happened up there wasn't your fault, Gabriel. It was her idea, but she needed you, didn't she? Because there were two of them, she needed you up there."

Without warning, Gabriel slammed his forehead hard into the cinder block wall. Before Julian could get around the desk that separated them, he did it again. Grabbing him, Julian spun him around. Gabriel's forehead was red and abraded, spots of blood showing.

"You don't understand her!" the boy wailed. "You don't understand her!"

"Then tell me!" Julian demanded.

They looked at each other and Julian could see the struggle in the other's face. After a moment, Gabriel simply murmured, "I can't."

Julian felt the elation of the day's events draining from his system and being replaced by a loathing for this bizarre couple that he could barely contain. He could see his chance of convicting the girl for the murders of Ryan and Rebecca falling away from him. The boy was a coward, more afraid of Morgan than the police.

"You're terrified of her, aren't you?" Julian hissed.

Something like dignity tried to make its way into Gabriel's face and failed. "We made a pact," he whispered. "We made a pact for as long as we live on this plane of existence."

Julian backed up a step, disgusted. "Get out of here. A medic will take a look at your head before you go back to your cell."

Alone, with his face in his hands, Julian weighed his remaining options.

☙

It was dawn when he had Morgan brought in. She looked exhausted but defiant. Julian knew that bail money for the both of them was enroute from her generous grandfather. He ignored the preliminaries, having made his decision in the quiet, predawn hours. Anything that was said in this room would never end up in a court of law.

They sat staring at each other like battle-weary vets. Tired, but not vanquished. Julian knew better than to bluff that her partner had squealed on her. She would find out the truth as soon as their bail arrived. No doubt, she knew her man pretty well in any case. Julian broke the silence.

"Morgan, I'm not going to detain you for long. As you know, our case against you for the manufacture and distribution of LSD is rock-solid."

"That's bullshit!" she spat out. "I'm a chemistry major and I've got the transcripts to prove it!"

Julian cut her off, "I'm sure you do. Not just any idiot can whip up a batch of acid. However, some of the chemicals you had in your possession are illegal in themselves, and taken together with your little set up, I don't think we'll have any problem proving our case."

He let her glare at him while it sank in.

"Your problems go just a little deeper than that though. You've got priors. Probation won't even be an issue in your case. You *will* do time. Five to ten years… for starters."

"What the hell is that supposed to mean—starters?"

Julian noticed that her choice of words and phrasing was cruder now than in their previous meetings. She was tired, ragged. He began the lie.

"It means this." He threw the ankh onto the desktop and let it lie there between them. For the first time, he saw actual fear in her face. She looked as if she wanted to run from the room. The expression was gone in a second, replaced by the roiling clouds of fury that seemed her natural state.

"Your boyfriend has already identified this as belonging to you, but I took it a step further. See where the thong is broken?" He held up the ends for her to see. "I had the prosecutor's lab take some scrapings from it for DNA analysis. It'll take a few days for the results. Then I'll be coming after you with a court order for some blood. I think you know what the results will be. How is your neck, by the way? All better?"

Like Gabriel, she stood up suddenly. Julian remained in his seat.

"You can stand, if you like, Morgan, but you *may* not leave." She glared at him. "So, you see, Morgan, that sample is going to place you at the scene—opportunity, it's called. Your fingerprints on the sheets of acid that Ryan got from you provide a motive. Motive, opportunity, and means. And the means were simple enough. You got them stoned and suggested a trip to the water tower. I imagine you guys had been up there before. It must be a great place to watch the world from when you're stoned. After they got settled, leaning over the railing and watching the world go by, you launched them. You took the girl, obviously, since we found your necklace in her hand. Gave you a bit of trouble, did she?"

"You're making all this up, you lying bastard!" she screamed.

Julian reached out and placed his hand over the ankh. "Morgan, you're going to spend the rest of your life in prison… following other people's orders. That'll be the hateful part for you, I imagine, no longer being in control and controlling others, but on the receiving end. That's what this has all been about, hasn't it? You lost control of Ryan, or thought you had, and he presented a threat to your little world, so you removed him... and the girl. Just to make sure. It wasn't murder, though. You were just sending them to the 'other side'... a little early, maybe. But rest assured that if anyone should dare to suggest the death penalty for you, I'll be the first to protest it, because that would be the easy way out for you, wouldn't it? After all, *you* don't fear the reaper, do you, Morgan? *Do* you?"

She launched herself at him, scratching three grooves down his cheek before Shane rushed in and dragged her back to her cell. Gabriel and Morgan were both released that same morning. Julian didn't have to wait long.

℮

This time the jumpers were spotted right away, thanks to the spotlights the borough had just placed at the bottom of the tower to illuminate the catwalk. Quite a crowd had gathered even before the police arrived. The girl wasted little time, according to witnesses, but dove with arms spread wide, flashing briefly in the glare of the lights before vanishing into the darkness at the base of the tower.

The young man remained motionless, with his back pressed against the wall of the tank, and the giant letters CAMELOT emblazoned above his head.

He was still there when Julian arrived and found Shane trying to talk him down with a loudspeaker. Leaving his car, Julian walked up to his perspiring partner. "Shane, when you get him down from there, bring him to me. He has something he can tell me now." With that, he turned and started back for his patrol car, thinking of two young people who would never grow old and their grieving parents and wondering if his own children were asleep yet.

Jack and the Devil
(2013)

When the old man awoke and pried his gummy eyes apart, he found the devil waiting. Sitting across from him in broad daylight, the brazen demon said what he always said at such meetings, "Stay with us, Jack... or you'll be mine if you don't." Jack's thready breath wheezed in his aching throat and his clumsy fingers scrambled for his Rosary.

"Looking for this?" the devil asked, draping the emerald colored prayer beads and crucifix over his horns. "Well, just jump up and get it," he laughed, and shook his head from side to side, making the tiny crucified figure dance before his black and sparkling eyes. Jack, with a near heart-stopping catch in his breath at such blasphemy, retreated back into unconsciousness and dreams of his life before the devil.

☙

It was mid-morning the next day and Jack eyed the bird uneasily. It sat on a branch outside the window of the den and eyed him back. To his experience it was uncommonly large and green, or at least greenish, and the thin mesh of the screen did not appear substantial enough to prevent its entering the room. He thought it appeared to be considering this as an option as it studied his emaciated, and helpless figure, prostrate on his daughter's sofa. He thought of his Irish grandmother's dark tales of the Morrigan, a female spirit of terror and greatness who would appear in the form of a crow to choose which champion must die on the field of battle and be feasted upon. But this was no crow. He pondered whether the devil had sent this creature to watch over him and decided that he had. He had found it hungrily watching him on several occasions.

The oxygen pump continued its comforting hum as it supplied him with breath but prevented him from hearing where his caregiver was in the house. The television set blathered on as well. It was left on for him all day, though he slipped in and out of sleep so often that he rarely understood what was happening on the programs. Increasingly, he found he didn't care.

He did care about the bird, though, and he shifted his watery eyes to the right to see if Brittany was anywhere close. The bird bent its head to scrape at its talons with a beak cruelly curved for rending, while the claws of its feet gripped the branch with a power that set the leaves into soft trembling motion. Still, it continued to regard Jack as it groomed itself, the ruby red eyes blinking from time to time in a speculative manner—a butcher preparing his knives.

"Britt," Jack managed to croak. The oxygen dried his mouth out, but he could scarcely take a sip of water without choking due to the cancer in his throat. He had no idea if he was being loud enough but thought it unwise to appear panicked before the green raptor. He whispered as loudly as he dared, "Brittany!" The bird's head came up and the eyes seemed to darken to the color of old blood.

There was a clatter of something metal from the direction of the kitchen and the sound of voices, a male's as well as the aide's. *Thank God... Julian's home*, he thought with relief. *He'll know what to do about the bird.*

A hot wind blew through the open window smelling of dusty feathers and rotting meat and Jack turned back to his tormentor. The branch swayed up and down... abandoned. From the front of the house a door slammed. Jack turned his head once more expecting his son-in-law to come striding in, but there was no one there. Irritated, he muttered something under his breath and after a few moments was asleep once more.

∽

"How are you, Jack?"

Jack glanced over at his son-in-law, embarrassed at having been caught talking to himself. Often, as he said his prayers, or the decades of the Rosary, he found that he would drift off to resume conversations with his wife, Marilyn, gone for twelve years now, or other people from his past and real life. It also irritated him to be interrupted at it.

"Couldn't get home for lunch, eh?" Jack offered as a greeting.

Julian, still in uniform, adjusted his sidearm so that he could slide into the wicker chair across from his wife's father. "It *is* lunchtime, Jack," he replied, then smiled. "Been missing me?"

"How can I miss anybody?" Jack croaked. "People never stop coming and going in this house—nurses, caregivers, priests... *others*... it's a feckin' parade around..." He choked and coughed, and Julian dipped a small sponge into some juice on the coffee table.

"Here," he urged. "Swab your mouth a little, you're dry as dust."

Jack snatched it from his hand and proceeded to scrub at his teeth, gums, and tongue—the apple juice as sweet as the nectar of the gods. When he was done he shoved the little sponge-on-a-stick toward Julian and released it before his son-in-law could react. Julian said nothing and picked it up. The nurse's aide appeared at his elbow and took it away.

"He's been a little worked up today," Brittany said over her shoulder.

"*Others…*" Julian enquired. "What others, Jack?"

The old man knew better than to cross the devil and held his peace.

Julian tried again, "What's worrying you today, Jack? Is there something you need? Are you in pain?" He knew Jack's pain was growing worse, but the old man would rarely admit to it.

Jack struggled to sit up a little straighter against the pillows piled behind him—he never lay prone anymore as it interfered with his breathing and hurt his neck. After some puffing, squirming, and a little alteration of his original position, he thrust a thin freckled arm at the open window. "That green bird was out there again."

Julian glanced in the direction of the pointing finger and studied the empty branch. He wondered if it might be too much morphine, or too little, then thought of how to reply. "How big is this bird, Jack?"

Jack used his hands to illustrate a space of nearly a foot. "Big bastard," he wheezed.

Julian ran a hand through his graying, close-cropped hair and agreed, "That *is* a big bastard… *green*, you say?"

Jack nodded his head, defiance written in his features.

"Well," Julian ventured. "It's possible that someone's had a parrot get loose, this time of year I would think a parrot could survive alright... for a while. I remember the Sawyers down the street had a parakeet escape a few years ago and we saw him flitting around the neighborhood for weeks... then the cold weather set in and we stopped seeing him."

Jack leaned toward his son-in-law and whispered, "He wants to get at me Julian... wants my liver." He turned a filmy eye on Brittany in the kitchen, then raised a finger to his lips to indicate that this was between the two men.

Glancing her way as well, Julian nodded his agreement, then stood up. The hallucinations, the delusions were getting worse, there was no doubt of that, he thought. But was it from dope, or pain? The doctor had informed Anne and him that too much pain could cause worse hallucinations than too much morphine, but with Jack it was difficult to know—he was such a stoic, insisting on the smallest doses of painkiller possible, as he wanted to keep a "clear mind" to attend to his affairs... and his prayers.

"How about we do your feeding now, you must be getting hungry?"

Jack nodded, and the bird forgotten, began to drag out the tubing he kept secured in his waistband that terminated within his stomach.

In the kitchen Julian opened the can of liquid that would serve as Jack's lunch and poured it into a container. As he suctioned up the prescribed amount into the plastic syringe he asked Brittany, "You haven't seen this big bird that keeps worrying him, have you?"

Brittany, a tiny, attractive girl of twenty-two, smiled at Julian and answered without a trace of irony, "No, I'm sorry, but I haven't."

Julian looked over the counter and into the den to see his father-in-law holding aloft the end of the uncapped tube like an offering, patiently awaiting his return. The former altar boy laid low, Julian thought. Not for the first time, he was overwhelmed by the sheer courage that the frail, helpless old man displayed, and recalled a remark he had made during the first few weeks after having moved in: "I'm not afraid to meet my Maker," he had rasped, "but I'm in no hurry to do it either." Then he had winked and begun the hospice program that would shepherd him to the end of his days.

With a sigh, Julian approached the dying man and began the task of administering his nourishment, being careful to avoid any splash-back onto the crisp uniform that he wore as Chief of the Camelot Beach Police Department.

☙

That night at dinner, Julian related his lunchtime experience with Jack. As he spoke to his wife of three decades he noticed her hands trembling a little. He stopped speaking and, reaching across the table, placed one of his hands on her smaller one. She looked up at him, the trembling having now migrated to her lips.

"Anne," he offered, "I'm sorry. I don't know why I bother you with this stuff. Jack's doing okay, he's not suffering." He felt a slight twinge of guilt for being less than forthcoming.

The sound of the TV reached them from the den; it was one of Jack's favorite game shows. He was a great lover of puzzles, a formidable crossword solver, and a sketch artist of some talent. Though, of late, Julian often found the daily paper's offerings unfinished; the penciled drawings the scribbling of a toddler. Jack's own life was becoming a confusing collage of fact and fantasy, reality and dream, as his mind began to pursue his body into death.

Anne shook her head and squeezed back on his hand. "It's not that," she assured him. "It's you... I feel so badly that you've inherited so much of the burden with Dad. You do everything for him, and between the department and here you're exhausted."

Julian smiled, touched by the tears that he knew now were partly shed for him. "It's not that big a deal," he assured her. "Now that we've got the nurses rotating through and Brittany coming each day, I hardly do a thing... I feed him his lunch.

"Fortunately, I'm the boss, so I can come home when I need to," he continued, "but you've got a classroom of kids. You can't just walk out on them each time a nurse calls or Brittany has a problem with Jack."

"It's you, Julian. He doesn't want anyone else doing for him but you."

Laughing, Julian answered, "Yeah, it's his punishment for me marrying his favorite daughter—at long last, the revenge of Jack!"

Anne laughed now, too, her green eyes still sparkling with tears, and Julian was reminded once again of how he would endure anything if it brought her happiness, or even the slightest chance of it.

He stood and began to help with clearing the dishes, while from the den he heard Jack croak out, "Woodrow Wilson, you igit!" A breeze blew through the open dining room window, clean and cool, with just a hint of smoke and dying leaves. It was early October and the evenings were, at last, breathing the promise of autumn after a long, stunningly hot summer. Anne had already begun to decorate the house for Halloween, the dining room walls festooned with a history of their grown children's trick-or-treat masks. But the season also brought the promise of darkness, of the end of life and youth. Julian shuddered, not just for Jack's dwindling days, but for his wife's coming loss, and at how death inched ever closer no matter where one stood.

When he entered the kitchen, he saw Jack trying to catch his attention with a now-familiar gesture: He held up a hand with his thumb and index fingers an inch apart. Julian saw him mouth the time-worn phrase, "A small one," and smile mischievously.

Julian smiled back and mouthed in return, "Coming right up," as he reached under the counter for the bottle of Irish whiskey that was a cure for all things in Jack's world. He knew that the old man would barely get a sip of it past his lips, but it pleased him so much to receive it that Julian was happy to serve it up.

With a shot glass in each hand, Julian joined Jack in the den, and the two began to negotiate which post-season ball game would be watched that night, though the outcome was a foregone conclusion: Jack assured his son-in-law that his Yankees were the only team worth watching and that Julian's Phillies were, at best, a jumped-up farm team.

"So I've been hearing for the past several decades," Julian remarked, then added slyly, "I'm surprised that your Yanks even bother to play anymore since they're *that* good."

Just as slyly, Jack responded, "It's only to keep in practice, in case they meet anyone worth playing."

❧

The following morning Father Gregory tapped on the door of the Hall residence. Within he could hear the chatter and predictable bursts of laughter provided by the television. He tapped a little harder.

He had spent the first few hours of his day making the rounds of the hospital-bound parishioners of St. Brendan's Parish, as well as tending to the needs and administering the Eucharist to any other errant Catholics he came across. Though he had been unable to manage breakfast with Chief J, as was often their habit when time permitted, he was well aware of the father-in-law's condition. It was a topic often on the policeman's mind and the Indian cleric could see the toll the situation was taking on his good friend—he appeared very tired most days, and his patience and concentration had clearly been affected. Dashing back and forth betwixt a stressful job and a dying relative, only to spend one's night trying to keep a delirious, and sometimes frantic, old man from climbing out of bed and falling onto the floor, could have no other outcome. The nights were hard on the dying, the priest knew well, but sometimes far worse on their loved ones.

The door was flung open by a large, heavyset woman with a mop of blonde curls. "Oh," she snapped, shifting a black, overstuffed bag onto her shoulder. "I didn't hear anyone at the door." Medical gear festooned the outer pockets of the carryall: a stethoscope, tongue depressors, and a host of digital apparatus that Father Gregory could only guess at as to their purpose. She stared down at the dark, little man. "You're here for Jack, then?" It was less a question than a statement.

Father Gregory took a step backward to avoid the bulk of the woman. "Ah, yes," he exclaimed, "exactly so."

From within the house, a more familiar female voice called out, "Who's at the door, Tessie?" Father Gregory remembered the aide from previous visits, a charming, if somewhat cloying girl— she was always hovering at one's elbow it seemed to the priest.

The woman who was Tessie barked over her heavily-laden shoulder, "It's a priest, got a funny accent." She smiled without a trace of sincerity and pushed past the clergyman, the odor of recently smoked cigarettes trailing in her wake.

Passing on into the house, the priest gently shut the door behind him. Brittany came around the corner drying her hands on a dishtowel. "Oh, hi," she said.

"Yes, hello," Father Gregory returned. "I hope I have not come at a difficult time," and glanced over his shoulder in the direction of the departing nurse.

"Don't worry about her," she laughed. "I don't think she much likes anyone… especially me," she added, smiling. "I don't let it bother me, it's just her way."

Father Gregory was impressed with the girl's equanimity and smiled back. "That is very admirable of you, dear girl. And how is Mister Jack today? Did he have a better night?"

Brittany's smile dimmed. "Not according to the chief. They were up with him several times. Jack kept shouting about a demon being after him."

The priest's smile also vanished at these words. "He spoke of a demon? Oh dear, this is not a good sign. In my experience, such visions mean the patient's mind is coming loose, and oftentimes, that the end is very near."

They walked into the kitchen together. "Don't you believe in demons and the devil?" Brittany asked. "You're a priest."

Glancing into the den, he saw that Jack was propped up on the couch in his usual position, the nasal cannula attached to his nostrils. The sounds of the TV and the oxygen machine prevented the old man from hearing them. "Oh yes, assuredly so," he answered, "without a doubt, yes. But I must say that, in this case, I think visitations by evil spirits to be quite out of the question, you see." The girl shook her head in puzzlement, as she did not see at all.

"No evil spirits would trouble Mister Jack," Father Gregory chuckled. "He is a most good man. He prays his Rosary every day and was an altar server until his illness, don't you know!" The priest held wide his hands, surely all was obvious now.

"Well," the young caregiver murmured, unconvinced, "I still think you'd better talk to him about all that."

The wattage of Father Gregory's smile dimmed. *I am forever having trouble communicating with these Americans,* he thought. A native Tamil speaker who was also fluent in Hindi and Latin, American English continued to confound him, though he never lost hope that he would become its master. *With the help of God,* he reminded himself.

Jack only noticed the priest as he approached and raised a shaking hand as if to ward him off. "Goddamn," he rasped.

"Mr. Jack," Father Gregory spoke in a gentle tone, "do not be afraid… it is me, Father Gregory from St. Brendan's."

Jack's hand came down by degrees and the little priest could see that he was panting for breath.

"Please forgive me, I have startled you," Father Gregory continued, seating himself in the same wicker chair favored by his police friend. "I am so sorry."

Jack's eyes came clear as he took in his visitor. "Yeah, I know who you are, Father… I remember you were just here a few days ago. I thought you might be…" he cast a cagey look at the curate, then went silent, his gaze drifting to the window and the beautiful day outside.

"You thought I might be who?" Father Gregory asked, resting his folded hands on his round belly.

He caught the old man sizing him up from the corner of his eye. "Nobody…" he answered, looking away again.

The priest was not to be put off. "Come now, Mr. Jack, I must insist. You are not to keep secrets from your confessor; surely you are aware of this fact?"

He knew that he was actually fudging things a bit, but since any moment could be Jack's last, nothing was unimportant as it pertained to his soul's preparation for the hereafter.

"I must insist," he repeated.

"Alright, damnit," Jack responded, "seeing as how you're my priest and all." He stopped and seemed to be considering how to proceed. "I don't think I've done anything wrong," he began, "at least, nothing serious. Anything serious I got taken care of long ago, right before Marilyn died. I didn't always do right by her, Father." He tapped himself over the heart out of reflex, as if in the confessional. "I still feel bad about it sometimes even so."

"Yes, yes," Father Gregory persisted, "but we must stick to what is the matter now! You are quite troubled, this I can see. Please tell me."

"I thought everything was set, you know. I've been faithful to God and the Holy Mother, but lately I've been getting scared."

"Of what are you frightened?"

There was a pause. "Things," Jack answered at last.

"Things… what are these things?"

Jack licked his chapped and flaky lips and glanced away as Father Gregory became aware that the girl had crept up on them and stood at his elbow. She held out a moistened sponge for Jack. "This might help," she said.

"Thank you… very good." The priest snatched the stick from her hand and passed it over to Jack who began to scrub at his mouth, a look of pleasure and relief transforming his pinched expression. "Now please leave us, dear girl. We need a few moments of privacy, if you would be so kind."

Brittany fled the room to make up Jack's hospital bed. This rested behind some screens in the living room as he could no longer climb the stairs to the extra bedroom. The advent of dying had all but robbed him of any privacy.

Jack flung the sponge onto the coffee table and regarded his interrogator anew.

"Please do go on, dear man. *Things…?*" Father Gregory prompted.

"The nuns in school called him the 'noonday devil,'" Jack answered at last, a look of fear in his rheumy eyes. "You heard of him, Father? You should have."

Father Gregory moistened his own lips as he contemplated the phrase, then lit upon its origin. "Ah yes," he exclaimed. "Psalms, yes… but, of course it is!" He was delighted at his recall and quoted the pertinent verse, "Thou shalt not be afraid of the arrow that flieth in the day… or of the noonday devil. Nothing shalt thou have to fear from nightly terrors… from the pestilence that walks to and fro in the darkness." Chuckling, he halted and said, "Oh dear, we are both remembering the old version, I'm afraid, but the revised is much less picturesque, though I shouldn't be saying so—the devil is replaced with the 'destruction' that wastes at noonday… not quite the same thing, I am thinking."

The clergyman glanced over at his charge and found the old man gazing out the window.

"My apology, Mister Jack, I do get carried away. Please tell me more about this 'devil.'"

Jack turned at the priest's words and regarded him with suspicion. At last, he spoke once more. "He sends a vulture, or some kind of bird, to keep a watch on me when he's not around," he whispered. "I'm afraid, Father. The devil tells me that there's nothing after this life… no heaven, no purgatory… just nothing. He even said that my Marilyn… my wife, is not waiting for me on the other side. I've been hoping that she would be, Father… along with my parents… I've always believed in that… always… but now…" He trailed off uncertainly.

Father Gregory heard the tears in the dying man's voice and felt a growing and righteous fury at this "devil," even if it was only the devil of "doubt." But wasn't that exactly how the church doctors had characterized the "Noonday Devil" of scripture, as the purveyor of doubt and slothfulness of spirit, the great distractor when it came to matters of salvation?

"Dear Jack," Father Gregory resumed, "what else does this devil say to you, good man, that he should shake your faith so? Tell me exactly his words."

The old man turned back to his confessor, tears now standing in his crusty eyes. "He says that I should hang on to life as long as I can, Father, no matter what, and no matter how bad it gets, because there's just nothingness on the other side... just nothingness and darkness, only the unending blackness of hell everlasting."

Rubbing at his burning eyes like a little child, Jack asked, "That's not true, is it, Father? That can't be true, can it?"

"No, Jack," Father Gregory said with absolute conviction. "It is *not* true... it is a *damned* lie."

The old man grinned at having provoked such language from a man of the cloth and dabbed at his eyes with a grey, unclean-looking handkerchief. "Got yer goat, did I, Father?"

"The Psalm also goes on to remind us," Father Gregory continued, "that the Lord set angels to watch over us and guard us from the devil and his minions. Call upon the mighty Archangel, St. Michael, the next time you are confronted by this demon and he will be banished. Of this you must have no doubt."

Jack nodded his head in tentative agreement.

"Do you know the prayer of St. Michael?"

Again Jack nodded.

"Then let us say it now together in order to gird your loins and banish this devil!"

The priest knelt next to the couch and seized Jack's dry, veiny hands within his own, and together they began to pray aloud.

Brittany, rounding the corner from the other room, took in the extraordinary tableau for several silent moments, then turned on her heel and fled into the kitchen to call her boyfriend and describe the remarkable proceedings occurring in the Hall household.

ॐ

That night was a restless one for Julian's father-in-law, as he was up several times to answer the old man's cries for help and his desperate attempts to escape the confines of his bed. So it was with the greatest reluctance that he agreed to meet his friend and priest, Father Gregory, for breakfast.

Julian staggered into the Luna Boardwalk Café having failed to shave before work for the first time since he could remember. He had chosen to wear "civvies" that day, thinking it would be easier than getting into uniform. Instead, he had somehow ended up wearing a dark blue shirt *and* sports jacket, and a tie that was a green tartan. At least with the trousers he had managed neutral beige. He hadn't notice that his socks reflected the difference betwixt his shirt and tie, each one supporting a different garment in the conflict.

Father Gregory was both shocked and amused at the appearance of the policeman. He motioned him over to their usual table by the window, where Julian plopped down.

"You are exhausted my good friend," he murmured, signaling the young man waiting their table for coffee.

Julian stared wordlessly out at the Atlantic, grey and heaving, despite the crystalline beauty of the autumn day. Strollers were on the beach, appearing carefree and happy, wearing scarves and light jackets and making the most of the good weather while it remained. He found himself envying them. Yet, soon, that would all change, he thought, as the sea was already warning of the coming winter… the inevitable season of darkness.

The coffee mug was smacked onto the scratched tabletop, causing it to slosh over the sides.

"Sorry," the young waiter apologized. "Sorry, Chief. I'll clean that up."

Waving him away with a smile, Father Gregory said, "Please do not trouble yourself, young man. We have plenty of napkins available to us and will attend to it. Thank you."

With a worried glance at Julian, the teenager fled the table and hurried towards the kitchen—he had heard of the young waitress arrested for murder in this very restaurant just a few years before and was made nervous by the man responsible.

"Our usual," Father Gregory called out to the retreating figure.

He turned back to Julian. "Please speak, my friend. Whatever is weighing on you cannot be as bad as all that."

Julian's bloodshot eyes swiveled to meet those of the cleric. "Sometimes, Father... sometimes, I wish it were all over... the dying, I mean," he whispered across the small tabletop. "God help me, there are moments that I've wished that... that Jack would just die and be done with it!"

Father Gregory was struck dumb for a moment by Julian's emotion, and the great and rising tide of guilt behind it.

"Yes, yes, it's perfectly understandable... anyone in your position has felt these very feelings. Your entire life is not only on hold, but the work and stress has all but been doubled by this responsibility. Only our Lord Himself would be unbowed before such an undertaking. Do not waste another moment punishing yourself for such errant thoughts—your actions remain noble, as they must, your true heart would never betray you."

"Anne and I were up so many times last night that I have no idea how she's going to get through a day with a classroom full of kindergartners. The morphine just doesn't seem to be working. He's getting worse and worse, and no amount calms him down. The hospice nurses have told me that he can receive a dose every hour if needed to keep him comfortable, and we're doing that... but it doesn't seem to be helping him. Nothing does. Maybe we're overdosing him... Christ, at this point I'm worried I'm going to kill him!"

"No, no," Father Gregory intervened, "you mustn't think so. Perhaps it would be helpful for you to know that Jack, too, is greatly troubled. Perhaps this lies at the center of his hallucinations."

Julian looked at the priest over a mug of trembling coffee. "What do you mean?"

"He says that he has been visited by a demon… the Noonday Devil, to use his own words. This devil is very wicked, Chief J., and taunts his faith and tempts him to despair. He is cruel with his poisoner's words, assuring dear Mister Jack that there is no afterlife, that his dear wife does not await him there in heaven with the saints."

"By God," Julian whispered, "he said that?"

Father Gregory nodded.

Julian looked out to the ocean once more. A single gull hung suspended above the waves like a kite on a string. "Poor Jack," he said at last. "He doesn't deserve this. I've never known a man with greater faith than him, and now, at the moment he needs it the most, it abandons him." He looked back at his close friend to find him studying a wrinkled piece of paper in his hands.

The priest slid it across the table to him. "Here is the face of the devil… Jack drew it for me."

Julian picked up the stained piece of lined notebook paper and looked at the face of Jack's infernal enemy. The rendering was certainly not up to Jack's old standards but served well enough to give an impression. The face of the devil was almost comically stereotypical with a pointed chin beard, curling mustache, exaggeratedly arched eyebrows, a great hooked nose and, of course, the required horns. Because it was a pencil drawing it failed to convey the skin coloring, though Julian guessed that had Jack had the means, it would've been a blazing red as befit most children's idea of the Evil One.

Their food arrived, and as the young waiter cautiously slid the plates in front of his customers, Julian folded the drawing up and placed it in a jacket pocket. "Mind if I hang onto this?" he asked Father Gregory. He didn't know why he wanted it, but a lifetime as a policeman made him reluctant to let go of anything that might be evidence… even if it was only evidence of Jack's crumbling mental armor.

"Of course," the priest replied, "if you find it helpful."

"Helpful?" Julian repeated vaguely, staring at his cooling eggs as Father Gregory tucked into his own breakfast with vigor.

☙

That evening, as Julian walked up the driveway to his home, he met the bird. He couldn't think what had drawn his attention to it; perhaps some slight movement had betrayed its perch amongst the leaves of the branch it sat upon. Or had he subconsciously been searching for it since Jack first told him of the creature?

He froze so as not to frighten it off. In the fading rays of the day's sun, it did appear greenish, but Julian's sharper, younger eyes could discern that it was just a trick of the light amongst the still-green leaves that gave it this tint. In fact, its breast was a speckled grey, while its wings, back, and head appeared a velvety blue. And he *was* a big bastard, just as Jack had described. He stood a foot in height and was nervously dividing his attention between Julian and the next-door neighbor's bird feeder, which was receiving a heavy traffic in much smaller birds. Clearly, Julian was interrupting the raptor's plans for supper.

Anne appeared at the front door, a hand raised to shield her eyes from the slanting rays of the sun. "What are you looking at?" she called out to her husband.

With that, the predator's nerve was broken, and he fell forward from the branch, throwing out his great wings all in a single motion. Julian ducked down out of reflex, and no small thrill of fear. With two powerful strokes of its broad wings the great bird disappeared into the darkening woods at the back of the house, his intended victims scattering in every direction at his passage.

Straightening up with a puzzled look, Julian answered, "Maybe the devil."

ℰℐ

The devil was waiting for Jack when he awoke. He had no idea of the time but thought that Julian had been home to feed him his liquefied lunch and had since returned to work. He blinked in the sunbeams slanting into the room and saw him sitting in the same wicker chair his son-in-law favored. He felt his bowels loosen in fear, and worse, the hot sting of humiliating tears spring forth from his sore eyes. The pain in his throat and lungs was acute and radiated from its source to the very skin that he wore. The devil, his face its usual rictus of malice, leaned towards him.

"Don't die on me, Jack. If you do, I'll eat that rotten liver of yours that you're always worried about. I'll save a bite for the big green bird, too. He'll enjoy that."

Jack cringed deeper into the cushions he lay helpless upon.

"You can tough it out, old man." The voice was mockingly young and strong. "The longer you last, the better it'll be for you when you do finally croak... scout's honor." The demon raised his right hand with the middle finger extended in parody of the time-honored salute, then chuckled.

Jack looked past his tormentor into the kitchen; as always when Satan made an appearance, Brittany was nowhere to be found. Perhaps the devil held her spellbound somewhere in the house. Then he thought of the prayer.

"Saint Michael the Archangel," he began, managing to unseal his coated tongue from the roof of his mouth, "defend us in the day of battle; be our safeguard against the wiles and wickedness of the devil."

The devil, half-rising from his comfortable seat, said, "What's that, Jack? What'd you say?"

Jack took strength from the words of the ancient prayer and struggled to raise himself. "May God rebuke him, we humbly pray, and do thou, O prince of the heavenly host, by the power of God…"

The devil leapt up and raised a large, long-fingered hand to point at Jack. "Stop that babbling, you old bastard. Nobody can even understand what you're saying anyway… and stay *down!*"

He pushed Jack deeper into the couch and the old man could see clearly the oily eyes set deep within the hideous, rigid face, eyes dancing with glee at his powerlessness. Rather than the devil's touch frightening him more, Jack found within himself a growing righteous anger.

"Cast into hell, Satan," Jack continued, ever more loudly now, even as there was a crash from the front of the house, "and all evil spirits that prowl about the world seeking the ruin of souls!"

And then the angel appeared. Just as he broke into a coughing fit for his efforts that he feared might rupture his spleen, a shadow passed across his vision, and the powerful Archangel swept down upon his adversary, his right arm raised in might.

With a bellow of fury, the angel struck down the squealing devil, now made small and ridiculous by this wrathful apparition, armed not with the sword or spear with which Jack had always seen him depicted, but with a lowly truncheon. Michael gave no heed to the devil's pleas for mercy, but rained blows down upon him, chastising the demon with a workman-like vigor and thoroughness. The girl, Brittany, screamed and screamed from somewhere nearby.

When, at last, the fearsome angel grew weary, he visited a final and terrible injury on his foe, ripping the hideous, taunting face of the devil clean of his skull and throwing it at the nurse's aide as she fled the house. But before the angel could turn and reveal his own radiant face, Jack felt himself slipping away into a warm, rushing darkness, a mortal tide that scoured his mind of all its fears and cleansed his body of all its pain. And as a long, rattling breath loosed itself from his body, a sweeter, warmer one brushed his lips like a feather, and he heard Marilyn say, "Hello, darling, I've missed you so much."

☙

Father Gregory sat with his grieving friends at their dining room table amidst the remains of a light dinner. It had been a long day for them all: Besides the arrest of the nurse's aide and her boyfriend, there had been the arrangements for the removal of Jack's body and all the notifications that had to be made as a result of his death. Julian and Anne had insisted that their priest stay for dinner, and wishing to be of some comfort to them, as well as being more than a little curious about the details of the day's extraordinary doings, he had agreed.

"So, my dear friends," Father Gregory began, "please explain to me how you determined that Mister Jack's devil was real. I must admit that I was floored when I heard, absolutely floored."

Julian smiled a little. "It was the bird. I met Jack's bird. He's apparently been haunting the neighborhood because of the bird feeder next door. It was a Goshawk according to the material I Googled, and it looked just like he described it, and that started me thinking: If Jack had been so dead-on about the hawk, might there be something to the devil story?

"So I took out the drawing he had made and showed it to Anne... she knew what it was immediately, and I should have, too: It was a rendering of a Halloween mask she kept hanging on that wall for decoration." He pointed to an empty space amidst an array of masks. "It was one our son had worn years ago, she felt certain of it. The only problem I had with that was that Jack couldn't get around on his own steam and hadn't been in this room since he got here. He had never spent Halloween here before either… so how did he know what this particular mask looked like? Admittedly, it was pretty generic, but after the bird sighting, well… you can see where I started to go with this."

Father Gregory nodded his round head in agreement, full of admiration for his friend. "It finally becomes clear to me why you are chief," he smiled.

"Well, thank you so much for noticing," Julian responded coolly.

"But why…" the little priest began.

"The same question I asked myself," Julian cut him off. "*If* someone was entering the house and wearing the mask, then *why* were they doing it? What was to be gained by it, besides terrifying a helpless old man?" Anne winced and Julian reached across and took her hand into his. "But when I really thought about it, it became obvious—the morphine. It had to be. What else did Jack have that anyone would want? It also made sense of what Jack told you, of what the 'devil' said about not dying… staying alive to avoid the nothingness of death. He just wanted Jack to hang on—in ever-growing pain since they were robbing him of his morphine, so that the drug would keep getting delivered to the house and they could keep stealing it, cutting it, and selling it— the morphine we were giving *him* was nothing but water.

"Once I had all that figured out, I put the house under surveillance… I didn't have to wait long."

"Their sin was very black indeed," Father Gregory murmured. "It was bad enough to torture the poor man, but to attempt to rob him of his faith... unforgivable! Well..." he corrected himself, "... *almost* unforgivable."

The priest rose and, murmuring his thanks for the meal, made slowly for the door. Julian and Anne, exhausted by the day and their loss, remained seated. With his hand on the door handle, Father Gregory paused and turned. Julian was waiting for it.

"This young man... this vile criminal... he made a mighty resistance to being arrested?"

Julian opened his mouth to speak, then shut it once more.

Anne turned her eyes to her husband as their confessor awaited an answer. "Julian...?"

"He is in the hospital, so I am told," Father Gregory added.

Julian maintained his silence, his eyes sliding away to study the now-empty spot on the wall where the devil's mask had hung.

After a pause, the little cleric opened the door to let himself out, and said, "One must not take too much pride even in beating the devil, Chief J, and wrath is *still* a mortal sin. I will see you this Saturday at confession, my dear friend... ten a.m. sharp," then closed the door behind him before he could be exposed to any rash or blasphemous replies.

Angela's Baby
(1992)

Julian made the mistake of walking into the dispatcher's area just as the call came in.

He'd been in the squad room for the past hour dotting i's and crossing t's on reports that had been dotted and crossed a week before. He had carefully re-read them to ensure thoroughness and accuracy and found them as thorough and accurate as the last time he had looked at them. Most days he avoided hanging out in the station, but today he was guilty of it and knew it. He kept trying to find a comfortable position to lounge in, but every time he got close the sergeant thrust his impatient head through the door. The sergeant held no great love for Julian and found his reasons for being off the road suspect. Any sign of comfort on the part of the patrolman and he would pounce. But Julian always managed to appear studious and the sergeant had finally withdrawn in a huff.

Moments later, Julian had heard the clang of the steel door leading to the carport and over his portable the voice of the sergeant signing on patrol. "Seven hundred to seven."

"Go ahead seven hundred."

"I guess I'm ten-forty-one. Let me know when we get another car on the road."

Even in the brief 10 code language used on the radio, the sergeant managed to convey his displeasure. Julian read the subtext as, "If I can't get an officer on patrol, I guess I'll have to do it myself!"

"Well that's stupid," he thought. "Why doesn't he just tell me to get on the road?"

He stood and stretched, smiling at having caused some irritation, and sauntered into the hallway. It was getting lonely in the squad room without his monitor.

Julian knew he was being contrary but couldn't help himself. He felt restless and cranky. It was day shift. The worst of all shifts in his opinion. Worse than that, it was day shift in the off season. The tourists were gone, leaving behind empty streets and houses. Even the mounds of beer cans and broken furniture left at the curb on Labor Day had long been carted away. Winter had crept in through fall, laying its spell on the town as surely as Merlin had cast his spell on its namesake, Camelot.

The calls on day shift were enough to make a saint weep. Old ladies who needed help in finding Foo-Foo, their toy poodle. Doors standing open on empty houses. Julian recalled one old girl insisting that the house behind her was suspicious, due to lights being on at night and it being unoccupied. No one had been there for months. On that point she was unshakable. Julian almost shot her new neighbors. And so it went, hours of boredom followed by moments of inanity.

That was why he was hiding out, opening and closing file folders, checking the tension on his ball-point's spring, drawing attention to areas the janitor missed, and generally being a nuisance.

Wandering toward the sound of the dispatcher's voice, he arrived just in time for the incoming call.

As he edged his way into the dispatch room, he looked for a comfortable chair. This would be a good time to go over the dispatcher's proper role in the police world, he thought. Settling into a cushioned office chair, he began to mull over examples he could use to illustrate his point. Subtly, of course. No sense in antagonizing anyone. The phone call Emma was fielding was taking much too long, perhaps he could start there. Just a few suggestions on asking the right questions to get the pertinent info. He began to listen in.

Emma, a large and formidable woman in her late forties, was having her usual chat, it seemed. She considered this one of her many privileges on the job and was less than tolerant of those patrolmen who might question them. Peering over glasses at Julian, she fixed him with her basilisk stare and then, to ensure there was no misunderstanding, pointed at him. This was in the way of letting him know that she intended for him to handle this call. She also favored him with a tiny smile, smug that she had headed him off at the pass. The sergeant had warned her that he was in one of his funks and might be headed her way.

Julian found a Most Wanted poster and studied it, avoiding even a glance at the gloating dispatcher. From what he had overheard of the conversation, words like plumber, gas, and no heat had popped up. He thought this an excellent time to hang the poster up in the sergeant's office. He stood to do just that and started for the door. Behind him he heard the phone receiver click into its cradle.

"I have a call for you, dear." The high-pitched voice with its peculiar drawl always had the same effect on him. To not do whatever was requested.

"Emma, I'm a little busy right now," he lied. "Don't we have a car that's free?"

The smile broadened, her glee evident.

"Yesss, but the sergeant said I was to give you the next call. I have the next call all ready for you. Are you ready for it?"

So they've plotted this out, have they? Julian fumed. Save the worst, most mundane assignment for Julian, and kick him out on the road with it! He envisioned himself executing various take-down tactics on a pleading dispatcher.

"What's it all about... *dear*?" he purred.

"It seems a lady over on Seventy-fourth Street has a problem with her plumber. She called him to take a look at her furnace. Which he did. He claims he couldn't find anything wrong with it. When he stepped out to his truck she locked him out! He says he's still got some tools inside and that she hasn't paid him."

"Oh, for God's sake, this is a civil matter!" Julian whined. "What was the original problem?"

"A smell of gas."

"All right, all right, I'll see if I can get this hashed out. Give me the house number once I come up on the air."

Julian left the station and cruised south.

The address was a two hundred number almost in the center of the block with a concrete porch spanning the width of the front. A set of sliding glass doors opened onto it.

Parking the squad car a few doors down, Julian walked up. He never liked to announce his presence until he was ready. The first thing he noticed was that the plumber had departed the scene. No truck or van was around. Emma had told him enroute that the lady in question lived on the first floor, so he avoided the slider, figuring from experience that it led to the living room, where she was probably waiting. Instead, he crept up to the kitchen door, on the side of the house, and peeked in.

The kitchen was a shambles. Every available surface was covered with crusty dishes and silverware. The sink was the only place spared. The trash can was filled to overflowing with disposable diapers. Through an open inner door he could make out a slice of the living area. It looked like someone had blown up a Good Will toy box. Broken, filthy toys were strewn everywhere. The one couch that was visible had obviously been supplied by the benevolent realtor. Julian made a mental note to avoid sitting on it.

One last look before entering, he thought, and knocked on the door, then walked to the front, ducking under the kitchen window as he passed, to arrive at the sliding glass door. He peeked in just in time to see a short, overweight woman walk through to the kitchen. He noted that she carried nothing in her hands. Good, he thought, at least she's not lying in wait for the plumber.

The living room was no surprise after the kitchen. The same designer had trashed both rooms. Besides the toys, second-hand furniture, and yet more dirty dishes, Julian noticed an empty playpen near the center of the floor.

Having satisfied himself, Julian rapped hard on the glass. The fat woman came striding out of the kitchen, a confused look on her face. Julian noted again that her hands were empty as she did so. He remembered from officer survival school that kitchens were notorious for supplying murder weapons.

Sliding open the door, her face had a look of bewilderment and agitation that was only partly due to Julian's methods. He could see in an instant that the uniform disturbed her. Her small, furtive eyes gave away the alarm that she was trying to hide.

"Yes Officer, is something the matter?" she inquired in a guarded voice.

Her face was nothing pleasant to look at, thought Julian. The hair was long, straight, and unwashed, and the eyebrows had been plucked out of existence. The heavy cheeks bordered on becoming jowls and along with her chin were lightly haired. Still, there was something about her... a gentle, beseeching quality that was attractive.

"You're having a problem with your plumbing?" Julian started, then realized that he was confusing her more. What was he going to do, pull out a wrench and go to work on the pipes? Before he could clarify his questions, she reached out and touched the sleeve of his jacket.

"Yes, yes please come in."

Julian did as he was bidden and entered the sour-smelling living room. She hurried to close the door behind him. Julian regretted that. Taking small, mincing steps now, like that of a child afraid of admonishment, she stood before him. She was just short of wringing her hands. The contrast to the purposefully striding woman he had glimpsed earlier was disturbing.

"I'm Patrolman Hall," he offered. "Julian Hall."

She seemed far away now, wrestling with something in her mind. She looked down and didn't respond.

"It's an odd name isn't it... Julian?"

No response. He decided to plow on, to give her time.

"My mother says I was named after a saint. A fella who took care of anyone that needed it. The sick, the lame, even lepers." Still nothing.

"My father, on the other hand, says I was named after a Roman emperor, called Julian the Apostate. His claim to fame was persecuting the Christians."

She glanced up at him.

"But I like to think I took after the first guy. Maybe that's why I got into this line of work. To help people. All people."

She smiled a little and said, "My name is Angela. I'm not a Christian, but I respect their values."

Julian smiled back.

"So, Angela, you've had a problem of some sort with the heater or the repairman?" He noted the chill in the house as he spoke.

She took a seat on a stuffed rocking chair, so he reluctantly perched on the very edge of the offensive sofa.

"It's the gas you see. I can smell it sometimes very strongly, like now. Do you smell that?"

Julian didn't. All he could smell was decaying food and the faint odor of stale urine. He was glad it was cold in the house. She was staring at him with a curious mixture of pleading and defiance. He lied a little.

"Yeah, now that you mention it, I do think I catch a whiff of something now and again."

She nodded her large head in agreement, leaning forward in her excitement.

"That man said he couldn't smell anything. He was lying. I don't know why he was lying, though. He may have been watching the house a few days ago. I'm pretty sure I saw him walk past the house several times."

Julian thought of the unlikeliness of that happening and began to ponder what he had walked into.

"I'll have to check into that," he murmured. "He did look around though, didn't he? To make sure there were no gas leaks?"

She wouldn't reply, so he stood and said, "How 'bout I take a look at the appliances? Just to make sure there's not a pilot light out."

"He did that," she said.

Julian walked into the kitchen, ostensibly to inspect the stove, but actually to buy a little time to think. In spite of it being cool in the house, he was starting to sweat a bit. A glance at the stove and oven showed all the pilot lights to be lit. The water heater the same. He had expected the stench of the diapers in the trash can to be powerful and was relieved that they weren't. He wondered why and peered down at the disgusting mound. He knew from when his own kids were babies that these were definitely not fresh. They were old—dry and crusted. Almost odorless. Thank God, he thought.

Stepping back into the living room, he saw at once that she was gone. A slight movement in the darkened hallway to his left sent a jolt of adrenaline through him and he spun around to face it.

She was standing halfway down the hall, silhouetted by the window at the rear of the house. He knew she was facing him when she spoke. For some reason he had been afraid that she had had her back to him. He knew he wouldn't have liked that.

"That's the furnace," she said, pointing at a large grate in the floor. The thermostat was at shoulder level on the wall to her right.

Julian took a breath, then walked down the hall to stand at the opposite end of the grate from Angela. Peering down into the darkness, he saw the living eye of the furnace—a small, dancing flame captured beneath a glass viewer. Its fits and starts were hypnotic in the gloom. It was an old, outdated style. He was not even sure that these were made anymore. They shouldn't be, he thought, they're dangerous as hell. The heating unit itself was set about three feet below floor level and provided gas-fed flames. These heated the air above and hopefully, but rarely, wafted currents of warmth into adjoining rooms. This one was shut off, denying it the chance to do even that much.

Remembering an identical floor unit in the home where he grew up, he thought of the faint, checkered scars on his palms. Scars from a fall onto that scorching grate when he was just a baby learning to walk. Just a baby.

"Angela, where is the baby?"

There was a long, still pause.

"Asleep. He's in his crib, asleep," she answered in a small, faraway voice.

For some reason that he couldn't fathom at the moment, a tiny alarm went off in his head. Even though he was perspiring, a chill from the dark house settled over Julian.

"Angela, maybe we had better turn on the heat for a little while. You know, it's awfully damp and chilly in here. The baby might catch cold."

She seemed to start awake, stung by his words. "No! The baby's fine! I would never do anything to hurt him. I haven't done anything wrong, have I? I can't turn on the heat or run the water because of the gas, don't you see? You smelled it yourself. You said so! It's poison gas! I've seen it!"

Julian stood stock-still as the winds of madness blew around him. He tried not to show his shock as her cries echoed off the walls. This was deeper than he'd thought. She was not just neurotic, she was in her own world and it was a nightmare place.

But something she said awoke a memory in Julian's mind. Just a brief, inconsequential flashback to the long-ago, warm summer. A call about a child locked in a running car at a local convenience store. He recalled a blonde-headed, happy baby smiling and laughing at the perspiring policemen trying to work the door open with a slim jim. And the mother, who had called them, standing at his shoulder, wringing her hands, unable to stop crying, saying, "I didn't do anything wrong! It was an accident!"

They had never thought otherwise and had paid her little attention. It had been Angela… and Angela's baby.

Now he stood with her in a darkened hallway in a dank, depressing apartment with flecks of her spittle drying on his face, separated by a furnace and a gulf of madness. He felt very much alone. He needed time and help and he needed a plan.

It was obvious to him now that he had to get Angela to the hospital for evaluation. Voluntary or not. And he didn't think it would be voluntary. He also had to get to the boy and make sure he was all right. The baby would have to be turned over to the Family Services people for a while.

She continued to stand in the hallway, blocking his access to the bedrooms at the rear of the house. He suspected that she had chosen that position on purpose. She was guarding her young. Guarding him from the authorities, poison gas, and whatever else she perceived as a threat. But how far was she prepared to go? How far had she already gone? The silence of the bedrooms, the old, stale diapers, and the cracked, waiting toys all weighed heavily on Julian's mind.

He could hear her taking rapid, shallow breaths in the dimness.

"You're right, Angela, of course. I wasn't thinking. That's not unusual for me. Now, about this gas. We're going to have to go over a few heads on this. Since it's obvious that the local workers can't be trusted, I think it's time we brought in a county inspector. It's the only way to get to the bottom of this. How's that sound?"

The sun was beginning its slow descent into late afternoon and a ray of it began to illuminate the hall enough for Julian to make out the wary, frightened face across from him. She seemed to be weighing his words, but he could also see that her mouth was set in a determined line.

"The gas is purple. I've seen it sometimes when I've had to use the sink. It comes out of the pipes. It seeps out from the stove and heater, too. It forms a haze around the ceiling sometimes and I have to open the doors and windows to keep it from building up. Tell them that."

Purple haze. Jimi Hendrix was right, Julian thought. "I will," he replied. "That's good information, something to work with.

"Angela, I'm gonna step out to my car to use the radio for the inspector. While I'm doing that, why don't you wrap up the baby and meet me out there. There's no sense in you two staying in a dangerous situation. We'll leave that to the inspector and come back when we get the all clear."

Palms sweating with tension, he wondered whether she would buy it or not. Either way, he had to go out to the car. He couldn't risk using her phone so he would have to use the one in the car. He didn't like it, but his sergeant had to be briefed and Family Services notified. Also it would avoid attracting the ghouls that monitored the police band. The situation was bad enough without onlookers cruising the street for a look at the madwoman of Camelot. And he couldn't risk a struggle alone with the woman. Psychotics could be inhumanly strong and dangerous. If the baby had been okay so far, then a few more minutes would probably not make any difference. If he wasn't then time was of no matter, anyway.

"All right," she said and smiled. It was not reassuring. She watched him walk towards the slider, not giving up her position. His back felt wide and vulnerable. Patting himself down, he said, "Where the heck did I put my keys?"

Digging into his front pants pocket, he came up with a handful of change, which he promptly dropped, scattering coins all over the floor. As he was gathering them up, he slipped a quarter into the track of the sliding glass door. Straightening up, he glanced over his shoulder at the silent woman in the darkness, smiled goofily, and walked out, praying she hadn't noticed.

Speaking directly to the sergeant, he explained as well and briefly as he could what he was attempting and asked for a back-up car to be in the area, in case things blew up. The sergeant advised him to switch his portable to channel two and that he would have the back-up car monitor the same. In the meantime he would contact the social workers and have them standing by at the hospital.

As he was cradling the phone to his ear, he saw her rush the door. "Oh, shit!" was his last communication to the sergeant as he dropped the receiver and began the fifty-yard dash. He could just make out her bulk behind the glass as she slammed it once again into the wedged quarter, the door tilting forward as it met resistance. She saw him coming and did an abrupt about face and charged back into the shadows. Julian had just time enough to catch a glimpse of a wrapped bundle in her right arm before she disappeared. Leaping onto the porch, he threw back the door.

Inside, it seemed darker than ever, as his eyes tried to adjust to the sudden transition, and he could just make out a large something in the center of the hallway. It was about three feet tall and seemed to be vanishing into the floor. Then it stopped and began to reverse itself, growing in height as it did so. An arm detached itself from the shapeless mass to lower the furnace grate back into the floor. Then Angela stood up, puffing. Leaning against the wall to her right, she covered the thermostat with her meaty hand. Julian could make out her face now, grim and wild, a sheen of sweat coating it.

As he took it all in, Julian began to feel a little sick. Angela had placed something in the furnace and that something had looked very much like a baby swaddled in a blanket, and she now stood in control of the thermostat. Her whole body was a picture of defiance, her face, a mask of cunning triumph.

But why hadn't the baby cried out? Surely, with all that jostling it would have been startled and cried. In fact, the whole time that he had been there the baby had not made one sound. Did that mean that he was already dead—that she had taken the ultimate step in protecting him from those mysterious and malevolent forces that crowded her world? Or was he drugged? With all the drugs that she had undoubtedly been prescribed over the years, it was a distinct possibility.

"Well, we're all set now," he began, feeling as if his mouth was filled with cotton. "The inspector's on his way, so we can get out of here. You about ready?"

She wasn't buying it. The trump card was in her right hand. "You get out of here," she hissed. "You think I'm crazy. I know what you're up to. No one's taking my baby. They sent you to get him, didn't they? I recognize you, even in that uniform. You don't fool me. I've looked out my windows and you've been there. Watching. I've seen you and the others standing in the darkness staring at my house!" Her hand convulsed on the thermostat.

Julian had to restrain himself from rushing her. He would never make it in time. They were only separated by about eight feet, but all she needed was a flick of the wrist. He imagined the quiet click of the thermostat, followed seconds later by the whoosh of ignited gas. A sudden roaring flame erupting around the child laying on the deadly jets. He didn't move. Neither did she.

He let his left hand drift to the portable radio on his belt. As he began to speak, he depressed the transmit button, and held it.

"Angela, you've gotten off your medication, haven't you?" he asked. "Sometimes when someone's been prescribed something, they forget to take it. Or they start feeling better and think they don't need it anymore. I think that's what's happened here, isn't it?"

She was silent, but he thought she seemed interested.

"That's all I'm concerned with. I don't want to separate you and the baby. I just want you to feel better, more comfortable. If we visit with the doctor, I think he'll get you set right up. A new prescription, maybe. But we have to get the baby out of there first. He can't be comfortable in there. The furnace is a dangerous place for him." He prayed that the back-up car heard the transmission and understood the situation.

She looked mesmerized. Her face was slack and dazed. She seemed to be reading his lips as he spoke, mouthing some of the words. He eased forward a few inches.

"No," she gurgled, rising slowly to the surface. "Please, no. I'm afraid. I can't trust you. They'll take my baby." She was almost moaning, the anxiety crushing her.

"Remember last summer, Angela?" Julian asked as he slid a couple more inches along the wall. "Remember when the baby got locked in the car, by accident?"

She looked at him sharply, remembering the incident.

"Remember how I got him out of the car? He was beautiful and happy, wasn't he? And I gave him right to you, didn't I? You were so worried that you were in trouble, but it was just an accident, and I handed him right over. You didn't do anything wrong. Let me help now."

Her arm drifted down from the thermostat a fraction. Julian could see that she was exhausted. She was looking at the grate. He crept forward again. She looked up, catching him at it. The arm shot back into place, the hand gripping the mechanism.

"Angela, don't!" Julian pleaded in a hushed whisper. "There's no going back if you do. Do you understand me? We can't undo this once it's done. Please talk to me. I won't make another move, unless you want me to. I promise." The hand didn't move and neither did the eyes as they searched his face. She wants to believe me, he thought.

Somewhere in the apartment he heard a clock ticking in the silence. The chill he had noticed earlier had gotten inside his jacket now and his teeth began to chatter with the cold and tension. The shadows had lengthened as the sun slid down the sky. A single ray of light had found its way through the rear window causing a halo around Angela, leaving her face in ever-deepening gloom. Something yellow bobbed into view on a rooftop that could be seen over her shoulder.

Julian tried not to stare as Large Albert's blond head popped into view once more, followed by his massive shoulders and arms lifting a ludicrously small Marlin carbine to his cheek. Albert was one of the best shots in the department and wouldn't miss the large silhouetted head of the unknowing Angela, even at fifty yards.

Julian's palms were sweating. Time was running out for her. He didn't want her to die, he knew that. Not standing there in front of him, listening to him, weighing his words, almost trusting him. There was a small click underneath Angela's palm. He could just make out a look of puzzlement cross her face.

The temperature! Jesus Christ! It was dropping by the moment. "Angela, set the temperature lower on the thermostat! Hurry, before it kicks on!" he pleaded.

She jumped at his voice and hesitated. There was another tiny click. Julian pictured the small bulb of mercury tilting over to make its connection. The electric pulse to the furnace would be a matter of seconds.

Suddenly she wrenched the dial forward, understanding coming late. There was another click as the circuit was disconnected. Silence followed.

Julian expected a nine millimeter bullet to erupt from her forehead after the sudden movement. He keyed his mike and began talking, trying to save her and the baby.

"Very good, very good! That was good, Angela. Now, I just want you to make sure it's on its lowest setting, okay? It's getting cold in here and we don't want any accidents, do we?"

He was babbling but couldn't help himself. She glanced at the dial and looked up at him with a frightened expression.

"Now then, let's get things wrapped up, Angela." He was going to take control now. "You love the child, anyone can see that. You don't really want any harm to come to him, so why don't you step back from the furnace now and let me get him out?" He could see tears glistening on her cheeks in the remaining light. She still didn't move. "Angela, the temperature's dropping by the minute. It can't be much above fifty degrees in this house right now. Even on its lowest setting that furnace is gonna kick on soon. Are you listening to me? We have to do something right away. The baby is in danger, Angela!"

A low moan broke forth from her clamped lips, sending a chill down Julian's spine. It rose higher as she wrapped her free arm around herself and began to rock. It was the sound of the lost in hell.

"I don't know what to do!" she cried. "This is my baby, he came from me. You didn't give him to me! He's not yours to take away! I love him but I have to be careful now. 'Specially now that I know what happens. They change them, you know. My little Timmy was changed! Did you know that? After they took him, he was programmed. They wouldn't give him back and when I went to see him, he didn't love me anymore! They brainwashed a little boy so that he wouldn't love his mommy anymore. They wouldn't let me take him back home and he... he ran from me when I tried to hold him." The confession was coming out of her in great, tearing sobs now. Julian felt his own eyes grow hot and moist as he watched her. He thought for a moment of his own children.

It was all becoming clear to him now, as he remembered that hot summer afternoon. A crying, hysterical Angela, even heavier than she was now, and a robust little boy, smiling and laughing at the efforts of his rescuers. Not an infant, but a little boy, that even then must have been a toddler. He couldn't be that tiny, swaddled bundle that Angela had carried so easily in one arm. It was all she had left of him, he guessed, a memory, a token, a favorite doll wrapped in one of his old blankets.

Her face was covered by her long hair as she hung her head and sobbed. Her hand slid down the wall. Julian took a full step closer, still wary of alarming her, keying his mike again as he did so. He spoke across the remaining few feet.

"Angela, he's not here is he?" She looked up at him, puzzled. Over her shoulder he saw Albert's head come up off the rifle. He was puzzled too. Julian could only hope that he would understand what was transpiring. "Let's go out of here now. It's cold and getting dark and we both need a rest. So I'm going to walk over to you now and I don't want you to be scared, okay?"

"What… what did you say?" she gasped.

"There's no sense in prolonging this anymore, Angela," he continued in a strong, level voice. "Let's go now before something bad happens." Julian took another step forward. He had one foot on the furnace grate now. Her arm shot back out to the thermostat.

"Stop!" she pleaded, panic rising in her voice. "Don't make me do it! I don't want to hurt him!"

"And you're not going to," he replied, "because he's not there."

"Oh yes, he is, he is!" She glanced down as if to reassure herself.

"And even if he was, you wouldn't hurt him anyway, would you?" Julian stood in the center of the grate now.

"Oh God, oh my God," she cried out. "You're making me do this!"

He reached out now with his left arm, releasing the mike button and severing his connection with the outside world. He placed his hand over hers.

As if freed from a tremendous inner pressure, she drooped forward into his arms, weeping, causing him to stagger back. His grip on her hand remained firm though and she let him gently peel back her fingers, dropping her arm to her side. He cradled her for a moment and rocked her from side to side. Behind her back he gave the all clear signal to Large Albert and saw him slide from view.

Next to him, he heard once again, the ominous metallic click of the heating control in the frigid silence. The sun slid out of the sky to the west and seem to suck the remaining warmth from the house. The furnace would activate itself, just as he had predicted. He thought of the flammable properties of the wool and plastic lying in the furnace and disengaged himself from the now docile Angela.

Learning over to pull up the grate, he heard the second click above his head. Not a moment to spare, he thought, and yanked up the covering, only to be greeted by the acrid smell of fresh urine and a tiny mewling sound in the darkness. The smallest of hands waved up at him.

Julian's sense of reality fell away from him in a sudden rush, making him feel as if he were about to topple into an endless hole. Flames erupted from the furnace, a terrified wail following it, and he dove forward, snatching the baby up and stripping away the smoldering blanket in a single movement. Behind him he heard Angela's anguished cry.

Holding the frightened baby at arm's length, he inspected it to find an unscorched and perfect little boy, maybe a month old—Angela's baby… her *second* baby.

With the infant still in his arms, he escorted mother and child to his patrol car, while praying that the next day, and every day thereafter, might be the most boring of his career.

Tomorrow's Dead

(2011) Nominated for Edgar and Derringer Awards

The old man opened his eyes and groaned. A string of reddened spittle spun from his busted lip and stretched itself impossibly upwards, crawling across his narrow field of vision in its quest for the ceiling of his car. He wanted to wipe it away, but his arms felt heavy and useless. He looked down to find his hands, but they were absent from his lap.

He thought irritably of his wife—perhaps she could explain; quite probably she was responsible. Wincing from the pain in his neck, he managed to turn towards the passenger seat. His wife hung motionless within her seatbelt, tendrils of grey hair floating above her head like that of a drowned woman.

He understood now; began to remember. There had been a truck—a very large truck with one of those great push-bumpers welded onto the front of it. It was the last thing he had seen as it T-boned them with such force that his car had been overturned and his wife killed. He had been given no time to be afraid or react. As he hung there studying the alien geography of his shattered windshield and the asphalt sky beyond, he began to grow angry. Not so much over the loss of his wife, as he had never had much use for her, but at being so roughly handled. He understood something of brutality, but only in the giving, not in the receiving.

With a great effort, fueled by his growing righteous fury, he willed his arms to return to his sides, to obey his commands, but like lumps of molded clay they dangled uselessly from his shoulders. Yet, a slight and painful tingling alerted him that they still lived, might still serve to release him from his entrapment given enough time. Once free of the seatbelt, he could crawl from the car and seek help; get proper medical attention and sue the towing company whose truck and drivers had done such damage. Because it *had* been a tow truck, there was no doubt in his mind on this matter, he remembered the crane-like appendage that jutted up from behind the cab. It had had a distinctive paint job, as well—blue and yellow; the cab occupied by two men so heavily tattooed that, in the brief moment before impact, they had appeared almost blue. *By God*, he thought, *they left me here to die! I'll wring them dry for this.*

As if summoned by his angry thoughts, the rumble of a large diesel engine entered his blood-filled ears. Wincing in pain the old man swiveled his head to peer out what was left of his driver's-side window. The distinctive blue and yellow color pattern rolled into his field of vision and stopped. *This won't do them any good,* he thought bitterly. *I had the right of way at the intersection and they were speeding on top of it; there's no way trying to be Good Samaritans now is gonna save 'em—they've broken my arms… and killed my wife, too,* he noted with a growing sense of indignation.

The truck appeared to sit there for a long time and he could see nothing but the huge knobby tires and the lower half of the door. *Where are the police?* he wondered. *Damn police should be here.*

He heard the squeal of rusted hinges and a pair of busted-up work boots dropped upside down into sight. A door slammed, then another. Both of the men were coming over, he observed. *Sons-of-bitches are not in any hurry,* he thought as the second pair of boots came into sight from round the truck—these were cowboy boots, shiny and new, the toes pointy and hard. Both sets of boots appeared aimed at him, immobile now—waiting.

What are they doing? the old man wondered, becoming uneasy. The amount of blood pooling onto the car ceiling alarmed him, though he was reasonably certain it was from his wife. *Even so, they should help,* he reasoned. *They should get me out of here... it's their fault, after all.* In the distance, a siren intruded into his panicky thoughts. *Thank God,* he thought, *someone has called the police.* The boots began to move.

Clipping across the tarmac, the cowboy boots took two steps for every one of the work boots. Both reached his window and halted, the old man's world reduced to a close study of men's footwear. He could see that the Western boots were covered in snakeskin while the work boots were scuffed and dusty, nondescript. "Help me," he croaked through a mouthful of blood and loose teeth. It sounded more like gargling, the words turned to mush.

Two faces appeared, close and upside-down. The tattoos flowed from beneath their collars and sleeves in a riot of swirling, maze-like patterns, occasionally interrupted by a recognizable image. The straining face of Christ, bloodied by his crown of thorns, peeked out from the open shirt of "Work Boots," while a serpent swallowing a naked woman crawled down the arm of "Cowboy."

Before he could wrench his attention from their illustrations and look into their faces, Work Boots produced a blade from somewhere, its cutting edge short but as curved as a parrot's beak. *He's going to cut me loose,* the old man thought, even as alarms began to clang inside his churning brain.

The larger man reached in as if to slice through the strap and the old man felt a sharp tug. But as his would-be rescuer retreated once more, he found that he was still suspended, though robbed of breath. A fine, crimson mist filled the car and though he comprehended its meaning, he no longer had the power to scream. A caul of blood masked his face and blinded his eyes. Even as his brain and heart began to power down in furious jolts and ominous lulls he wondered why. *Why have you cut my throat?* he wanted to ask, but the ones who could answer were already driving away in the stolen car they had parked nearby just a few hours before.

ↄ৸

Snagging the phone before the third ring, Byron flipped it open and mumbled, "Chief Patrick here." The voice on the other end made him sit bolt upright in bed, his gummy eyes fluttering open. The digital clock glowed redly from its perch—it was three-thirty in the morning.

"Byron?" the woman's voice sounded uncertain. "It's me, Reba."

Byron pictured his best friend's wife in faraway Atlanta, a genteel, classy woman. The soft lilt of home bled through the tension in her voice. "What's wrong?" he asked. Something had to be wrong, of course, for her to call at this hour; for it to be her instead of Tom. He thought of Tom's recent heart problems. "Is Tom okay? What's wrong?"

There was a pause, and then she answered, a tremor entering her voice now, "He's gone, Byron. I don't know what's happened, but he never came home from his office on Tuesday."

Byron's free hand slid across the smooth, unwrinkled sheet of the far side of his bed. It remained as empty as when he had turned in for the night. He remembered that it was now Thursday—Tom had been gone for over twenty-four hours. Julia had not come home either, but he was growing used to that—they were not Tom and Reba.

Reba went on, "I've called everyone we know; everyone I could think of. No one's heard from him or seen him. Then I thought of you. I knew it was a long shot, with you being way up there in New Jersey, but I thought maybe… maybe he just needed some time with an old friend. He's seemed worried lately… preoccupied." Another pause ensued, this one charged and dark as a thunderhead. "He's not there is he?" she asked at last, the tears in her voice betraying her fear.

"I'll catch the very first flight I can," Byron replied, even as his mind raced through all the details of handing over the reins of his department to his second-in-command. "I should be there by late afternoon. Call me right away if he comes home in the meantime."

ಌ

Byron sat in the faux leather chair that Thomas Llewellyn should have occupied and swiveled from side to side. The seventh-floor office overlooking Peachtree Street was not cooperating. The large chair and the scarred metal desk it faced were the only signs of permanence, and even these were devoid of character, being standard issue in cubicles across the nation. The shelving along the walls was constructed of thin, wobbly railings supporting dusty cardboard boxes; most appeared in danger of imminent collapse. The few filing cabinets were tilted and dented, as if accustomed to suffering the kicks and blows of angry men. The ragged files they contained meant nothing to Byron and shed no light on his friend's disappearance. Tom's laptop, the only computer he possessed, Reba had explained to him, was nowhere to be found.

He had visited the office only once before and that had been many years ago on one of his annual trips to see his mother. Whenever possible, Byron engineered a stopover with the Llewellyns on his way to their mutual hometown of Columbus, yet a hundred miles further south. It seemed more than a lifetime ago when they had all attended the same high school together; lived in the same neighborhood.

At the time of his first visit Tom had been in the midst of getting moved in, just beginning his consulting business. And now it seemed to Byron that almost nothing had changed in the room since that time, and this gave him an anxious, uneasy feeling. Thomas had done very well in life, had a good income and a beautiful home in a leafy, much-sought-after suburb, yet his office reflected none of this. In fact, Byron thought, it was a decidedly mute environment—any single one of his officers' lockers back in New Jersey displayed more character, more personality, than this dim, silent room.

Byron had opened every drawer, closet, and box in his blind search for any clue as to where Tom had gone—or been taken. Reba assured him that Tom had no enemies, none that he had ever spoken of. "He's a municipal planning consultant," she reminded Byron. "He visits towns throughout the Southeast—by invitation mind you—conducts interviews with employees, observes procedures, and writes up his thoughts and recommendations on streamlining operations.

"He's never the one that actually does any firings, you know, if that's what you're thinking. He's long gone before anything like that gets done. People *like* Tom, Byron; you know that. They always have."

It was true, Byron agreed—Tom had always had an easy, witty charm about him. He wasn't the kind to make enemies. In that way they were very different men. Byron smiled at the memory of Tom's sardonic banter, the arched eyebrow, the curved upper lip that belied his innate good humor. He moved easily amongst men, Byron reflected with only a little envy. But even as he remembered his best friend, his hands, patting and probing without need of his direct attention, discovered the envelope and drew it forth. It had been taped to the bottom of the battered desk's slide-out typing shelf—an anachronism concealing a secret.

As the yellowed, brittle newspaper clippings spilled forth onto the desktop like ancient leaves, Byron felt a darkness, the shadow of a black wing, sweep across his heart. He did not need to read the terse accounts to know the story they told; he recognized his old home in the grainy photos, his own mother and father, decades younger, but the strain and heartache already permanently etched into their faces. Worse still was the tiny inset of a school photo the police had used in their investigation—a boy of ten sporting the lacquered, thrust-up hair of the era; his smile wide and toothsome—a boy that might have been Byron himself but for his blondness. "Daniel," he whispered.

Leaping to his feet, Byron swept the clippings back into the envelope. A list of names and addresses written on a strip of white paper, obviously much newer than the articles, caught his eye amongst the tobacco-colored shards, and he studied it for a moment. All of the addresses were in Columbus, but the names themselves meant nothing to him. He returned the list to the envelope and stuffed the entire package into his jacket pocket. Within minutes he was in his rental car and speeding southward on I-85 through the wind-swept night.

 batch

The shell of a house peeked whitely out from its nest of riotous shrubberies and questing vines. In the moonlight it reminded Byron of a skull sinking into the overgrown, humid earth. The entrance was only partly covered by a piece of warped plywood. *Probably neighborhood kids*, he thought, *the house would certainly qualify as haunted.* He could picture the local kids taking the dare to enter the decrepit blue-collar bungalow; he might have done the same thing himself once upon a time.

Something flexed and popped beneath his shoe and he flashed a quick beam from his penlight onto it. A "For Sale" sign lay rusting and forgotten in the tall, rank grasses, while the house still lay empty after thirty-five years—a testament to the fate of its original owner.

Daniel's body had never been found, his abductor and murderer never apprehended by the police. But the man responsible *was* identified, Byron recalled in a frisson of loathing tinged with guilt. Justice had been served, and more importantly, Daniel had been avenged. Of this, and not very much more, he was certain. Just as he was certain, when he discovered the clippings regarding Daniel's kidnapping in Tom's office, that his missing friend had discovered something new in the decades-old case, possibly something dangerous to them both. Otherwise Byron would never have returned to this house just two blocks from where he and Thomas grew up, never returned to the only place on earth where he had been responsible for the death of another human being—where they had killed his brother's murderer.

The list of names meant something to Thomas and now he had disappeared. Was he being blackmailed? Had they been found out after all these years?

Pushing through the tall grasses, Byron mounted the few, cracked concrete steps leading up to the gapped entrance. With just a pause to illuminate the interior and ensure that a floor still existed, he squeezed through and stood inside.

The climbing tendrils that threatened to pull the tiny house down had not yet obscured all the windows, and through these poured a faint, phosphorescent light. Byron stood still and allowed his eyes to adjust. Gradually, objects once recognizable as furniture coalesced into view—a moldering armchair trembling with hidden mice, a pile of unidentifiable debris seemingly swept up into one corner, a two-legged coffee table that appeared to be kneeling like a dog. He glanced down the short hallway and risked a brief flash of his light. The kitchen at the other end of the house remained impenetrable to the weak illumination, but no noose hung there, no corpulent little man dangled kicking and purple-faced, his eyes black with engorged blood; there was no toppled chair.

Something fluttered on the door frame and Byron sought it with the beam of his light. He half-expected to find a dusty, irritated moth, but found instead a square of paper tacked to the warped, peeling wood, its edges trembling in the slight breeze. Like the list with the yellowed clippings, this also appeared fresh and recent in its brilliance. Byron trod cautiously down the corridor, his heart thudding louder with every step that drew him closer to the kitchen and its dark memories.

It had all started with their dog "Buddy"—he was the first to go missing. In reality, he had been Byron's dog, an amiable mongrel that he had adopted off the street and then left behind as he entered his teens. Daniel had been only too happy to inherit the black and white cur. In just a short while, Buddy had successfully, and far too easily as far as Byron had been concerned, transferred his allegiance to the younger Patrick—he became Daniel's shadow and constant companion; there was not one without the other. That is, until Buddy failed to show up for breakfast one hot, sticky morning a month into their summer vacation.

By the second day of Buddy's absence, Daniel was inconsolable, suffering the loss as a fresh and open wound. It had been Byron who suggested his little brother stop his sniveling, wipe his snotty nose, and go from house to house to make inquiries. Byron had not expected this tactic to produce any actual results other than occupying Daniel's attention for a few days and putting an end to his bawling. This cynical suggestion would haunt Byron for the rest of his life.

Armed with a crayon depiction of Buddy scrawled onto a page of lined notebook paper, Daniel sallied forth into the early morning neighborhood with full confidence in his brother's idea. He never came back. The portrait of the dog was later found in a garbage can set out to the curb. The can bore the sloppily painted numbers that once were attached to the decaying house in which Byron now stood. The former, and deceased, occupant denied any knowledge of little boys or missing dogs. No one believed him.

He was an older man who lived alone. So far as anyone knew there had never been a missus or a girlfriend, and there had been rumors long before Daniel disappeared. Some of Byron's friends hinted at hidden knowledge, kids in the neighborhood who went silent when the subject of Mr. Virgil Curtsie came up—children who went dead white and stared at their feet. When Byron suggested the door-to-door campaign to Daniel, he had forgotten Mr. Curtsie; he had forgotten the spider that crouched within the heart of their neighborhood, the small, soft man who always found something to do in his postage-stamp-sized front yard when school let out. The grubby little man with the thick, greasy glasses that insisted trick-or-treaters come into his home on Halloween to receive their due.

Even so, the police search revealed nothing useful to their investigation within his walls. Half the neighborhood, adult and child, had stood vigil outside his home the day of the search. When Curtsie had escorted the last officer to the door, Byron recalled the little smile that had lifted his pursed and purplish lips—a tiny, furtive smile of triumph. Thomas had nudged him hard in the ribs that hot day as the sun sank like a ball of fire into the faraway ocean. "We should git'im! You wanna git'im?" he had asked. "If it was my brother, I'd damn sure git'im!"

They were both big boys at fourteen, and athletic, and what they did was not hard to do once they made up their minds. Thomas had been startlingly adept at violence, pummeling and overpowering the smiling Curtsie as he answered their knock at his back door. Binding him with the clothesline they had brought was the work of only a few moments. The remaining length had been fastened round his fleshy neck and pulled through a lamp hook fastened to the ceiling and tied off to the oven door. Byron remembered being amazed and intimidated by his best friend's unexpected proclivity for violence and his adult-like confidence. From the moment they had entered the house, Thomas moved with assurance.

The entire episode had unfolded in the slow, detail-laden way of dreams, only the moments of violence achieving rapidity, the images blurred and seeping colors. Byron had intended that they should interrogate the grimy little man about Daniel's whereabouts, but Thomas, in his righteous zeal, had rendered the man's mouth incapable of forming coherent words. Now their plan to threaten him with hanging unless he came clean would appear to have no real purpose. Nonetheless, Thomas herded their prisoner onto the chair and threaded the hangman's rope to its anchor. Mr. Curtsie swayed from side to side and appeared dazed, unsure of what was happening to him. Just as Byron prepared to intervene—after all it was Daniel's whereabouts that they had come for—Thomas suddenly put a finger to his lips and pointed to the front of the house. "Did you hear a car pull up?"

Sprinting for the front door, Byron peered cautiously through the curtains. The mailman's jeep was just pulling away from the Curtsie postbox. He nearly passed out with relief. When he returned, the chair lay on its side and the man responsible for his little brother's disappearance dangled from the ceiling. "The bastard jumped," Thomas whispered at the awe-inspiring sight and pointed to the back door. "Let's go," he commanded the mesmerized Byron, "Now!" Together, they had fled the house like two boys running from a broken window, shouting and laughing with relief when they were safely away. It was only later that Byron realized that Tom untied the dead man's hands before they escaped.

Snagging the folded note from the door frame, Byron opened it. In the beam from his penlight, he read the words, "Waiting for you."

∽

The Chief of the Columbus P.D. was a large, heavy man not much older than Byron, early fifties, he guessed. He had the look of a college football player gone to seed. The chief slid a paper cup of coffee across his desk and regarded his visitor. Byron saluted him with it, saying, "I appreciate you seeing me, Chief Tanner, I'm sure you're busy."

"Call me Steve," he replied, suspicion written all over his face. "How can I say no to a fellow chief... even one from New Jersey?" he added with just the hint of a smile.

Byron smiled back. "I grew up here... born and raised. My mama still lives here."

"Columbus High?"

"No, Pacelli."

Chief Tanner took a noisy sip of his coffee and leaned back in his leather chair. "Is that right? You gotta go somewhere, I reckon. Well how in the hell did you end up stranded in the frozen north, pray tell?"

"Pretty easy, actually. I met and married a Jersey girl while I was serving in the army. You know how it goes, when we decided to get out of the service she wanted to settle down close to her folks, and I just wanted her to be happy for a change. It worked… for a while."

Tanner smiled more broadly now, as if Byron was just then exhibiting recognizable human features. "Wives," he waved his meaty paw across the top of his desk, "they're something, ain't they?" He didn't require an answer. "Looks like they've treated you pretty good up there, didn't they, Chief… for a Southern boy?" He slid Byron's police ID card across his desk to him.

"Yep," Byron admitted, "They sure as hell have."

Tanner gazed across the desk at him with an expression of benevolence. "So then, what is it we can do for you?"

"My best friend, has gone missing and I have reason to believe he may be somewhere here in Columbus… his wife is frantic," he added for emphasis.

"Grown man?" Tanner asked. "He might not thank you if you find him, Byron. Besides, you know as well as me that the police can't involve themselves with runaway husbands."

"It's not like that." Byron leaned forward. "I think he's gotten into some kind of trouble. I don't know if he's running to, or from, something, but it's also possible he was taken."

"Taken?" Tanner echoed. "If you had any proof of that the FBI would already be involved, wouldn't they?" He didn't wait for an answer but continued. "I'm still not hearing why this might be a police matter, Byron, and to tell you God's honest truth, we're a little bit busy around here just at the moment. You may not be familiar with the little crime wave we're having, but the press is having a field day." He shoved the morning's *Ledger-Enquirer* across his desk to Byron and pointed at a photograph of an overturned car with spectators kneeling and peering at something dangling within. Chief Tanner stabbed a thick finger at it, saying, "Had his throat cut, by God! Run off the road and murdered for no apparent reason, his wallet left behind. It don't make sense and it's not the first—we're rackin' em' up day by day. I've got a city of over a quarter million people, Byron, and less than five hundred cops to take care of 'em. Like I said, we're kind of preoccupied just now."

Byron had stopped listening, his attention having been arrested by the name of the elderly victim—Nicholas A. Strohmayer. His finger hung above it like a wasp, hovering and uncertain, unable to move on. He fished the list of names he had taken from Tom's office out of his jacket pocket and scanned it. N. Strohmayer appeared third down. His eyes flicked back to the newspaper to confirm the spelling, then up to the face of his counterpart.

"Steve," he asked, "you said there have been other unexplained murders recently—like Strohmayer?" The Columbus chief nodded his large, bullish head. "What were their names?"

Tanner paused for just a moment, then answered, "Fletcher Robson and Claudius Forrester... Claude to his friends when he was still breathing. Why do you ask?"

Byron's finger trailed down the list stopping on the two names printed as C. Forrester and F. Robson. He looked back up at Tanner. "I think I may have a list of the victims," he answered, handing the paper to him.

Tanner studied it for several long moments before saying, "I'll assign you a liaison officer, but you'll have to share a desk."

❧

Vanda Tucker did not recognize Byron by either name or
appearance, and he said nothing to enlighten her. On the other
hand, he had recognized her instantly in spite of the many years
that had passed since their brief acquaintance. He actually felt
himself blushing upon introduction. She was in a gray pants
suit that had become a little too snug and sported a detective
sergeant's badge on the leather holder attached to her belt. Byron
had to keep biting his lower lip to keep from smiling. Escorting
him into her small, basement office, she threw him a suspicious
glance as she pushed open a frosted window. The narrow view
revealed little but a concrete runway leading to the basement
steps at the other end of the building. Several trash cans were
lined up opposite, their lids invisible from the acute angle. She
fired a cigarette and waved the smoke out the opening. "What's
the grin for, Chief? Something strike your funny bone this
morning?" She took a quick glance in a mirror hung on the brick
wall and pushed at her dark hair a little. "Hmmm?"

"No," he lied, "just the awkwardness of the situation, I guess."

She didn't appear to buy that but went on anyway. "Alright
then, the chief says, that is, *my chief*, that I'm to bring you up to
speed on these cases—our little murder spree, so let's get to it."

She signaled for him to sit, so Byron eased himself into the
ancient wooden school chair that was wedged next to her desk.
If someone opened the door too wide he would be banged in the
knees with it. She threw a number of files onto the desk but did
not bother to sit herself.

Puffing away she narrated in fine detail the apparently
senseless murders of three men. He already knew the manner of
death of the most recent, Strohmayer, but the previous two bore

no resemblance other than the cold-blooded ferocity of their execution and the lack of any appreciable motive. "Oh yeah," she added. "In all three cases the victims were elderly men, though I'm sure you've already noted that.

"Also," she continued, "witnesses have testified that the killers were two heavily tattooed white males. They don't seem to be making too much of an effort to conceal their identities—our forensic artist is working something up for us and it should be ready soon."

She flicked her latest cigarette out the window and turned back to Byron. "I'm sorry about all that," she said. "I've tried to quit a bunch of times, but every time I do I blow up like a balloon. Even now, I can hardly button these pants." She laughed.

It was not her pants that drew so much of Byron's unwilling attention, but her blouse, whose buttons appeared to be straining with the effort of containing her. The memories of their first and, until now, only meeting, came rushing back to him, flooding his senses, making him as testosterone-charged as an adolescent boy, as the fifteen-year-old he had once been when they had met that long-ago autumn night.

"Goodness gracious you are easily embarrassed." She laughed again, mistaking Byron's discomfort to be about her remarks. "Don't they have any girls up there in New Jersey?"

"Yeah," he admitted as thoughts of Julia rose like snow dervishes, instantly cooling him. "Maybe we should consider re-interviewing the families of the victims," Byron offered.

Vanda's smile vanished with Byron's and she responded, "To what end?"

He told her about Thomas and the list.

"What's your friend got to do with all this?"

"I don't know," Byron answered, "I really don't."

∽

The widow Robson greeted them from her front porch swing. The early sun had yet to reach her and she was wrapped in a hand-knitted shawl in shades of orange and green. Byron thought her thin white hair resembled a halo as it floated above her tiny, fragile skull. Pointing to two rusty metal rockers that faced the street, she asked pleasantly, "Could I get ya'll some coffee?"

"No ma'am," he declined, "we've had our coffee, thank you." He could hear his drawl seeping back into his speech with every word—it was like a first language that returned when back in the land of one's birth, smoothly, without conscious thought.

"We just wondered if we could ask you a few questions about your husband?" he continued. Vanda smiled at the old woman and took a seat, while Byron half-sat and half-leaned on the porch railing.

Her smile vanishing, Mrs. Robson snugged the caftan around her narrow shoulders as if she had just felt a chill. "More questions, then? I don't much see the point, I must say. The harm's all been done, nothing we say here's gonna change any of that."

"Harm, ma'am... you mean your husband's murder?" Vanda asked.

The old woman looked down at her lap, her large-jointed fingers knitting restlessly together. "Yes," she answered after a moment. "That's harm too, isn't it?"

Giving a puzzled glance at his partner, Byron answered, "Of course it is, and men are still being murdered, Mrs. Robson. We'd like to put a stop to it, that's why we're here."

She looked back up at him, her eyes misty and frightened. "I don't really know anything," she pleaded.

"Maybe you do, ma'am," Vanda intervened, reaching over and patting one of her veined hands. "Sometimes we know more than we realize."

"Did you, or your husband, know a man named Thomas Llewellyn?" Byron asked.

The old woman shook her head. "No, I'm afraid that doesn't ring any bells. I'm sorry." Byron thought she seemed relieved. He thrust the list at her.

"How about any of the names on this list? Take your time, Mrs. Robson, and be sure." He watched her peruse the roster from the top down. The paper began to vibrate in her fingers, and she went to hand it back to him. "Which ones do you recognize?" he asked, refusing to take it. "Point at them."

She looked up at him with pleading, yellow eyes. "Do it, ma'am, right this minute." He felt Vanda's gaze on him. The old woman unfurled a talon-like finger and tapped a name on the list, then another and another. One name had been that of fellow victim Claudius Forrester; the second, however, still lived… at least for now.

"How about the name Virgil Curtsie… does that do anything for you?" She kept her face pointed down at the quaking paper clutched in her spiderish hands. "That name isn't on the list, so why don't you look up at me and answer?"

Vanda had risen to her feet and appeared on the verge of intervening. "Hey now," she began, but Byron cut her off.

"Look at me and answer," he almost shouted, snatching the list from her.

Mrs. Robson raised her pale, ghostly face, her mouth parted, tears trembling in her eyes. "How did you know?" she asked. "How could you know?"

"What's going on?" he heard Vanda ask from somewhere far away. "Chief?"

Byron ignored her and pressed on. "Did your husband keep an address book… where is it, Mrs. Robson?"

She pointed at the screen door. "Just inside by the telephone… I don't know why you're shouting at me," she sobbed. "I didn't do anything!"

"Get it!" he barked at Det. Sgt. Tucker.

"Yes sir!" she barked back, throwing open the door and letting it slam behind her. When she returned moments later with the book, it was to witness Byron stalking away toward the car. She hastened to catch up. "We'll return this after we're done with it," she promised the old woman over her shoulder.

"I don't want it," she cried in return as she scurried into her house.

"Sir," Vanda called out to Byron's back, hurrying to catch him, "Sir!… Chief or no chief, you've got some explaining to do! What *was* that back there?"

Byron had already reached the car and started it. He began to pull away from the curb before she could even close her door. The acceleration threw her back into her seat. "Damnit, Chief! You mind not killing us… at least not before you've explained what's going on." She snapped her seatbelt before turning to study Byron's hardened profile and lighting a cigarette. She didn't bother opening a window. "It's not fair to sit down at *our* table with cards up your sleeve—it's just not polite, especially when you're a guest. So how about it, Chiefie? You about ready to spill your guts, or do I have to smoke you out?" She laughed at her own joke in a way that made Byron feel both warm and challenged.

"Yeah," he answered, glancing over at her, noting the sparkle in her green eyes. "I'm about ready… just open that damn window."

He aimed the car for downtown and the Rankin Bar.

❧

Byron knocked back his second bourbon and set the glass down next to his cooling cup of coffee. Vanda sat across the small table from him sipping at a steaming cup of chicory, the Rankin Bar being one of the very few places in town where they served the Old South coffee substitute. The Detective Sergeant studied her charge with some amusement.

"Hey there," she said, "let's not forget it's only eleven—that's a.m., by the way." Glancing around the cool dark room she added, "Ain't it a shame you can't even smoke in bars anymore? Good Lord… this used to be a place of sin and iniquity… now look at it, all dolled up for church."

Byron took in his surroundings for the first time. It was true… this bar, like most of downtown, had become so gentrified since he had last lived in Columbus that it was almost unrecognizable. What had once been a decaying business district in a dying mill town had been transformed. Gone were the sleazy hole-in-the-wall, drink-standing-up or go-outside-to-fall-down bars where textile workers used to donate their hard-earned paychecks. Even the gritty, massive brick buildings that had once ground and roared twenty-four hours a day and housed thousands of workers had fallen silent, their operations spirited away to exotic lands like Mexico and Indonesia. Now, those that remained had been converted into high-end lofts with views of the river that had once powered their turbines, the rest having been plowed under for strip malls or preserved as seldom visited museums. Like elsewhere, Byron thought through the calming haze of Maker's Mark, Columbus had surrendered its blue-collar soul for a place in the land of cubicles, replacing its mills and foundries with insurance companies and credit card corporations. As if conjured up by his ruminations, an old tramp made his unsteady way past their window, blinking and uncertain in the new day—a working-class Rip Van Winkle awakened to a future that held no place for him. Byron raised a finger to the bartender.

"Hold that thought," Vanda commanded both Byron and the mixologist, stopping the latter with his hand on the neck of the preferred bottle. Receiving no encouragement from Byron he drifted away into the shadows. "Still waiting on you, professor," Vanda smiled across the table at her new partner. "Let's have it, shall we, before you render yourself incapable. Tell me about that list."

"When I realized that some of the names on Tom's list were also your victims, I knew that I... *we*," he corrected himself, receiving an encouraging nod from Vanda, "had to find the connection—that there had to be something that tied them all together. So, when I saw the old woman, Mrs. Robson, I decided to take a chance and show her the list. She knew the other names, and more importantly, her husband had known them as well... she also knew Virgil Curtsie."

"Who the hell is he when he's at home?" Vanda quipped. "His name wasn't on that paper."

"No," Byron conceded, "but she knew him, which meant her husband knew him, and my friend Tom Llewellyn knew them all... or at least their names."

"Why?"

"I'm not sure."

Vanda took a breath, "Do you think it could be your friend is behind these murders?"

Byron took a moment before answering, "I don't know anymore, but it's something I have to consider."

Vanda reached over and patted his hand. "How did you know to show the old lady the list, Byron? What significance do those names hold for you? 'Cause if you don't mind my saying, that scene on the porch came across as a little personal to me."

"You really don't remember me, do you?"

Vanda tucked her chin in and pursed her lips as if she had been considering this very thing, then tapped the tabletop with a long, lacquered nail before answering, "There *is* something about you that is *so* familiar." Her eyes narrowed in concentration. "High school?" she asked.

"Pacelli," he answered, just as he had done in Tanner's interview.

Vanda shook her head. "Nope... Baker." She arched an eyebrow at him. "A Catholic boy, huh, they can be awful sweet," she observed.

"Please, Lord above," she continued, "do not tell me that I *should* remember you, if you know what I mean, and I pray you don't." She shook a cigarette out of her package, then not finding an ashtray, managed to break it in half while trying to get it back in. "There was a time there... a short period, mind you, after my husband left me, when I'm afraid I kinda went off the deep end a little... did a little too much partying... woke up in a few too many strange places with a few too many strange... well, I don't have to tell you, you're a mature man, after all." She took a deep breath. "You are not *one* of those men, are you? *Please* say no.

"You can't be," she answered herself, "you've been living up north all this time! Oh my God, that's a relief! Only why in the world do I run my mouth so, besides you're the one that's supposed to be talking. You did that on purpose!" she accused Byron.

He laughed. "I'm sorry, I do have the advantage, as I remember you explicitly."

Vanda propped her chin in her hand. "Explicitly... oh dear... well do tell, get it over with."

"It was at Baker High School," Byron began, his voice becoming soft and smoky with the memories of a long-ago evening. "Some classmates and I crashed one of those famous teen dances at your school gym. One of the coaches that guarded the entrance was the older brother of one of my school buddies and he let us in. We hardly knew what to do once we breached your battlements, so we just stood around in a knot trying not to look conspicuous and achieving the exact opposite, I'm sure. That's when I saw you. You were dancing away and the center of attention, at least my attention, and I made up my mind right then and there to ask you to dance. I couldn't stop looking at you."

"Oh how you do go on!" Vanda said in her best tidewater drawl, then "Pray continue."

Byron chuckled. "Well, I asked... I asked you to dance and you did. I think my legs were shaking, I was so nervous. Then, at some point, the band switched to something slow and I'll never forget the sensation of holding you close. Remember, I'd been attending a Catholic school, and it was the seventies you know, so I hadn't had a lot of experience with girls yet. Then I did something that I've never forgiven myself for." He glanced at Vanda whose hand had drifted to her cheek.

"Oh my God," she whispered.

"I let my hand brush up against your left breast, I distinctly remember which one, and said, quite romantically I'm sure, 'I'd really like to do it with you.'"

Vanda's mouth fell open. "*You!*" she managed to say. "That was you?"

"So you do remember me?" Byron laughed.

"I do now, you naughty boy! I was so disappointed that you didn't stick around for an answer, you took off from there like the devil was on your heels."

"I lost my nerve and so also the lady fair... but I never forgot her."

Vanda blushed in spite of herself. "How you do talk, suh, I declare!"

"So now you know my deep, dark secret."

"Darlin', if that's the worst of it you've *got* to keep trying."

Byron glanced down at his empty tumbler and Vanda followed his gaze. "But that's not all, is it? Maybe I should buy you another after all, it appears firewater puts you in a confessional mood."

He glanced up just as her cell phone began to ring. "Detective Sergeant Tucker," she answered, then went silent. After a moment more she said, "Five minutes, we're just around the corner from the station." Turning to Byron, she explained, "We've got to roll... it seems a package arrived at the station that's causing quite a stir... and it's for you."

⁊

They met Chief Tanner in the evidence processing room on the second floor. He was waiting for them at the end of a long table on which sat a single cardboard box. The box appeared to have been roughly torn open, the brown wrapping paper and string that had bound it had been left hanging from its crushed sides. It was smeared with fingerprint dust as well. Several men in lab jackets were arrayed around the table in various attitudes; none appeared happy with the box.

"We had the robot open it when we saw it was addressed to you," Chief Tanner informed Byron as he and Vanda walked into the room. "There was no return address and after what just happened, I thought it best we didn't take any chances."

Byron stopped at the far end opposite his counterpart and asked, "What *did* just happen?"

Tanner pushed the box several inches further away just using his fingertips and said, "We went right over to Mister Timothy Wakely's house after I got a look at that list of yours—he was the next on it; still living so far as we knew—we now know that to be incorrect."

"Murdered?"

"Very much so," Tanner assured him. "Had his head removed with the family sword. My boys here," he nodded at the gloomy technicians, "assure me that the sword is a genuine Confederate issue; probably a family heirloom. Not that that matters much for Mr. Wakely, as it appears he had no children of his own to hand it off to—a confirmed bachelor as they used to say in the old days."

Vanda, who had been edging up to the open box, halted and said, "Please tell me that his head is *not* in that box." Her face went a shade lighter.

Tanner gave her a look, then said, "Byron, I'm afraid this might be bad news for you, but what came in this box has to do with your missing friend, Llewellyn."

Byron noticed Vanda sidling a little closer to the box. He remained still. "Bad news?" he repeated.

Vanda reached the box and peered in. Byron heard her say, "Oh my God!"

"Pretty bad, yeah," Tanner continued, softening his voice a little. "Some sonofabitch sent you his index fingers."

Byron felt himself take a step back then stop, then heard himself ask, "You sure they're his?"

"Yeah, 'fraid so, we rolled one and sent it through AFIS. It was a match from when he applied for a pistol permit in Atlanta a few years ago. We couldn't lift any prints from the box itself. Whoever sent it was careful enough."

"Any chance for Thomas?" Byron asked.

"It's possible" Tanner answered, his expression unconvincing; "… he could still be alive. It would depend on whether they stanched the bleeding… or whatever else they may have done to him before, or afterward. I'm sorry, Byron, I know you were good friends."

"That's it then?"

Tanner shook his big head. "No, I'm afraid not… there's a note." The Columbus chief slid a clear plastic evidence bag containing a handwritten note on lined paper to Byron. Byron noted the rusty-looking stains that decorated the margins, as well as remnants of clear tape that had been snipped near their middle. It read, "Tell Byron to hurry up—I'm almost done. Thomas wanted to point the way." He looked up at Chief Tanner as Vanda placed a hand on his arm. He could feel himself shaking. "His fingers were taped to this page?"

Tanner nodded. "Each was pointing in the opposite direction of the other—a joke."

"Who's left now?"

"Just one according to Llewellyn's list—a Randolph J. Carruthers, white male, aged seventy-six. He lives alone since his mother died a few years ago. We've got undercover with him now."

"Anyone assigned to the night shift yet?"

"You and Tucker I expect," Tanner sighed.

"That'd be fine… thanks," Byron said.

Tanner called over to Vanda, "Tucker, you in?"

She turned from the window overlooking the patrol parking lot and answered, "Neck deep, Chief."

"Byron, go get fitted for a vest and draw a weapon from the armory… you comfortable with a .45 cal?"

"That's what we qualify with."

"Good. Tucker, will you stop mooning around and escort Chief Patrick to the armory, please ma'am?"

As they walked down the hallway together Vanda turned and said, "He might still be alive, Byron. I know it's not likely, but we don't know why he was taken in the first place. He may have some value to them."

Byron said nothing, as he was wondering what that value might be.

"Besides," she added with a weak smile, "at least now you know that he's not the one behind all this."

✑

Randolph J. sat in the shadowed corner of his cluttered, dusty living room and eyeballed the two officers that had relieved his previous guardians. They didn't look like much to him. When he had been the man's age, he reflected, he could have taken him easily; as to the woman… well, that was obvious. He had spent nearly his entire life in school gyms teaching kids the rudiments of sports and the basics of developing a strong physique and knew two losers when he saw them. Smokers and drinkers… soft and slow—this was what stood between him and… something… a painful death, maybe. He shuddered and the damned woman noticed as she made her rounds of the windows checking latches. She quickly turned away. He hoped that they could at least shoot well, if it came to that.

The man reentered the room from the kitchen after spending what seemed an inordinate amount of time in the back rooms of his house. He was drying his hands with a ragged dish towel. "Find anything to interest you?" Randolph J. asked.

Byron regarded him for a moment before asking in his turn, "What do you think?"

The old man reared back in his stained and tattered lounger, "I won't tolerate disrespect—I demand respect."

Byron turned away and went to the front door. "Uh huh," he answered.

Sidling up to him, Vanda whispered fiercely in his ear, "Do you mind? We've got to spend all night here with this old boy, so do you think you could give your feud with the elderly just a slight hiatus?"

Byron jiggled the doorknob and double-checked the deadbolt without answering.

Vanda's forehead furrowed with a new thought. "Wait a minute," she continued with just a glance over her shoulder at Carruthers, "*did* you find something?"

Byron turned back toward the kitchen and Vanda followed. "I'll make some coffee," he said.

When they had entered the tiny, fly-blown kitchen, she seized his elbow. "Byron?" she demanded, then folded her arms waiting.

He looked over her shoulder into the darkening living room. Carruthers studied them both with open suspicion, his long, sagging face, pale and stubbled, pursed in distaste; his tiny, deep-set eyes glittering with malice. Turning back to Vanda, Byron answered, "He has a drawer full of children's underwear in his bedroom," he said, then resumed his preparations, rinsing out a greasy coffee pot and spooning some stale grounds into a filter basket.

"Might be grandchildren," Vanda offered.

Byron glanced over his shoulder at her, then returned to his task.

She looked once more to where the man they were to protect glowed like a fungus in the deepening shadows of the oncoming evening. "Oh Lordy," Vanda whispered, "I won't sleep a wink in this house."

"Am I allowed to use my own bathroom?" their unhappy host called out to them. "Would that be a Goddamn problem, do you think?" He began to hoist himself up on shaky, spindly arms.

"It's your house," Byron answered, "do what you want. All we ask is that you not go outside and to keep all the curtains closed and the doors locked—the rest is up to you."

"So I can go to bed if I want to?" Randolph J. persisted, beginning his unsteady exit of the close, malodorous room.

"It's up to you," Byron repeated. "Don't let us stop you."

The old man made his way like a great, white spider into the dark recesses of the house and vanished from sight.

↻

When they came for him it was not in darkness but just as the sun began to rise over a murky horizon. Vanda had not been as good as her word, but had fallen asleep on the old man's seedy, sprung couch sometime after three a.m. Byron had succumbed in an armchair facing the front door some time before, confident that the sound of anyone attempting to gain entry would rouse him.

It was the crash and grind of the approaching garbage truck that awakened them both. Byron stood and stretched before going to the window to take a peek, and heard bones cracking in his back.

Parting the thick, dusty curtains, he peeked outside. The garbage truck trundled noisily into view, an institutional green monster, spewing diesel smoke and dripping an unsavory stew of fluids from various leaks within its carcass. With a hiss and a squeal it halted in front of Carruthers' house and the man in back leapt down from the maw of the vehicle. Byron dully registered the worker's scroll of tats and began to turn away. *He's going to ruin those fancy cowboy boots*, he thought.

"Anything showing?" Vanda asked as she made her way to the kitchen to begin a fresh pot of coffee.

Byron heard the crash of metal as Randolph's garbage can was slammed into the lip of the receiving end of the truck outside. "No," he began, "just the garbage pick-up. That's one job you couldn't pay me to…" The boots niggled at his subconscious and he turned back toward the window, but it was the sound of running footsteps that interrupted his sentence. "What the …?" he began.

Throwing back the curtain, he was just in time to see Cowboy Boots returning the now-empty and very dented can back to the side of Carruthers' house, even as a second heavily-tattooed man charged up the walk wielding a cinder block. Byron just had time to think, *Two white males, heavily tattooed*, before the concrete was launched and he hurled himself to the floor in a shower of broken glass and shards of jagged wood.

From the kitchen, he heard the sound of something clattering to the floor and Vanda's voice crying, "Byron!?"

He had fallen onto his right side, pinning his gun beneath his frame. As he scrabbled to flip himself over and bring it into play, Vanda rushed in with her weapon already drawn and pointing at the destroyed window. In that split second, the face of Cowboy Boots appeared framed in the wreckage and Byron noted his long, curly hair, clean and shining in the light of the new day, swinging about his shoulders like a model's in a shampoo commercial. In spite of the tattoos concealing so much of his features it was clear to Byron that he could not be much more than twenty-five. The tattooed man tossed the grenade into the room and vanished before either he or Vanda could fire a single shot. Byron thought his expression was damned cheerful for the occasion.

The resultant explosion concussed Byron and slammed him back to the floor clasping his ears, deaf, writhing, and blind as a mole. He could not know what might have happened to Vanda. Though his senses had been scattered by the bang and flash of the stun grenade, he understood that he was still alive for the moment, yet helpless and at the mercy of his enemies.

It was the terrified screams of Randolph J. that first pierced the swirling disorder of his mind and ears. Through a white haze he was startled to see that the two tattooed men were already in the house and carrying the old man between them, as neatly wrapped in a blanket as a cigar. Byron sat up feeling for his gun. The driver kicked him in the forehead as he passed with his load and Byron went back down, the gun forgotten.

Byron dragged himself toward where Vanda lay as a trickle of blood began to stain his vision. He could see that she was still breathing, but unconscious. He felt something metal beneath his hand and seized it, then made for the destroyed doorway like a slug—unable to comprehend what had transpired in the lost time from the moment of the explosion until now.

As the sun rose like an angry red eye over the misty treetops and damp roofs, he saw his adversaries toss Carruthers onto the drooling lip of the garbage truck's compressor. Byron's vision cleared enough to witness the younger of the two men throw the lever to commence the downward progress of the great blade as the older held their victim in place, smiling all the while. Carruthers screamed and flopped about like a monstrous cocoon while watching his death come to him with the inexorable whine of hydraulics.

Byron's first shot went wide of the larger, older man, but pinged off the metal hide of the truck in an unnoticed shower of rust and paint. The killers were unable to hear the report above the screams and machinery, so he tried again. This time the younger one went down, his hand releasing the deadly lever, but without missing a beat his partner took over his duties and resumed the downward progress while pinning Carruthers with a corded, muscular arm. He glanced back towards Byron with a patient hatred, as if he had all the time in the world. As Byron tried to steady himself for his next shot, the great, filthy blade arrived, beginning its crude vivisection—there was no chance for the victim now, the voice of his terror and pain arcing ever-higher, then halting with the sickening snap of metal meeting metal.

With only the briefest of pauses to ensure that his partner was truly dead, the big man stalked away in the direction from which the truck had come. By then so many people had come out to see what was happening that Byron had no chance for another shot. Wisely, no one made a move to stop the man. The screaming of the shocked witnesses almost masked the banshee wail of fast-approaching sirens, while behind him Byron heard Vanda cough and groan.

"Don't open your eyes," he mumbled through a mouthful of blood, then laid his head down on the filthy floor and closed his own.

✌

It was mid-afternoon by the time Byron and Vanda were released from the emergency room at Saint Francis. Tanner was waiting for them in his office. He could have been happier.

The two of them gave their account of the debacle at the Carruthers home, and with their stories being in accord with the facts found on the scene, Tanner had little to say except, "Well, maybe things will settle down now since they got everyone on the goddamn list. Hopefully that made the surviving sonofabitch a happy camper." As they made their way for the door, he added, "By the way, I'm glad those bastards let you two live—they did, you know. Any thoughts on that, Byron? I'm sure it's crossed your mind too."

Turning back to Tanner who looked tired and as creased as old leather, Byron said, "I'll probably never know now. They did what they set out to do, I think. It's over." He didn't tell Tanner or Vanda of the note he had found tucked away in his pocket. One of the assailants had slipped it into his jacket as he and Vanda had lain unconscious after the concussion grenade had done its work. It read, "Think simple and you'll know what to do—come alone." It was written in the same crude lettering of the note contained in the bloody package.

Outside of Tanner's office Vanda took Byron's hand and looked up into his face. "You shouldn't be alone tonight, Byron—I know I don't want to be."

Byron found that he couldn't even smile. "God, I spent my whole youth and a good part of my adulthood fantasizing about this moment."

Vanda sighed and took a step back, releasing his hand. "But…?"

"The memory of us… of what could have been, is all I've had to keep me going at times… a lot of times. My life is a shambles right now… my wife… I don't even want to go there. The truth is I can't afford the risk of losing you by having you. I'm afraid to take the chance, Vanda."

The corners of Vanda's mouth turned up a little. "My God, I can't believe I'm being turned down in favor of a fantasy—even if it is a fantasy about me. You are a dreamer, Byron Patrick, and a little bit of a poet, and very sweet, and I'd really like a chance to kick your wife's ass." The little smile vanished. "You're also something of a liar, Chief Patrick. You're keeping something back in all this and I know it has to do with your little brother's abduction all those years ago."

Byron reared back as Vanda continued, "Yeah, that's right, I know about your little brother and Virgil Curtsie—I had one of our computer geeks Google you the day we met—I may be a hot little number, Byron, but I am also a pretty damn good cop. That list your friend Llewellyn had is connected to that event. You know the rest, I think, or have figured it out by now."

Byron stared hard at her for several moments before saying, "Tom and I killed Virgil Curtsie, Vanda, the man who took my little brother. We were just kids, and I don't think we set out to do it, but to be honest with you, I don't really know anymore. But now, all these years later, it seems someone wants revenge for that killing—that's why they took Thomas.

"As to the list, I'm just not sure. It became apparent to me during this investigation, and to you as well I suspect, that the list was a roll call of pedophiles, all of an age to have been contemporaries of Virgil Curtsie. What Tom was doing with the list?—that's where things start to get hazy. At first, I thought it might be Tom behind the murders, but after the index fingers, I knew better."

Vanda glanced at Chief Tanner's closed door. "You poor baby, you've been carrying this around all these years and then… this. It must seem like a nightmare."

Byron nodded, adding, "It's been a nightmare since I sent Daniel out to look for that damned dog of his. The killing of Curtsie seemed just another part of it all. It's why I left Columbus all those years ago; it's probably why I went into police work in the first place—penance. Now it's come full circle somehow and here I am again."

"What will you do now?" Vanda asked. "What will you tell Tom's wife?"

"What'll I do?" Byron repeated, then lied, "Go back to my motel room and get drunk. Then sometime after that call Reba and give her the news that Tom's not coming back—not now, probably not ever."

Vanda took his jacket by the lapels and pulled him down to her, planting a moist kiss on his stubbled cheek, then just brushing his lips with hers. For a brief moment he felt her fingers stray across his ribcage, then withdraw with a final, urgent tug on his jacket. "Call me if you change your mind," she said, her eyes never leaving his own, "… and don't go roamin' around after dark, okay? I'll be watching you," she promised.

Byron nodded back, the note in his pocket as heavy as death.

☙

Curtsie's house appeared just as he had last seen it—bathed in moonlight and sagging beneath the weight of climbing vines and cloaking branches. The plywood door covering still hung tiredly from a single nail as Byron slipped behind it and entered.

A wavering yellow light flickered in the short hallway leading to the kitchen, and Byron walked toward its source. He did not try to hide his coming as he knew that he was expected, and the creaking floorboards would not allow stealth in any case. Even so, he walked slowly and gently, his hands empty, palms sweating.

The kitchen chair—could it possibly be the same one?—had been placed in the middle of the room once more, its spindly metal legs, rusty and loose with age, shifting dangerously with the weight of Thomas Llewellyn. Lit candles gave the long-abandoned kitchen the sepia tone of an old photograph. His hands had been tied behind his back and Byron could see the crude, dirty bandages they sported; he also had a filthy rag tied around his mouth. A rope circled his neck, running through a chandelier hook above his head. It terminated in a sturdy knot. The knot lay in the hands of the large, tattooed man who had written Byron's invitation to the party. From time to time the man would give a little tug on his end in order to observe the resultant actions on the other. Tom's predicament appeared to provide him a quiet amusement.

"Figured it out, yet?" he asked Byron in the sand-papered voice of a heavy smoker.

Byron studied the features camouflaged beneath the swirling body art, the faded blue eyes, the stubby nose flattened now by some past violence, the sandy hair gone grey with hard years, still shaggy as a rock star's. "Some, Danny... not all," he answered. His throat felt swollen and his vision blurred for a moment.

"It's all about your friend here, brother; your friend... and his friends—men like Mr. Curtsie."

Byron shook his head and took a step back, feeling as if he might pass out.

"You never knew when we were kids that Tom knew Curtsie?" Daniel asked. "I'm shocked, big brother, after all he was your very best friend wasn't he?"

Byron looked to Tom whose streaming brown eyes were wide with fear and panic. "Tell me," Byron said, turning away from him to face his brother.

"He was Curtsie's 'boy.' That is, until he reached fourteen. Curtsie liked 'em a little younger. That's where I came in. *I* was a little younger." He gave the rope a slight tug and Tom teetered first to one side, then the other, before regaining his balance once more. Byron could hear his mewling through the filthy gag.

Lighting a cigarette with his free hand, Daniel continued, "Curtsie threatened to sell him to someone who liked his age group unless he recruited a replacement—that was me. Are you beginning to get the picture there, Chief?"

Byron nodded, saying nothing.

"Ol' Tom here took advantage of my search for the dog to make sure I stopped in at Virgil Curtsie's. He told me he was pretty sure that Curtsie had taken our dog in and was keeping him for the owner to claim. I went there, of course. What did I know?—I was only nine years old. He had a cozy room set up for me in his basement, and if the heat hadn't been brought on him so soon, he might have 'recruited' me to take Good Friend Tom's place and let me go—that's how it went with you, didn't it, Good Friend Tom?" He placed a work-booted foot against the chair and pushed it several inches. Tom's squealing grew more frantic. From somewhere outside Byron heard a car gliding down the deserted street, then another. They stopped several houses away.

"As it turned out," Daniel continued, crushing out his smoke with his heel, "Curtsie had 'friends' and he was able to hand me off before the police came in to search. I think you know the kind of friends I'm talking about, Big Brother; you've got a list of them from our friend Tom, I think. He got that list from our Mister Curtsie and has been making money from it ever since... can't say I blame him too much on that account. He deserved something, too, I reckon, for all *his* sufferings." He turned to regard Tom once more. "Even so... I did a little suffering myself." He shoved the chair a few more inches and drew up on the slack in the rope. The toes of Tom's shoes danced on the edge as his eyes began to bulge and grow dark with blood.

Daniel turned back to Byron. "For the next seven years I got traded. I didn't even know who I was anymore... who I belonged to—I was newly adopted, a visiting nephew or grandchild, a runaway daughter's illegitimate son.... I had so many different names, that if it weren't for Tom's list there, I might not remember them all.

"In the end, I was dumped out of the other end of the pipeline—too old... at sixteen. Can you beat that? I never went home; the thought never even crossed my mind. I wasn't 'that' little boy anymore. I went to all the places people like me go and made my way in fits and starts to prison—it wasn't hard... in fact, it seemed kind of like a natural progression. It was a good environment for me... I kinda liked prison, really."

He studied Byron in silence for a moment before continuing, "I met a fella inside that had done time in New Jersey, courtesy of you, he said. 'Course he didn't know we were brothers. Boy was I surprised—my big brother, a cop—and in New Jersey for God's sake! That guy hoped to kill you next time he got up north... but he fell to death in the showers before his time was up."

From outside, Byron heard the distinct snick of car doors being carefully shut.

"Friends of yours?" Daniel inquired, and when Byron didn't answer he continued his narrative as if nothing was happening. "If you and Tom hadn't killed Curtsie they might have found me, brother. That was Tom's plan all along, you know—he never intended for the old man to be able to talk to anyone... about anything, if you know what I mean. He brought you along for extra muscle and, if it all went wrong, fall guy."

Byron looked at his little brother and asked, "Why now, Daniel—what's happened?"

"I was released, Byron... sent back out into the good old world to finish dying. I've got AIDS as it turns out... clock ticking, that sort of thing. It just occurred to me to tie up some loose strings. I did that and just have this one left. I knew you'd come when I took Tom—I hoped you would. You're a loose end, too, and I wanted you to know." He grinned up at Tom and poked him hard in the ribs with a stiff finger. His victim supplied a corresponding muffled squeal. "You want to help?"

Tom's pleading eyes met Byron's, but he turned away.

"Who was it that I killed?" Byron asked.

"A good friend of mine from prison... somebody like me really, there's a lot of us out there. I don't think he cared too much that you killed him, big brother, if that's worrying you."

"I have a lot to answer for, Danny. I didn't look after my little brother and look what it's come to—Mom and Dad killed by the strain of it all, you... ruined, and me—my whole life an attempt to escape the past, each day, each tomorrow, dead—stillborn. Just look at us." The brothers' eyes met in the flickering, haunted room.

"But we were kids, little brother, victims, even Tom—though he still has a lot to answer for. But I can't just stand here and let this happen, because if I do, I will never, ever, be able to recover from it, and everything will just continue instead of really ending. I'm gonna take him out of here, Daniel, and I'm gonna see to it that everyone knows what he did, and more importantly, why you've done the things you've done. I owe you that much, Danny—people should know, and you should be there to tell them while you can.

"Tom sent you into this house a long time ago and I wasn't there for you—please, Danny, now that I've found you all these years later, let me take you out of here... if not for your sake, then for my own—I need you, little brother, and there's not a lot of time left to us. Isn't that why I'm really here?"

Byron reached across the short distance between them and took hold of Daniel's end of the rope. Daniel stared back hard at him, his grip firm.

"Please," Byron pleaded.

"You should have gone with me, Byron," Daniel answered, tears leaking from his fierce, bloodshot eyes. "I needed you." His grip loosened and Byron untied the knot, then gently threaded the rope back through the ceiling hook. Still holding one end, he guided Tom down from the rickety chair and led him toward the door like a dog on a leash, not bothering to remove his gag or ligatures. He felt Daniel looming close behind.

As he neared the doorway, Byron called out to the officers he knew had surrounded the house, "Vanda... Chief, we're coming out! Hold your fire! I've got the one responsible for all this and I'm sending him out first!" With that, he kicked his old friend hard enough in the backside to propel him through the doorway, taking out the plywood sheet as he tumbled down the steps into the tall, rank grasses of the front yard. A murmur arose at the trussed suspect's violent expulsion.

"Vanda, I'm coming next, but I've got company so don't anybody get antsy, you hear? You'll recognize him but take it easy! He's ugly enough to scare anybody and that's for certain, but he's with me... it's my brother!" And with that Byron turned and took Daniel's arm, and together they walked out of that house and into the warm and living night.

Made in the USA
Monee, IL
13 August 2022

11458839R00174